Feminist Popular Fiction

Also by Merja Makinen

FEMALE FETISHISM: A New Look (*with Lorraine Gamman*)
JOYCE CARY: A Descriptive Bibliography

Feminist Popular Fiction

Merja Makinen
Principal Lecturer, English Literary Studies
Middlesex University
London

First published 2001 by
PALGRAVE
Houndmills, Basingstoke, Hampshire RG21 6XS and
175 Fifth Avenue, New York, N.Y. 10010
Companies and representatives throughout the world

PALGRAVE is the new global academic imprint of
St. Martin's Press LLC Scholarly and Reference Division and
Palgrave Publishers Ltd (formerly Macmillan Press Ltd).

ISBN 0–333–79317–X

This book is printed on paper suitable for recycling and
made from fully managed and sustained forest sources.

A catalogue record for this book is available
from the British Library.

Library of Congress Cataloging-in-Publication Data
Makinen, Merja.
    Feminist popular fiction / Merja Makinen.
        p. cm.
    Includes bibliographical references and index.
    ISBN 0–333–79317–X
    1. Feminist fiction, English—History and criticism. 2. Women
and literature—Great Britain—History—20th century. 3. Women
and literature—United States—History—20th century. 4. Popular
literature—Great Britain—History and criticism. 5. Popular
literature—United States—History and criticism. 6. American
fiction—Women authors—History and criticism. 7. English fiction–
–Women authors—History and criticism. 8. American fiction—20th
century—History and criticism. 9. English fiction—20th century–
–History and criticism. 10. Feminist fiction, American—History and
criticism. I. Title.
    PR888.F45 M34 2001
    823'.914099287—dc21
                                                            2001031311

10   9   8   7   6   5   4   3   2   1
10   09 08 07 06 05 04 03 02 01

Printed in Great Britain by Antony Rowe Ltd, Chippenham, Wiltshire

To Nicholas,
for putting up with my preoccupation

Contents

Acknowledgements

I would like to thank the following, for discussing ideas, reading chapters, or suggesting further reading: David Drake, Aline Ferriera, Lorraine Gamman, Farah Mendlesohn, Sarah Niblock and Victoria De Rijke. Thanks to Clive Bloom, for encouraging the initial project, and to the English Literary Studies Department at Middlesex University for granting a sabbatical, and for their continuing support and leniency throughout the assignment. Thanks go to Joanne Winning for her internet detective skills in tracking down the image for the cover. Thanks also to the students who have taken my MA module 'Women's Writing and the Question of Genre' over the years and who have helped me hone my views. Grateful thanks to Vicky Newell and Janice Williams for helping to keep me sane, and to Nicholas for reminding me of my priorities. Finally, thanks go to Jo North for bringing a consistency to my erratic typescript, and to the Library Staff at Middlesex University, particularly Rachel Morgan, and to the Staff at the British Library.

Introduction: Unleashing the Genres

Are romance, or fairy tale, or detective fiction inherently conservative formats? The received assumption is that they are. Researching the feminist debates within each of these genres, I have been struck by the marked similarities. Each genre has been having basically the same dispute. Feminist theorists assert that the conventions of the genre are conservative and therefore inimicable to feminist writers, whereas the genre historians argue that the genre contains subversive and proto-feminist examples. Thinking through the question of why the same debate was surfacing in all the genres has brought me to the conclusion that no popular genre can be called 'inherently conservative' because they are all such loose, baggy, chameleons.

Genre or canon?

What feminist historians in each genre have uncovered, by their rediscovery of its invisible history of women authors, is the gargantuan mutability of their genre. This rediscovery further highlights the fact that what feminist theorists are looking at, when considering the conventions, the format, or the inherent structures of a genre, is not the genre itself, but the canon created from within that genre. It is the genre canon that is conservative because, like most academic canons until the 1970s, it privileges conservative and phallologocentric values in its choice of favoured texts. The construction of a 'classic' (sic) format out of the canon, allows commentators to call it conservative and allows feminist theorists, turning to look at the impact on women readers, to argue the same. But canons deliberately expel the subversive and the challenging; and structuralists in defining the format deliberately ignore important cultural and historical

1

differences. Each genre is more than, and other than, its canonical construction.

Detective fiction: an example

Any number of books[1] will tell you that classic detective fiction starts with Edgar Allan Poe's short story 'Murders in the Rue Morgue' (1841), develops into the series format with Conan Doyle's Sherlock Holmes (1887–1927), and further develops between the wars into the ratiocinating puzzle of who-dunnit with the British 'Golden Age' writers, Agatha Christie, Dorothy Sayers, Patricia Wentworth, Ngaio Marsh and Margery Allingham. From this history, develops the classic format: starting with a disruption of the status quo (the crime) which the detective, representing overdetermined individualism and a triumph of logical, rational thought, proceeds to make sense of, discover the criminal and eradicate his/her disruption, thereby restoring the status quo. The 'establishment', the police, judiciary, or the upper-class amateur detective restores order and stability to the closed, hierarchical community of the country house, the aristocracy, the church, cruise liner or college. In America, the Hard-Boiled School of Hammett, Chandler and MacDonald develops alongside the British format, reifying the integrity and toughness of a machismo individualism, which locates corruption within those who reject social, bourgeois values in favour of greed and power. In all the genre formats, female sexuality is posited as a site of social disruption and crime. Such a canonical history, and the 'classic' format could be argued to be inherently conservative and phallologocentric.

Michelle Slung[2] and Patricia Craig and Mary Cadogan[3] were among the first to argue for a different history which incorporated the profusion of 'lady detectives' and earlier women writers. The first 'lady detectives' were published in the early 1860s with W. S. Hayward's *The Revelations of A Lady Detective*[4] and Andrew Forrester Jnr's *The Female Detective* (1864). Both had upper-middle-class women attached to the Metropolitan Police, exuberantly solving a number of crimes in milieux where men could not infiltrate. The lady detective became a stalwart of both male and female writers from the 1880s–1930s, for example, Dorcas Dene, Miss Butterworth, Hagar, Gypsy Rose, Miss Lois Caley, Hilary Wade, Florence Cusak, Dora Myrl, Loveday Brooke, Madelyn Mack, Violet Strange, Constance Dunlap through to Lucie Mott, Miss Pinkerton, Emma Marsh and eminent psychologist Mrs Bradley, with honorary degrees from every university except Tokyo.

The first Anglo-American detective novel is usually argued to be Anna Katherine Green's *The Leavenworth Case* (1878) which became a runaway bestseller and so overshadowed Seeley Register's *The Dead Letter* of 1866, both well before Conan Doyle. Women writers have always been an important presence in detective fiction, although writers such as Green, L. T. Mead, Catherine Luisa Purkis, Baroness Orczy, Mary Roberts Rinehart, Gladys Mitchell, E. Phillips Oppenheim, Josephine Bell, Christianna Brand, Charlotte Armstrong, Mignon G. Eberhart and Hilda Lawrence are mostly out of print. In 1909 Rinehart's *The Man in the Lower Ten* made the British bestsellers list and throughout the 1920s either Rinehart or Oppenheim appeared on the lists. Rinehart's average yearly sales were 300 000 copies.[5] Ros Coward and Linda Semple,[6] editors of Pandora's 'Women Crime Writers' series in the late 1980s, argued that the more subversively feminist texts were the very ones allowed to go out of print. Kathleen Gregory Klein's 1994 collection traces 117 widely read women writers, while Victoria Nichols and Susan Thompson[7] have a shopping list of 600 series detectives written by women.

Alongside the silence about the women writers and 'lady detectives' came a denigration of certain sub-genres of detective fiction which, perhaps not coincidentally, were written by women. This sub-genre, which became known as the 'Had I But Known' school, and has an 'amateur' retrospectively tracing the mystery she has been caught up in, was denigrated by the Detective Club of Great Britain as not 'true' detective fiction because it solved the mysteries through intuition and feminine knowledge. Mary Robert Rinehart wrote in this sub-genre, and the dismissal of these 'too fanciful' works thereby consolidates the ratiocination of the classic canon. But only by ignoring much of the hugely popular women's detective fiction which relied on intuition and a knowledge of personality to solve the crimes, rather than on material evidence and rationality. The expanded detective genre encompasses other forms of validated knowledge alongside the phallologocentric.

A further exploration of the range of detective fiction outside the canon uncovers the early socialist critiques of writers such as Fergus Hume, Izaac Zangwill and Arthur Morrison. Fergus Hume's Hagar, *Hagar of the Pawnshop* (1898), was one of the early female detectives who broke the ranks of gentility as a gypsy. Hume's short story 'The Lone Inn' was serialised in 1894 in Keir Hardie's *Labour Leader*. Zangwill and Morrison, better known for their East End social-protest novels, both wrote detective fiction. Morrison created two detectives.

Martin Hewitt was a critique of Holmes's flamboyant individualism, whereas his Dorrington, *Dorrington Deed Box* (1897) and Zangwill's Grodman, *The Big Bow Mystery* (1891) are both dishonest detectives who implicate the judiciary in protecting a corrupt capitalism (which is the true villain in both texts). While Dorrington, having discovered the perpetrators, uses that knowledge for extortion rather than justice, Grodman reveals himself as the murderer of the idealistic Labour supporter. This ability to critique bourgeois law and order by implicating the police was another of the things the Detective Club ruled out from their putative canon in 1929, but that did not prevent its being a motif in non-canonical detective fiction.

A knowledge of the wider genre history of detective fiction uncovers a gargantuan discourse of competing formats, where the ability to question the social status quo, masculine overvaluation of ratiocination, and to assert female agency were already present well before feminist writers brought their own critiques to bear on it in the 1970s. An acquaintance with this wider history precludes the argument that detective fiction *per se* is inimical to feminist writers.

Feminism and popular genres

Within the feminist debates in detective fiction, any number of critics argue for the inherent conservatism of detective fiction. Kathleen Gregory Klein's *The Woman Detective: Gender and Genre*[8] upholds that because all popular genres are conservative, feminist attempts to appropriate them must fail, and therefore the changes in recent fiction are only superficial 'variations in style, dress and custom'.[9] Despite having a detailed knowledge of the history of the genre, Klein's 'conspiracy theory' model of popular culture prevents her theorising detective fiction as potentially transformable.[10] In contrast Maureen Reddy[11] and Rosalind Coward and Linda Semple[12] were arguing for the genre's potential to be appropriated by feminists by looking at the history. The debate about whether or not detective fiction is an unsuitable genre for feminists has raged from then on.

The same debates can be found in the criticism of fairy tales, beginning with Andrea Dworkin[13] arguing for the genre's patriarchal prescription of good women as passive, and active women as villains, in contrast to Alison Lurie's[14] contention that while the male editors privileged these stereotypes, the wider range of oral tales contain many proto-feminist protagonists and so are admirable texts for young girls to read.

In the romance genre, Tania Modleski[15] and David Margolies[16] argued for its inherent patriarchal inscription and this model remained firm for a long time as the debates shifted to a cultural discussion of what women readers did with romance fiction. Latterly though, a focus on historical specificity by Nickianne Moody[17] and Jay Dixon[18] has begun to argue for a wider assessment of the model of the genre.

Science fiction does not really have the same debates, perhaps because feminist concerns have so spectacularly appropriated the genre, especially the utopian sub-genre. The development of 'soft' social science fiction in the 1960s, in contrast to the 'hard' technological science fiction, means the debates may well have come much earlier while the explosion of sub-genres such as utopias, fantasy and sword-and-sorcery, means that critics find it harder to talk about an inherent patriarchal and bourgeois conservatism. The debates still seem to be how to distance science fiction from other genre fiction, in order for it to be taken seriously as literature. An inherently conservative and conformist thrust to the criticism, that ignores the validation of popular culture, brought about by cultural studies in the 1980s.

It is surprising that in the early 1990s, when so many feminist detective writers were so successfully going mainstream, such notable critics as Ann Cranny Francis[19] and Paulina Palmer[20] still had such trouble with reconciling feminist and lesbian attempts to appropriate the 'conservative' genre, because they were still accepting the canonical view of the genre. Which is not to say that all the hugely popular feminist detective fiction is successful within feminist terms. The debates still need to be had in relation to those texts which, in a simple role reversal, substitute a 'strong woman' for the male detective, and those works which self-reflexively interrogate the format and the conventions of the canon. But it is time to acknowledge the work of the genre historians and to argue that popular genres are not fixed, but that like any popular product they are continually adapting to and contributing to their historical contexts, and that at times of gender modification and magnification, as at the turn of the century with the 'new woman', or in the 1970–80s, genres have assimilated the conflicting discourses on gender.

Genre's fluidity

Not all of a popular genre is radical. Much of it remains within the canonical format and the majority of it conforms to readerly expectations (an important element in genre formation), but each is a broad enough church to harbour a number of contending sub-genres, some of which are subversive and self-critical, and the existence of these prevents the assertion that the genre in itself is inherently conservative. One can only assert that the most favoured – whether the most popular or the most canonical – are conservative. And when it comes to popularity, given that genre audiences consist of a number of different constituencies, one cannot even say that of detective fiction any longer, as my local library's crime fiction shelves pile Christie and Dexter alongside Valerie Miner and Barbara Wilson.

This study had the good fortune to span a number of genres and hence to notice the similarity of the feminist critical debates. While the critical debate exists within each genre, there has not been an overview to realise and then question why the debates are all converging, and recognise the canonical imperative at work. Klein, Dworkin and Modleski were not wrong, canonical detective fiction, fairy tale, and romance are conservative and phallocentric. But that is not the whole picture and a different canon could elucidate a different, even a subversive format. I would not go so far as to argue that all genres are equally subversive for feminist practice, some are easier to appropriate than others, but I would and do argue that all the genres are potentially and inherently transformable. Cultural studies now argue for a fluid model of popular discourses, where context and audiences influence the production. Literary criticism also has a model of a fluid genre, in Frederic Jameson's discussion of the magical realist genre shifting from the medieval to the eighteenth century.[21] As I examine in my first chapter, Jameson argues that medieval romance is 'reinvented' in the eighteenth century by replacing the medieval positives such as magic with newer positives such as theology and a nascent psychology. The basic form remains the same but the 'ideologemes' have shifted because of the new historical context. Jameson's model suggests that the same features can carry radically different meanings within different cultural contexts. After all, serial romance was (and still is by some[22]) seen as the genre quintessentially inscribed by patriarchy, until lesbian romance took its format and transformed the codes and ideologies.

1

Feminism and Genre Fiction: the Preliminaries

The 1980s saw the rise of feminist popular genre fiction, the appropriation of a variety of formulaic narratives by feminist writers. This book is in part a textual study of the tensions that arise from such appropriations, both to the genre and to the feminism. By looking at the history of each genre, the chapters begin with the premise that genres are transformable, that they have adapted to cultural shifts and transformations like any other narrative, and so are also open to the specific cultural changes that began with the Women's Liberation Movement in the late 1960s and the 1970s, in the US and in Britain. As such, the book questions certain feminist assumptions that generic formulae are fixed and inherently conservative categories. If the genres are open to ideological appropriation, then one of the interests is how that same ideology has endeavoured to appropriate the different genres. By viewing a range of feminist genre fiction, the book is able to compare the narrative strategies used in relation to the conventions of each genre's narrative format. It is a study that encompasses: a history of the genre, reinstating women's contributions; the main feminist critiques of each genre and the feminist appropriations; followed by case studies of specific texts in order to explore in more detail the narrative strategies at play in the appropriations. As a literary analysis of the genre fiction, this is not an examination of audiences and of readership, but no discussion of popular fiction can ignore this issue altogether, nor can it assume an unproblematically singular form of feminism, to which it can refer. So this opening chapter is in part a methodological discussion of the issues of the popular, pleasure and the audience, the issue of feminism(s), and of the transformability of formula fiction.

Feminism and the popular

Feminist literature in Britain and America during the rise of the Women's Liberation Movement, initially took the form of the realist 'coming to consciousness' novel, a form of *bildungsroman* of the feminist consciouness in the female protagonist. Erica Jong's *Fear of Flying* and Marilyn French's *The Woman's Room* are two best-selling landmarks in this type of feminist fiction which Nicci Gerrard has defined as 'the literature of personal angst and domestic oppression ... in which pain is worn like a badge of moral superiority'.[1] But during the later part of the 1970s and progressively in the 1980s, feminist fiction began to branch out into exploring the popular genre format, giving rise to a whole wave of self-consciously styled feminist detective fiction, feminist science fiction and feminist fairy tales. Feminist publishing houses, such as Pandora and the Women's Press, set up their own genre series of detective fiction and science fiction, while the more mainstream and genre presses welcomed self-styled feminist writers.

This choice to move into popular genre forms was not an arbitrary one. It could almost be argued, as Judith Williamson did in 1986 in the left-wing journal *New Socialist*, that during the 1980s, the left as a whole discovered popular culture:

> It used to be an act of daring on the left to claim enjoyment of *Dallas*, disco-dancing, or any other piece of popular culture. Now it seems to require equal daring to suggest that such activities, while certainly enjoyable, are not radical.[2]

Citing the 1986 'Left Alive' conference hosted by *Marxism Today*, which included top designers, fashion writers and television advertisers amongst its speakers, Williamson was speaking out against what she saw as the left's wholesale embrace of the popular. She located this shift in the left as a reaction to Thatcher's swingeing popularity and the apparent hegemonic success of the market economy. Herself a left-wing writer on popular culture, Williamson's main thesis was that in their urge to be in touch with 'the people' the left should not abrogate their political critique of the popular.[3] Her critical assessment that the shift in the left had gone too far, elucidates the fact that such a shift had indeed taken place in Britain:

> It is, of course, intended to show how out of touch the left had been until it discovered marketing and consumerism. (An ad for the

future: 'I thought the working class was a man with a ferret until I discovered ... marketing.')[4]

The shift was one that feminist thinkers were taking a central part in. In a talk given in 1980, and published in 1982, the Marxist feminist Michèle Barrett was arguing for 'feminists ... attempting to influence the mass media and reach a wider audience'.[5] Rejecting the elitism that dismisses mass culture as conservative escapism, Barrett argued for a two-pronged advance, of feminist avant-garde writers trying to create a feminine language, and of feminists moving into popular culture: '... a small popular change is *relatively* just as significant as a large minority change. There may be at least as much potential for change in a tv soap opera as in agit-prop theatre.'[6] She concludes that as feminists,

> [w]e take some responsibility for the cultural meaning of gender and it is up to us all to change it. But this struggle cannot rest on a challenge to ideological dimensions of the old-master paintings – it will also have to engage with the aesthetic pleasures of advertisements.[7]

So the move into popular culture and popular fictions during the 1980s was one of the agendas for left-wing feminists, and was to some extent part of a larger attempt to wrest cultural signification away from the right's successful harnessing of the popular with images such as the 'yuppie'. As Jean Radford argued in the mid-1980s in her introduction to a collection of essays arising out of a History Workshop conference at Ruskin College, Oxford,

> the contributors ... see an anlogy, I think, between their work on popular culture and socialist attempts to understand the popularity of right wing, conservative politics in Britain and the US at present. Recent analyses of political populism argue that we have to ask what it is so many identify with in conservative ideology (and *why*) ...[8]

Feminists, during the 1980s, identified a need to address the popular viewpoint, to change cultural opinion, and the attempt to appropriate popular culture and popular genres was part of that procedure.

As Anne Cranny-Francis has argued in her useful analysis of the structures of feminist genre fiction, *Feminist Fiction: Feminist Uses of Generic Fiction*:[9]

> But why genre fiction? The answer lies in the synonym by which these texts are described – popular. People enjoy genre fiction; it sells by the truckload. As a conscious feminist propagandist it makes sense to use a fictional format which already has a huge market.[10]

In Britain literary novels tend to have a very small print run, perhaps only 2000 copies in hardback.[11] The feminist publishing house Virago, had an average print run for paperbacks of 6000–7000 in its heyday in the early 1980s.[12] Even a relative feminist success, such as Angela Carter's *Nights at the Circus*, published by a mainstream paperback publisher Picador/Pan, could hope to achieve sales of around ten times that.[13] In contrast, some genre fiction, romance for example, sells titles in the millions.[14] Where romance and detective fiction sell well, however, fairy tales and some science fiction would not have quite so huge an audience. Nevertheless, they would share along with the other popular genres a new, fresh, audience for feminist fiction.

But what is the impact of moving into popular culture for feminist writers? What happens, if anything, to the ideological intent when addressing the wider audience, and not simply addressing the already converted? Having interviewed a number of women writers for *Women's Review* during the 1980s, Nicci Gerrard raised this issue when she questioned the impact on feminist writing of going mainstream:

> Entering the mainstream holds a host of opposing interpretations: selling, or selling out; gaining access, or losing substance; making more money, or taking fewer risks; becoming part of the larger world, or relinquishing the female world. It is 'coping practically and courageously' with the world in which we live, and it is weakly swimming with the tide. It implies success to some and failure to others.[15]

Whether feminist genre writers have managed to 'sell' and gain a wider audience, or have 'sold out' in order to attract a market, will depend upon the specific writer and the specific text, and the case studies in the ensuing chapters explore this. One also needs to consider which sort of feminism you judge that decision by, as the section on 'issues of the feminist text' exemplifies below. But, despite these problems of assessing the ideological effectiveness of the fiction, in choosing to become genre writers feminist writers have clearly made a bid for a wider readership.

Issues of pleasure and the audience

> Popular formulaic fiction is usually defined as fiction that is read purely for pleasure, as a form of escapism. This is the sort of fiction that is read wholly for pleasure and is therefore part of one's leisure activity ... the popular novel is there simply to entertain and to divert; if it fails to do this then it fails in its main function.[16]

The concept of escapism is no longer seen perjoratively within much cultural studies work, in contrast to literary studies. Richard Dyer's 'Entertainment and Utopia'[17] argued in relation to audiences of Hollywood films, that they escape the exhaustion and dreary monotony of their lives by vicariously experiencing the activity, potential and full emotional responses on the screen. The experience the film offers is a utopian one to counter the mundane stresses of their normal existence. For the period of watching, they are transported outside of themselves. This accords with Janice Radway's sample of romance readers in her seminal sociological study of why women read romance fiction, *Reading the Romance*. Her small audience said they read 'for simple relaxation' and 'to escape from daily problems'. Radway enumerates this in her statement that:

> romance reading is valued ... because the experience is *different* from ordinary existence. Not only is it a relaxing release from the tension produced by daily problems and responsibilities, but it creates a time or space within which a woman can be entirely on her own, preoccupied with her own personal needs, desires and pleasure.[18]

The more recent *Star Gazing*,[19] by Jackie Stacey, develops this concept of being transported into another world, in an analysis of British wartime audiences at the cinema, with its aura of glamour and its star system. Transportation into another world, she argues, involves a loss of self as a part of that escapism: 'This loss of self enabled women to hide from the stresses of everyday life, from their own feelings of inadequacy, and to imagine themselves in the utopian world of Hollywood stars for a short time.'[20] But while she allows for the regressive element of escapism involved in such transportation, she also cites Ien Ang's argument that such fantasising can be viewed more positively as well. Ang's *Watching Dallas*[21] took issue with Michèle Barrett's assumption that the implicit fantasies of powerlessness inscribed in soap operas lead to political passivity in the women viewers. She argued instead for the need to acknowledge the nature of fantasy as something different from how we live our real lives. Just because we enjoy reading fantasies of powerlessness does not mean we will translate that into how we live our real lives. It is the 'playfulness', the 'trying out' of fantasy that needs to be acknowledged, and hence its potential to generate fictional selves:

> producing and consuming fantasies allows for a play with reality, which can be felt as 'liberating' because it is fictional, not real. In the play of fantasy we can adopt positions and 'try out' those positions, without having to worry about their 'reality value'.[22]

This aspect of the more liberating and creative activities of escapism, as well as the transportive escapism, are important for the consideration of feminist popular fiction, because such texts by their very nature argue for a challenge to the social constructions and constrictions of femininity within the particular genre conventions. A recognition of this by the reader calls for something more active than just transportation and loss of self, in the pleasures of the reading.

Clive Bloom, in *Cult Fiction*, argues that feminist critics do not really like the popular and are simply 'using the material as an *excuse* in the war over "gender" definitions and control'.[23] While I cannot deny that this is sometimes true, and true of feminist writers as well as critics, as my discussion of *Fairytales for Feminists* in Chapter 3 and *Passion Fruit* in Chapter 2 substantiates, it is not true of all feminist critics and writers. In the following four chapters, I review the main feminist critiques of each genre and amply illustrate that many of the feminist critics are as much 'knowledgeable fans', as Bloom positions himself. Bloom attacks feminist readings of popular fiction for valuing it in terms of the 'self-reflexive, subversive and radical in order to be good popular fiction'.[24] The implication is that, since feminist critics are looking for the wrong things in their assessment of popular fiction, popular fiction texts themselves cannot be subversive and radical.[25] It would also follow that feminist appropriations, because they are subversive, radical, and often self-reflexive, cannot be true popular fiction. This is in accord with Mann's view of popular fiction as 'simply to entertain and to divert ... The light novel is not a challenge to society and is much more likely to be reassuring rather than challenging.'[26]

However, it needs to be noted that Bloom and Mann are dealing primarily with the adventure story and the romance, which tend to invoke conservative inscriptions of machismo and femininity. Not quite the same certainty of argument about the absence of radical subversiveness could be applied to the genre of science fiction for example. But Bloom's assumption, in his argument against feminists, is that the negotiations that genre readers of pulp have with the text is simple and uncomplex escapism. Because the characteristic element is formulaic – the element of sameness as much as of difference, the recognisable – does not mean that the audience consumes the fiction without critical comment.

Stuart Hall argued for three kinds of reading in 'Encoding and Decoding in the Media Discourse'.[27] 'Encoded' reading is where the audience adopts the ideologies in the text, 'oppositional', when the audience rejects the mores, and 'negotiated', where the audience accepts some and contests others. This middle position, 'negotiation', Christine Gledhill suggested, in relation to women viewers, is a more accurately fluid way of describing the relations between audiences, media products and ideologies.[28]

Elizabeth Flynn, looking at women reading books, in 'Gender and Reading',[29] gave a similar three interactions between readers and texts. In the reader-dominated interaction, the reader resists the text, becomes bored and probably discards it. In the text-dominated inter-action, the reader's self is effaced and 'the text overpowers the reader and so eliminates the reader's powers of discernment'.[30] The text-dominated model is implicit in Mann's view of the escapist popular reader. Flynn's third position is a model of mutual dialogue, where 'reader and text, interact in such a way that the reader learns from the experience without losing critical distance'.[31] This more active model allows the reader a critical engagement with the book, and is one I want to make available for the popular reader. I want to complicate Flynn's model, though, because I do not think any reading involves just one of these positions, and most readings involve all three. There are moments in any book, where one is bored and tempted to skim read, points where one is completely 'transported', and other points where one is critically engaged in the process of the story. This is as true for genre reading as it is for literary reading, although the balance of boredom, transportation and criticism may vary.

The fact that popular genre readers consume vast amounts of their chosen genres is often taken as being a sign of their complete lack of discernment, and therefore evidence of the text-dominated reading position. In fact it is often quite the opposite: the reading of large numbers of works of one genre allows the ordinary, non-academic reader a level of authority because of their overview of their subject. They come to hold a body of knowledge about the genre that informs their judgements about any particular text, however personal that judgement might be for their own uses. When he is not being antagonistic to feminism, Bloom argues this point well: 'Liking popular fiction and the popular arts is (as any fan knows) to create a hierarchy of taste and a popular set of canonical rules – an aesthetic of the popular which is at one and the same time a social negotiation.'[32] Sally Munt pushes this further, in relation to feminist readers, arguing that they are 'a community of readers who actively interrogate the texts they see as "theirs" for an affirmation of sub-cultural belief, and an exploration and dissemination of ideals.'[33]

But I want to look specifically at romance readers, since they are usually assumed to be a book-dominated or encoded readership, and cultural feminist investigation from the mid-1980s has challenged this view of romance readers as passive dupes. Bridget Fowler argued that 77 per cent of the romance readers she surveyed enjoyed reading romance because they took pleasure in a formula, as much as in the pleasure or distraction it afforded.[34] They clearly illustrate a level of critical engagement with the generic conventions. Janice Radway cites the occassion when her romance readers rejected one book, despite its being marketed as romance and by a successful romance writer, because it did not conform sufficiently to the genre format.[35] Radway links this critical engagement to the pleasures of reading the genre and concludes, in relation to reader expertise, that a sense of authority is part of the reading pleasure:

> ... the narrative discourse of the romantic novel is structured in such a way that it yields easily to the reader's most familiar reading strategies. Thus the act of constructing the narrative is reassuring because the romantic writer's typical discourse leads the reader to make abductions and inferences that are always immediately confirmed. As she assembles the plot therefore, the reader learns in addition to what happens next, that *she* knows how to make sense of texts and human action. The reader thus engages in an activity that shores up her own sense of her abilities.[36]

Rowan McCauley, in a paper 'Romance and Women's Pleasure',[37] elaborated on this active pleasure of the expertise, open to the woman reader conversant with the codes of romance and therefore knowing more than the heroine, still locked in the process of believing that the hero is indifferent.

Despite the formulaic nature of the fiction, and its escapist properties, genre readers are no less active than other readers, indeed they may even be more so, in the employment of their expertise of the genre. Because they are active, though, does not mean they are necessarily being radical, subversive, or challenging the ideologies of the text. As Jackie Stacey rightly points out, 'Activity in itself is not a form of resistance: women may be . . . *actively* investing in oppressive ideologies'.[38] Judith Williamson had also argued that because a lot of people engage with popular culture and find it enjoyable, does not necessarily make the genre radical:

> A more complex view would be that often *potentially* radical drives and desires take the forms offered within the status quo (e.g. charities are fuelled by altruism, wearing 'way out' clothes may symbolise the wish to disrupt etc.). *But that doesn't make the forms themselves radical.*[39]

I wanted to make available a model of the genre reader as active and potentially critical, but the active reader is not automatically a feminist reader just because she reads romances actively; far from it. It does, however, open up the position where readers could read feminist examples of the genre and enjoy reading them as part of a genre, without stepping outside of their reading engagement (of rejecting the book as not generic), even while they engage at some level with the feminist ideology. The reader of feminist detective fiction is, after all, no more engaged with formulaic differences than the reader of the British golden-age stories picking up an American hard-boiled novel. Raymond Chandler is very different from Agatha Christie, but a reader expert in the codes of detective fiction can appreciate the ways in which the formulae have been stretched and transformed without being broken. Such a genre transformation, or appropriation, is also open to the feminist writer as I discuss below, but it also means the genre is available to reach a wider public. As I have argued elsewhere,[40] there is a wide constituency of potential readers who satisfy the minimum requirement of having an awareness that feminist texts challenge sexist constructions. One does not need to be a feminist to enjoy feminist detective fiction, for example, though it certainly helps. But the reader needs to be able to appreciate the way that the woman detective both conforms to some of the genre codes for the detective, while simultaneously challenging other, more sexist, assumptions of the formula. If the plot and the writing are effective, the reader will be held and the appropriation will have been successful.

So far I have been discussing the audience as if they were homogeneous, but the readership of any text, verbal or visual, is never unified in its reception. Cultural Studies investigations, such as the BFI *Women Viewing Violence*,[41] have shown how women react differently to viewing the same film or television episode, that they often divide along class, age, or ethnic lines, and in relation to whether they have had some personal experience of the things being viewed (in this case, violence). Bridget Fowler's ethnographic study of romance readers reinforces how they too divide along lines of class and economic dependency.[42] My study is a literary analysis, with its focus on the textual, and as such I will be basing my argument in relation to the readerly positions the texts set up. But that does not imply that I think readers necessarily have to adopt the text's reading position, in a text-dominated or encoded interaction, nor does it mean that I expect all readers will take the same reading of the text.[43]

I do, however, believe that texts are active and do set up readerly positions which the reader can then conform to, or resist, or adopt a complex oscillation betweeen the two. Flynn argued for a dialogue of mutuality in her third readerly position, and such a model implies an active text, alongside the active reader. All texts convey an implicit complex of discourses, and textual analysis discusses them and their effectiveness. All the texts I examine are self-confessedly feminist texts, and I will be examining the various feminist readerly positions they employ, since I believe the genres under study are all open to a feminist appropriation of some sort.

Genre as transformable

Some feminist critics have assumed that the formula of genre fiction is static, a fixed category and thereby, in some sense, inherently conservative, whatever readerly positions are available. Tania Modleski's influential discussion of women's genres across the media, *Loving with a Vengeance: Mass-Produced Fantasies for Women*,[44] challenged the view of women as passive imbibers of patriarchal ideology in their consumption of Harlequin Romance, the female gothic and soap-opera. The assumptions that she makes about each of the genres, implies that they are static forms. Her challenge is to the assumptions of the readerly positions women can take in relation to their chosen genre. Modleski traces the antecedents of each genre, but she never goes on to explore the changes within the genres themselves, thereby implying that they have each remained an unchanged formula throughout the twentieth century. In her introductory discussion of women's gothic, she traces it from Daphne du Maurier's *Rebecca* in 1938, through the 'gaslight' film noir of the 1940s, to the contemporary narratives of the 1980s. 'For Gothic novels have continued to this day to enjoy a steady popularity, and a few of their authors, like Victoria Holt and Mary Stewart, reliably appear on the best-seller list.'[45] That the 1940s' films have the same format as the 1980s' novels is implicit in her discussion, as it is in her chapter on the Harlequin Romances which, she claims, have not changed from their inception in 1958 through to the 1980s: 'the formula rarely varies'.[46]

To be fair to Modleski's deservedly influential study, her enquiry was not about the variability of genre fiction, but her assumption that genre fiction is not transformable is a common one. The belief that feminists who aspire to appropriate genre fiction inevitably do damage their feminism has been prevalent across the various genres, as Andrea Dworkin argues in relation to fairy tales in *Woman Hating*.[47]

Generic fiction has to subscribe to certain conventions in order to be accepted as generic fiction. A feminist fiction that failed to have a crime that is finally solved by the detective, may well be good fiction but it would not be good detective fiction. Detective fiction needs a crime and it needs a detective, and certain expectations have developed in relation to that detective, whether amateur or professional, which the individual writer needs to some extent to engage with – but not necessarily subscribe to. This series of expectations between audiences, writers and publishers marketing the fiction, is the formula or format of that genre. Its rules can be stretched but they cannot be broken, if the work is to remain within the category of that genre. And it has to be acknowledged that those generic formulae carry with them certain ideological implications and assumptions. But that does not mean that the genre itself is monolithic, or that it is unchanging. Formulae adapt over different historical times, they shift and interact with the cultural changes and expectations of their audiences, as a glance at the history of any genre will illustrate. Fairy tales, for example, embodied an aristocratic ideology of appropriate behaviour for children in France during the eighteenth century, shifted to conveying a bourgeois view during the industrialised nineteenth century in Germany and England, and were open to a feminist appropriation in the late twentieth century, at a moment when society is undergoing huge changes in relation to gender. In adapting and working with the format, the genre is at any given moment a complex amalgam of both preceding conventions and the current usage.

Frederic Jameson's model, in his chapter 'Magical Narratives: on the dialectical use of genre criticism', in *The Political Unconscious*,[48] does proper justice to this complicated mix of the conservative and the transformable aspects of genre fiction. Jameson's discussion centres on one of the more traditional and wider uses of the term 'literary genres', looking at romance literature from medieval times to the eighteenth century, but his model is as useful for the popular formulaic genres.

Jameson opens the chapter by describing the genres as 'literary institutions' and, as such, are 'social contracts between a writer and a specific public'.[49] Analysing the mechanisms of genre he decides:

> by means of radical historicization, the 'essence', 'spirit', 'world-view', in question is revealed to be an ideologeme, that is, a historically determinate conceptual or semic complex which can project itself variously in the form of a protonarrative, a private or collective narrative fantasy.[50]

But these ideologemes are not fixed for each genre. Discussing Stendhal's *La Chartreuse* he argues that one passage marks 'the rationalising interiorisation of the form by way of the assimilation of historically new types of content'.[51] Jameson is arguing that genres are transformable, in this specific instance that medieval romance can be 'reinvented' in the eighteenth century by replacing medieval positives such as magic, with newer positives such as theology and a nascent psychology. The basic format remains the same but the 'ideologemes' have shifted because of the new historical context. Of course it is not quite as clear-cut a shift as that. As Jameson develops the model, the genre is transformable within different historical moments but its format continues to carry some of the earlier ideological implications as a kind of residual 'sediment':

> Let us now look more closely at this type of construction, which we will designate as a model of formal *sedimentation* . . . in its emergent, strong form a genre is essentially a socio-symbolic message, or in other terms, that form is immanently and intrinsically an ideology in its own right. When such forms are reappropriated and refashioned in quite different social and cultural contexts, this message persists and must be functionally reckoned into the new form . . .

The ideology of the form itself, thus sedimented, persists into the later, more complex structure as a generic message which co-exists – either as a contradiction or, on the other hand, as a mediatory or harmonizing mechanism – with elements from later stages.[52]

This model of a synchronic text allows for the tensions and contradictions of the variant discourses at play when feminists attempt to appropriate various genre fiction formats. A model that is available to all the genres, since I argue that all genre fiction is potentially transformable.

Cranny-Francis' study asserts that some genres are available for political resistance, such as utopian science fiction with its history of nineteenth-century socialist utopias,[53] but other genres, such as romance, are inimicable to feminist appropriation. 'Romance is even less accessible for feminists, premised, as it is, on an unequal relationship between women and men.'[54] Comparing the feminist criticism across the various genres has led me to a different conclusion. While the genre canon is conservative because, like most academic canons until the 1970s, it privileges conservative and phallologocentric values in its choice of favoured texts, the canon is not symptomatic of the whole genre. In focusing on the 'classic format' Cranny-Francis does not always give due weight to the complex and changing histories of the genres, nor to how the formats and conventions have often contained the subversive and the challenging at some earlier historical moments. Each genre is more than, and other than, its canonical construction. Popular genres are not fixed, but fluid and often very amorphous at their boundaries. Like any popular product they are continually adapting to, and contributing to, their historical contexts. And, when that historical context has included times of gender modification and magnification, as at the turn of the century with the 'new woman', or the 1970s–1980s with second wave feminism, the genres assimilate the conflicting discourses and become a means of exploring feminist or proto-feminist concerns.

I would not go so far as to argue that all genres are equally subversive for feminist practice, some are easier to appropriate than others, but I would and do argue that all the genres are potentially and inherently transformable. The elements of genre 'sedimentation' are a problem that feminist appropriation needs to interrogate, if it is to be judged as effectively feminist, but Jameson's model suggests that the same features can carry radically different meanings within different cultural contexts. Popular genres are fluid and constantly developing.

Feminism and the issue of the feminist text

During the 1980s, not only was feminist fiction branching out, but so was feminist theory. Feminism, no less than generic fiction or the genre audience, was neither static nor monolithic. The concept of what is meant by 'Feminism' and what is meant by feminist writing and feminist literary criticism, had by this time become problematically fragmentary. Rosemary Tonge's *Feminist Thought*[55] delineates seven different feminist positions in 1989: liberal feminism; Marxist feminism; radical feminism; psychoanalytic feminism; socialist feminism; existential feminism; and postmodern feminism. It was no longer possible to talk accurately about Feminism as if it was a unified and singular position. By the end of the 1980s, one needed to acknowledge a range of feminisms. The divergence within feminism developed within feminist *literary* theory and criticism. In the same year as Tonge, *Feminist Readings/Feminists Reading*[56] gave examples of eight, feminist literary critical practices, ranging from sexual politics, to authentic realism, gynocriticism, the anxiety of authorship, French feminisms and Marxist feminism. The 1996 second edition added lesbian criticism and post-colonial feminist theory to the list.[57] While Elaine Showalter's gynocriticism, for example, would focus on the unique differences of women's writing within the dominant male culture, looking for the 'double-voiced discourse' and for the muted 'other voice' of feminine values, French feminism questioned the very values that have been associated as feminine within a phallocentric culture, and looked instead for the disruptive discourse of the semiotic, and for the excesses of masquerade in the descriptions of gender construction. While Marxist feminist critics looked for the silences, the 'not saids', and the lack of closure in the texts, in order to uncover and destabilise the patriarchal ideologies at play in the texts, queer theory looked to destabilise the sexual identities in order to focus on the arbitrariness of gender positions present in the texts. Each feminist critical position looks for variant things within the text and has often made claims for being a superior or more effective form of feminist practice than its colleagues. Never more so than during the early 1980s, the time of the Anglo-American/French feminisms divide when, for example, Moi argued that gynocriticism had thrown the baby out with the bath water when it was unable to incorporate 'Virginia Woolf as the progressive, feminist writer of genius she undoubtedly was'.[58] In the 1990s, the debates raged less internecinely, and began to acknowledge the strengths and the limitations of all the different reading positions. Although some are invariably valued more than others, all have some value for feminist practice.

These contending debates and the issue of a range of feminist practices obviously raise the question of what is a feminist literary practice, in relation to the texts I examine, and moreover what critical assumptions am I making about effective feminist criticism in my examination of the case studies? The first is the easiest to answer, for there are some basic political requirements as Cranny-Francis notes in her introduction to *Feminist Fictions*:

> In feminist fiction, including feminist genre fiction, feminist discourse operates to make visible within the text the practices by which conservative discourses such as sexism are seemlessly and invisibly stitched into the textual fabric, both into its structure and into its story, the weave and the print.[59]

It is this 'disarticulation' of the conventions which is the key to feminist practice, not simply a role reversal, where women do the male tasks (though that can be an important element) but how the narrative 'actively interrogates and destabilises the institutions in which those conventions have become embedded',[60] as Lynne Pearce and Gina Wisker demand of rescripted romance.

The answer to the second question must be a more heterogeneous one, if it is going to do justice to the various and contending voices. Barbara Johnson opens her 1998 *Feminist Difference: Literature, Psychoanalysis, Race and Gender*[61] with a discussion of the 1995 MLA forum on 'Feminist Criticism Revisited' attended by a range of feminist theory practitioners including herself, Elaine Showalter, Jane Gallop, Nancy Miller and Bonnie Zimmerman. Rather than confrontation, the mood was one of ambivalence. Asking, 'Is there something about contemporary academic feminism that requires ambivalence?' she concludes in the face of contending feminist positions that ambivalence is *the* feminist position of the latter half of the 1990s, a 'simultaneity of contradiction and transformation'[62] that rejects a position of assurance and exclusiveness in answering what feminist criticism is. 'If resistance is always the sign of a counter-story, ambivalence is perhaps the state of holding on to more than one story at a time.'[63]

Johnson's ambivalence allows a validity to a heterogeneous range of feminist practices and, moreover, these various practices need to be placed within their own historicity. As Lynne Pearce and Sara Mills point out in their conclusion to the second edition of *Feminist Readings/Feminists Reading*:

> no matter how hybrid or heterogeneous our textual practices become, it seems important to remember that all 'feminist readings' bear the mark of a particular *political* commitment and, as such, come with a history attached.[64]

In my analysis of the feminist appropriations and the feminist critical debates on genres, I think it is important to acknowledge the range of viable feminist positions and not to seek, as some feminist critics have done, to dismiss those works that do not hold their own positions as thereby, *ipso facto*, not effectively feminist.

All the texts addressed position themselves self-conscioulsy as feminist texts: in relation to their authors' position, the dominant reading position offered by the text, and sometimes also by the marketing and distribution of the text. These are avowedly feminist texts and the textual analysis of them takes account of a number of feminist practices in the examination of their strengths and weaknesses as feminist texts, and of their ability to gain a popular audience within the chosen genre.

Finally, it needs to be said that I am not setting up the choice of the texts used as the best of the feminist appropriations, but rather from the wealth of material, as cases that elaborate on issues raised through the examination of the history of the genre and the feminist criticism of the genre. Also, I have necessarily had to limit my examination of the genre criticism to the more mainstream feminist publications, in books or in feminist journals, because to incorporate the criticism within the small-circulation magazines and fanzines as well, would have been beyond the scope of this project. There is still an interesting study to be done, in relation to them, but on the whole they have not had a significant impact on the principal feminist debates about the genre.

2
The Romance

There has long been a convention amongst some feminists that romance fiction is all the same: with a young, innocent, virginal, heroine who desires but repudiates the attentions of the older, richer, sardonically experienced, hero until he finally proposes. Feminist theoreticians from Tania Modleski in 1982 to Cranny-Francis in 1990 have asserted this view (Cranny-Francis argues that the strong male figure is one of the two main ideas of romance). But others, such as Anderson, Moody and Dixon have focused their study on the genre at specific periods in order to demonstrate a more complex and changing script for romance fiction through the century. Their research demonstrates that the kinds of role available to the heroines changed at differing cultural moments, as did the kinds of 'male object' that proved popular, and the configurations of what was important for women.

Many critics of the romance genre have traced the antecedents for the genre to the works of Richardson, the Brontës and Jane Austen, but I will be following Rachel Anderson's model[1] of beginning the genre with the more 'popular' texts rather than the more literary classics,[2] because these focus on the emotional intensity of love. As Janice Radway's Smithton romance fans argued, '"Not all love stories are romances." Some are simply novels about love.'[3] The romance's formula whether it is a gothic romance, an historical romance, or an erotic romance, concentrates on the emotional intensity of the experience of the protagonist falling in love and carefully prolongs the process of anticipation, bewilderment and desire that she experiences as she is pursued and/or played with by the 'hero'. It is the reader's vicarious participation in this heightened state of desire, this 'falling in love', the experience of being courted, that marks out the romance genre format. The clearest examples are those of the formulaic series romances from publishers such as Mills and Boon, Harlequin and Silhouette, where the detailed presentation of the experiential minutiae of the attraction and the set-backs necessitates two-dimensional representations of less important elements such as background, minor characters, and even plot. The same focus on emotional vicissitudes is present in the whole range of the genre, historical romances, gothic romances, and mystery romances, although these obviously display more contextual detail and more convoluted plotting.

Romance can voice a repressed feminine desire in the only genre dominated by women, both as writers and readers, and it can reach a phenomenally huge popular audience. Romance readers consume more texts than most of the other genres put together. That not all women hold feminist views is axiomatic, and a large number of romance texts promulgate phallocentric attitudes towards feminine desire, but the range of the representations allows for more contestation within the genre, than some critics concede.

A history of the genre

Anderson credits circulating libraries such as Mudie's Select Library (1842–1880s) as developing the wider-circulation popular fiction. By the turn of the century, most publishing houses had a cheaper series devoted to adventure and romance fiction, retailing at around two shillings, though some were as cheap as seven old pence.[4] The popular romance in the late nineteenth century translated desire into a more acceptable sacred fervour, with the innocent upper-class women saved from enforced marriages or threatened dishonour because of their spiritual goodness. The works of Charlotte M. Yonge set a trend at the turn of the century. Roda Broughton and Ouida had introduced a less demure concern for the sexual passions in the 1860s, and these also proved popular. Mary Elizabeth Braddon's mystery romance *Lady Audley's Secret* (1862) complicated the formula even more with a female protagonist who proves to be less than innocent (having murdered her husband). The book was a runaway success, selling out its first three editions in ten days and eight editions within three months.[5] Nevertheless, though successful, the erotic and the nefarious heroines were not typical of the majority of the genre during the late Victorian and Edwardian periods. As a publisher's circular of 1897 stated, 'Of all forms of fiction, the semi-religious is the most popular.'[6]

The beginning of the twentieth century brought a more worldly fascination with aristocratic society, as in the works of Mrs Bailie Saunders and Frances Hodgson-Burnett. The romances lavished details on the milieu of tennis parties and grand balls and their plots hinged upon the more material concerns for reputation, dowries and inheritances. Elinor Glyn's *3 Weeks* (1907) continued the erotic sub-genre, with its tale of a passionate affair between a mature European princess and a young British traveller, and proved so successful that it was still in print during the 1930s, having sold over five million copies. The semi-religious form had not disappeared, however. Florence Barclay's *The Rosary* of 1909 was also successful. Ethel M. Dell varied the sub-genre by introducing more adventurous settings in far-flung posts of the British Empire, where her innocent heroines had to contend with religious doubts alongside tempests and brutal husbands. Marie Corelli's religious romances remained firmly within conventional London 'Society' but proved less than conventional in their unorthodox representations of religion. Corelli, having seen angels as a girl, believed herself to have a special calling to endorse a more variant spirituality. Her brand of intense, passionate religiosity was phenomenally successful and she proudly numbered monarchy among her readership (including Victoria and the Prince of Wales).

Though smaller in number, the erotic romances continued to be produced and they had their own runaway success in 1919 with E. M. Hull's *The Sheik*. Hull adopted the more exotic settings of Etel M. Dell, and added erotic adventure, with the abduction of its English heroine by a passionate sheik who forces her into his harem. (An explosively transgressive situation that is superficially disarmed by the discovery that he is the son of a Scottish earl and a Spanish princess, no true Arab at all.)

At the turn of the century two distinct sub-genres of romance had already established themselves: a strand that presented love as a semi-religious fervour; and a strand that celebrated the more sensual passions. Both strands conformed socially, being set within the distinctly aristocratic social milieu.

1909 also saw the beginning of a small general publishing house that was to become synonymous with the romance genre. Mills and Boon began by publishing a number of well-known literary names in its fiction lists, such as Hugh Walpole, P. G. Wodehouse, E. F. Benson and Jack London. It also published non-fiction and educational books.[7] Their early romance writers, such as Louise Gerard and Sophie Cole, had upper-class protagonists in London society or in Africa, Burma and India, locations related to the British Empire. While the foreign locations sported traditional Imperial heroes, the society novels illustrated a different gender configuration. Jay Dixon notes in her study of the history of Mills and Boon, that during the first decade of the twentieth century, they had mature female protagonists whose attractions were to give 'succour' and stability to the male hero.[8] This gender configuration was also true of Mills and Boon's 'city and country' romances which brought in the first middle-class protagonists. In these, while the wives remained at home in the country, surrounded by the stable virtues of nature and domesticity, their husbands' work in the city left them vulnerable to the heady temptations of the metropolis. In both the society novels and the country-and-the-city novels, it is the women who provide the solidity and security for their more fallible men.

During the 1920s and 1930s, the heroines become younger, more glamorous and sophisticated, reflecting the advent of a new form of 'society' during the period of the gay young things. She lived in Mayfair, smoked cigarettes and drank cocktails. By the mid-1930s she was also economically independent for the first time, usually working in something creative or fashion-orientated, with a busy nightlife crammed with cocktail parties, night-clubs and West End shows. Berta Ruck, Ruby M. Ayres, Netta Muskett and Denise Robins were the most popular writers of this type of romance.

Dixon situates this shift within the historical context of five million women working, between the wars. While the literary novels of the day ignored this phenomenon, romance fiction explored the incumbent concerns of both work and independence, albeit in a highly fantasised configuration.

This economic independence transmuted both the erotic and the semi-religious sub-genres. The earlier religious fervour became converted into an equally innocent, maternal concern for the hero, who became particularly boyish during the 1920s (and hence less sexually intimidating). Not only were the heroes younger, but they were also predominantly poorer and less well-educated than the female protagonists. These more vulnerable boy heroes appealed to the women's desire to nurture. Dixon suggests that the memory of the 'golden youth' lost in the First World War, and the crisis of masculinity that arose with shell-shocked soldiers diagnosed as 'neurasthenic' (believed to be a woman's disease), may have led to the preponderance of boy heroes.[9] While possibly true, this does not explain the crossing of class boundaries implicit in the representations, that links more closely to women's migration into the wider arena of the workplace.

Economic independence also fuelled the erotic sub-genre which, inspired by the success of *The Sheik*, had a whole raft of financially independent women travellers encountering passionate Mediterranean lovers. Desire and passion, between the wars, were located within the European, rather than British masculinity.

In the 1930s, Mills and Boon began to specialise in romance fiction, and during the depression their brown covers, the 'books in brown', were a mainstay of the twopenny commercial libraries. The romance hero developed into a more mature and solid country-gentleman (the representation women had held in the 1900s), with a focus on companionship rather than passion, leading Anderson to argue that the romances of this period were 'shallow, flaccid and unspirited'.[10] During the 1940s, the genre focused upon the protagonists' respectablity even more. 'The War had finally killed off any of the last remaining traces of the reckless spirit of E. M. Hull and E. M. Dell or Elinor Glynn,' Anderson argues. 'Heroines were never again to know the wild sweet joy of mad, passionate love.'[11] (It needs to be borne in mind that Anderson was writing before the advent of the 1970s 'erotic romance' series.) Some of the 1940s romances had a war setting, often with the protagonists in uniform, and a spate of injured heroes began what would later become the doctor/nurse sub-genre. The majority of romances at this time offered an escape from the hardships and rationing by portraying a time of stability and plenty, celebrating the more domestic values of women's lives. Where there were still wealthy heroines, their wealth was now seen as a 'problem' to the relationship, and only the rival 'other woman' could have a glamorous career. Authoritative father-figures became the new objects of desire, expurgating the erotic to such an extent that eye-contact, rather than kisses, became the site of ardour. Dixon argues that Mills and Boon romances tended to contextualise the war only in the 1950s, with the returning heroes, traumatised by their experiences, being healed by the love of a good woman. The maturity of the heroes remains an important configuration, with the hero often distinguished as the 'real man' amongst the 'boys'. It is only during the 1950s that the conventional stereotype becomes established. The variety of ages and the transmutaion of the authority narrows to the reification of masculine domination, with the hero as a man of the world, thirty-five, sardonic, and wealthy, in contrast to the heroine in her early twenties, a virgin and with few protective relations. Desire remains pure, with the protection of the protagonist's chastity as the main discursive narrative.

In 1949, Harlequin set up as a Canadian reprint operation buying in titles from, among other publishers, Mills and Boon. The late 1950s saw the decline of the lending libraries, one of romance's major outlets, and readership declined. In 1957, Mills and Boon chose to concentrate solely on the romance market because of its popularity and, following the example of Harlequin, launched its own paperback series in 1960.

During the majority of the 1960s, modesty and chastity remain the ideological norms of romance fiction, despite the historical context of the 'Swinging Sixties' and the 'permissive revolution'. Barbara Cartland's heroines exemplify the genre during the decade. The stereotyped older, experienced and wealthy hero continued to pursue the virginal, younger woman, although she was allowed to return to a glamorous, fashionable job in some exotic location. Towards the end of the 1960s, the suppressed erotic sub-genre made itself partially felt, with the return of machismo Latin or Arabic lovers, though censorially the protagonists just manage to remain chaste until the altar. This reinforcement of virginity as the essential aspect of desirable femininity, shows romance fiction at its most conformist, at a time of real change and flexibility in relation to sexual mores.

It was not to last long; the 1970s saw the return of the repressed, with the phenomenal success of the 'bodice-rippers'. The erotic strand of the genre reappeared in the historical romances of Kathleen Woodiwiss, closely followed by Lolah Burford and Rosemary Rogers. Danielle Steel and Janet Dailey then took the erotic element into more contemporary settings. Harlequin reacted to the market response by separating its output into two distinct series, adding 'Presents' to its 'Romance', thereby codifying the two main sub-genres of romance fiction through the years. The 'Presents' protagonists experienced more detailed and turbulent erotic desires, though still retaining their virginity until marriage. The 'Presents' heroes were more aggressive and passionate with 'feisty' heroines who fought back. During 1977–8 this led to a preponderance of 'rape' plots, an effect some critics have suggested of feminism's raising of cultural awareness of male violence. From 1979, the male characters developed as 'other'. They became unknowable, antagonistic, and constructed as very different from women, often literally strangers. Frenier suggests, in her analysis of the changing roles of heroes during the 1970s and 1980s, that this may be linked to the publication of Nancy Friday's research, showing that the main fantasy of American women at the time was having sex with a stranger.[12]

In the early 1970s Harlequin proved so successful that it bought up

Mills and Boon, and in 1971 employed W. Lawrence Heisey, a Proctor and Gamble salesman, to initiate a marketing strategy that sold fiction like magazines, stocking them in supermarkets rather than bookshops, focusing advertising on the Harlequin package rather than on individual books, and issuing new titles monthly. Heisey also undertook market research, to cater plots and characters to audience preferences. In the 1980s, Harlequin became a sales phenomenon. In 1979 it was claiming to have an American readership of sixteen million, and issuing twelve books a month, six 'Romance' and six 'Presents'.[13] Janice Radway points to this change in the marketing of the product, to explain the contradictory rise of both phenomenal romance fiction sales and the impact of feminism on British and American society.

In 1980, Simon and Schuster began the Silhouette series, as a challenge to Harlequin–Mills and Boon's virtual monopoly on romance, looking to focus groups to tell them what the American public really wanted, while poaching some of Harlequin's most successful authors, such as Charlotte Lamb and Janet Dailey. Their 'Candlelight Ecstasy' series brought out more realistic gender roles, sexier but with gentler heroes. In 1982 this mutated into the 'Desire' series with explicit premarital sex and sold so well that Barbara Rudolph argued at the time that 'Harlequin is a classic case of missing out on a changing market. Its staple was innocent love, but readers gradually developed an appetite for less naive heroines and spicier plots.'[14] Although Rudolph seems to be referring to the Harlequin Romance series, rather than its 'Presents', Harlequin took note of Silhouette's success and in 1984 brought out its 'Temptation' series with more mature protagonists than their Romance heroines. (They also bought the Silhouette imprint from Simon and Schuster in 1985.) Temptation heroines, as Nickianne Moody notes, are sexually experienced, have engrossing jobs but, having reached a pinnacle of success in their thirties, are ripe for something different in their lives. Although she does not argue for a 'radical change' in the Temptation series, Moody does note a definite shift in the 'structural portrayal of the gender relations'.[15] In Temptation fiction it is often the hero who holds back from sex, until he is sure that it will be a loving consummation, and helps the heroine to resolve a past hurt and to convince her that marriage, and particularly motherhood, is a viable proposition.

> The 'temptation' (from a feminist perspective) experienced by the 1990s heroine is not to surrender her precious virginity, but to commit the post-feminist sin of giving up her hard-won independence.[16]

Although the romances still uphold monogamy and marriage as normalised ideals, the relationship between the two sexes has had to be re-drawn to adapt to social changes and expectations. The heroes and heroines of the 1980s and 1990s romance have gentler, more consensual relationships, where women are again economically independent and more likely to continue working after marriage. Women are able to voice their desire and initiate sex which is presented as more enjoyable and diverse, and less violent. In the 1990s it is the woman who needs to be coaxed into agreeing to marry, rather than the man, thereby acknowledging that marriage, as a patriarchal structure, holds more perils for women.

A look at the history of romance fiction identifies that erotic passion is not solely a phenomenon of the rise of the Women's Liberation Movement, as many feminist critics, comparing only the 1960s with the 1970s, have argued. Physical passion has been a staple from the genre's inception. Nor has the shift to less authoritative, gentler heroes been only a late twentieth-century phenomenon. In fact, the 1940s representations, running through to the 1960s, which are usually assumed to constitute the tradition of the genre, are actually atypical in censoring the more erotic aspects of women's romance fiction. Second-wave feminism has had an important impact in developing the representations of female desire and social equality, but it did not initiate them. Indeed the impact of feminism on romance was initially counter-productive, as Ann Rosalind Jones' examination of Mills and Boon output makes plain.[17] In 1983–4, economically independent women had to defend themselves rigorously from the charge of being feminists, while the men treat feminist claims dismissively, and are shown to be right. A common implication of these books is that feminists are simply afraid of men, and of male potency. The underlying ideological import is that feminism itself is unnatural and misguided. That the romances need to bring in feminism, and yet display 'a multilevelled incoherence in dealing with it', shows the genre's resistance to feminism at this time, even while the plots often accord with feminist views such as the woman's right to continue working after marriage.[18] Catherine Kirkland's 1984 PhD thesis[19] agreed with this ambivalence towards feminism but argued for a more diverse response from romance writers. While some romance writers saw the genre as one of the last bastions against feminism, others willingly identified themselves as feminists.

When it comes to feminist appropriation, it is hard to make generalisations about romance fiction as a whole, given the huge output of romance material during the 1970s–1990s, particularly when the more gentle, chaste Harlequin Romance sells alongside the Harlequin Temptation. Certainly no avowedly feminist writers have written romance fiction and no mainstream romance texts have been sold on a feminist byline, but as will be seen below, some feminist critics point to writers such as Charlotte Lamb, Victoria Kelrich or Susan Napier, as pushing the construction of femininity, along pro-feminist lines.

Feminist criticism and appropriation of romance

In 1970, Germaine Greer's social criticism *The Female Eunuch*[20] had one of its chapters devoted to romance fiction and she, like Kate Millett[21] and Shulamith Firestone,[22] saw it as creating a false consciousness, an opiate for downtrodden women. Greer argues that the romance hero of the rich and powerful father-phallus who will adore the heroine, lures women into ignoring reality and distorting their actual behaviour. But women are complicit in their collusion: 'This is the hero that women have chosen for themselves. The traits invented for him have been invented by women cherishing the chains of their bondage.'[23]

1974 saw the publication of Rachel Anderson's *The Purple Heart Throbs: the Sub-literature of Love*, a book-length study of the early history of the genre. Anderson's book established the genre as worthy of serious study but, in its sub-title made no claims to challenge the canon of 'literature'. (Romance was one of the genres to benefit from just such a challenge during the following decade.) Starting with Charlotte M. Yonge's *The Heir of Radcliffe* (1853), the book charts the romance authors through to the early 1970s, with a subtext that privileges the exploration of the erotic and disparages the rigid codification into chaste respectability in the 1950s. 'It used to be possible for the hero to be considerably younger than the heroine – now such an idea has a hint of wilful non-conformity, even of obscenity about it.'[24] Focusing on the history of the genre allows Anderson to argue that romance shifts and changes through the decades.

The 1980s saw a profusion of texts on romance, debating their patriarchal inscription or their subversive potential. Tania Modleski's seminal book, *Loving with a Vengeance: Mass-Produced Fantasies for Women* (1982), opened the debate by arguing that the cultural critics' decision to ignore romance, while considering detective fiction, is yet one further way of devaluing women and women's interests. The book looks seriously at Harlequin Romance, gothic novels and films, and soap-operas, investigating why women should get such pleasure from them. Her psychoanalytic study of the romance texts argues that they speak covertly to women's deep-rooted anxieties, desires and wishes, within a hostile culture. Romance allows them to experience regressive fantasies of rebellious anger and of being cherished and protected. Women gaining pleasure from romances, she argues, are therefore actively engaged in adapting their circumscribed lives. However, the rebellion is neutralised by the narrative desire for a happy closure, subverted by the reader's wish that the hero will see the woman as cute rather than aggressive. The construction of these hostile heroes, moreover, teaches women to 'read' men's behaviour and perpetuates the confusion around male sexuality. Looking at Harlequin in the late 1970s, she argues that the formula rarely varies from the idealised passivity of the young, inexperienced woman confused by the mocking, older, wealthy man. Such a rigid formula 'inoculates' women against social inequities. As such, romance novels, though they give women pleasure, prevent women rebelling.

David Margolies, in 'Mills and Boon: Guilt without Sex'[25] agrees that reading romances allows an expression to the emotions starved in everyday life, but that the narratives serve to naturalise male aggression and female obsessive concentration on men. The women's 'insecurity' in relation to the hero and her 'guilt' in misunderstanding him and in arousing his desire, are also naturalised as part of being a woman. Margolies' Marxist analysis of a few months' output of Mills and Boon argues that, being market-led, they reflect attitudes already accepted by the majority of the readership and so reinforce the status quo.

Ann Barr Snitow's 'Mass Market Romance; Pornography for Women is Different'[26] agrees with Margolies that Harlequin romances are accurate reflections of certain aspects of accepted cultural femininity, but focuses the pleasure women get from reading them into an erotic frame, asserting that they illustrate how women's 'pornography' is different from men's. With the two genders constructed as separate species, the books focus on a 'phallic worship'[27] of unknowable, magical maleness, where coldness and cruelty are accepted as just part of the package. The protagonist exists in one of two states: either fighting his physical effect, when present, or waiting absorbed, for the next encounter. The tension created is titillating and erotically pleasurable, thus allowing women a sense of excitement, adventure and fulfilment. While these highly eroticised narratives valorise woman's passivity in a manner similar to male pornography, the female versions bathe the sex in a romantic glow. Harlequin texts thereby allow women to experience erotic feelings safely within the social double standards. Snitow accepts that feminists are quite right to dislike the passive elements ascribed to feminine sexuality, but she points out that the genre illuminates how female arousal is dependent on a complex social and emotional negotiation: female sexual desire combines romance, security and eroticism. So, while acknowledging the social reinforcement of feminine passivity and phallocentricism, Snitow argues that romance allows women an experience which, though socially circumscribed, nevertheless points towards a more accurate representation of what constitutes female desire.

1984 saw the publication of perhaps the most influential book on how romance is discussed, Janice Radway's *Reading the Romance: Women, Patriarchy, and Popular Literature.*[28] Radway shifted her analysis from the textual reading, to an ethnographic examination of the reading habits of a specific group of romance readers. As well as looking at how the texts construct the implied reader, Radway examined how actual readers constructed the texts. Such an analysis complicates further the discussion of whether romance reading is resisting or reinforcing patriarchy, because as well as the text, there is the action of reading it. The women saw this act as 'combative' because for the period of reading, they resist the demands of their families in order to devote time to themselves, to their own pleasure, and to forging an imagined community of other women readers. Radway accepts that romance as a text is a contradictory narrative that allows the voicing of women's anxieties and desires within patriarchy, while revealing its 'role as conservator of the social structure and its legitimizing ideology',[29] by its marital happy-ending. What Radway's group took from the narratives however, were stories of female triumph, where intelligent and 'feisty' women defy the heroes and transform them into people who can love and care for women as they wish to be loved. The readers revel in the self-sufficient initiative of the defiant heroine, as much as they do in the final mutual capitulation. In their readings, the ending has the hero softened into the same attentive, intuitive, caring behaviour as women accord to men. By examining women reading romance, rather than assuming she knows what they do, Radway is able to argue that women use romance fiction as a cognitive exploration for adapting their ordinary lives:

romance is never simply a love story, [it] is also an exploration of the meaning of patriarchy for women. As a result, it is concerned with the fact that men possess and regularly exercise power over them in all sorts of circumstances. By picturing the heroine in relative positions of weakness, romances are not necessarily endorsing her situation, but examining an all-too-common state of affairs in order to display possible strategies for coping with it.[30]

Like Modleski she is arguing for a complex process of reading that is both oppositional and capitulating, but Radway's main focus is on the uses real women put romance texts to. As she points out, many romance readers do not want feminism's autonomous, work-orientated ideal, being more concerned with how to effect the broadening of femininity (sexual passion and feisty independence) within their traditional institutions of marriage and family. Radway argues for romance's value in serving ordinary women's needs within an oppressive system. Romance fiction also charts the small changes that feminism has effected within the major social institutions. Romance preferences point to a contemporary shift in the kinds of masculinity women desire. Her mid-town, middle-aged group rejected brutal heroes in favour of ones that are nurturing and tender. Using a psychological model drawn from Chodorow,[31] Radway argues that this preference points to a regressive fantasy to be mothered, that women repress in infancy. Following Chodorow's view of 'sex imprints' as fixed, Radway's liberal feminism (even in the 1991 introduction) argues that 'in ideal romances the hero is constructed androgynously'.[32] A more post-structuralist view of gender would argue that her readers were pointing to a preference for a new, broader inscription of masculinity, alongside the newly 'feisty' femininity, rather than a denial of the masculine altogether. Nevertheless, Radway's book has been extremely influential in shifting how the romance genre is discussed, particularly within cultural studies. The main problems with it lie in its attempt to universalise the conclusions from the Smithton group, to all women.

Kay Mussell's *Fantasy and Reconciliation: Contemporary Formulas of Women's Romance Fiction*[33] of the same year argued a more conservative view of romance as a bastion against feminism, for women who felt threatened by the changes to their traditional roles. Romance, with its certain moral order and its focus on the traditional feminine concerns of mate selection and homemaking, offered a predictable safety. The main focus of the book is the clarification of the typology of romance into six sections: series; erotic; romantic suspense; gothic mysteries; romantic biographies; and historical romances, though Mussell is forced to admit that these typologies overlap. Which type is favoured in which periods, she sees as an indicator of the rapidly altering cultural shifts in women's experience; 'the formulaic variations ... mirror the concerns of the readers'.[34]

Also in the same year came a third way of developing an analysis of romance, in an important essay by Alison Light, 'Returning to Manderley – Romance Fiction, Female Sexuality and Class'.[35] Taking issue with Margolies' model of the texts 'reflecting' society, Light argues for a much more flexible model of reading that takes into account the fictionality of the literature, arguing that while not 'progressive', romance reading could be seen as symptomatic of women's discontent and, as a technique of survival, 'transgressive'.[36] Romance creates a fantasy where 'relations [are] impossibly harmonized; it uses unequal heterosexuality as a dream of equality and gives women uncomplicated access to a subjectivity which is unified and coherent *and* still operating within the field of pleasure.'[37] The essay goes on to give a materialist post-structuralist analysis of *Rebecca* that argues for the social construction of bourgeois femininity in the narrator's collusion with the male (Maxim), and in the self-suppression (murdering) of the disruptive alternative of sensual and independent femininity (Rebecca). The text therefore acts out what all women go through in constructing their femininity, but despite the text's suppressive closure, the reader's identification with transgressive femininity 'can never be fully contained nor its disruptive potential fully retrieved'.[38] Like Radway, though from a different feminist stance, Light is arguing for an appreciation of how romance works as a space of psychic and cultural resistance and pleasure, even though it is not a site of open rebellion.

The following year Janet Batsleer, Tony Davies, Rebecca O'Rourke and Chris Weedon brought out *Rewriting English: Cultural Politics of Gender and Class*[39] as part of the challenge of the canon, and the ideology underpinning the academic concept of 'literature' undertaken by the Birmingham Centre for Contemporary Cultural Studies. One chapter was devoted to romance fiction, and another to an examination of women's actual reading practices. Romance was positioned as reinforcing ideological conventions of sexual division and the inferiority of women. Acknowledging the historical changes in the romance narratives, they yet argue for a similarity of plot around the taming of women (as opposed to Radway's taming of men). Focusing mainly on Barbara Cartland, they argue that romance marks out femininity as domestic, dependent and sexually passive, fore-grounding familial relationships. The genre focuses on a common structure of experience that largely excluded women from the public sphere, and evaluated the domestic as at the 'heart' of society. Romances reinforce sexual double-standards, while allowing women an erotic titillation. Despite this reading of romance's reinforcement of patriarchy, the authors do not go on to condemn romance reading. Perhaps in the light of their later chapter,[40] they conclude that it should not be assumed that women are incapable of 'recognizing a fairy-story when they see one',[41] and romance reading illustrates a daily dissatisfaction with the reality of women's lives.

At the end of the year, Deborah Philips[42] concentrated on the publishing phenomenon of romance, detailing the millions of titles sold by Harlequin, Mills and Boon, and Silhouette, dismissing the products as unchanging as bars of chocolate in their perpetuation of the patriarchal construction of female desire.

In 1986 feminists began to consolidate a more positive reading in romance fiction. *The Progress of the Romance: the Politics of Popular Romance*,[43] edited by Jean Radford and arising from a conference at Ruskin College, placed analysing romance as a left-wing challenge to canonical assumptions of English Literature, and a left-wing attempt to understand the popularity of conservative politics. As feminists, the contributors rejected the view of the woman reader as a passive imbiber of ideology. Adopting a model of the reader informed by Radway and Light, the introduction argues for plural and contradictory effects produced by the texts, and the way they speak to women's lives and their subjectivity. Jean Radford's own essay[44] argues for Radcliff Hall's *The Well of Loneliness* being a popular lesbian romance while Michele Roberts' contribution[45] explores the difficulties, for a feminist writer, inherent in writing romance fiction. Ann Rosalind Jones' article on 'Mills and Boon and Feminism', pointed to the novels' defensive negation of feminism as a label, even while they accommodated some of its claims for independence.

In the States, Carol Thurston's *The Romance Revolution: Erotic Novels for Women and the Quest for a New Sexual Identity*[46] was also making feminist claims for the importance of romance fiction in women's lives, though her claims were less divided in their praise. Thurston argued that in the 1970s and 1980s, the American romances of Silhouette and Ballantine began to voice a new sexuality, starting with the historical romances (the 'bodice-rippers') and extending into the contemporary romances. Responding to both feminist challenges of ideology and market forces of what readers wanted, the books developed a different plot structure where the challenge was to find a mutually respectful love, rather than overcoming obstacles put in love's way. Echoing the 'New Man' construction, the heroes became more sensitive and vulnerable, while the protagonist became more powerful in the public world of work, and expected to remain so after her marriage. The American romances thereby argued for a heterosexual relationship of equals, 'one that frees respect and the right of self-determination from gender'[47] and, through its confident and independent heroines, is able to disseminate the feminist vision to readers who might otherwise reject its ideology (though she argued research had shown that in fact romance readers were not anti-feminist). For Thurston, therefore, 1980s Silhouette and Ballantine romances were to some extent feminist appropriations.

Jay Dixon's article, 'Fantasy Unlimited: the World of Mills and Boon'[48] didn't quite go as far in its claims, acknowledging that in one sense Mills and Boon and the Women's Liberation Movement are antithetical to each other. Nevertheless, she saw romances as positive fantasies for women, putting women first, celebrating women fighting for what they want, and controlling their own destinies. Masculinity, defined as sexual and financial power, is overwhelmed by the woman's emotional power, and so it is the heroine that triumphs. Although the essay largely ignores the fact that the patriarchal institutions remain intact its claim for a positive reading of romance is the opposite of Deborah Philips', two years before in the same journal.

Amal Treacher's 'What is Life Without My Love? Desire and Romantic Fiction'[49] in a book dedicated to women and popular fiction, also argued that while not a radical intervention to phallocentric culture, an analysis of romance does offer insights into how women negotiate their fantasy lives within a patriarchal culture and begin to understand how we are gendered with contradictory and ambivalent desires. Romance revels in the primitive and the emotional, offering a utopian distraction from the mundane and the difficult. This psychoanalytic feminist examination rejects a more didactic moralising to suggest that the study of romance helps to uncover how 'seemingly undesirable phantasies remain obstinately erotic',[50] arguing that the dominant and yet caring hero is a projection of the ideal father *and* mother, combining their total, unconditional love in the adult relationship. Informed by Snitow's reading of the sexual fantasies present in romance, Treacher goes on to argue that not only is feminine desire described in contradictory terms, but masculinity is too, and that romance fiction is able to give coherence to the wildly contradictory and ambivalent phantasies.

Frenier's *Goodbye Heathcliffe: Changing Heroes, Heroines, Roles and Values in Women's Category Romances*[51] in 1988 takes Thurston's distinction between Silhouette and Harlequin to chart the rise of the independent, intellectual and sexually desiring heroines and sensitive, caring heroes from the late 1970s to the early 1980s. Although the links it makes to the cultural shifts are shallow and the analyses are descriptive rather than analytic, the book makes a case for romance changing in relation to feminism, and continues the positive reading of romance as symptomatic of cultural changes.

Helen Taylor's 'Romantic Readers' in yet another book on gender and genre, *From My Guy to Sci-Fi*,[52] acknowledges the popularity of the genre and feminists' critical interest in it, from their early dismissal to the 1980s' celebration. This feminist interest has led to a new breed of romance writers and to new developments within the genre. In contrast to Frenier, she claims the representation of masculinity does not change, nor does the marital ending. Other women's fiction, the family sagas and lesbian romance, have successfully challenged these aspects of patriarchy. Feminist critics' focus on the readers is praised as one of the most exciting aspects of the romance discourse, although Taylor finds problems with the unified models imposed, and argues for more awareness of the audience's age, class and ethnicity to complicate the psychoanalytic 'universal' model, drawing on her forthcoming study of readers of *Gone With the Wind*, *Scarlet's Women*.[53]

As Taylor describes, there has been a shift during the 1980s, from a rather apologetic analysis of romance – as something patriarchally inscribed, but still important to women readers – to a view of it as potentially transgressive and even celebratory. This shift arose with the change from studying them as literary narratives, to viewing them as symptomatic of women's needs as socially gendered subjects, within a changing culture. The 1990s saw an intensification of this kind of debate, alongside a questioning of how feminist romance itself, as a genre, could be claimed to be.

Ann Cranny-Francis' *Feminist Fiction: Feminist Uses of Generic Fiction*[54] considered a range of feminist attempts to reappropriate genre fiction. In the chapter on romance,[55] she claims that, since the genre is premised on an unequal relationship between genders, it is impossible for feminists to appropriate it. Romance 'encodes the most coherent inflection of the discourses of gender, class and race constitutive of the contemporary social order'.[56] Fetishising patriarchal marriage, romance channels the erotic drive into an economic desire for wealth, security and status by marrying the man that embodies both erotic and economic power. The protagonist does that by being the most patriarchally 'feminine'. Romance therefore reinforces not only patriarchy but the bourgeois ideology as well. Cranny-Francis contends that while feminist writers cannot appropriate the romance discourse, they have interrogated it within their fiction, in novels which have romance writers as characters, and which contain examples of romance prose within the narrative.

Bridget Fowler's *The Alienated Reader: Women and Romantic Literature in the Twentieth Century*[57] agrees that romance is one of the least rebellious of the popular genres, due to its feudal origins. Fowler places romance's precedents in the fairy tale, where women were dependent vassals. Adopting a method similar to Radway's of studying a group of actual readers, Fowler problematises both the romance genre and the readership, in ways Radway never does. Fowler's study distinguishes between romance texts, arguing that where series romances naturalise patriarchal and bourgeois norms, a sub-genre of family sagas by Cookson, Holt and Taylor Bradford stretch the formula to challenge feminine dependency. She similarly makes distinctions within her group of readers, noting how her Scottish women's responses divided along lines of class and economic dependency. Poorer, more dependent, readers chose Mills and Boon as a conservative escape from drudgery and insecurity, while more aspiring and economically comfortable readers went for the more questioning, resistant sub-genre. Fowler brings a much-needed refinement to the ethnographic study of the romance genre. Like Cranny-Francis, Fowler concludes that the romance formula colludes with dominant patriarchal institutions, but that it also provides 'the heart of a heartless world'[58] to the alienated woman reader.

1995 saw the publication of two diametrically opposing views of romance: *Their Own Worst Enemies* and *Romance Revisited*. Daphne Watson's *Their Own Worst Enemies: Women Writers of Women's Fiction*[59] argues that romance writers and contemporary blockbusters create acceptable selves for the women readers which are conservative and patriarchal. Turning in her fourth chapter to Mills and Boon,[60] she attacks Radway and Modleski for their 'political correctness' in not wishing to attack either the texts or the readers, and rejects the idea of the active reader for one of the dupe. The texts portray aggressive, dominating men demanding subservience from the insecure and fragile heroines, and provide all the comfort of a warm bath or a cuddly toy, while subtly damaging the reader's sense of femininity. While Watson continues Fowler's questioning of Radway's conclusions, her reasoning and vitriol go right back to Germaine Greer's attack on the genre, 25 years earlier.

In contrast, the *Romance Revisited* collection of essays argued that now was the time to put romance 'back on the feminist agenda'.[61] The editors interrogate why the desire for romance continues in our culture, while traditional relationships are breaking down. Arguing that the structural properties of the classic romance have become dislocated and transformed within postmodernity, they claimed a need for feminists to re-theorise romance. Pearce and Stacey proposed the 'newer' methodologies of discourse theory and dialogics as capable of moving the feminist analysis forwards. These predicate the 'historical/cultural situatedness' of romance and its unstable 'provisionality' and constant transformation. Such a reading would allow us to view romance reading as open to 'the radical questionings of subjectivity and gender-identity', rather than as just 'fantasy and wish-fulfilment'.[62] The significant collection of essays discusses feminism's impact on the discourse of romance,[63] and how the romantic discourse in contemporary culture is changing.

Lynne Pearce continued this argument in her 1998 collection, *Fatal Attractions: Rescripting Romance in Contemporary Literature and Film*[64] co-edited with Gina Wisker, around the issue of whether the concept of love, or romance, had itself renegotiated in relation to feminism and socialism. At issue, was how in contemporary films and fiction, the romantic desire (for union, merger, closure), the property of everybody, could be dissociated from the institutions of romance (heterosexuality, marriage, racial purity). Their ideal subversion involves the separation of the psychic foundations of desire from the cultural institutions which are thereby exposed. Perhaps not surprisingly, only two of the essays focused on formulaic romance, as opposed to romance within non-genre novels and films: Nickianne Moody's essay on the 'Temptation' series, and Paulina Palmer's consideration of lesbian romance.

1999 saw the publication of Jay Dixon's in-depth study of the history of Mills and Boon's output, *The Romance Fiction of Mills and Boon 1909–1990s*.[65] Situating herself as a former M&B editor, feminist and avid-reader of romances, Dixon argues they depict the difficulties specific to women within a patriarchal world. Going further, she makes the rather dubious suggestion that they may even be Cixous' 'woman's voice'. But the main thesis of the book is that Mills and Boon novels are not 'all the same'; that in each decade of this century, they have reflected the cultural moment. Mills and Boon texts have consistently seen women working outside the home, even when they are married. The romance world, where women's love prevails, shows the male world becoming conflated with the feminine, as the woman changes the hero into the man she wants as a partner. Because of this empowering of the female sphere, she concludes that 'Mills and Boon romances and feminism have differing political frameworks, but it may just be that under the skin they are sisters.'[66] While such a claim goes way too far, contemporary feminist debate on the romance genre does not always assume that it is a genre completlely incapable of appropriation.

Feminist debate has produced some significant shifts in how we discuss readership, in resisting the denigration of the women who read romance in such large numbers. The debate about whether romance itself encodes patriarchal gender assumptions and institutions is less divided than at first it seems, because most critics agree that they do (even if only on the closure of the marital happy-ending). Where they divide is in how women access the texts and use them for their own, possibly transgressive, ends. The critics also divide on whether the romance plots and gender roles have shifted in relation to changing cultural expectations, or remained the same.

The attempt to re-appropriate romance by avowedly feminist writers, however, has been less significant when it comes to heterosexual romance. Anne Cranny-Francis claims that feminist writers find it hard to negotiate a genre predicated on the unequal power relations between men and women, where getting the man is the happy solution to the woman's worries, thereby underwriting her dependency on the male. Although this is not quite accurate in its depiction of romance's history, it is for the most part the overall assumption about romance prevalent in the 1980s and so, as Cranny-Francis accurately points out, few feminist writers have tried to appropriate the genre.[67] What they have been more likely to do is to comment obliquely on the romance discourse, by incorporating it into their plots. She cites Margaret Atwood's *Lady Oracle* (1982) and Fay Weldon's *Life and Loves of a She-Devil* (1983) as two examples where the novelists include a romance writer as a main character, and the narratives interrogate how the romance discourse obscures and damages women's view of life. Helen Taylor[68] adds Marilyn French's *The Bleeding Heart* (1980) and Jill Tweedie's *Bliss* (1985) to this list of feminist 'reworking and pastiche' of romance novels, but also puts forward the collection of stories edited by Jeanette Winterson, *Passion Fruit: Romantic Fiction with a Twist* (1986) as a further interesting feminist reworking. Although I would agree on their interest, I would question their status as feminist re-appropriations of the genre, because to return to Radway's readers – '"Not all love stories are romances." Some are simply novels about love.'[69]

But another impact of feminism, the setting up of feminist publishing houses, brought a much more radical challenge to traditional romance fiction, with the introduction of the lesbian romance imprint by Naiad Press in the mid-1970s. Long before feminism, some of the smaller romance imprints[70] had story-lines including lesbians, usually as the third party who comes between the protagonist and her lover/husband. The dénouement tended to have the protagonist returning to the man's arms, having learnt the error of her ways, while the lesbian takes to drink, or becomes insane. Despite the condemnatory closures, these earlier narratives had allowed some brief exploration of women's love for another woman. Naiad Press's narratives were much more openly celebratory. Initially their main writers were Sarah Aldridge and Katherine V. Forrest (who also wrote feminist detective fiction), followed by Michelle Martin, whose lesbian regency romance, *Pembroke Park* (1986), was highly successful. In these overtly lesbian romances, it is the lesbian lover who rescues the woman from an unhappy heterosexual relationship, the preponderance of rape scenes between the male lover and the protagonist serving to highlight the failings of heterosexuality. Naiad romances also challenge the usual power politics between the romantic couple. Since both of them are women the naturalised dominant-submissive enactment is exposed for what it is, and variant more mutual relationships develop. Naiad romances also question the dénouement, since the institution of marriage is not an option, and the novels tend to question the validity of promises of long-term monogamous commitment in relation to desire.

Feminist theory debates whether traditional series romance reinforces patriarchal constructions of femininity as functioning in relation to men, and being consummated by the institution of marriage, or whether, given its commercial sensitivity to reader preferences, it gives voice to women's real concerns and desires, in relation to their own roles and to the behaviour of men. Clearly it serves a need for huge numbers of women, and its narrative structure also reifies men's phallic power as central to a woman's life and positions marriage as the solution for women's happiness. But where this is all true for heterosexual romance, it is anything but true for lesbian romance. By placing women in both roles, of protagonist and hero, the chased and the chaser, it is able to question the way gender roles have been portrayed as 'natural', in relation to sexual difference. Lesbian romance has the potential to transform the conventions of the genre – the ability of a woman's love to transform the powerful other – without reinforcing the phallocentric idealisation of masculinity, since the powerful 'other' is also a woman. Bonnie Zimmerman[71] argues that the lesbian viewpoint, 'outside' so called normal life, allows it to show how gruesomely abnormal, 'normal' relationships are, and to call into question a whole set of assumptions about the naturalisation of unequal gender roles, and the de-centring of the powerful bonds between women. Irigaray[72] argues that lesbianism represents an alternative sexual economy to the phallocentric model endorsed by the dominant culture. And her very presence shows up the male inscription of traditional femininity. In contrast, woman identified woman has the potential to put forward alternative models of femininity untainted by the phallocentric and thereby open up another concept of femininity to all women, heterosexual as well as lesbian. Of course, this is just the potential. As Lynne Pearce and Gina Wisker have pointed out there is still the narrative propensity for a lesbian romance (they cite Jane Rule's 1964 *Desert of the Heart*) to leave 'the cultural institution of heterosexuality' untouched in its retelling of the romance with 'different players'.[73] Paulina Palmer's image for the lesbian romance writer, in 'Girl meets Girl: Changing Approaches to Lesbian Fiction',[74] is of a tight-rope dancer having 'to perform a precarious balancing act, maintaining an equilibrium between, on the one hand, respecting the conventions of the chosen genre and, on the other, subverting the attitudes informing it.'[75] Palmer's preferred strategy for doing this is parody. Irony allows the narrative a distance from the conventions, which realism does not, in order to quote and to question simultaneously.

Case studies: Susan Napier (Mills and Boon), *Passion Fruit*, and Lisa Shapiro (Naiad)

Susan Napier's *Deal of a Lifetime*[76] was first published by Mills and Boon in 1991 in Australia, the Philippines and Britain. Its reissue in 1995 in the 'Duet' series (omnibus reissues of established popular authors), indicates that it was very successful when first published.

Deal of a Lifetime is unusual in its open acknowledgement of feminist issues, with the narrative reinforcing the feminism, rather than denigrating it, as Ann Rosalind Jones found in her study in the 1980s. Set within a large Australian company, Concorp, the text highlights the unequal power structures between the genders at work, at home, and in personal life, and suggests how these can be reworked more equitably. Misogynistic attitudes are presented in a number of the male characters and condemned as a weakness in men who are afraid of female competition. This includes the hero's uncharacteristically sexist aggression, when he fears he is losing her. (An exploration of the repressed internalisation of machismo, in the hero.) The book celebrates the importance of a career for some women, arguing that women should be free to follow their vocation whether domestic or public, and it thereby opens out representations of feminity, rather than striving to essentialise all women into the one role. In the early stages, Emma, the protagonist, also comments on the conspicuous consumption of the family owning Concorp, refusing to sympathise with the the hero's having to fly 'economy' like an ordinary mortal, and wryly assessing that the Conway women's hopelessness at sewing is an economic outcome of their wealth, 'They could afford to be!' (p. 42). But this class issue is not pursued past chapter 3, and the usual silence about issues of race prevails.[77] Nevertheless, this text is not afraid to use the term feminism and talks easily about 'sexism'.

Emma, Concorp's legal executive and in the running for promotion as its managing director, is defined as having 'feminist principles'(p. 120) and the hero turns out to be the 'feminist mentor' who has taught his son to use the word '"women" instead of "ladies" or "girls", too fine a distinction for one so young to understand' (p. 82). The narrative endorses Emma's overtly feminist statements such as,

> 'Let a man discover that you could cook like a dream and he'd have you chained to the kitchen in no time flat, never mind if you had a brain like Albert Einstein.' (p. 46)

> 'He said that children needed a stable constant of at least one parent at home ... but it never occurred to him that *he* take any time off from his career to be the constant parent – oh, no, that was strictly a female task.' (p. 126)

And in answer to the hero's comment on their mutual attraction:

'I don't have any problems with the idea of combining business with pleasure....'
'You aren't a woman. It's always the woman who gets fired.' (p. 72)

The plot turns on the chauvinist expectations of family, business colleagues, and a former lover, all of whom have conditioned Emma into fearing marriage and children as a threat to her career. The hero understands and is attracted by the protagonist's aggression, her incisive mind, and her ambition. The narrative hinges on his proving to her, through all the complications and misunderstandings, that not all men are chauvinist, and that marriage to him means she can keep her successful career alongside love and children. In contrast to the former lover, the hero proposes that she would return to work while he brought up the children, with the aid of a nanny. 'As long as our children are well-loved, darling, they're not going to lack for anything just because their mother has another kingdon to run. They'll be as proud of you as I am' (p. 186). What is notable is the lack of opprobrium in this statement. Women following their own vocations are being unequivocally celebrated, though it is not the only possible role offered to women by the text. The narrative is careful to propose a range of viable feminine positions. Frazer's first wife, Sally, and the nanny, Jen, are characterised as loving domesticity without thereby having to forfeit their feisty independence of mind. Emma and Trixie, a mechanical engineering student, want to pursue a career. The text stresses that the important thing is that the women should not be prevented from following their own choice.

Frazer's brief running of Concorp involves a 'feminising' of the workplace, breaking down the rigid hierarchical structures and addressing all the workforce on first-name terms. A change that the chauvinist rivals cannot encompass, while Emma and her supportive male secretary thrive. The text challenges the polarity of the work/home divide, when Emma negotiates arrangements with the various young Conway children, indicating a re-evaluation of the skills of domesticity. Frazer's negotiations with Emma are a far cry from the more traditional domineering masculinity. Showing Emma that she is still defensively living by ideals she had in her teens and now needs to look for a less-restricted option, Frazer does not seek to dominate her but leaves her to make up her own mind. Having awoken the strength of her desires, he 'had made his point, and now it was up to his cautious, impulsive Emma to come to terms with it in her own inimitable fashion' (p. 132). In *Deal of a Lifetime* the ideal romance hero treats the woman with an equality of respect. The text is careful to ensure Frazer resists approaching her at work (which could be construed as 'harassment'), insists on an equal activity in their sexual encounters, and in the mutual vulnerability that ensues from desire. While Emma may be feeling overwhelmed by the passions awoken, so too does Frazer: 'He had known she aroused him, he just hadn't realised how vulnerable that made him' (p. 94). In one sense, the gender constructions and the relationship between the genders are being recast. And this sits uneasily alongside more traditional romance conventions that argue that love and passion should be at the centre of a woman's life, with marriage to the hero as the solution to all her problems. There are points at which the two ideologies conflict and the narrative becomes strident or opaque. Frazer's acknowledgement of cultural constrictions on gender sits uncomfortably alongside his essentialist insistence that her sexual attractiveness and passion is the real 'woman' in Emma, and his attraction to her is being 'a man', linked to his 'virility'. Frazer's constant forcing of this issue pushes Emma to exclaim, quite explicably within this feminist context, '. . . stop equating my sexuality with my identity as a woman' (p. 110). For this equation *is* what lies at the heart of the romance ideology. But having voiced the criticism, the text cannot sustain it. Emma immediately questions 'What on earth was that supposed to mean? She sounded like a naive schoolgirl'; it is the only time Emma's feminism is overtly criticised, and Frazer smoothly interjects the more essentialist view that she is afraid of 'an emotional commitment to your womanhood' (p. 110) by which he means her emotional and sexual side, leading inevitably to marriage and babies. And yet this coexists with a Frazer who does not 'subscribe to the garbage' (p. 124) about women's emotionalism preventing their ability to analyse. Frazer still initiates the sex, takes the lead and teaches Emma her own sexual desires. At the point of consummation, the conservative essentialism becomes overt, because the task is given such seriousness: he devotes 'himself fiercely, single-mindedly to his task' (p. 169). However, alongside this essentialising is a different narrative construction of sex that gives a more fluid construction of playful dominance and submission, with each of them alternating as 'sadist', while she, the 'boss', 'let an employee have his way' (p. 188). That sex can be treated lightly and with humour undercuts the essentialist importance of the act. The contradictons of these two representations of sex are never resolved, or even acknowledged by the narrative. Frazer is still ten years older than

Emma, richer and more powerful. Emma is only twenty-six, which is unrealistic given the acheivements in her career, but it is only with the introduction of the 'Temptation' series that heroines were allowed to be in their thirties. Frazer gives her the promotion, although the text highlights the difference between patronage and earned advancement, by having Emma initially turn it down 'hating him for making it sound like a beneficent gift on his part, rather than a reward for work well done on hers' (p. 139).

Deal of a Lifetime is shot through with contradictions between the essentialist ideology of traditional romance, and the feminist questioning of the gender roles within society. But it is a Mills and Boon text that treats feminism generously as a valid viewpoint and overtly questions the power structures within personal and public institutions. It ends up reinforcing marriage – but the marriage it endorses has changed to one of equality and mutual support, where the man has had to learn how to 'read' the career-minded woman, and to persuade her that marriage and babies are not a 'trap'. This is a complete gender-switch from the 1950s and 1960s, where the innocent, domestic woman had to tame and 'capture' the roving, dominant worldly man. *Deal of a Lifetime* may not be the most subversive of feminist texts, but it *is* a feminist text of sorts and, since it is distributed by Mills and Boon, reached thousands of readers, twice over. It raises issues of gender and treats feminist questioning positively, and allows the career-dominated protagonist to succeed within its own terms. I am not, here, claiming that all Mills and Boon novels do this, or even that all Susan Napier novels do,[78] but that, in the 1990s, some formulaic romance have sought to come to terms with feminism and feminist issues and, responding to women readers' changing expectations, Mills and Boon has published texts which no longer denigrate feminists but accommodate their views. Moreover, that such a text was not a 'mistake' to be buried as soon as issued, but proved popular enough to be reissued in their prestigious Duet series.

Passion Fruit: Romantic Fiction With a Twist[79] edited by Jeanette Winterson for the feminist publishing house Pandora, in 1986, is a very different kettle of fish. To begin with, it is a book of short stories, rather than one piece of fiction, but given serial romance's simple plot and brevity (50 000–55 000 words to fit the 191-page format), this is perhaps less a contrast than a more complex longer novel. Both focus on the romance, the relationship between the couple with little subplotting. And the stories are by major feminist writers looking at romance. Winterson edits, but does not contribute a story. The thirteen contributors include Lorna Tracy, Sara Maitland, Fay Weldon, Josephine Saxton, Marge Piercy, Fiona Cooper, Angela Carter, Aileen La Tourette and Michelene Wandor. Only three stories had appeared elsewhere, Carter's, Mason's and Tracey's, and Tracey developed hers further for this collection. So what we have are a number of stories setting themselves up as a take on romance from a feminist angle. But it is just a take, as the title indicates – these stories all give the concept of romance a definite 'twist'. Indeed, the twist is so unbridled that I would argue only three of the thirteen could even be described as commenting on the romance genre, rather than simply rubbishing the cultural concept of romance. Not all stories about love are romances, and these are, in the main, realistic stories about dysfunctional relationships. One quarter of the stories feature at least one of the protagonists as insane, as if romance in the 1980s can only be explained as madness.[80] The sense of fantasy and passion, and of how it feels to be swept up by 'love' are evoked and critiqued only in Sara Maitland's 'Heart Throb',[81] Laurie Colwyn's 'French Movie'[82] and perhaps Michelene Wandor's 'Some of My Best Friends'.[83]

Sara Maitland's 'Heart Throb' exposes the physical and psychic damage inflicted upon women in order to sustain the myth of romance, conveyed using the breathless prose of the infatuated woman narrator. Divided into two sections, the first half describes the illusion concocted by the illusionist, the 'most romantic act in town'. The play essentialises femininity as created by man for the adoration of his importance. Once the woman 'realises there is a whole world to enchant and not just him' (p. 23), he chops her up and recreates her as focused solely upon him. This performance is an enormous hit because of their 'relationship with each other, and that comes over, a kind of romantic excitement' (p. 25). The second half of the text, the commentary on this phallocentric mystification, unmasks the 'romance' as predicated upon the woman's sexual, physical and economic exploitation, and on her collusion in this exploitation. The voice of the former capable hooker deteriorates into the breathless adoration of the masochist, willing to allow herself to be hacked to pieces so long as it proves he 'needs' her. Once she has experienced 'how far he was prepared to go with my body and how I was prepared to follow him there' (p. 32), he is 'my whole world. Without him I did not exist. I loved him most terribly' (pp. 32–3). The catalogue of his abuse, from the beatings to the drinking of her blood, the stealing of the profits and the spending it on other women, also charts the increasing insanity consequent upon a man believing in the phallic

mystification. The breathless and inane prose of the protagonist parodies the narration of the romance genre as she utters the platitudes
that reify masculinity at the price of denigrating femininity, and
suggests how romance is predicated upon a sado-masochistic relationship that abuses and objectifies the woman. Maitland's story
effectively parodies the romance genre, in Linda Hutcheon's description of parody, because it both imitates and critiques the genre, but it
is a parody that never stretches to being an appropriation. The text
does not wish to recreate the discourse, newly inflected by feminism,
but to make a feminist comment upon the current version of the
discourse.

Laurie Colwyn's 'French Movie' also evokes the intensity of passion,
in its realistic story of an adulterous liaison. Here it is the realism of the
details that constantly comments upon and 'corrects' the romance
version of a love affair. Everything about the tale is anathema to traditional serial romance. The participants are both the wrong side of
middle-age, not young and beautiful. The narrator has no concern in
objectifying herslf, reifying beauty, or fetishising clothes. She lives in
shapeless sweaters that are cast offs of her male relatives, since clothes
always 'took against her, and rucked or wrinkled or caused its seams to
go awry' (p. 102) and her lover quips, 'You really go all out for a guy'
(p. 105). She is undomesticated, cannot cook, but hard-headed,
straightforward and an economic historian.

The lover is not the sole focus of her attention, and their recipro-
cated love is not the solution to the woman's dilemmas, it is itself the
dilemma. The woman is not romantically unattached to anyone
within her society, ready to be swept off into his world, she has
friends, a job and a husband. This is an adulterous affair, the very
anathema to the wholesome myth of the family, and both partners
care for their spouses. Love, desire, is constructed as something that
occurs, that creates pain and pleasure, but that is incidental to real
lives, not all-consuming. In detriment to the romance genre's
ideology, other things are more important than love, ordinary,
mundane things. The text critiques the elemental claims of romance
by their acknowledgement that there is no future for their desire, it is
an 'irritant' or a 'thorn' and yet it is an irritant that creates a 'fresh-
water pearl' (p. 102). Love, as a concept, is not being rejected here but
contextualised within more realistic life choices and ties. Rather than
have the ending solved by the lovers declaring their commitment to
each other, the anticlimactic closure has love acknowledged as something precious but not the most important thing in either of their

lives. The very indecision of the conclusion points to love's insignificance: 'They might part forever, but it didn't matter. These moments, so vivid and sweet were inalienably theirs – a created thing – as specific and available as a piece of music' (p. 116). Love is created by the people who experience the desire, and it does not sweep all before it. It is not the very centre of a woman's life, eclipsing all other relationships. Colwyn's narrative obliquely comments on the aporia of the romance genre, particularly in relation to the female protagonist who is usually stripped of all the meaningful accoutrements of a life, in order to allow her to focus upon, and succumb to, the dominant man.

Where Colwyn comments on the role of love within the personal sphere, Wandor situates the same problematic nature of desire securely within the socio-political sphere, when two of the organisers of a gay rights march, a lesbian and a homosexual, fall surprisingly in love. While they are busily continuing to align themselves with the gay movement by refusing to be 'going straight', and rejecting the concept of bisexuality as woolly liberal, the antagonism of their community apes the intolerance of the heterosexual world for the gay community.

The narration evokes the prose of besotted infatuation, but knowingly, with a comment on how the aura of romance emanates from lust:

> It was as if he brought with him some sort of aura, that made the air round him clearer and brighter than the air round everyone else. reader, i fancied him … all i felt was perked up, terrific energy, my heart beating faster. (p. 146)

These 'hallmarks of love and romance' (p. 150) are resolutely politicised. In this narrative of the marginalised, love is not elemental and life-solving with a happy ending. Desire has political ramifications for the sexual choices the protagonists reinforce, brings more problems than it solves. Love ends unhappily, even disastrously, because of the intolerance of others. A story that focuses as much on the closed communities of the marginalised, it also contextualises the natural, elemental 'love' as socially interpellated and often in conflict with society. The story exposes the unspoken institution of heterosexuality within traditional romance formats.

These three feminist romance fictions with a twist, pastiche and parody the romance genre in order to critique the phallocentric misogyny inherent within the traditional format, the unrealistic reification of love over other more important personal and social ties, and the politicisation of heterosexuality as the norm in series romance. Their analysis of romance from a feminist perspective is more profound, witty and iconoclastic than *Deal of a Lifetime* but would certainly have reached far less of the genre audience, if indeed any of it at all. Like *Lady Oracle* and the other feminist novels, this is a text that engages with the genre only peripherally and is marketed for a feminist audience who would have had only incidental interest in the romance genre. It is therefore writing within the ghetto, in Nicci Gerrard's terms. The text does not offer the same pleasures of emotional intensity and escapist fantasy, which both my first and third texts do. As such, the collection does not set itself up as appropriation of the genre, but as an interesting and effective parodic critique.

My final text, from the lesbian Naiad Press's romance genre series, clearly does set itself up as appropriation, and by that appropriation, effectively critiques the traditional genre's ideology. *Color of Winter* by Lisa Shapiro[84] is a series romance from Naiad Press, 'the oldest and largest lesbian/feminist publishing company in the world' (p. 202) as they advertise themselves, and this book's blurb calls it 'Romantic love beyond your wildest dreams' (p. 202). Unlike *Passion Fruit*, *Color of Winter* follows the genre format of focusing on the two lovers, on the feelings of being pursued and of the emotional struggle against the conventions that preclude their relationship. Sandra Ross, the protagonist, is professionally competent but emotionally scared and repressed in a manner very similar to the protagonist of *Deal of a Lifetime*. She has also been damaged in the past, preventing her from embracing relationships, and it is the acceptance of desire that heals the pain and transforms her view of herself. 'Love, for her, was neither hard nor soft, not difficult or simple. It was, at that moment, the only place to stand' (p. 99). Such paeans to the power of love to overcome everything are *de rigueur* in romance texts. But this paean is not timeless, but quietly relative in its claims 'at that moment'. Love reforms the protagonist and the 'hero', and its force is strong enough to overturn all the conventions, but it is not seen to last for ever. The two protagonists commit themselves to each other but committing themselves to a lifetime together, in a lesbian imitation of marriage, is not the inevitable outcome. The fantasy happy-ever-after is quietly discarded as the lovers acknowledge that something else is more important to both women than love: their vocations. Where Frazer's love is able to show Emma that she does not need to choose between a vocation and marriage, but can have both, Sandra and Jay's love allows them the strength to acknowledge their needs publicly and to encourage each other to pursue their vocations at the expense of their desire. Where the Mills and Boon heterosexual feminism may change the institution of marriage but not destroy it, the lesbian romance argues that love is not about ownership, but about selflessly setting the other free to be themselves. The very concept of romance itself is being renegotiated by challenging the traditional closure. Desire is not 'for ever'.

The balance of authority, wealth and status is also interrogated by the two lovers. Sandra Ross, the 51-year-old history lecturer at Berkeley, loves cooking, is sexually timid and confoms to rules. With her full figure and 'soft waves of grey hair' (p. 2), the protagonist challenges the ageism of traditional romance heroines. But where she has the authority and the status, since she is supervising Jay's proposal, Jay, the 29-year-old rebellious daughter of wealthy philanthropists, holds the wealth, social ease and the sexual confidence of the younger generation of West Coast lesbians. Jay, with her more aggressive attributes, 'the snapping intensity in her copper-colored eyes ... straight black slashes of brow collided in concentration' (p. 4), strides long-leggedly from confrontation to confrontation. The dominant positions of age, authority, worldly experience and arrogance are shared out between them, neither allowed to hold all the cards.

The conflict to their desire is social expectations but not, cleverly, in relation to their lesbianism, which is received relatively unproblematically by their joint milieux. The real adversaries are money, influence, departmental politics and parental pressure and these become the institutional enemies that uphold the social status quo and which seek to prevent these two women finding happiness. Families are seen as damaging social institutions. 'Each generation entrenched habit and defended custom, sacrificing preference on the altar of tradition' (p. 165). Jay's powerful mother, sacrificing her daughter's artistic gift as a sculptor of wood, in order to gain an inheritance, and manipulating Sandra's appointment at the university, is the focus of this institutional, familial demand for self-sacrifice. In a foil narrative, Sandra's artistic father compromised his talent, becoming a lawyer to fulfil his family's expectations, and committed suicide. Sandra voices an anger against her mother's inability to love him *enough* to 'help him find his own convictions' (p. 119) and defy protocol. Love, in this context, becomes something other than a thing in itself, to enfold the couple in bliss. Love is 'no safe haven' (p. 189). It is an active desire to serve the other's best interests, to support the other and push them into risking their own passions. Love and commitment are being rewritten, freed from the traits of ownership and possession.

Sandra will help Jay find the artistic conviction to brave the 'exposure' of her work to the public, and to pursue her artistic talent in New York, away from her. Jay's love for Sandra is equally beneficial, since it forces her to reject the conformist behaviour, evoked by her father's suicide. Since he was unable to live by the rules, she fears that her lesbianism, discovered in her thirties, will lead to a similarly self-destructive exile from society. Jay's beauty and rebelliousness teaches her the strength to embrace a 'Situational ethics ... Honour your own truth' (p. 160). Sandra's internal malaise, signalled by her constant drinking, her insomnia and her writer's block, is reformed by the end. Alone in California, 'Her own transformation seemed equally invisible but creativity had not, after all, been abandoned. Line after line, her work grew in substance, and she had no doubt that the words would carry her through to the spring' (pp. 200–1). This text, celebrating the powers of love, ends with the lovers apart, having loved each other 'enough' to put the other's true happiness first. And that happiness, that following of a vocation, or 'nature', is set up as more important than their desire. Love is not all-encompassing in a woman's life.

There is no irony in the novel's representation, no knowing distance to comment on the romance format, since that would prevent the straightforward identification with the protagonist which is one of the hallmarks, and pleasures, of the genre. It is the content of the lesbian lifestyles that requires a thorough overhaul of the usual plot conventions. Lesbian romance problematises the ideology of heterosexuality by its very characterisation. And, though Jay invokes certain 'masculine' elements, and Sandra certain 'feminine' ones, as already stated their characterisation complicated the usual power structures. Jay initially pursues Sandra and makes her desire known, but accepts Sandra's refusal, on professional grounds, and it is then Sandra who pursues Jay. The pursuer–pursued dichotomy is overturned for a more equitable sharing of the dynamics of desire-overcoming-fear in both of them, and is cut loose from constructions of the inherent 'nature' of masculinity and femininity. Both characters have come from dysfunctional heterosexual families, and the plot shows how families are unable to nurture the individual's needs, but force her to compromise her nature resulting in unhappiness. It needs courage to strive for the freedom from rules that can bring fulfilment and happiness, and that courage comes from the love and encouragement of like-minded souls. *Color of Winter*, like other lesbian texts, includes more detailed secondary characters who support the couple and help them discover their way forward and this challenges the usual representation of the two lovers alone and isolated from the rest of the world in their 'natural' coupledom.

The plot of creative fulfilment versus family conformity has a subtext that evokes acknowledging lesbian desire and braving 'coming out' as a lesbian. The true 'sin' of Eve is said to be 'To accept another's thoughts but ignore your own' (p. 126). And Jay's fear of showing her sculpture is couched as 'If you had the opportunity to show your most private self in public, would you bare your soul to the world?' (p. 177). This is linked to the 'coming out party', where the 'formidable and elegant' black academic, Audrey Linden, is found to be gay also. 'Lesbianism isn't new to me. Openness is new', she explains, and Sandra acknowledges, 'Exposure isn't easy for anyone' (p. 183).

Lesbian romance celebrates lesbian desire and discusses the social exclusions it brings. By invoking the genre format, it also subverts certain inherent ideologies, by rewriting the traditional naturalisation of heterosexuality, the institutions of family and marriage, and the centrality of love to a woman's life. *The Color of Winter* problematises the power structure of the older, wealthier, more experienced man transforming the younger, less wealthy, less experienced woman. Just as the power structures are shared between them, so the transformation is a mutually enlightening one. It rewrites the usual silences around same-sex desire and issues of race,[85] and class, and by its closure problematises the power and importance of love even as it invokes it. To appropriate Bonnie Zimmerman, lesbian romance by its very existence highlights some of the abnormalities present in the 'normal' romance genre.

All three texts negotiate the romance genre from a feminist stance. With *Passion Fruit*, the feminism overrides the romance genre. *Deal of a Lifetime* walks a difficult tightrope of feminist comment within a series romance that exhibits the dislocation of the competing ideologies, and for some readers the romance format might be said to override the feminism. *Color of Winter*, by reviewing and rewriting the formats that challenge a lesbian ideology, creates the more subversive and reappropriated feminist romance. However, though it may be more successful in ideological terms, it is less far-reaching in its popularity. Alice Walker's novel *The Colour Purple* was emphatically more subversive in its writing about African-American lesbianism than the soft-focused Steven Spielberg film of the book, but the film, with its wider distribution, produced more cultural discussion about the issue of black lesbianism than the book ever has. Whether *The Color of Winter*, *Passion Fruit*, or *Deal of a Lifetime* is the more effective feminist text depends on one's particular standpoint of effectiveness, in the balance of ideology and wide readership. Two of the three texts manage to appropriate the genre format to the contemporary cultural transformations taking place in relation to gender, to shift the discourse of romance. It is not the first such change the genre has undergone in its history, nor will it be the last. For the romance genre by its very focus comments on the changing cultural construction of femininity and the more fluid this becomes, the more the traditional format has to rewrite itself.

3
The Fairy Tale

Fairy tales, as we have come to recognise them, are literary appropriations of oral folk tales, traditionally believed to be collected from
peasant women. Women told them amongst themselves while spin-
ning, carding, or collectively performing other monotonous tasks.
These tales were also recounted to their children and to the children of
the aristocracy and the bourgeoisie, by peasant nurses. For the
purposes of this chapter, I will be focusing on fairy tales that conform
to this short story format. During the nineteenth and twentieth
centuries, there have been a large number of books which have
employed fairy tale elements within longer narratives,[1] but I want to
concentrate on the 'classic' format of the genre as it developed from
Perrault, the Grimms and Andersen.

The oral tale of Little Red Riding Hood, as far as we can apprehend
it, is very different from the story as it has come down to us through
Perrault and the Brothers Grimm. The oral original is a specific
warning against werewolves that were believed to lurk in forests, and
has the resourceful peasant girl outsmart the animal and escape.[2]

'The story of Grandmother', collected by Paul Delarue,[3] is a more
complex and troubling tale, with a happy resolution of the dangers.
The girl is unnamed and not described, she is simply asked to carry
milk and a loaf to her grandmother, by the mother, and does so,
meeting a wolf on the way. She answers the wolf's query by telling him
where she is going, via the path of needles rather than of pins. She
stops to collect needles, allowing the werewolf to arrive first using the
path of pins. The werewolf kills the granny and puts some of her meat
and a bottle of her blood in a place where the girl, on arriving, can eat
them in exchange for the milk and bread. As the grandmother's cat
condemns her action, the werewolf begins a series of commands for

her to undress herself and dispose of each garment in the fire. Getting into bed, it is noticeable that the large attributes focus on the wolf/grandmother's needs, rather than in relation to the girl – the big shoulders are to carry wood, rather than arms to hug the child, the nostrils are to snuff tobacco rather than to smell her. The mouth/teeth remain focused on the girl at the climax of the question and answers but instead of the wolf succeeding in eating her, this peasant girl claims a need to go outside to relieve herself. When the wolf fastens a rope to her leg and allows her outside, she ties the rope to a plum tree and escapes.

Yvonne Verdier has argued that the tale is linked to peasant girls' initiation at puberty into needlework apprenticeship, symbolically displacing the older generation (the grandmother). Verdier argues that the oral tales, recounted by women, refer to women's acquisition of different knowledges at different physical maturation points, such as needlework at puberty and cookery when procreative. The telling of such an oral tale is therefore related to the successful induction into domestic knowledge within female peasant society.[4]

Hans Peter Duerr's work, *Traumzeit. Über die Grenze zwischen Wildnis und Zivilisation*[5] is used by Zipes in *Fairy Tales and the Art of Subversion* to argue for a different more positive reading of the werewolf in the oral folk tale:

> in the archaic mentality, the fence, the hedge, which separates the realm of wilderness from that of civilization did not represent limits which were insurpassable. On the contrary, this fence was even torn down at certain times. People who wanted to live within the fence with awareness had to leave this enclosure at least once in their lifetime. They had to have roamed the woods as wolves or 'wild persons'. That is, to put it in more modern terms: they had to have experienced the wildness in themselves, their animal nature. For their 'cultural nature' was only one side of their being, bound by fate to the animal fylgja, which became visible to those people who went beyond the fence and abandoned themselves to their 'second face'.
>
> In facing the werewolf and temporarily abandoning herself to him, the little girl sees the animal side of her self. She crosses the border between civilization and wilderness, goes beyond the dividing line to face death in order to live. Her return home is a move forward as a whole person. She is a wo/man, self-aware, ready to integrate herself in society with awareness.[6]

Verder and Zipes use a knowledge of medieval peasant culture to argue for a positive reading of the girl in the Little Red Riding Hood oral tale, in contrast to Perrault's negative commodification of the passive, weak and beautiful protagonist in his version. I would not want to disagree with these readings but rather to push them further, in a recognition of the liminal states being invoked both at the time of initiation and at the crossing of the boundary of phallocentric civilisation.

Linked to this is one of the genre's main conventions, that of fantastic and of the carnivalesque. Lucy Armitt argues in *Theorising the Fantastic*[7] that fantasy is posited upon lack, and that the pleasurable-ness of the fantastic is located in the reader's experience of this uncanny liminalness:

> In this sense, all fantastic fictions of otherness become projections of the uncanny derived from that primary site of boundary negoti-ation which marks us all as aliens and exiles. This also feeds into Kristevan readings of the abject, which takes that same image of maternal body as a crucial determinant of the way in which we, as a society, perceive the Other as alien. The maternal, as our first site of licence and prohibition, takes on territorial identity. Simultaneously familiar and unknowable, it is our primary metaphor for the defamiliarised explorations into home territory that we project outwards as speculative fictions.[8]

Having developed this link to the maternal body, and to a space avail-able for *écriture féminine*, feminine writing, Armitt goes on to problematise the carnivalesque in highlighting how the fairy tale's use of fantasy and magic, at its best, genuinely discomforts the reader through its darker, dangerous and more atavistic element. Carnival humour is based upon horror and a genuine excess in relation to the disgusting and the licentious. Carnival transgresses the limits and boundaries in ways that genuinely disturb and unsettle prohibited taboos, she reminds us. Fantastic fiction, according to Armitt, is fiction that is obsessed with the precariousness of apparently fixed structures. Marina Warner also links the transgressive element to the marvellous, though in a more celebratory way that ignores the abject. 'Fairytales concern themselves with sexual distinctions and with sexual trans-gression, with defining differences according to morals and mores. This interest forms part of the genre's larger engagement with the marvellous, for the marvellous is understood to be impossible.'[9] One of the major conventions of the fairy tale is its use of magic, its potentially transgressive disposition, and its ability to unsettle and disturb the traditionally male reader.

A history of the genre

The earliest European written forms were texts such as Boccaccio's *Decameron* and Chaucer's *Canterbury Tales* in the fourteenth century, Straparola's *Tredici Piacevoli Notti* and Marguerite de Navarre's *The Heptameron* in the sixteenth century, and Basile's *Pentamerone* in the early seventeenth century. All have a gathering of characters who choose to pass the time together by recounting tales.[10] Most of these characters are themselves women, or claim to have heard the story from a woman.[11]

Perrault's *Contes du temps passé* (Tales of times passed) in 1697 was the first to eschew such a framework, presenting the tales on their own merit. The sub-title, or alternative title, was *Contes de ma Mère l'Oye*, and in Britain it was published under this alternative as *Mother Goose's Tales*. The inference of the title was that these tales came from peasant women. Perrault introduces the form of the fairy tale as we have come to recognise it, by taking oral tales from the French peasantry, and adding a rhymed moralistic (and hence overtly ideological) 'explanation' to each tale. Perrault wrote for the court of Louis XIV, and the tales similarly address both an adult, aristocratic, audience and a juvenile audience. In targeting the latter with his appended morals, the tales fit into a discourse on childhood and the appropriate training for children which begins during the sixteenth and seventeenth centuries.[12] Zipes argues in relation to their production and reception:

> This *discourse* had and continues to have many levels to it: the writers of fairy tales for children entered into a dialogue on values and manners with the folk tale, with contemporary writers of fairy tales, with the prevailing social code, with implicit adult and young readers, and with unimplied audiences.[13]

Jack Zipes has further argued that Perrault's literary version of the oral tale shifts the popular folk warnings and utopias (happy endings) into a more socialising, admonitory product. Perrault's heroine in his 'Little Red Riding Hood' conforms to the contemporary aristocratic ideals of femininity: she is helpless and naive and pretty. In some sense she is also blameworthy, since she is devoured by the wolf. Perrault's undressed little girl sliding into the bed with the wolf and commenting with innocent curiosity on his large appendages, clearly addresses adult titillation alongside childhood suspense. Perrault's 'Little Red Riding Hood' invoking the *femme civilisée*, warns young girls against sexual predators, urges self-control of her natural desires, and threatens dire consequences if she does not repress feminine desire.

As I began this section by arguing, Perrault's *Contes du temps passé* is a literary appropriation of the oral tradition, configuring in that appropriation a seventeenth-century aristocratic ideology of gender whereby civilised femininity is passive, beautiful and obedient and civilised masculinity is active, resourceful, quick-witted and brave. Perrault it is who makes Little Red Riding Hood pretty and doted upon, and he gives her the red cloak synonymous in the Catholic Church of the time with sin and temptation. Perrault's tales have a courtly rationality that eschews the magical where possible, although the tales still bring with them a sedimentation of the peasant oral tales. His morals have an ironic worldliness appropriate to his aristocratic audience. The moral for 'Sleeping Beauty in the Wood' is:

> A brave, rich husband is a prize well worth waiting for; but no modern woman would think it was worth waiting for a hundred years. The tale of Sleeping Beauty shows how long engagements make for happy marriages, but young girls these days want so much to be married I do not have the heart to press the moral.[14]

And his 'Sleeping Beauty', unlike the earlier Strapola version, is not impregnated by the prince until they have been securely married. She too is passive when her children are threatened by the prince's mother. However, the courtly advantages can outweigh passive good looks: 'Ricky with the Tuft' reifies charm and wit in women above beauty.

Perrault's *Tales* created a tremendous vogue for fairy tales, which was supplied in equal measure by women writers as well as men. The literary salon women, the *précieuses*, including Marie-Jeanne Lheritier, Marie-Catherine D'Aulnoy, Charlotte-Rose Caumont de la Force and Henriette Julie de Murat, made it their oeuvre. This vogue for reading simple peasant tales continued in France among the aristocracy and the rising bourgeoisie right up to the French Revolution.

The next significant development in the history of the written fairy tale comes in Germany during the late eighteenth and the nineteenth centuries, as part of the German Romantic movement. Early Romantic writers such as Tieck, Novalis and Goethe wrote fairy tales or *marchen* primarily to celebrate the power of fantasy and the imagination, but also as part of the cult of the natural. Later writers such as Brentano, Eichendorff and Hoffmann continued the tradition, critiquing the rising middle-class commodification of culture. In Tieck's *The Runenberg* of 1803, for example Christian abandons a successful farm and a gentle wife and children, obsessed by a beautiful fairy and the jewels lying beneath the mountain. Where the other characters see only pebbles and a wizened wood-woman and assume Christian is insane, Christian's wild, imaginative alternative to the ordinary and everyday remains the crux of the tale. Hoffmann's later *The Sandman* (1817) is an even more open critique of the bourgeois life where people, like the Sandman's beautiful daughter, have been turned into automata. The German Romantic writers utilised the format of the genre to create challenging and disturbing stories of their own, to critique the cultural changes taking place in Germany.

In contrast, the Brothers Grimm collected original German folk tales in the early nineteenth century as part of a nationalist attempt to unify the German nation (unification came in 1871). These oral German tales were used to demonstrate a particularly German national spirit. And again, the documentation shows that most of the tales were collected from women.[15] The brothers also focused on an adult audience for their two volumes of *Kinder- und Hausmarchen* (Children's and Household Tales) of 1812–15 and 1819, but published a shorter edition specifically for children. Jakob and Wilhelm Grimm therefore continue the form of fairy tale developed by Perrault, and indeed their versions are the most widely circulated to date. Like Perrault, they did not simply transcribe oral tales but adapted the stories to the ideology and cultural expectations of their time, by altering or omitting the aspects deemed inappropriate for a domestic audience. The *Tales* went through a number of revisions and new editions, developing them from the bald story to more elaborate, and more literary interpretations, and there are numerous instances of Wilhelm suppressing certain aspects to privilege more acceptable, bourgeois and patriarchal views.[16] However, as part of the German Romantic tradition, they valued the darker, more disturbing, magical aspects that Perrault's seventeenth-century rationality had rejected.

More appropriate to the nineteenth century's passion for compiling and classifying, the Grimms' *Tales* ran to over two hundred stories. Oral tales are no respecter of geographical borders, so many of the tales collected to develop a national sense of identity actually came from France or Italy. One such tale was 'Little Red Riding Hood' which the Grimms entitled 'Little Red Cap'.

The Brothers Grimm version, 'Little Red Cap', omits the sexual connotations that Perrault's more libertine age countenanced, as part of the reification of the middle-class nuclear family. The character is still culpable, but this time the transgression is one of obedience and the breaking of a promise: she strays from the path to pick flowers after she promised her mother that she would not. As Zipes has pointed out in *Trials and Tribulations of Little Red Riding Hood*, in the more bourgeois culture where sex is expurgated for women and children, the crime becomes the breaking of a contract.[17] Little Red Cap does not undress and get into the bed with the wolf, he springs out and devours her.[18] The Brothers Grimm reinvent a happy ending, taking one from another folk tale, 'The Wolf and the Seven Kids'. A hunter saves Little Red Cap and her Granny by cutting open the wolf's belly, letting them out, and then filling the belly with stones. The women are therefore rescued by the male, who alone is powerful enough to subdue nature.

The tale has a second episode, though, where the girl and her Granny combine forces to vanquish a second wolf who tries to tempt Little Red Cap. Although it is there to demonstrate the child has learnt her lesson, i.e. internalised the prescriptions on her behaviour, it does show the grandmother outwitting the wolf, with the obedient girl's help. The notion of a generational succession has been replaced by a successful amalgamation of forces so long as the young girl complies. The Brothers Grimm's protagonist has less focus upon her beauty, she is 'sweet' rather than 'pretty',[19] but she is still helpless, naive, and now timid as well. Perrault's sexuality and retribution have been toned down and the longer story now focuses purely upon regulation by social precept. Given these moralistic encodings, it is unsurprising that Grimms' *Tales* became part of the Prussian elementary school syllabus beginning in 1850.[20]

While Perrault and Grimm dominate the traditional fairy tale genre, a number of developments continued in the nineteenth century. Hans Christian Andersen, writing in Denmark between 1837 and 1875, created a corpus of 156 fairy tales, aimed specifically at children, which brought him immense fame. From a peasant family, Andersen was brought up by a middle-class family that recognised his gifts and he ended up under the patronage of the King of Denmark. In stories such as 'The Ugly Duckling' or 'The Tinderbox', lower-class protagonists are humiliated but, through diligence and perseverance, their true worth is appreciated and they are rewarded with entry into an elevated milieu. Like the earlier tales written for children, these are socialising tales that conform to nineteenth-century bourgeois values.

Female characters are particularly self-effacing and decorous as with 'The Little Mermaid'. If they are not, like the protagonist of 'The Red Shoes', then they are punished for their self-concern.

Oscar Wilde published his first book, a selection of fairy tales *The Happy Prince and Other Tales*, in 1888. Wilde's mother, Speranza, collected Irish folk tales from the locals, and his doctor father often accepted tales as payment from his poorer patients.[21] Wilde's knowledge of oral folk tales may be one of the reasons why his fairy tales are a direct play on, and critique of, Andersen's literary and conformist tales. Wilde's 'Star Child' and his 'The Fisherman and his Soul' are the antitheses to 'The Ugly Duckling' and 'The Little Mermaid'. Wilde's tales overtly critique the simplistic moralising of Andersen's fairy tales, showing by their disturbance of the conventions a questioning of contemporary society. Recently, critics have begun to analyse his tales for early queer theory readings that reject social conformism, for an acceptance of difference. 'The Happy Prince', for instance, castigates the self-satisfied blindness of the town's rulers to the needs of the poor and rejects any happy resolution for the more grim continuance of the social inequities. The good go unappreciated. Wilde's utilisation of unhappy endings, unlike the Perrault endings, does not serve as an admonishment to conform to accepted codes of behaviour, rather it serves to question the duplicity and inequity of the status quo.

Andrew Lang published the *Blue Fairy Book* 1889, followed by *Red Fairy Book* etc., through a whole range of colours beyond the four primary ones at the end of the nineteenth century. Continuing the classical tradition of Perrault and the Brothers Grimm, in Britain, Lang's compilations do not initially stray far from the normative moralising. However, Alison Lurie has pointed to a shift in the later collections. Acknowledging that the *Blue Fairy Book* lacks stories of female initiative, Lurie argues that in order to continue the successful series, Lang was forced to include stories of active heroines from the thousands known to him as a folklorist, once he had exhausted the more passive female protagonists.[22] Marina Warner has further pointed to Lang's use of a team of women editors, transcribers and paraphrasers to compile the volumes, and his reliance on his wife, Leonora Alleyne, to edit the later volumes.

From the genre's written inception at the end of the seventeenth century, to the end of the nineteenth century, there had been a double strand of fairy tale writing: the first a transcription of oral folk tales as a recording of popular culture, with at least some demand for authenticity; the other the creation of original stories utilising the format of the fairy tale, with the focus on more literary and aesthetic demands. Neither are as polar opposite as this suggests, for a study of the Brothers Grimm's three editions of their tales shows a shift from the early bald story to a more elaborate, expanded narrative that clearly aspires to more literary pretensions.

The history of the fairy tale genre shows continuous adaptation and appropriation. Like any other cultural product, it was part of the complex cultural debates of its time. The fairy tale has primarily been seen as a genre of socialisation when addressed to children and so has carried an overt ideological didacticism, whether the stories were 'transcribed' folk tales or newly created fairy tales. Stories addressed to a more adult audience have had a greater focus on the aesthetic component and are often more subversive and questioning – playing upon the palimpsest of the moralistic juvenile's format. However, tales addressed to children, such as Wilde's, could also be less conformist.

Looking at the history of the fairy tale genre illustrates how the overt moralising has always been a site of contest. Each culture has imposed its own set of norms as a repression of earlier practices, though aspects of them remain sedimented within the more magical, inexplicable aspects of the tale. Perrault's tales obscure and rewrite the autonomy and agency of the peasant protagonists, particularly when they are women, to correspond to the mores of the time. The Brothers Grimm further appropriated the tales for a nineteenth-century middle-class conception of appropriate behaviour. The German Romantics and Wilde wrote their tales as an ironic comment upon the more classic conventions of the genre, critiquing and re-appropriating the genre in new developments of its form. Each historical moment has shaped and changed the genre to the needs and expectations of its time.[23]

Feminist criticism and appropriation of the fairy tale

During the 1970s, feminist criticism took two opposing positions on whether the fairy tale genre colluded with patriarchy or could be a site of contestation. Feminist social critics like Andrea Dworkin pointed to the most well-known fairy tales as reinforcing patriarchal gender steretypes. Feminists who worked within the genre acknowledged that patriarchy privileged certain tales but argued for strong, active female protagonists in the wider range of fairy tales. At the end of the 1970s there was also a move to harness fairy tales as encoding a woman's voice and women's preoccupations. Some used a psychoanalytic model to argue this, such as Gilbert and Gubar's 1979 study, or Shuli

Barzilai's in 1999. Others, such as Marina Warner and Heather Lyons do so from a historical perspective. During the 1990s the same debate about collusion or contestation has taken place, in microcosm, amongst Carter scholars in relation to her re-written fairy tales, *The Bloody Chamber*.

Alison Lurie's article 'Fairytale Liberation' was published in the *New York Review of Books* during the Christmas period of 1970, and clearly implied that Lang's fairy tales would make a good present for a girl because of their subversive elements. 'Often, though usually in a disguised form, they support the rights of disadvantaged members of the population – children, women, and the poor – against the establishment.'[24] Criticising feminists for seeing the genre as chauvinistic brainwashing in its promulgating of passive, obedient heroines,[25] she recognises that this is the type favoured by Walt Disney and so most prevalent in America, but argues that the opposite is true in the European tradition which 'is exactly the sort of subversive literature of which feminists should approve'.[26] The article claims that there are many active heroines present in fairy tales and many powerful witches and stepmothers. As oral tales told by women within a popular genre, women were naturally the central characters and the issues were those of concern to women, family relationships, work and survival. Since these tales were transcribed by upper-middle-class men they selectively chose a canon that reduced the role of the women characters, but larger, more comprehensive collections of fairy tales, such as Andrew Lang's later books (largely compiled and revised by his wife), contain many courageous and resourceful heroines. In many ways, Lurie's article contains in embryonic form many of the strands of the feminist debates.

In 1972, Marcia K. Lieberman took issue with Alison Lurie's claim that the Lang fairy tale books could be seen as potentially empowering to girl readers. As already mentioned, Lowrie's argument was that once he had embarked on such a successful series of books, Lang was forced to scour further for his stories and begin to encompass ones with active heroines. Lieberman, ignoring this thesis, returns to the earliest *Blue Fairy Book* to analyse the gender constructions being promulgated and finds that the women are praised for being passive and the men for being active. One of the earliest second-wave, liberation movement, feminist criticisms of fairy tales, Lieberman's 'Some Day my Prince Will Come'[27] introduces the character analysis that was to predominate in feminist criticism in the 1970s. Analysing the female characters in Lang's chosen tales, she divides them into young and old. The young women are rewarded if they are beautiful and meek, but are constructed as bad-tempered if they are ugly. So beauty becomes a moral attribute to aspire to, and the girls who are singled out to win are those who are deemed 'the fairest of them all'. Young women are predominantly passive, awaiting rescue and reward, and many are specifically victims, thereby glamorising martyrdom. The reward system for the young female characters revolves around them being attractive, being chosen/rescued, and becoming elevated in their social status through marriage (to a prince). In contrast, the older women are often active and even powerful, but this is invariably portrayed as unattractive, if not repulsive. There are good, powerful women but they are always remote and transient fairies, and so not aspirational to the reader. The bad women, whether ogres or human, are invariably ugly and this in itself is often the explanation for their wickedness. Lieberman's conclusion is that fairy tales convey a dichotomy of models for the women reader: the young, passive, gentle and fair; the older wicked, active and ugly. Assuming, as many of the feminist critics do that women readers will only relate to the female characters, and ignore the uncanny, magical aspects of the tales, Lieberman's assessment of the encoding of femininity in the fairy tales sets the agenda for later critics.

Andrea Dworkin, in *Woman Hating*[28] in 1974, develops Lieberman's thesis that written fairy tale reinforces patriarchal ideologies and argues that Grimm and Perrault teach girls that fear is a function of their femininity:

> The lessons are simple, and we learn them well. Men and women are different, absolute opposites. The heroic prince can never be confused with Cinderella, or Snow-white, or Sleeping-Beauty. She could never do what he does at all, let alone better.... Where he is active, she is passive. Where she is erect, or awake, or active, she is evil and must be destroyed.[29]

Dworkin sees the unfettered cruelty as spelling out the punishment for rebellion or dissent:

> There are two definitions of woman. There is the good woman. She is the victim. There is the bad woman. She must be destroyed. The good woman must be possessed. The bad woman must be killed, or punished, or nullified.[30]

For Dworkin, the tales are not weapons of understanding or change, but parables handed out to children to knuckle down to fitting the uncongenial shapes society forces them into.

But Dworkin's is not the only radical feminist viewpoint available. A year earlier, Lea Kavablum in a less well-known text, *Cinderella: Radical Feminist, Alchemist*[31] held Cinderella up as a model feminist who rejected the competitive, opportunistic behaviour of her sisters but resourcefully escapes the domestic entrapment of the kitchen and fireside. Reading her 'prince' as symbolic of her inner strength, and reading the Freudian symbolism of the slipper as a vagina, Kavablum claims Cinderella as an independent woman regaining her own sexuality.

In 1975, Kay Stone[32] located the gender stereotyping analysis within its historical period of twentieth-century America. Her research into the popularity of specific fairy tales in America discovered that the most popular favoured the docile heroines. Of the massive compilation of tales in the Brothers Grimm collection, only 25 or less were known to contemporary American children. Only 20 per cent of the Grimms' tales have passive heroines, but these make up 75 per cent of the North American versions. Cinderella, she argues, succeeds because of her excessive kindness and patience; Sleeping Beauty and Snow White are so passive they have to be reawakened to life by men; and innocent heroines like the Little Goose Girl and Six Swans are victims of scheming and ambitious wicked women. This American role model of patience, kindness and passivity is reinforced by Walt Disney. Stone thinks it is no accident that the three films Disney made himself all focus on the passive pretty heroine victimised by female villains: *Sleeping Beauty*, *Snow White*, *Cinderella*. Where the heroes succeed because they act, because they overcome obstacles, the heroines are already perfect and, according to Disney, simply need to remain what they are (a beautiful face, a tiny foot, and a pleasing temperament). His film of *Sleeping Beauty* never tells us, as the original did, that the prince impregnates her while she is still asleep. So, while acknowledging the patriarchal reification of the more passive heroines in 1950–1960s America, Stone also shifts the focus by arguing for a wealth of autonomous models in the repressed tales that have been ignored.

In Britain, in 1978, Heather Lyons writing for the Open University 'Literature and Learning' course also argued for a more historical awareness. In 'Some Second Thoughts on Sexism in Fairy Tales'[33] she suggests that feminist dismissal of traditional fairy tales stems from a lack of understanding. Summarising the debates she argues that there are both passive and active heroines, depending on which tales are chosen, and that the canon of passive gender steretypes is the result of the mediation of the printed word. A consideration of the teller of the tale can also alter the inflection, so that hearing a role reversal tale where the men are portrayed as foolish, when told by a woman to an audience of women, may be woman-centred without being anti-men:

> the mockery is affectionate and implicit and from a feminist point of view reveals the possibility of a world not entirely made up of capable men and incapable women, but of human beings equally capable of error and foolishness.[34]

Lyons continues this thesis by arguing that while some fairy tales are misogynistic, it is the telling that determines the level of mysogyny. She gives two versions of 'The Fisherman and His Wife' in which the first has the wife greedy and over-demanding, while the second portrays her extravagant wishes as marvellously daring and challenging to patriarchal decorum. Misogyny is not inscribed in the tale so much as in how the version is told. One answer for the feminist, she concludes, is not only to write new fairy tales but also to begin to orate the old ones giving them this new feminist inflection.

Gilbert and Gubar and Karen Rowe, writing at the end of the 1970s, focus on the allure of fairy tales and cite Bettelheim[35] as one way of discussing this attraction. Sandra M. Gilbert and Susan Gubar, in their influential *The Mad Woman in the Attic*[36] of 1979, have a chapter entitled 'The Queen's Looking Glass' where they discuss the psychoanalytic potency of fairy tales and myths for describing cultural codes of femininity. Citing Bettelheim's description of the Queen and Snow White in an oedipal battle for the affections of the king/father, Gilbert and Gubar argue that the Queen's 'narcissistic' turning to the mirror is in fact a turning to the internalised prescriptions of patriarchal approval. They argue that the excess of the Queen's rage against Snow White needs to be explained in other ways. Developing their book's thesis of the female writer struggling for creative topos within a culture that dismisses women, they argue that the Queen, active and imaginative, is symbolic of the writer who needs to destroy the mythic nullity of Snow White, the blank page of the 'angel in the house'. Between the glass coffin of the feminine selflessness and the mirror reflecting patriarchal inscription, the woman writer must negotiate a way to write. Gilbert and Gubar utilise the earlier feminist identification of the angel/ogre dichotomy, but argue that more complex psychic negotiations are necessary for women.

In the same year, Karen E. Rowe in an essay 'Feminism and Fairy Tales'[37] identified the enduring fairy tale romance motif in women's magazines and romance genre fiction. She uses Bettelheim's discussion of the adolescent girl's ambivalent desire for both independence and the safety of childhood, to analyse the reading of the wicked witch (preventing maturity) and the fairy godmother (nurturing) that allay such separation anxieties. She also employs his analysis of the beast marriages, where the young girl must transform her aversion for male sexuality into a romantic commitment. Rowe accepts Bettelheim's reading of the fairy tales' psychoanalytic content but foregrounds the self-sacrifice demanded by the women characters, the self-effacement and glorification of passivity that the texts' enchantment espouses. Rowe concludes that fairy tales are dangerous because while they speak to adolescent anxieties about maturing into women, they advance an ideology that trades feminine selfhood for subordination, and sees marriage as a haven from the harsh realities of life. Rowe argues that this romantic myth informs many women's expectation of men and marriage, rather than their actual experience.

The main development in the 1980s was not critical analysis of fairy tales but a plethora of books linking fairy tales to a range of myths around the mystical woman as wise woman or as goddess, and the move to a more separatist stance that took the tales as symptoms of a missing woman's voice.[38] Patricia Monaghan's *The Book of Goddesses and Heroines*,[39] Sylvia Brinton Perera's *The Descent of the Goddess*,[40] Marta Weigle's *Spiders and Spinsters: Women and Mythology*,[41] and Barbara Walker's *The Woman's Encyclopedia of Myths and Secrets*,[42] were only the tip of the iceberg.

The 1990s saw a shift towards a consideration of fairy tales not from the feminist point of view, so much as the 'woman-centred', as perhaps befits a period at times defined as 'post-feminist'. Shuli Barzilai argued for a woman-centred psychoanalytic reading of 'Snow White', while Marina Warner's book, *From the Beast to the Blonde*, argued for a woman-centred historical account of fairy tales. Perhaps noting the trend, Bloomsbury brought out a collection of Alison Lurie's earlier essays under the title, *Don't Tell the Grown-Ups: Subversive Children's Literature*.[43]

In 1990 Barzilai's 'Reading "Snow White": the Mother's Story' was published in the influential feminist journal, *Signs*.[44] It took issue with Bettelheim's psychoanalytic approach to Snow White, because he imports the absent father figure, and with Gilbert and Gubar's feminist psychoanalytic reading because they omit the crucial mother–daughter relationship. Noting that both interpretations place the phallus, or male rule, at the centre of the women's conflict, Barzilai questions how competent their readings can be if they ignore fundamental elements of the story. Considering a range of 'Snow White' type tales, she notes that while many aspects of the story change from tale to tale, what remains a constant is the pattern of jealousy and expulsion between an older mother figure and a young girl.

Barzilai proceeds to give a psychoanalytic reading. Placing oral tales as a women's genre, she argues that 'Snow White' inscribes the difficulties inherent when the mother–daughter relationship goes awry. Seeing it as an aspect of the separation anxiety of both the daughter and the mother, told from the point of view of the daughter, she argues for the Queen initially experiencing the wish fulfilment of a dream motherhood, then turning bitter when the seven-year-old child, no longer docile, seeks independence. Using Lacanian psychoanalysis, Barzilai argues that the Queen undergoes a regressive 'mirror' stage and loses her sense of wholeness when the daughter asserts her otherness. With the separation of the child comes a passage of decline linked to ageing so that the Queen's mirror is not the voice of patriarchy but a reflection of her own separation anxiety. The Queen's spell on Snow White is a way of reincorporating her back into passive babyhood. In this reading, Barzilai argues that 'Snow White' is a story exploring the relationships between women, unmediated by any male figures.

Marina Warner took a similar approach from a socio-historical approach four years later in her book, *From the Beast to the Blonde: On Fairy Tales and their Tellers.* The first half of the book looks at the 'tellers' of the genre, documenting how the tales originated from women and exploring the images of women as tellers. While men may dominate the written form of the tale, the stories originate from women and Warner suggests a rethinking of 'what different ways the pattern of fairytale romancing might be drawn when women are the tellers'.[45]

The second half of the book considers the meanings of various tales or motifs within the tales. It examines the rival relationships between women in 'Cinderella' and 'Sleeping Beauty', and explores the romance element in the 'Bluebeard' and the 'Beauty and the Beast' stories. The book also considers the significance of 'blondeness' in fairy tales and the muteness of many of the heroines. Rejecting the universalising of psychoanalysis for a new historical focus on material specificity, Warner claims that fairy tales illuminate 'how human behaviour is embedded in material circumstance, in laws of dowry, land tenure, feudal obedience, domestic hierarchies and marital dispositions'.[46]

Despite her refutation of psychoanalytic readings, Warner's analysis of the tales bears a strong similarity to Barzilai's concerns. *From the Beast to the Blonde*'s consideration of the wicked stepmother motif also foregrounds the tales as inscribing women's concerns and fantasies:

> The experiences these stories recount are remembered, lived experiences of women … they are rooted in the social, legal and economic history of marriage and family, they have all the stark actuality of the real and the power real life has to bite into the psyche and etch its design: if you accept Mother Goose tales as the testimony of women, as old wives' tales, you can hear vibrating in them the tensions, the insecurity, jealousy and rage of both mothers-in-law against their daughter-in-law and vice versa, as well as the vulnerability of children from different marriages. Certainly, women strove against women because they wished to promote their own children's interests over those of another man's offspring; the economic dependence of wives and mothers on the male bread-winner exacerbated – and still does – the divisions that may first spring from preferences for a child of one's flesh. But another set of conditions set women against women, and the misogyny of fairy tales reflects them from a woman's point of view: rivalry for the prince's love.[47]

Warner and Barzilai both castigate 'the feminists' for importing paternalism into the tales and for 'tarnishing' fairy tales as simple vehicles of gender stereotypes. Nevertheless, both of their studies are appropriate for later feminist critical dvelopments. Warner and Barzilai are not rejecting feminism but disputing earlier feminist stances as too narrow for effective analysis and putting forward their own strategies for reading gender.

Feminist fiction writers took up the challenge of the fairy tale during the 1970s and 1980s, both re-writing classic stories and creating new ones to challege the patriarchal inscriptions and to put forward new ones informed by feminism. Since the traditional tales were seen as didactic, there were less qualms about masking the newer ideology of the appropriations. Some writers, such as Yolen and Carter had an understanding of the history of the fairy tale (see below), while others took Grimm or Perrault at face value in their re-writings. Some addressed juvenile audiences, while others focused on the adult market. On the whole, as Zipes has argued,[48] the children's tales concentrated upon active, emulatory heroines whereas the adult texts focus on the clash between male and female characters and critique the social constrictions of femininity more widely.

In 1971, the American poet Anne Sexton published *Transformations*, her retelling of Grimms' fairy tales in verse such as Little Red Riding Hood or Cinderella, framed by modern experience. Her poems question the consolatory role these narratives have on our consciousness, and demonstrate how they can circumscribe feminine expectations. In the same year the British fantasy writer Tanith Lee published *The Dragon Hoard*, followed by *Princess Hynchatti and Some Other Surprises* (1972) both for children. Her adult re-writings, *Red as Blood or Tales from the Grimmer Sisters*, came in 1983, following Broumas' and Carter's. In 1974 the prolific American fantasist, Jane Yolen, began her series of children's fairy tales, *The Girl who Cried Flowers, Moon Ribbon and Other Tales* (1976), *The Hundredth Dove* (1977), *Dream Weaver* (1979) and *Sleeping Ugly* (1981). Writers of fantasy, science fiction and other speculative fictions seem to have an affinity with the fairy story genre. Joanna Russ' fantasy novel, *Kittatinny* (1978), for example, contains a significant critique of 'The Little Mermaid' as part of its narrative.[49] (See also Ursula Le Guin's 'The Wife's Story' of 1983.)

In 1977, while Ann Tompert was publishing *The Clever Princess* for children, the American poet Olga Broumas followed Anne Sexton's example in using fairy tales in her more explicit poem *Beginning with O*. Two years later, Angela Carter, another writer whose work contains a range of speculative narratives borrowing from the fantasy and the gothic, published *The Bloody Chamber and Other Tales* in Britain, the explicit and erotic nature of which had to be signalled in the American edition, *The Bloody Chamber and Other Adult Tales*, in 1981.

Alongside individual writers using the genre for more or less feminist aims, were a number of avowedly feminist collectives, such as the Merseyside Fairy Tale Collective, who published *Little Red Riding Hood*, *The Swineherd* and *Snow White* in 1978, and the Irish Fairy Tales for Feminists collective who published, *Ride on Rapunzel* (1992), *Ms Muffet* (1990), *Mad and Bad Fairies* (1990), *Sweeping Beauties* (1989) and *Cinderella on the Ball* (1991).

Feminist editors were also bringing out selections of traditional tales, highlighting subversive female protagonists, both for children and adults. Alison Lurie edited *Clever Gretchen and Other Forgotten Folk Tales* in 1980, Letty Cottin Pogrebin edited *Stories for Free Children* in 1982, while the feminist publishing house Virago brought out two volumes of the *Virago Book of Fairy Tales*, the first edited by Angela Carter in 1991, the second begun by Carter, and completed after her death by Marina Warner in 1992.

Case studies: Jane Yolen, Fairytales for Feminists, Angela Carter

All three, Yolen, Carter and the Fairytales for Feminists collective are avowedly feminist writers and the dominant readerly position produced in *Moon Ribbon*, *Bloody Chamber* and *Sweeping Beauties* is a feminist one. All three texts also sold well.

Jane Yolen is a prolific writer and editor of fantasy and children's stories. The cover of *Sister Light, Sister Dark*, claims it as her hundredth book, and there have been many since. She has written both novels and non-fiction using the fairy tale. *Briar Rose*[50] in 1992, written for the Tor Fantasy 'Fairy Tale Series' is an adult novel placing the story of Sleeping Beauty within World War Two, and the holocaust. *Touch Magic: Fantasy, Faerie and Folklore in the Literature of Childhood*[51] is non-fiction and claims a need for myths to enrich our lives. The book's first section, 'The Tale and the Teller' gives a knowledgeable account of the oral folk tales transcription by Perrault and others, and a distinction is made between Perrault's transcriptions and Andersen's literary, or art, tale. This distinction, in section two 'Touch Magic', is applied to her own work which, she claims, is a blending of folkloric elements with original themes to create a literary tale. Interestingly, she argues that Cinderella was more active in the original fairy tale and blames Walt Disney for creating 'a helpless, hapless, pitiable, useless heroine' and thereby the 'story has been falsified and the true meaning lost – perhaps forever'.[52] Quite what she sees as the 'true' meaning is never explained.

Moon Ribbon and Other Tales[53] is a children's book, with black and white full-page illustrations by David Palladini, and large print. It is aimed at a fluently reading pre-teen market. The book is dedicated to a number of leading American feminists of the period, 'Dale, Nancy, Shulamith and Monday Eve'.[54] The strength of the book is its haunting evocation of the magical and the fantastic, an element that is often missing in feminist re-writings. The narratives present both the plausible and the unsettling qualities that allow the magical to challenge what constitutes 'the real' and to inscribe a feminist fantasy.

Some of the tales are re-writings of earlier fairy tales: 'Moon Ribbon' replaces 'Cinderella', 'Rosechild' 'Thumbelina', 'Sans Soleil' 'Sleeping Beauty', and 'Moon Child' 'The Ugly Duckling'. This reappropriation is never made explicit, although this knowledge obviously adds a further level of meaning to the reading.

Published in 1977, when the feminist critique of gender stereotyping was dominated by critics such as Lieberman and Dworkin criticising the reification of passivity, Jan Yollen's tales quietly challenge the conventional expectations of both genders, but go further in using magic as a paradigm for a feminine wisdom, an 'other' knowledge, particularly symbolised by the moon (a conventional symbol for both femininity and for otherness that is adopted by a number of essentialist feminists during the 1980s). The narrations are uncomplicated in voice, tone or tense, framed by the orthododx opening for the genre's speculative fiction: 'Once', 'Once there lived', or 'There once was'. The tales follow a simple linear chronology, and mainly have a satisfying 'happy-ending' closure, though a few have no closure and one, 'Sans Soleil' ends on a moral.

The issue of beauty, a significant one for contemporary feminists, is questioned in two of the tales. Sylva, the protagonist of 'Moon Ribbon' is plain, thus raising the importance of beauty in relation to femininity. In 'Sans Soleil', the protagonist is beautiful but the main object of beauty is the prince, thus confounding the usual gender expectations in the genre. 'Sans Soleil' seems to accept the reification of beauty, where 'Moon Ribbon' rejects it, but both tales problematise its use, calling attention to a generic orthodoxy.

Sylva's house had belonged to her mother and only passes to the father on her death. A similar matrilinear tradition belongs to the moon ribbon she bequeathes her daughter (and which Sylva will, in her turn, put by for her own daughter):

> It was a strange ribbon, the color of the moonlight, for it had been woven from the gray hairs of her mother and her mother's mother and her mother's mother's mother before her. (p. 1)

Sylva's opening construction is as loving, good-hearted and docile. She does not complain about the harsh treatment of the stepmother and stepsisters who treat her as their servant and push her in to sleeping, initially, on the kitchen floor and then outside with the animals. Through the magic of the moon ribbon and the matriarchal silver-haired woman, Sylva is taught that passivity colludes with the exploiter – 'No one can take unless you give ... there is always a choice' (p. 12). The end of the adventures sees her courageous, independent and assertive so that, in contrast to Cinderella, she can defy the unjust step-mother herself, with her 'I *will* not' (p. 14), and vanquish all three opponents to take her rightful place in the mother's house.

'Sans Soleil' has a similar female protagonist, though this one does not need to learn how to be strong-minded and enterprising. In contrast to the girl, the men are fearful and superstitious. A prophecy decrees that the prince will be struck dead if the sun should ever see his beauty, but Viga, the duke's daughter, rejects the superstition as irrational. 'The sun is not harmful. It nourishes. It causes all things to grow' (p. 32). She bravely challenges the king and the courtiers, and is rewarded with the prince as a bridegroom. It is the male who is the passive reward for female enterprise, in this reworking. Passionately desiring her husband to remain with her during the day, she has the ingenuity to imprison all the kingdom's cockerels so that they cannot warn him of the sun's approach. In this tale it is the woman who is not only cunning and intelligent, but also sexually active. However, she cannot modify male superstition. Touched by the sun, the prince falls down dead and the saddened Viga herself reasons the moral of the tale: 'Sometimes,' Viga would say, 'what we believe is stronger than what is true' (p. 39). Where earlier fairy tales would have punished the young woman for her wilful scheming, this tale twists the ending to foreground feminine sense and courage in contrast to men's lack of sense. The moral posits 'beliefs' as cultural constructions in contradistinction to the truth. The tale is not simply a role reversal, though it certainly is that, it also gestures towards the fluidity of gender constructions.

A similar motif and trope are found in the brief tale 'The Honey-Stick Boy'. In this story the husband is conformist and fearful of the rule of the spirit of the hive, whereas his wife has the temerity to name her own desire, and autonomously create a son out of sticks and honey. The boy is nurturing, sweet-natured and self-sacrificing, and the text foregrounds this alternative gender construction, in the exchange between the couple: 'Where is it said that a boy should be sweet?' asked the old man gruffly. 'All people should be sweet,' she replied (p. 18). When the spirit of the hive tricks the old man into losing the boy in the river, the woman does not become the sharp-tongued scold of the reader's expectations (for example, the nagging wife in Perrault's 'Three Wishes'). Again, the narrative twists gender and genre orthodoxy, to focus on the woman's benevolent acknowledgement of her fortunes, 'sadly, but ... not ... bitterly. For she had her dear husband safe and she had her memories, and it was hard to say which she treasured most' (p. 22).

This positive feminine, loving heart is also evoked in the short 'Rosechild' where an old woman, finding a minuscule baby in a rose, asks three male authority figures how she should look after it. Each of the men refuses to take her question at face value and projects their own preoccupations on to the question and thereby give her the wrong information. Her own heart teaches her how to care for the babe as later the girl cares for her. The story gently mocks how patriarchy mis-hears women and obstructs their ability to create nurturing, reciprocal relationships with each other.

The final story, 'Moon Child' is more accusatory in its narrative address. Again men are superstitious, worshipping the sun and fearful of the dark, including the forest of Swartwood. The whole community reject Mona, the pale moon child, because she is different and difference begets fear and victimisation. Learning the wonders of the forest which refresh her, Mona initially teaches the children to wonder at the moon-flowers and the moon-stones she brings out to them, but the adults evict her from the village. She lives a self-sufficient exile in the cool of the forest. In direct contrast to the phallocentric community, superstitious and fearful, the woman as 'other' is constructed as brave, autonomous, and able to see clearly because she rejects the patriarchal precepts. Rejected by the conformists, she repudiates victimisation for an embracing of difference and, as I discuss below, a crossing of the boundaries that create distinctions.

Alongside these five challenges to the gender stereotyping of the orthodox fairy tales, Yolen gives one story that does not. In 'Somewhen' the protagonist is male and enterprising, going off to seek adventure, and the woman is the more usual reward system: 'a lovely girl whose hair was brushed with sunlight and whose hands were meant to rock cradles' (p. 44) with whom he settles down. Standing on its own, it could easily be argued that this colludes with phallocentric values, but in the context of the other five stories it could be an attempt to inclusively embrace a positive masculine role, in order to encompass a variety of readerly positions (the young boy's as well as the girl's), and to resist a gender stereotyping in reverse.

The familial structures displayed in Yolen's tales argue for a range of different, viable relationships, none of them the ideal American nuclear family. 'Sans Soleil' has only the father–daughter, or father–son relationship, dealing as it does with public standards and actions, and Viga's challenge to the patriarchal view. In 'The Honey-Stick Boy', the child is created by the woman out of sticks and honey; in 'Rosechild' the old woman finds the tiny girl in a rose. Neither mother is thus a blood relation, for all their loving nurture. In 'Moon Ribbon' the main relationship invoked is that of the greedy step-mother and stepdaughters, but this is countered by a maternal, sisterly hierarchy of knowledge. In 'The Moon Child' the parents are blood relatives but they shun their daughter and collude in her banishment. Yolen's fairy tales problematise familial relationships and give a range of alternatives none of which, except for the atypical 'Somewhen', normalises the nuclear family as the natural arrangement.

Yolen's evocation of the magical, with its focus on otherness, allows for a more symbolic rendition of the potency of femininity and this is particularly so in the two tales that use the symbolism of the moon. Both tales evoke an ambivalent and liminal state, the exact opposite of the more fixed and superstitious boundaries created by the male char-acters. The moon ribbon in the first story is described as 'rough and smooth at once' (p. 3). Turning magically into a river, it floats the protagonist to a place where she is unsure if she is dreaming or dead. At the door of the house 'that was like and yet not like' (p. 5) the one she has left, Sylva 'feared to knock and yet feared equally not to' (p. 5). Part of this dichotomy belongs to the girl's lack of integration at the beginning of the adventures and the more courage and independence she gains, the less ambivalent her experience becomes. But it simulta-neously invokes the blurring of fixed boundaries and this is nowhere more evident than in the magical, silver-haired woman. She is invoked as the mother, when Sylva is still timid and dependent, and as her sister, when Sylva becomes more strong-minded. She is either, though, only 'if you make me so' (pp. 8, 12) pointing to the power of percep-tion, the relativity of reality, and the need to actively create one's own destiny.

The moon child's description of the wonders of Swartwood is a similar irresolution of opposites: 'There is a place ... deep in the wood where it is neither night nor day, where sunlight and shadows meet and dance together in ever-changing ways' (p. 51). The fearful, conformist community destroy her presents and evict her, but they are unable to erase the impression she has made on their children. The text reinforces the power of her presence when, years later, the chil-dren search the forest for her:

where she waited, further out, always further out, in the places past the darkness where the sunlight and shadows met and danced together in ever-changing ways. (p. 54)

As with the moon-ribbon, this children's tale evokes in simple form a feminine fluidity, an acceptance of antinomies, and the blurring of those distinctions that create hierarchical oppositions. Women, as 'other' to phallocentric conformism, succeed when they have a matrilinear relationship, but without it must become either self-sufficient outcasts, or reconcile themselves to the unremediable nature of their men. The ambivalent and liminal magical province inscribed within the texts is clearly linked to femininity and a feminine way of viewing the world, that invokes otherness without rejecting a pragmatic rationality. Yolen's stories, aimed at a juvenile audience, inscribe complex Anglo-American liberal feminist theories in an accessible form that awakens a questioning readerly stance, and affirms a feminine one, without any overt moralising.

The stories in *Sweeping Beauties* are the exact opposite. Written for an adult audience, they demonstrate, for the most part, little detailed knowledge of the fairy tale genre they utilise, alongside an overtly self-referencing use of feminism. Fairytales for Feminists, an Irish collective of women writers, published a series of books for the feminist publishing house, Attic Press. *Sweeping Beauties*[55] was the fourth in the series. Most of the stories neither appropriate the genre nor parody it, rather they quote conventions of plot or character for their own purposes. All but one of the tales follow Lieberman and Dworkin in viewing fairy tales as vehicles of social codification, rather than as a literary genre. They therefore target cultural mores and pay little attention to the generic conventions or format. Such tales lack the depth of awareness necessary for parody. As Linda Hutcheon has argued, in relation to historiographic metafiction, 'To parody is not to destroy the past; in fact to parody is both to enshrine the past and to question it.'[56]

What I mean by 'parody' here ... is *not* the ridiculing imitation of the standard theories and definitions that are rooted in eighteenth-century theories of wit. The collective weight of parodic *practice* suggests a redefinition of parody as repetition with critical distance that allows ironic signalling of difference at the very heart of similarity.[57]

Most of the stories by the Fairytales for Feminists collective remain at the level of Hutcheon's 'ridiculing imitation', though some do not have sufficient similarity to be imitations, simply referring to certain characters, such as a princess, or Snow White. The texts show a dismissive lack of appreciation of the vehicle they employ, and this leads to narratives that are shallow in their attempt to be fairy tale, though their purpose often makes humorous and satisfying reading as feminist stories. Marguerite D'Arcy's tale, however, shows an appreciation and a valuing of fairy tale as a genre, through its detailed 'repetition' allowing it to be a successful appropriation or parody, in Hutcheon's terms. This appreciation leads to a denser, generically satisfying text that incorporates the feminism without sacrificing the aesthetic pleasures of the fairy tale conventions.

The two main targets of the critique of the social conventions are the unappreciated domestic industry of women and the feminine mystique that expects women to be simpering, eyelash-fluttering incompetents, to flatter male importance: two major themes of the liberal feminists during the 1970s, and important ones, but they were becoming hackneyed by 1989.

Two examples of the 'ridiculing imitation' of the genre can be found in 'The Fairy Godmother' by Elaine Cowley and Anne Le Martiquand Hartigan's 'A Tale to Remember'. A comparison of their treatment of magic highlights how generic conventions can aid the critique of social mores. Cowley's story has a young princess being groomed to be married off by her father, since it is a woman's role and women are property:

> 'Women were made for marriage and besides I have lost my fortune – we are very poor. But you are very beautiful and I know just the prince for you.' (p. 5)

The fairy godmother, a straight-talking women's liberationist, arrives to disabuse the princess and to argue that in contrast to the olden days, gifts of 'patience, tolerance and forgiveness.... All virtues to help a girl not go mad and kill herself or her husband after marriage', she now bestows 'A true value on yourself, independence of spirit and, the important one, being able to earn your own living' (p. 8). The bestowing of this 'gift' is done not by magic but by talking, by consciousness-raising. The plot and character of fairy tales are being imitated solely to comment didactically upon the earlier versions' reproduction of feudal system of women as property. While the feminist reader may well enjoy the ideological twist, the polemic would be off-putting to the general reader of the genre. 'A Tale to Remember', by including some rendition of the magical, manages to evoke the genre while still treating it primarily as a promulgator of social codes. The brilliant, academic princess who reverts to a tittering dullard when she marries, while her less-gifted husband's career prospers, clearly challenges the social convention that devalues intelligence in women. The princess's wit when he is absent, and her vacuousness when he is present, critiques women's collusion in the feminine mystique, but this point is never overtly made by the narrator. Instead the narrative constructs the transformation as an 'evil enchantment', evoking the appropriate magical convention. In this instance, less is more. By withholding direct polemic, and allowing the reader to make the inferences, the tale more effectively mimics the genre. Although it still relies upon a feminist readership for its pleasure, and the magic has none of the disturbance of psychic taboos discussed by Armitt, its use of the 'evil enchantment' as a metaphor for the collusive containment of women, a metaphor that simultaneously captures and critiques the social effect, works well. Patriarchy itself becomes indicted as the evil that blights women's intellectual growth. The feminist thesis of 'A Tale to Remember' is no more or less strong that that of 'The Fairy Godmother', but Anne Le Marquand Hartigan's more careful use of fairy tale conventions means that, aesthetically, it functions as a form of simple mimicry rather than as dismissive ridicule.

The stories of O'Neill, Healey and Corcoran are the low point of the collection as far as the appropriation of the fairy tale genre is concerned. These simply take the names of fairy tale protagonists for their own uses and have no pretence at being fairy tales *per se*. This is not to deny that they give pleasure to many feminist readers – the fact that the series ran to four successful volumes is clear evidence that they have a market – but they do not (and do not aim to) reach a wider audience by their use of the popular genre. To cite Nicci Gerrard's phrase, they are writing firmly within the ghetto, and to the already converted. 'Ms Snow White wins case in High Court' purports to be the report of a court case granting Snow White an injunction against the seven men who have exploited her youth and vulnerability in making her their domestic slave. The main narrative interest lies in the application of legal jargon to a known fairy tale, to give a feminist perspective on the plot, and after the initial interest in the presentation, this palls. An interest in word-play and in twisting a familiar narrative is the substance of 'The Revenge of the Sisters Grimm', based on the 'Emperor's New Clothes'. The Patri-arks have suppressed women by hiding the history of the Matri-arks, who originally held power and lived in harmony with nature. The Grimms, following their feminine 'insight' and 'instinct', uncover this history, run 'feminars and consciousness-raising sessions' (p. 13), and infiltrate the instruments of social power, revealing the Patri-arks on national television without their clothes. The uninventive and unproblematic reproduction of such 1970s radical feminist clichés as a hidden matriarchy and a passive, nurturing disposition closer to nature, in 1989 reveals a level of complacency that can alienate even many feminist readers.

> They learned about a time and place where woman ruled in harmony with nature. All the natural laws were strictly observed. In fact, nature was their religion. They took nothing from the earth without giving something in return. Their laws were based on love, justice and respect for all and violence was alien to their lives. All was not good, however. A certain breed of man was not content with peace and harmony. These men, known ever after as Patri-arks, wanted to upset this natural order. (p. 12)

The generalisation manifested in this schematic short-hand also lacks any aethetic pleasure, only partially because of its complete dismissal of the fairy tale it seeks to criticise. Such a narrative does leave itself open to Bloom's assertion that feminists use genres as an excuse in the war over gender definitions, rather than from any love of the form.

Grainne Healey's 'Snow Fight Defeats Patri Arky' has a level of inventiveness in the naming of the characters, if not in its plot. Snow Fight (as opposed to White, to ensure we recognise the active role model) goes to live with her cousins the Arkys: Matri, Patri, Olig, Hier, Mon and Noh. The brother, Patri, joins forces with the Crat brothers, Otto and Techno, to drug Snow Fight's soya milk and it takes Ann Arky's return, as a world famous scientist, to revive Snow Fight and take over the house as a separatist collective. The play on such words as anarchy, hierarchy, and autocrat, is witty and more developed than the O'Neill story, but the transparently heavy-handed moralising is the same and prevents any real engagement with the issues. These tales rely on like-minded readers recognising their 'political correctness' and enjoying that recognition. During the opening years of the Women's Liberation Movement, reading such a shared vision gave a pleasurable sense of cohesion similar to that experienced in real life in the consciousness-raising groups of the day. To be producing the same thing 15 years later has a different, less ground-breaking effect, that suggests a regressive desire for an orthodoxy in its way just as 'normalising' and oppressive as the phallocentric. These are tales that chance nothing, not even a flight of fancy, let alone the unsettling uncanny, or the blurring of boundaries. Few of them even tackle the darker, harrowing elements of phallocentrism. In this feminist landscape, women are oppressed by housework and the demand to be coquettes, they band together, realise men are a joke, and prevail.

The final story, 'Grainne's Version of the Pursuit' by Rita Kelly, offers a much more problematic, less self-congratulatory view of feminine sisterhood. The first-person narrative is more complex and the characterisation more detailed, as it explores a transgressive alternative to the pariarchal nuclear family. Here the princess is constructed iconoclastically as foul-mouthed, sexually active, and a lesbian. Rejecting her prince suitor for his beautiful sister, the two women wittily refute the usual representations of feminine decorum, culminating in the sister's revelation of a taste for sadomasochism:

> It went with the territory, she informed me, and what the hell did I think she majored in while on scholarship in Ohio if not S&M. Me, poor fool, thought it had something to do with female spirituality. (p. 63)

Kelly's exuberant tale voices contemporary 1980s debates within lesbian feminist circles and for the first time in the volume problematises the relationships between women, by pointing out that not all female relationships are nurturing and supportive, particularly once desire makes its unruly presence felt. This is a more satisfying story theoretically, while the tongue-in-cheek play on the fairy tale format works better than dismissive rejection. Nevertheless, its focus is on its feminist audience, rather than on the popular genre. It is left to 'The Budgeen' to seriously attempt an appropriation of the fairy tale genre in this collection.

'The Budgeen' by Margaretta D'Arcy has an appreciation of the genre that allows a densely satisfying appropriation. In this tale all the people wear veils and live in fear. The protagonist, a questioning, bold girl discovers it is because the men's noses fall off. Fleeing the retributive male violence, she finds the enchantress who bakes the budgeens (noses) out of dough. This woman, unlike the princess in 'A Tale to Remember', is angered by men's appropriation of her industry and refuses to make any more. The exploration of the frailty of phallocentric power is rendered with an inventive detail and an unsettling fantasy reminiscent of a folk tale.

> Old Morrigan got hold of her bellows and began puffing the air between Macha's feet so vigorously that the girl lost her balance and floated up into the air, out of the window, and over the trees. As she went, she heard Morrigan's voice like a thin pipe following her: 'You have already one gift, the gift of fearlessness: I give you two more – the gift of speed and the gift of the budgeen-recipe.' (pp. 52–3)

While the narrative eschews overt comment, the feminist critique of male aggrandisement through unacknowledged female industry is effectively reinterpreted when the young girl, the true inheritor of the matriarchal magic, mockingly rebirths the king.

In relation to feminist theory, 'The Budgeen' is no more advanced than 'A Tale to Remember' or 'Miss Snow White Wins Case in High Court', and certainly not as complex as 'Grainne's Version of the Pursuit', but as a generic appropriation of a fairy tale that appeals to a wider audience without sacrificing its feminist premise, it is by far the most successful of the tales. The unsettling opaqueness of the symbolism of the budgeen, the men's secrecy about their fragility, and their artificiality, allow an inclusive role for the reader. The sincerity of the presentation of the generic conventions produces an effective feminist re-writing.

Overall, *Sweeping Beauties* is a mix of the good, the bad and the indifferent. Apart from D'Arcy the writers show no real knowledge of the fairy tale genre, relying on a cultural assumption of passive princesses and a focus around the character of Snow White. They also rely upon a common consensus of feminist values which was already being challenged in the late 1970s and the 1980s by a range of other feminist voices. The tales, however, are clearly and unambiguously feminist in ideology, even if for the most part they are not fairy tales.

Carter's tales, in contrast, while clearly re-writing fairy tales, so disturbingly raise issues of the uncanny and of problematic sexuality, that some critics have raised the question of whether they are feminist. Angela Carter was the author of some nine novels and four collections of short stories. Her interest in fairy tales began during the folk music boom in the early 1960s, when she was reading medieval English at Bristol University. Two of the progenitors of the fairy tale, Chaucer and Boccaccio, were firm favourites.[58] In 1977 she translated *The Fairy Tales of Charles Perrault*[59] for Gollancz's children's list. The 'Foreword' praises Perrault's good-natured cynicism. It gives a knowledgeable account of Perrault's life and the cultural context of the tales and makes distinctions between the original, oral version's 'succinct brutality' and Perrault's modification of it 'by the application of rationality', going on to compare Perrault's ironic and sensible style to the later Grimms' 'savagery and wonder and dark poetry'.[60] The Foreword acknowledges that there are more troubling, darker and sexual aspects to 'Little Red Riding Hood', which Perrault's version ignores:

> Let's not bother our heads with the mysteries of sado-masochistic attraction. We must learn to cope with the world before we can interpret it. Modern savants with a psychoanalytic bent tend to ignore or berate Perrault because he incorporates certain troubling and intransigent images into a well-mannered schema of good sense, so that they cease to be troubling at all.[61]

Perhaps understandably, given the context of promoting the book, she does not discuss the sexism but instead praises Perrault as a 'humane, tolerant and kind-hearted Frenchman'.[62]

Two years later, Carter published *The Bloody Chamber*, her own highly literary versions of fairy tales where the tales contain all the sexuality and the troubling intransigence she claimed Perrault's had suppressed. But before considering the tales, I'd like to consider another aspect of Carter and the fairy tale genre. During the 1990s, she edited two volumes of fairy tales for Virago, the second edition being completed on her death by Marina Warner. In the 'Introduction' to the first, *The Virago Book of Fairy Tales*,[63] she discusses the history and the nature of fairy tales and folk tales. Fairy tales are seen as the 'unofficial' transmission of history, sociology and psychology, recording 'the real lives of the anonymous poor with sometimes uncomfortable fidelity'[64] but in an unashamedly fabulist form, 'dedicated to the pleasure principle'.[65] The recording of folk tales has been for 'a wide variety of reasons, from antiquarian to ideology'[66] but she focuses on their use for nationalistic purposes. During the nineteenth century, she argues:

> The excision of references to sexual and excremental functions, the toning down of sexual situations and the reluctance to include 'indelicate' material ... helped to denaturize the fairy tale and, indeed, helped to denaturize its vision of everyday life.[67]

Carter's own re-writings of fairy tales ten years before had given a voice to a feminine desire by revitalising just such erotic and indelicate subject matter.

The Bloody Chamber and Other Stories[68] consists of ten stories that comment upon a number of the classic fairy tales from Perrault, the Bothers Grimm, and Madame Le Prince de Beaumont.

Her tales textually invoke the earlier fairy tales in Hutcheon parodies that invoke the earlier form both in the narrative detail and in their uncanny disturbing savagery, but they also comment upon the earlier versions with a critical distance informed by feminism. Carter's 'The Company of Wolves', for example, not only re-writes 'Little Red Riding Hood' by giving the girl an active sexuality, it also encodes the previous versions intertextually so that it critiques Perrault's earlier, misogynistic version, and quotes the original 'Tale of Grandmother' in a complex palimpsest:

> What big teeth you have ...
> All the better to eat you with.
> The girl burst out laughing; she knew she was nobody's meat. She laughed at him full in the face, she ripped off his shirt for him and flung it into the fire, in the fiery wake of her own discarded clothing. (p. 118)

'Company of Wolves' is also prefaced by two other werewolf stories, locating it in a superstitious, peasant folklore, as is the earlier 'Werewolf' where the protagonist conforms to the social codes and rejects her *fylgja* for a comfortable prosperity. 'The Courtship of Mr Lyon' reproduces faithfully the snowy scene of the father's stranding, though now it is a motor car rather than a carriage, and the mysterious mansion to which he gains entry. The 'Snow Child' however, twists the 'Snow White' story while making overt the female rivalry between queen and girl for the king's attention, implicit in the Perrault. Here, it is the king who wishes to have a child 'as white as snow' and 'as red as blood', rather than the queen, and the shift in sex changes utterly the semantics of 'to have' as he sexually possesses her corpse (as the prince, in Strapola's version, has sex with Sleeping Beauty's somnalescent body). In the title tale, 'The Bloody Chamber', as Robin Ann Sheets demonstrates, the text intertextually refers to the fifteenth-century serial killer Gilles de Rais, whom many folklorists see as an important source for the Bluebeard story.[69] The anachronistic details, the telephones, motor cars, the stock-exchange, running alongside the obsolete relationships where women remain property to be bartered or bought, calls attention to the outmoded nature of these feudal relationships continuing within the modern world. Carter's tales not only reappropriate the fairy tale genre, but create complex Hutcheon parodies that both enshrine and question the genre simultaneously.

Their highly sexualised, erotic explorations have, however, led some feminist critics to brand them as phallocentrically pornographic and unfeminist[70] while others have defended their attempt to re-write a feminine sexuality.[71] As the editors to a 1997 collection of essays on Carter have observed, 'these stories have never ceased to engage – and enrage – their readers, who continue to debate whether Carter's revisionary handling of European legends contests or colludes with patriarchal values.'[72] The debate amongst Carter critics is therefore almost identical to the debate amongst feminist critics of the fairy tale genre itself. My own reading will argue for *The Bloody Chamber and Other Stories* as an attempt to decolonise women from a phallocentric view of themselves as passive objects. Carter has written of her interest in:

> questioning ... the nature of my reality as a *woman*. How that social fiction of my 'femininity' was created, by means outside my control, and palmed off on me as the real thing.
> This investigation of the social fictions that regulate our lives – what Blake called the 'mind-forg'd manacles' – is what I've concerned myself with ...[73]

and her re-written fairy tales explore women's ability to negotiate sexual relations without reproducing the phallocentric view of them as passive victims in the sexual act, the masochists within a sado-masochistic transaction. The tales directly engage with this issue and argue for women's transformation if they can escape the indoctrination, the 'mind-forg'd manacles' of their own view of desire. The opening tale 'The Bloody Chamber', based on Perrault's 'Bluebeard', has the male locked into his role of violator, though the bride can at the end step outside of the role of victim. The 'Lady of the House of Love' explores the victim–violator dichotomy with a twist, since it is the woman who is the blood-sucking predator, and the young man who is the beautiful, virginal prey. But the young man's uncomprehending acceptance and pity for her, and the vampire's own love for him together manage to rupture the ordained structure in a way figured by the tale's motif: 'Can a bird sing only the song it knows, or can it learn a new song?' (p. 103). Since for Carter, the sexual act is not 'natural' but culturally determined,[74] the question is answered in 'The Company of Wolves' when the girl's refusal to be a victim ('she knew she was nobody's meat' (p. 118)) turns the wolf into a 'tender' being. Likewise, the pitying and uncomprehending acceptance of the Duke by Alice, in 'Wolf-Alice' transforms the werewolf who has no reflection in a mirror, into something more human, 'as if brought into being by her soft, moist, gentle tongue, finally, the face of the Duke' (p. 126) is reflected. Unlike the monstrous Marquis of the opening story, the monstrous Duke of the final story, furnished with his own 'bloody chamber' (p. 123), can be transformed by the end because the transaction has been transformed through the play of the ten stories. The structures of relationship are not fixed, but dynamic, but it takes the women's rejection of the victim role to bring about this transformation of the unequal sado-masochistic interchange. As the narator of 'The Tiger's Bride' argues, 'The tiger will never lie down with the lamb; he acknowledges no pact that is not reciprocal. The lamb must learn to run with the tigers' (p. 64). 'Wolf Alice' has a similar argument when wolves are described as 'Unkind to their prey, to their own they are tender' (p. 121). But it lies with the women to transform the relationships, 'grace could not come to the wolf from its own despair, only through some external mediator' (p. 112, 'The Company of Woves'). Women need the psychic strength to learn new ways of relating to men that incorporate a sense of their own power, it takes the 'strong-minded child' (p. 113) who does not know yet know fear to bring about the transformations of the wolf and the vampire.[75] Carter's women need to learn to reject treacherous attractions of objecthood. As E. A. Kaplan has theorised in an essay questioning whether there can be such a thing as a female subject of desire, within the phallocentric framework, if a woman 'is to have sexual pleasure, it can only be constructed around her objectification; it cannot be pleasure that comes from desire for the other (a subject position)'.[76] Indeed, she goes further and argues, 'Women have learned to associate their sexuality with domination of the male gaze, a position involving a degree of masochism in finding their objectification erotic.'[77] Carter's tales explore these erotic attractions in 'The Erl-King', 'The Courtship of Mr Lyon', where the girl figures herself as 'Miss Lamb, spotless, sacrificial' (p. 45), and most notably, 'The Bloody Chamber'. In this first tale, the male gaze objectifies the girl who initially colludes in her masochism:

I saw him watching me in the gilded mirrors with the assessing eye of a connoisseur inspecting horseflesh.... When I saw him look at me with lust, I dropped my eyes but, in glancing away from him, I caught sight of myself in the mirror. And I saw myself, suddenly, as he saw me.... And for the first time ... I sensed in myself a potentiality for corruption that took my breath away. (p. 11)

No, I was not afraid of him; but of myself. I seemed reborn in his unreflective eyes, reborn in unfamiliar shapes. I hardly recognized myself from his descriptions of me and yet, and yet – might there not be a grain of beastly truth in them? ... I blushed ... to think he might have chosen me because, in my innocence, he sensed a rare talent for corruption. (p. 20)

However, when her aroused desire for 'the thousand, thousand baroque intersections of flesh upon flesh' (p. 22) which his libertine experience promises, turns out instead to be destruction, she finds within herself defiant 'nerves and a will' (p. 28). She recognises that she has had no choice, but has been an unequal partner in the transaction written for her by patriarchal precept.

I had played a game in which every move was governed by a destiny as oppressive and omnipotent as himself, since that destiny was himself; and I had lost. Lost at that charade of innocence and vice in which he had engaged me. Lost, as the victim loses to the executioner. (p. 34)

Collusion with victimhood, and imprisonment within the objectifying male gaze, need to be rejected in order to attain a female subject position of desire, as the two re-writings of the 'Beauty and the Beast' tales develop. In the idyllic fairy tale 'The Courtship of Mr Lyon', Beauty initially sees herself as victim, as sacrificial lamb for her father, and is appalled by the Lyon's 'bewildering difference from herself' (p. 45). Although she sees herself as powerless, the narrative consistently rejects this view, arguing that the beast is more afraid of her and with better reason. This bourgeois virgin is afraid of experiencing desire, of experiencing otherness, and when he kisses her hands in an eroticised description that recalls the Marquis's kisses,'she felt his hot breath on her fingers, the stiff bristles of his muzzle grazing her skin, the rough lapping of his tongue' (p. 46), we are told she 'would retreat nervously into her skin, flinching at his touch' (p. 48). But the rejection of experience is regressive, 'grazed by the possibility of some change, but finally, left intact' (p. 48). When she returns to the dying beast, she can no longer sustain the victim role, and in acknowledging that, also acknowledges the falsity of his role as violator, transforming him into a man as she reciprocates his earlier gesture in the reciprocity of equals: 'She flung herself upon him, so that the iron bedstead groaned, and covered his poor paws with her kisses' (p. 50).

The more worldly and materialist rendition of the same story, 'The Tiger's Bride' accords more to Carter's view of folk tales as it reproduces the material conditions of a Beauty tied to a drunken gambler of a father who views her solely as property.[78] This protagonist has 'the cynicism peculiar to women whom circumstances force mutely to witness folly' (p. 52), for she has a much more material oppression but rejects any notion of self-pitying martyrdom. She has learnt a different, more earthy, view of sexual relations from her peasant maids. She is as curious about 'the exact nature of his "beastliness"' (p. 55) as he is curious 'as to the fleshly nature of women' (p. 64) When his demand is to see her naked, she refuses to be made the object of his gaze, opting instead for the less victimised role of the working whore. With an unladylike guffaw she answers his demand with,

> I will pull my skirt up to my waist, ready for you. But ... I shall be covered completely from the waist upwards, and no lights. There you can visit me once, sir, and only the once. (p. 59)

His second demand to see her naked is also rejected, forcing him to disrobe himself, at which point she can do so as an equal and receive the 'marvellous wound' of acknowledging his otherness, his nature outside of the patriarchal. She learns to run with the tigers and renounces her return to patriarchy, where she has functioned as a 'simulacrum' of a woman, an 'imitative life amongst men', and resolves to live a life of otherness, becoming transformed in this trans-action into an equal beast of power: 'And each stroke of his tongue ripped off skin after successive skin, all the successive skins of a life in the world, and left behind a nascent patina of shining hair' (p. 67).

The final tale, 'Wolf-Alice', explores this issue of femininity outside of the patriarchal discourse, with the girl raised by wolves, the descrip-tion of which brings in many of the motifs of the earlier tales:

> If you could transport her, in her filth, rags and feral disorder, to the Eden of our first beginnings where Eve and grunting Adam squat on a daisy bank, picking the lice from one another's pelts, then she

might prove to be a wise child who leads them all and her silence and her howling a language as authentic as any language of nature. In a world of talking beasts and flowers, she would be a bud of flesh in the kind lion's mouth: but how can the bitten apple flesh out its scar again? (p. 121)

Carter's view is a materialist one, not a mystical one, Alice is now within culture and subjecthood cannot be dissociated from cultural forces. She learns to recognise her self as a self, to wear clothes and tend the monstrous Duke, yet she is still enough in touch with her own inviolability to bring about the Duke's transformation. The women in Carter's fairy tales learn to reject the phallocentric roles and to inhabit a new subject position that is alien, that is other, to patriarchy. Like the peasants of Duerr's vision, they have abandoned a damaging civilisation to experience the 'wildness in themselves ... the animal *fylgja*'. As I have argued elsewhere,[79] Carter's fairy tales embody powerful representations of women as subjects of desire, and at a moment when feminist debate was focusing on whether such a possibility could exist. Lynn Segal's analysis of the feminist pornography debates of the late 1970s and the early 1980s, the time of *Bloody Chamber*'s publication, argues that at the crux of feminist concern was the question: 'Is it, or is it not, possible for women to conceive of, and enjoy, an active pleasurable engagement in sex with men? Is it, or is it not, possible to see women as empowered agents of heterosexual desire?'[80] These tales therefore engage theoretically with the contemporary feminist debates of their time, and argue a complex material position. They are, however, resolutely representations of heterosexual desire. As a number of critics have persuasively argued, this text does not allow for a desire of women for women.[81]

Sweeping Beauties, with some exceptions, takes the fairy tale genre as a symptom of a patriarchal society, and dismisses the genre in its discussions of social concerns. Its focus on cultural stereotypes and the creation of alternative, feminist stereotypes, result in its failure to write fairy tales. Published by the feminist Attic Press, it has a small but committed audience and the fact that the series ran to five volumes points to a certain success. It does not aim at a wider genre audience, talking instead to like-minded feminists who will appreciate the knowing references. *Moon Ribbon* and *The Bloody Chamber* were both published by more mainstream publishers, and address a wider audience. Yolen was published by Dent, in Britain, and Carter initially by Gollancz, Penguin acquiring the paperback rights in 1981. Both texts develop a more complex appropriation of the genre, fuelled by a better grasp of its tradition and history, and have a more general appeal to the fairy tale reader.

As the history of the genre shows, the folk tale genre originally had a strong focus on women and women's issues. Women told the tales, and the content was often of female concerns and female apprenticeships. When male writers adapted the form they brought to it an overt ideological content, alongside the magical sedimentation with its channels to the uncanny. This overt ideological signification shifted to accommodate changing times and mores. Such an openly ideological narrative lends itself readily to feminist appropriation, and presents no serious pressures upon the genre's poetic conventions. One avowed ideology is simply being changed for another, equally avowed. The fact that for most readers, the fairy tale has been allocated to children's literature has allowed it to remain within a feminised domain. Yolen's appropriation is the least confrontational, generically and narratively speaking, and as such the most effective for the widest readership. It mirrors the shifting cultural changes in Britain and America post the Women's Liberation Movement, just as the Grimms' reinforced the bourgeoisification in the first half of the nineteenth century. Carter's appropriation of the adult, literary format is a similar generic shift to that of the German Romantics, such as Hoffmann and Tieck. However, since this adult format, in contrast to the juvenile, is less well known *The Bloody Chamber* appears at first, less an appropriation of the fairy tale format, and more of a hybridisation – a parodic mixture of the childhood fairy tale and the adult erotic tale. That said, the Carter text has proved the most popular of the three case studies. Penguin is one of the major popular paperback houses, reaching a large audience, and *The Bloody Chamber* has run to numerous imprints, never having been out of print in twenty years.

4
Detective Fiction

There are two standard assumptions about detective fiction, that it is a male-based genre because of its ratiocinating puzzle-solving element, and that it is an inherently conservative genre because its resolution involves the reinstatement of a hierarchical status quo. Both assumptions are challenged by a detailed look at the history of the genre. (The assumption that detective fiction valorises individualism is less easy to question, before the feminist appropriations.)

A bowdlerised view of the genre's history runs from Poe, through Conan Doyle, to the British Golden Age, with American hard-boiled adaptation of Hammett and Chandler as a reaction to the staid Golden Age. Agatha Christie is the singular acknowledged female writer of any standing. Such a canon argues that women characters in these stories of the authoritative detective pursuing the wrongdoers, are relegated to victims and the occasional love-interest that blossoms with the hard-boiled variety, into the more sinisterly dangerous construction of the vamps. Such a view ignores the fact that women have consistently written detective fiction, and in large numbers, and that the character of the woman detective, or the 'lady detective' as she was described in the titles, was a mainstay of detective fiction for writers of both sexes from the 1860s through to the Golden Age. Michelle Slung,[1] Patricia Craig and Mary Cadogan[2] rediscovered the wealth of female detectives during the 1970s and the 1980s but this alternative history has not affected the common assumption.

The view that detective fiction is a conservative genre is less easily demolished, if the social context is of a fixed, hierarchical stereotype, as in much Golden Age fiction with its village life of the squire, the vicar, the major, and the middle-class families serviced by a devoted, unsavoury or ingratiating working class. In such cases the resolution of the status quo is conservative, because the whole world-view is conservative. But not all detective fiction is Golden Age. The genre is much bigger and more diverse than that. Initially, the focus on the crime – on the things that *disturb* or disrupt societies – was much less comfortable, as in Andrew Forrest's 1864 *The Revelations of a Lady Detective*, and this element has developed into the crime fiction of writers such as Patricia Highsmith whose work focuses on the criminal, rather than the detective. Forrest's detective acknowledged a certain sleaziness in spying on society, to uncover the secrets of the crimes, and this sleazy, outcast status has come down through to the hard-boiled private eye, on the edge of society. The amateur detective's snooping on their acquaintances is an unsavoury characteristic which the Golden Age either circumvented by making their detective an aristocrat (and therefore beyond reproach), or adapted the stereotype of the nosy, elderly spinster. But not all detective milieux have been so conservative and writers from the early Chesterton through Hammett, to Walter Mosley and William McIlvaney have used the genre to portray a much darker, shifting, and corrupt society in which crime is always endemic and life is often iniquitous. In these novels a faith in authority is questioned rather than invoked because the law itself is often in corrupt hands, individually or socially. There has been a small but steady strand of left-wing writers who have used the genre, from Israel Zangwill and Arthur Morrison in the late 1890s, through to the 1930s writers such as C. Day Lewis (Nicholas Blake), the Fabians G. D. H. and Margaret Cole, and the Marxist Christopher Caudwell (Christopher St John Sprigg). Indeed, partly because of the tradition of seeing detective fiction as a more intellectual form of popular fiction, and therefore accorded a higher status than romance,[3] a number of literary writers, academics and artists have written for the genre, often using a pseudonym.[4]

Enough variation exists to be able to argue that although canonical detective fiction may have a conservative formula, the genre as a whole is much more variable and particularly open to exploring the individual in relation to the social and legal matrix. Looking at the 'conservative' thriller, but including many detective works in his argument, Steven Knight argues that they have the potential to be radical because of their very focus upon, and re-perception of, urban tension, professional skills and 'crime'.[5] Rosalind Coward and Linda Semple argue in relation to women's detective writing,

although certain conventions within detective fiction pull towards

tradition and repetition, and towards that particular brand of individualism and faith in authority, nevertheless there is nothing
necessarily conservative in the form. Different writers do, and have
always done, very different things with these generic constraints.[6]

They go on to argue that women, implicated as they are in the
concerns with violence, social conflict, victimisation and protection,
have always been attracted to detective and crime fiction. Women's
gender-specific view allows for a potentially radical input, even if
many of the women detective writers have been neither radical nor
feminist.[7] Knight, Coward and Semple argue that the form is not
necessarily conservative, though it has often been used to reinforce
that ideology, and point briefly to the forgotten history of more
radical and subversive writing within the genre to support their
arguments.

A history of the genre

Edgar Allen Poe's story, 'Murders in the Rue Morgue' (1841), with its
mystery of two women murdered within a sealed room, is usually cited
as the first detective short story of the intellectual puzzle type. Two
more stories followed, 'Mystery of Marie Roget' (1842–3) and 'The
Purloined Letter' (1845). Dupin, Poe's detective, with his seclusion and
his hauteur, sets the model for authoritative intervention as he solves
each of the cases. Poe divided these three stories from his horror
stories, as 'tales of ratiocination'. Ian Ousby affirms Poe 'first brought
the ingredients of detective fiction together'[8]: the baffling crime; the
eccentric, intellectual detective; and the solution achieved by method-
ical ratiocination, revealed at the closure. The author's interest, at this
point, was neither justice nor social order but the pleasure of the
puzzle for its own sake. The focus on the solving of the puzzle distinguishes the detective format from the sensation novels of Wilkie
Collins' *The Woman in White* (1859–60), *The Moonstone* (1868), Mary
Braddon's *Lady Audley's Secret* (1862) and Dickens' unfinished *The
Mystery of Edwin Drood* (1870) where detective characters also appear.
Partricia Craig and Mary Cadogan argue that while sensation fiction
focuses on the victim's experience, detective fiction focuses on the
investigator uncovering the identity of the villain.[9]

Two works introducing the 'lady detective' as a fictional characterisation appeared in the 1860s, well before such a profession was open
to women in real life, as Michelle Slung indicates.[10] In 1861 *The*

Revelations of a Lady Detective was published in Britain and in 1864 *The Female Detective* was published in America.[11] *The Revelations of a Lady Detective* by W. S. Hayward (initially published anonymously) has Mrs Paschal as the first female sleuth. Verging on forty she takes up detection as an escape from genteel poverty and is attached to the Metropolitan police. Upper middle-class and well-educated, she exuberantly solves a range of mysteries of forgery, blackmail, stolen jewels and missing wills. Andrew Forrester Junior's heroine of *The Female Detective*, is deliberately anonymous and more subdued as a narrator. Also attached to the Metropolitan police, she solves a similar range of crimes. These women detectives are able to infiltrate places where a man would look out of place, and employ a 'feminine' knowledge (about clothing or dressmaking, for example) which often holds the vital clue to the mystery. Both employ disguises and a flair for acting during their investigations, particularly Mrs Paschal. *Revelations* was part of the popular 'yellowback' tradition[12] of fictional memoirs of detectives that had become popular since the British publication of the French detective, Vidocq's *Memoirs* in 1829 (in France in 1828/9) and developed by fiction writers such as Thomas Gaspey's *Recollections of a Detective Police Officer* of 1856.

Both lady detectives predate Gaboriau's *L'Affaire Lerouge* (serialised in France in 1865, book 1866). Gaboriau's first amateur detective 'Père' Tabaret is outwardly unimpressive, but intellectually brilliant. In *Le Crime d'Orcival* (1866–7) and *Le Dossier no. 113* (1867), however, Gaboriau presented his more famous police detective, Monsieur Lecoq, also known for his ordinariness, a professional, middle-class, urban detective, and another master of disguise. *Monsieur Lecoq* (1869) invokes the conflict between monarchist, conservative landowners and the liberal bourgeoisie, an overt engagement with French social and political issues. Stephen Knight argues that though Gaboriau's work may seem reactionary today, in its period with the aristocracy trying to curb the force of the rising bourgeoisie, *Monsieur Lecoq* was radical both in form and content.[13]

The canon usually cites Sherlock Holmes as the next important detective characterisation, but between Lecoq and Holmes, came Anna Katherine Green who, Michelle Slung argues, was the first known woman detective writer, and hence 'the mother of the detective novel'.[14] Green's career started with *The Leavenworth Case* published in America in 1878 and ended with her final novel in 1923. *The Leavenworth Case* was a runaway bestseller, thereby overshadowing Seeley Register's *The Dead Letter* of 1866 which has the prior claim to being the first detective fiction by a woman writer. Green's first novel had a male detective but in her second, *That Affair Next Door* (1897), the crime is overlooked by an elderly, aristocratic, inquisitive, and astute spinster, Miss Butterworth, who becomes the detective's amateur helper in solving the murder. Slung calls Miss Butterworth the 'first truly important innovation'[15] for the woman detective and argues she is the prototype of the Golden Age elderly, female busy-bodies, Miss Marple and Miss Silver. Miss Butterworth reappears in *Lost Man's Lane* (1898) in a slightly more gothic case of disappearances and clandestine burial. In 1915 Green created a younger, attractive and more socialite female detective, Violet Strange in *The Golden Slipper and Other Problems for Violet Strange*, when the younger, winsome women detectives were in vogue. Violet Strange has an aristocratic fastidious-ness against sleuthing but cannot prevent herself becoming absorbed by the puzzle element of her mysteries.

Clarice Dyke the Female Detective by Harry Rackwood was published some time before 1883 (the known date of the reprint). Clarice is the wife of a detective and assists her husband in a subservient role in solving the cases, a model that was to burgeon in the 1930s detective couples (Nora and Nick Charles, Tom and Tuppence Beresford, Simon and Steve Temple, and the Lockridges).

In 1887 Conan Doyle's first Sherlock Holmes story, 'A Study in Scarlet' appeared in *Beeton's Christmas Annual* (book form 1888) followed by *The Sign of the Four* (1890). Success came when Conan Doyle started writing Holmes short stories for *Strand Magazine*, the first series collected as *The Adventures of Sherlock Holmes* (1892), the second series as *The Memoirs of Sherlock Holmes* (1894). Conan Doyle's boredom with the formula led him to kill Holmes off in 'The Final Problem', the last of the *Memoirs* stories. His resolve was unable to withstand public outcry and his publisher's lucrative incentives and, in all, the Holmes phenomenon spanned forty years, running to four novels and fifty-six stories.

Holmes borrowed the narrative motif of the admiring friend presenting the detective's exploits from Poe, but developed the worthy, plodding unimaginative character of the loyal Watson in much more detail. Holmes' intellect prowess, his arrogance and his aloofness alongside his eccentric dandyism (taking cocaine and playing the violin) became a model for later detectives. He operates a methodology of scientific rationalism, of studying the evidence, and has a near superhuman expertise in varieties of tobacco ash, news-paper typefaces, and little-known poisons. Initially solving crimes for their own intellectual sake, the later Holmes has an increasingly moral incentive, in exonerating the falsely accused. Conan Doyle has little interest in the law and the bumbling Lestrade. Of the sixty plots only eighteen end in arrests and legal punishment, eighteen end in some form of natural justice, and in eleven cases Holmes lets the perpetrator off.[16]

Following the enormous success of Holmes, the detective genre burgeoned during the 1890s. The genre was also taken up by left-wing writers. Israel Zangwill, a working-class Jewish writer most known for his social realist exposés of ghetto poverty, such as *Children of the Ghetto* (1892), wrote a locked-room puzzle novel, *The Big Bow Mystery* (1891). Set in the East End amongst the Labour movement, suspicion for the murder falls upon a rising Labour leader. The private detective, Grodman, finally reveals himself as the murderer, implicating detective and the police forces as corruptly protecting capitalism. Zangwill's fellow social realist of the East End, Arthur Morrison (*Tales of the Mean Streets*, 1894 and *A Child of Jago*, 1894) created a series of stories around two detectives, Martin Hewitt and Dorrington. The Hewitt stories, collected as *Martin Hewitt, Investigator* (1894), *The Chronicles of Martin Hewitt* (1895) and *Hewitt: The Third Series* (1896) were created as a critique of Holmes, eschewing flamboyant gestures, for a detective who prosaically tails his suspects. The crimes were often commercial, implicating capitalism as the real villain of the tale, as in 'The Avalanche Bicycle and Tyre Company' story in *The Dorrington Deed Box* (1897). Dorrington was an unscrupulous and near-criminal detective who, having found evidence, used it as a means for extortion rather than for arrest. Like Zangwill, Morrison used the detective genre to question the robbery implicit in capitalism and to question the role of the police as safeguarding capitalism. This theme is also present in the early G. K. Chesterton detective novel, *The Man Who Was Thursday* (1905) though less apparent in the later Father Brown stories.

In the wake of the cultural phenomenon of the 'new woman' at the turn of the century, a plethora of lady detectives took their place amongst the stories of lady balloonists, lady bicyclists, nurses and journalists. Grant Allen, best known for the novel *The Woman Who Did* (1895) about a 'new woman' who rejects the hypocrisy of marriage, on finding herself pregnant, also created two female detectives for *The Strand* in 1898: Miss Lois Caley and Nurse Wade. Neither has the social critique of the social-realist writers. Both detectives travel the world solving mysteries, aided by feminine intuition and, in the case of Nurse Wade, a photographic memory. More interesting lady detective representations came with George R. Sims' *Dorcas Dene Detective* (1897–8), Fergus Hume's *Hagar of the Pawnshop* (1898) and 'Old Sleuth' (Harlen Page Halsey's) *Gypsy Rose the Female Detective* (US 1898), alongside A. K. Greene's two Miss Butterworth novels. Unlike Miss Butterworth, these detectives are young and attractive. Dorcas Dene is supporting a blind husband by the use of her intellect and a flair for disguise. Hagar is a Romany beauty with lustrous black hair and vivid clothing, who has fled her gypsy clan and solves the mysteries surrounding objects brought in to be pawned. She finally marries one of the early clients and eschews sleuthing for marital bliss. Knight argues that an earlier Hume novel, *The Mystery of a Hansome Cab* of 1886, set in Australia, was a radical portrayal of mushrooming capitalism, and 'the first best-seller in all crime fiction'.[17] His 'The Lone Inn' was serialised in Keir Hardie's *Labour Leader* in 1894.

The beginning of the twentieth century saw the continuing rise of the lady detective and of the woman detective writer. L. T. Meade (Elizabeth Smith) collaborated with Robert Eustace, a medical expert, to create a number of medical mysteries, *A Master of Mysteries* (1898), *The Sanctuary Club* (1900) and four short stories for the *Harmsworth Magazine* (1899–1900), involving the young detective Florence Cusak. M. McD Bodkin (QC) created *Dora Myrl, the Lady Detective* (1900) enthusiastically solving crimes on that Edwardian symbol of female independence, the bicycle, and able to pick locks with a hairpin. In the 1909 *The Capture of Paul Beck*, however, she is pitted against Bodkin's other, male, detective, eminently more capable and experienced. Bodkin marries them at the end, whereupon Dora renounces detective work for motherhood, and gives birth to the junior member of the team, *Young Beck, a Chip Off the Old Block* (1912). In the same year as Dora Myrl, Catherine Louisa Purkiss published *The Experiences of Loveday Brooke, Lady Detective* (1900). Loveday Brooke owes similarities to Andrew Forrester Junior's anonymous protagonist, in her deliberately nondescript, self-effacing character. Loveday is a far cry from the flamboyance of Baroness Orczy's famous Lady Molly. Baroness Orczy created a self-effacing male sleuth in *The Old Man in the Corner* (1909), who solves the mysteries brought to him by a young female journalist, from his chair in the pub. But a year later she published *Lady Molly of Scotland Yard* (1910). Entering the profession to prove her imprisoned husband's innocence, Lady Molly solves a number of crimes with a good deal of feminine intuition and lucky coincidence, before freeing her husband and renouncing detection. Hugh C. Weir's American *Miss Madelyn Mack, Detective* (1914) had an equally flamboyant female detective, whose character owes a lot to Sherlock Holmes, wielding as she does a magnifying glass, proceeding from deductions of the evidence, and having recourse to narcotic 'cola berries'. Madelyn Mack is a representation of the 'exceptional woman', a dazzling intellectual genius, and so the usual closure of marriage-and-renunciation-of-detection is handed down to her chronicler, the young reporter Nora Noraker. Richard Marsh created a slightly different young female detective in *The Adventures of Judith Lee* (1916). A teacher of the deaf by profession, Judith Lee's ability to lipread helps her solve her crimes. These flamboyant and feminine middle-to-upper-class socialites with their 'new woman' attributes do not persist much after the First World War. Two American versions, Arthur Reeve's *Constance Dunlop: Woman Detective* (1916) and Jeanette Lee's Millicent Newberry in *The Green Jacket* (1917) are more low key and employ the feminine stereotype of reforming saviour.

Another tradition replaced the Holmes clones and the 'lady detective' on either sides of the Atlantic after the war. In Britain, this was predominantly the 'Golden Age' tradition while in America it was the 'Hard-boiled' tradition. Chandler argues for Hard-boiled coming from a reaction to the unreality of the Golden Age fiction, but the dates of Hammett's first work point to a simultaneous switch in different directions.

In 1918, twenty-five women were appointed to the Metropolitan Police Force to patrol London but denied the powers of arrest. Derided by the public and their colleagues, they were disbanded in 1922 but in the same year the CID appointed a woman to help interview female and child victims of sexual assaults. Despite this context, the Golden Age fiction has few professional women detectives, leaning instead heavily to the elderly busybody spinster. Again, women provide a large number of the writers. The 1920s saw the start of Agatha Christie (with Poirot), Dorothy L. Sayers, Margery Allingham, Patricia Wentworth and Josephine Tey, as well as the male writers Freeman Wills Croft, Frances Iles and in America, Ellery Queen and S. S. Van Dine. The 1930s saw the continuance of these writers, with Christie developing Miss Marple and Sayers Lord Peter Wimsey alongside John Dickson Carr, Michael Innes, Ngaio Marsh and Nicholas Blake, with Rex Stout beginning in America.

The Golden Age novels shift the focus from the detective to the 'world' of the crime, often a closed world of a village, university college, cruise ship, or country house where the body is found (for Golden Age crime narrowed down solely to murder). The puzzle of the crime is shifted more directly on to the reader, becoming more game-like and, Priestman argues that 'literary intellectuals in this period were engaged *en masse* in a love affair with the form'[18] citing W. H. Auden, George Orwell, William Empson and T. S. Eliot as public fans. The 'world' evoked is a complacently upper-middle class one, usually with a well-born male detective (Sayers, Dickson Carr, Innes, Allingham and Marsh) dispensing literary allusions alongside his authoritative analysis. This convention of focusing on the puzzle and eliding the social issues is unfortuntaely just as true of the left-wing writers such as G. D. H. and Margaret Cole and Nicholas Blake.

In 1928 the Detection Club was formed in Britain. Its founding members included Chesterton, Bentley and Sayers. The Club resolved to reject unfair resolutions which the reader would be unable to decipher for themselves. In 1929 Ronald Knox, detective writer and Balliol scholar and clergyman, codified this into a 'Decalogue' that ensured technical rigour and a spirit of 'fair play'.[19] The gentlemanly detectives, suave connoisseurs, use an orderly method to apprehend the villain and return society to order. The Club effectively designated a canon of 'true' detective fiction and an ideology of readership that accorded to a 'gentleman's agreement'. This canon rejected the more feminine conventions of the genre, by ruling out 'intuition' by the detective, and denigrating the highly successful feminine 'If I Had But Known' school. Constructing the genre as an intellectual puzzle effectively also rules out the social exploration of disruption and inequity. The Detective Club created a supremely conservative canon of what the genre 'should be'.

Other versions of the genre continued, however. Josephine Bell evoked the darker side of working-class life in *The Port of London Murders* (1938), while in the States, career girls such as teachers, journalists and particularly nurses continued to sleuth. Mignon Eberhart's Nurse Sarah Keate mysteries began with *The Patient in Room 18* (1929) and ran for over sixty novels while Mary Robert Rinehart's nurse, 'Miss Pinkerton' began in *The Buckled Bag* (1925) and ran for just under twenty years. These 'Had I But Known' mysteries relied heavily on feminine intuition, and were denigrated by the Detective Club as inferior. Slung links the denigration specifically to their focus on the 'clutter and flutter' of the feminine,[20] and certainly they carry on the tradition of amateur women sleuths. In 1909 Rinehart's *The Man in the Lower Ten* made the British bestsellers list and throughout the 1920s either Rinehart or E. Phillips Oppenheim (another woman detective writer) appeared on the lists. Rinehart's average yearly sales were

300 000 copies.[21] The denigrated 'Had I But Known' school has an 'amateur' retrospectively tracing the mystery she has been caught up in. Mary Robert Rinehart wrote in this sub-genre, and the dismissal of these 'too fanciful' works, by the Detective Club, thereby consolidates the ratiocination of the classic canon. But it does so only by ignoring much of the hugely popular women's detective fiction of the period, which relied on intuition and a knowledge of personality to solve the crimes, rather than on material evidence and rationality. This expanded genre format encompasses other models of validated knowledge, alongside the phallologocentric.

Nowadays, the best known of the female sleuths of the 1930s are the canonical Miss Marple, Wentworth's Miss Silver and Gladys Mitchell's Miss Bradley, the three grandmotherly amateurs, whose age prevents their sexuality creating a conflict of representation with their effective ratiocination. Christie's strength as a writer was the ingenious plot, and her characters remained of secondary consideration, often a stereotype. Miss Marple, of *Murder at the Vicarage* (1932), 'stands for intelligent, moderate conservatism although, in the tradition of the deferential female, she is always hesitant about proffering an opinion'.[22] Patricia Wentworth's Miss Silver, beginning with *Lonesome Road* (1937) falls into a similar mode, accompanied by one of two young policemen. Miss Silver is a former governess and innocent, romantically involved couples seek her aid. This grandmotherly protection of young love further softens and 'feminises' the authority of her intelligence. Mitchell's Mrs Bradley is a very different proposition. Beginning with *Speedy Death* (1929), Mitchell tends to problematise the moral issue of crime which traditional Golden Age ignores, and her protagonist is the very antithesis of the modest, deferential Misses Marple and Silver. A distinguished psychoanalyst and academic author, holding honorary degrees from scores of universities, twice widowed with a successful barrister son, Mrs Bradley is extravagant, exuberant, incisive, and so old that she is 'saurian'.

Dorothy L. Sayers introduced a younger, more eligible woman, Harriet Vane, as a love interest for her main detective, Lord Peter Wimsey. In *Strong Poison* (1930) Vane is a writer of detective fiction wrongly accused of the murder of her lover, whom Wimsey exonerates. In *Have His Carcase* (1932) she takes on a subordinate role in solving the murder, but in *Gaudy Night* (1935) she investigates some poison penletters in an Oxbridge women's college and, although it is Wimsey who finally arrives and provides the solution, it is Harriet's ratiocination that is foregrounded. *Gaudy Night*, with its subtext of an intelligent woman's role in society and the choice between marriage or an intellectual career, has fuelled a debate amongst feminist critics of detective fiction, as to whether its subversive content is proto-feminism, although many have been disappointed that the conventional dénouement remains marriage to Wimsey. *Gaudy Night* is an exception though. On the whole, Golden Age fiction codified the narrative to a puzzle ('whodunnit') and reified the aristocratic male detective to reinforce phallocentric and class-ridden stereotypes.

The Hard-boiled American tradition began with Dashiel Hammett. Hammett had been a Pinkerton 'operative' from 1915–22. Starting with bounty hunting in 1850, the Pinkerton Detective Agency specialised in security work for large companies during the twentieth century, solving bank and railway thefts. Its trademark of an eye, with the motto 'We Never Sleep', originated the slang name for American detectives, 'private eye'. Hammett's first short stories were published in *Black Mask* (one of the many detective magazines that along with the dime novels were the American equivalent of the British 'yellowbacks') in 1923, with his detective Continental Op (short for operative). Continental Op stories continued in 1929, alongside *Red Harvest* and *The Dain Curse*. *The Maltese Falcon* followed a year later, *Glass Slipper* in 1931, and the final *The Thin Man* in 1934. Hammett gave the narration to the detective, rather than an observing friend, and the spare, wise-cracking, slang-ridden narration created much of the character. 'Stirring things up rather than thinking things out'[23] became the tradition, since logical deduction by the narrator would reveal the suspects much too quickly to the reader. The plots became more adventurous with the detective implicated in the events as he embarks on an urban picaresque of high society and seedy criminality. The whole milieux, big business, the police, and the rich clients, are tarnished by crime. Only the cynical wise-cracking narrator has a moral integrity, a code of honour. In 1939, Raymond Chandler began the first of his seven Philip Marlowe novels, *The Big Sleep*, developing the honourable image of the detective as alienated knight errant. Chandler claimed a contemporary authenticity and a social, urban realism missing from the hide-bound Golden Age. The American villains of the 1930s were more likely to be corrupt groups of individuals in high power, rather than the British version of the aberrant, crazed individual. Power, not madness, became implicated as the site of disruption. Ross MacDonald continued the hard-boiled tradition with his Lew Archer novels, and James Hadley Chase tried the same formula in a British context.

There are few women detectives in this mould, though Rex Stout's nubile Dol Banner, *The Hand in the Glove* (1937) aggressively rejecting patronising men, and Will Oursler's Gale Gallagher, *I Found Him Dead* (1947), case-hardened and stunning, sporting a Colt .32, are examples. The main female detectives of the 1930s and 1940s were the boyish girl detectives in girls' magazines such as Nancy Drew and Judy Bolton. During the 1930s extreme youth or extreme old age effectively elided issues of women's sexuality, allowing the female detectives an agency without challenging the cultural stereotypes of femininity.

George Simenon's Maigret introduces a new dimension to the detective format, that of police bureaucracy. Writing ten novels in 1931, and eighty by 1972, his stolid and unromantic detective is a bureaucrat, depending heavily on the back-up of his colleagues. This portrayal of the detective paved the way for the more realistic 'police procedurals' of Hillary Waugh's *Last Seen Wearing* (1952) and Ed McBain's 87th Precinct novels, beginning with *Cop Hater* in 1965. In these, the emphasis is on team work and the routines of police investigations. Alongside the police procedurals developed the crime novel, where the focus is on the psychology of the criminal rather than the detective. Francis Iles' *Malice Aforethought* (1931) and James M. Cain's *The Postman Always Rings Twice* (1934) begin this tradition but it is Patricia Highsmith who makes it her own, beginning with *Strangers on a Train* (1950) and then embarking on the first of her Ripley series, *The Talented Mr Ripley* (1955).

By the mid-1960s the development of the genre becomes a more eclectic mixing of the forms, rather than any new adaptation. Contemporary detective fiction needs to take account of the traditions of police procedure and of the psychology of the criminal alongside a more realistic social milieu. This shift away from the 'great detective' to a broader focus on tracking down the criminal(s) produced a shift in the naming of the genre. Contemporary bookshops are more likely to have a 'crime fiction' section rather than a 'detective fiction' section, to signal the wider gamut of the genre. In America the private eye tradition continues, while Britain favours the police detective series, such as P. D. James' Adam Dalgleish (beginning with *Cover her Face*, 1964), Ruth Rendell's Wexford (*From Doon with Death*, 1964), Colin Dexter's Morse (*Last Bus to Woodstock*, 1975) and Reginald Hill's Dalziel and Pascoe (*A Clubbable Woman*, 1970). Britain has also returned to working-class milieux and concerns, particularly in the works of William McIlvaney, *Laidlaw* (1977) and *The Papers of Tony Veitch* (1983) and Ian Rankin (*Rebus*, 1987). In America, the focus on the hunt for serial killers in Elmore Leonard and James Ellroy, also incorporate a gritty realism. The late 1970s saw the arrival of specifically feminist writers and detectives (see below) to interrogate the sexism of the genre and, in 1990, Walter Moseley's black detective Easy Rawlins (beginning with *Devil in a Blue Dress*) used the detective genre to interrogate racism in American society.

The bestselling detective novels in the 1990s accept women in places of high office, by Lynda La Plante or the phenomenally successful Patricia Cornwall, and any mainstream bookshop or library will feature a large number of feminist detective writers in its crime section. Interrogations of class, gender and race sit alongside puzzle plots, police procedurals unquestioning of the law and order enforced, and crime exploring the psyche of the psychopath. The variety and eclecticism of the genre in the 1990s holds a multiplicity of ideologies within its distended format.

Feminist criticism and appropriation of detective fiction

In 1975 Michelle B. Slung's *Crime on Her Mind: Fifteen Stories of Female Sleuths from the Victorian Era to the Forties*[24] began the work of uncovering the literary history of the 'lady detective' by both male and female writers. Her introduction argues for well over 60 women detectives from the mid-nineteenth to the mid-twentieth centuries, 'from Edwardian débutantes to ingenious flappers, from elderly busibodies to hard-boiled molls'.[25] Slung links the appearance to the cultural emergence of the 'new woman' who rejected domesticity for excitement and a career, although she notes women were unable to be police detectives in reality. The characterisations of the early detectives were over-endowed with femininity to compensate for their profession, and solved the mysteries by feminine intuition. During the early twentieth century, the stereotypes began to entrench, with a prosaic feminine common sense for the women detectives, while their male counterparts had the ratiocinating 'pyrotechnics' of solving the crimes.

Earl F. Bargainnier continued Slung's task by editing *10 Women of Mystery* in 1981[26] with ten introductory essays on women writers from Green and Rinehart to Sayers and Amanda Cross. The introduction argues that detective fiction is unique in allowing women writers with women protagonists a widespread success that is read equally by men and women. The introduction of women detective writers has continued apace; Kathleen Gregory Klein's 1994 edition *Great Women*

Mystery Writers: Classic to Contemporary[27] gives entries of 117 popular women writers.

During the mid-1980s feminist criticism began to appear, mostly in small genre journals such as *Clues: a Journal of Detection*, where the level of feminist analysis, or originality, was thin. Jane S. Bakerman's 'Cordelia Gray: Apprentice and Archetype' argues Cordelia as a feminist *bildungsroman* protagonist with no analysis of 'feminist', but the focus solely on the *bildungsroman*.[28] Similarly, Jane C. Pennell's 'The Female Detective: Pre- and Post-Women's Lib'[29] turns on whether the women detectives choose a career over marriage. However, Jeanne Addison Roberts, 'Feminist Murder: Amanda Cross Reinvents Womanhood',[30] gives a perceptive analysis of how Carolyn Heilbrun's feminist theory has affected her later detective fiction as Amanda Cross, and how the development of Cross' feminism has changed the protagonist from 'androgynous' to 'autonomous'.

In 1986 Patricia Craig and Mary Cadogan brought feminist detective fiction into the mainstream when Oxford University Press published their *The Lady Investigates: Women Detectives and Spies in Fiction*[31] and the feminist debate around detective fiction takes off from the late 1980s. *The Lady Investigates* considers the lady detective at different historical periods on either side of the Atlantic, comparing the manifestations. The analysis is detailed, authoritative, and grapples intelligently with issues of feminism. Christie, for example, is acknowledged as transmuting gossip and nosiness into something more socially useful in Miss Marple, but in her simpering and dithering she still reifies the deferential female. The lady detective, they conclude, after a sentimental beginning and an eccentric middle period, is finally becoming a character of substance, efficacy, and with Cordelia Gray and Kate Fansler, feminist in the 1960s and 1970s. The lady detective, as a characterisation, has been 'the most economical, the most striking and the most agreeable embodiment of two qualities often disallowed for women in the past: the powers of action and practical intelligence'.[32]

In the same year, Cora Kaplan was considering whether detective fiction was 'An Unsuitable Genre for a Feminist'.[33] Looking at the new breed of liberated, smart and sexual women detectives such as Cordelia Gray and Jemima Shore, she argues that while they have the ability to challenge the fictional conventions of the detective, they are unable to affect the conservative politics of the genre itself. Many of the 'great' women writers such as Christie, Sayers and James, wrote sexually and socially conservative themes, both in seeing women's sexuality as the disruptive agent of crime, and in positioning individual responsibility as the cause of crime. While feminist writers are using male villains to represent social pressures and using promiscuous protagonists to challenge representations of feminine sexuality as the trigger for social disruption, their protagonists are still safely bourgeois, urban professionals upholding conservative social values. Caplan ends with the question of whether true feminist detective fiction, if it were to exist, would lose the narrative pleasure of the genre.

1986 also saw a conference on detective fiction at Wesleyan University, Connecticut, with a section devoted to 'Women and Crime Fiction'[34] and the keynote speech by Carolyn Heilbrun/Amanda Cross. The proceedings were published two years later, *The Sleuth and the Scholar: Origins, Evolution, and Current Trends in Detective Fiction*.[35] Heilbrun's 'Keynote Address: Gender and Detective Fiction' argued that the English detective novel had always been androgynous, with its charming and effete male detectives, and American detective fiction had lately adopted the format. Setting androgyny up as the opposite to sexual stereotyping, Heilbrun argued that detective fiction challenges gender stereotypes, and women have transformed the genre.

1988 saw two books dedicated to gender which held opposing views on the impact of feminism: Reddy's *Sisters in Crime* and Klein's *The Woman Detective*. Kathleen Gregory Klein's *The Woman Detective: Gender and Genre*[36] argues that because the genre is conservative, the changes brought about by placing a woman at the centre are only superficial. Unlike Reddy, Klein looks at the history of the genre, from Forrest and Pachal through to Paretsky and Grafton. In limiting her analysis to professional detectives, though, Klein ignores the amateur tradition which has proved to be the more subversive strand, and which already did many of the things she called upon a feminist detective fiction to do. Klein accepts the Frankfurt School thesis of popular culture: 'the producers ... have a vested interest in certain arrangements of the status quo which they are unwilling to see challenged in the materials they finance'.[37] This 'conspiracy theory' view of popular culture prevents her fully developing the detailed gynocritical readings of the protagonists and forces her to conclude that genre triumphs over ideology when the woman's script and the detective's script try to mesh.

Maureen T. Reddy's *Sisters in Crime: Feminism and the Crime Novel*[38] looks at the recent diversity of women protagonists, the amateur, the academic, police, hard-boiled and lesbian detectives. Reddy, too, argues that detective fiction is conservative but is able to argue for feminist transformation by dividing up the genre. 'Detective fiction' is masculinist, defined by the Decalogue golden rules of fair play, reassuring in its linear procedure and the masculine authority figure who banishes disruptive elements. Feminist writers have set up a countertradition that is less monologic, which she terms 'crime fiction'. Looking for a precursor to this 'crime fiction' she ignores the history of the genre, turning instead to the gothic. On the recent genre she is on stronger ground. Rejecting simple role reversal as keeping the conventions in place, she argues for feminist rewriting through 'the violation of linear progress, the ultimate absence of authority as conventionally defined, and the use of a dialogic form'.[39] While Lilian O'Donnell's Norah Mulcaheney novels change only the gender of the protagonist and remain patriarchal texts, Paretsky's V. I. Warshawski redraws the hard-boiled boundaries and forces readers to reconsider their usual reading strategies. The most radically subversive texts come from the growing sub-genre of lesbian detective fiction which challenges generic conventions and critiques social constructions.

Sally Munt's chapter, 'The Inverstigators: Lesbian Crime Fiction',[40] in the same year develops this discussion of the lesbian transformation of an 'historically monological mysogynistic megalomania'.[41] Effective lesbian detective fiction critiques the Manichaean morality of good and evil, natural justice, tidy textual closures and above all unified subjectivity. The narrative pleasure of detective fiction comes from discovery, and the most subversive lesbian detectives discover that identity is a transitional process reflecting the diversity and complexity of desire.

In the following year, Rosalind Coward and Linda Semple, who as Pandora's series editors of 'Women Crime Writers' began reissuing forgotten works by women to create a more radical canon of detective fiction,[42] published 'Tracking Down the Past: Women and Detective Fiction'.[43] Pointing to the current renaissance of women writers of detective fiction, they detail the hidden tradition of earlier women writers and pose the question of why women are so good at crime? They reject the view that the genre is necessarily conservative and phallocentric, because they argue the boundaries of the genre are fluid and often subversive. Female writers are not necessarily more progressive, but many have taken issues such as illegitimacy, abortion and the powerlessness of women, from the 1940s onwards. Contemporary women have added pornography, rape and sexual violence to examine the gender issues of victimisation. Detective fiction, they argue, is a literature of transgression and, with the amateur sleuths, of ambivalence to law and order. Closed communities have allowed the exploration of complex relationships between women, extending the community in radical directions. Women have always been attracted to crime writing because its concerns and conflicts are particularly relevant to women.

Four essays were published in 1990, addressing the question of feminist appropriation. Maggie Humm's 'Feminist Detective Fiction'[44] argued that feminist detective writers were questioning the limits of women's contemporary experience by questioning the limitations of the genre. Using Mary Douglas' anthropological work on boundaries to codify gender, Humm argues that where the traditional detective fiction polices the boundaries to expel deviants and reinforce the moral consensus, feminist detective fiction crosses the boundaries, by connecting sexual politics to economic and patriarchal repression. While their books reject linearity and the individual scopic gaze, their detectives act more collectively, as mediators between groups, and focus on more domestic issues, rather than the public. The feminist writers therefore challenge the conventions of containment and displacement.

Maureen T. Reddy's 'The Feminist Counter-Tradition in Crime: Cross, Grafton, Paretsky and Wilson'[45] continued to detail how feminist writers create a counter-tradition. Feminist ideology informs the source of the detective's authority and power, while corruption is linked to capitalist patriarchy. Truth is shown to be relative, order is often the source of the crimes, and relationships are often seen as more important than abstract justice. The feminist detectives are implicated in the events and the closure hinges on relatedness, an egalitarian sisterhood, rather than romance or solitude.

Lyn Pykett's 'Investigating Women: the Female Sleuth after Feminism'[46] is more sceptical about the new 'Queens of Crime', arguing that not all of the women writers seriously challenge the conservative values of the genre, but that some do. Where Fraser, James and Cross merely 'update' the genre by placing more modern, younger women as the detectives, the feminists 'appropriate' the genre by questioning its politics. Addressing issues of race, class, gender and sexual preference leads to novels of ideas, where the detective figure is transformed.

Anne Cranny-Francis' chapter 'Feminist Detective Fiction'[47] argues that detective fiction upholds bourgeois ideology (invoking the traditional canon and the gothic for her history of the genre), so feminists need to reposition the reader and challenge the conventions in order to effectively appropriate the ideology of the genre. Feminist detectives have professional jobs, to transgress the stereotypes, creating economically independent, sexually autonomous, intelligent and courageous protagonists who engage physically in their investigations. The criminals tend to be implicated in patriarchal, bourgeois values but with the more experimental (the amateurs) the criminal and the victim blur. However, Cranny-Francis is sceptical of the attempt to appropriate the genre, arguing that serious ideological challenge leads to a diminution of suspense (and hence an inability to remain within the conventions). The 'genre conventions are encoded with ideological discourses'[48] that prevent feminist appropriation. So the more radical fiction is not properly within the genre.

In contrast to Cranny-Francis' careful interrogation of the genre conventions and her consequent pessimism, Marion Shaw and Sabine Vanacker's more lightweight *Reflecting on Miss Marple*[49] argues optimistically for a feminist revision of Agatha Christie. They too agree that the genre is conservative, though their concept of ideology is flawed,[50] but argue that Christie 'feminised' the genre. The fussy, pottering detection, the social oddity of spinsterhood, and the minute observation of human nature, are all validated by Christie's allowing Miss Marple to invade the male territories of logic and rationality and solve the crime. Acknowledging that Christie was no feminist, but an arch conservative, they yet go on to make the startling claim that recent feminist detectives are Miss Marple's 'afterlife': the inter-war marginalised spinster now becoming the similarly alienated lesbian sleuth.

Paulina Palmer's essay 'The Lesbian Feminist Thriller and Detective Novel'[51] of the same year is more substantial in its consideration of the genre, but equally positive in its view of the possibility of some appropriation. Asserting that the conventions are conservative and at times openly racist and mysogynistic, Palmer argues that lesbian writers have to find ways of transforming the attitudes. Most lesbian detectives are hard-boiled because this places greater emphasis on the critique of social hierarchy, legality, and racial and gay discrimination. The lack of firm closure also accords with feminist fiction. Lesbian writers have confronted the difficulties surrounding the detective figure by inventing new ways to deconstruct self-sufficiency and individualism. They have also been able to confront issues surrounding collective action, such as antagonism and competitiveness between women. The hard-boiled's tradition of sexual conquest allows them to write about lesbian sex, exploring issues of dominance and subordination, and the scopic gaze. Lesbian hard-boiled fiction, for Palmer, succeeds in interrogating the conventions and re-writing a feminist detective fiction.

David Glover and Cora Kaplan's brief 'Guns in the House of Culture? Crime Fiction and the Politics of the Popular'[52] (1992) acknowledges the impact of feminist crime writers, in the change to the assumptions that are now made about the limits of female agency. But these shifting representations of femininity and masculinity are, they note, often located within highly violent narratives. Eschewing the usual critical condemnation of violence, they ponder the narrative pleasure of positing utopian changes to identity alongside such violence.

Sally Munt's book-length study of contemporary feminist detective fiction, *Murder By The Book?: Feminism and the Crime Novel*,[53] acknowledges the different kinds of feminism in use, liberal and socialist feminisms, race, lesbian, psychoanalytic and post-modern feminisms. Munt challenges the idea that detective fiction is inherently masculine and misogynistic, arguing that feminists have adopted a satiric form to parody patriarchal norms and forms. Genre is dynamic, 'a cultural code in which meanings are consistently contested'.[54] Her informed analysis contends that feminist detective fiction exposes sex and gender oppression, while making guilt collective and social. The politics of the gaze is foregrounded, to unmask its sexed, gendered and racial paradigms. While some feminists adopt a counter-discourse to heroism, others explore the fractured self and the importance of *communitas*. Munt concludes that the heyday of the feminist genre was linked to the decade of Thatcher and Reagan, which reified the individual, and that it has declined in the 1990s, along with the feminist presses.[55]

In 1995 Kathleen Gregory Klein edited *Women Times Three: Writers, Detectives, Readers*.[56] In her opening discussion, she acknowledges that the genre is transformable, a dialogue between writers and readers (she ignores the publishers) and that feminists have overwritten the palimpsest of masculine conventions, sustained by a feminist readership. The majority of the eleven essays utilise a reader-response reading to argue that Paretsky's traversing of Chicago, makes a Chicago critic re-evaluate her own autonomy,[57] or that Claire Molloy as a single working-mum, speaks to many female readers.[58] The majority simply validate 'strong woman' role models, but Liahna Babener's 'Uncloseting Ideology in the Novels of Barbara Wilson'[59] offers a more complex analysis. As detective fiction supports a conservative ideology, feminist attempts to appropriate the genre are mostly unsuccessful because they do not dismantle these patriarchal ideologies. However, Wilson's Pam Neilsen series does succeed in breaking the narrative codes (through interrupted momentum, retarded dénouement, polyvocal narration and dialogic speech), undermining heteronormativity and replacing it with a positive, resistant lesbian and feminist community. So, while it is fraught with difficulties, Wilson proves it is possible to destabilise the lexical systems of the genre and write feminist detective fiction.

Feminism in Women's Detective Fiction, edited by Glenwood Irons, contains essays on gender issues across the history of the genre, from Amelia Butterworth to Sara Paretsky. The debate about feminist appropriation is split between the contributors, some arguing the detectives are an important role model, while others argue the detectives have lost the 'otherness' that is feminine, and have been co-opted by the male-centred status quo. Kathleen Gregory Klein's 'Habeas Corpus: Feminism and Detective Fiction'[60] adopts Liahna Babener's thesis that Barbara Wilson is able to deconstruct both femininity and the genre conventions to establish the prospect of a truly feminist genre.

In 1997, Peter Messent's *Criminal Proceedings: the Contemporary American Crime Novel*[61] contained three essays addressing feminist issues. Sabine Vanacker's 'V. I. Warshawski, Kinsey Milhone and Kay Scarpetta: Creating a Feminist Detective Hero'[62] assumes a strong female protagonist makes a text feminist and so is able to include Patricia Cornwall's fiction despite its Manichaean reinforcement of good and evil. Paulina Palmer's 'The Lesbian Thriller: Transgressive Investigations'[63] reiterates the thesis of her earlier 1991 essay, with a detailed criticism of Wilson, Wings and Schulman and an overview of the debate about feminists venturing into the popular arena with the feminist thriller. Christopher Gair's 'Policing the Margins: Barbara Wilson's *Gaudi Afternoon* and *Troubles in Transylvania*'[64] continues the discussion of Wilson with the question of whether her feminist fragmentation and post-modern sensibility prevent her writing a generic detective fiction. The lack of a crime, the fluid, chameleon-like identity of the protagonist, and the decentred perspective while undermining and deconstructing notions of identity and parental structures, also stretch 'the genre of crime fiction to such an extent that it eventually implodes'.[65]

Priscilla L. Walton and Marina Jones' excellent *Detective Agency: Women Rewriting the Hard-Boiled Tradition*[66] continues the feminist criticism to the end of the century, with a sophisticated analysis of the contemporary, mainstream, hard-boiled tradition. They combine this with a detailed consideration of issues of production and popularity. Informed by cultural studies, they reject the view that the genre is inherently conservative, arguing that it is audience-led and potentially subversive. They contend that feminist agency renegotiates the 'generic contract' precisely because it does address the conventions. In contrast to many feminist critics, who have singled out the hard-boiled as the most inimical to feminist appropriation, they argue that feminist hard-boiled reinscribes the discourse by refusing the stereotypes while revealing their contradictions. The hard-boiled feminist narrator is able to recast subjectivity, question the politics of the gaze, and address her vulnerability in order to construct a resistant speaking subject that has proved particularly accessible to racial and ethnic configurations. The protagonist's marginalisation allows an interrogation of the borders of law and crime while criss-crossing the borders of sex and gender, performing gender (since they mimic the masculine with a difference) in a way most critics only allow for the lesbian amateur detectives. The hard-boiled sub-genre, they conclude, successfully allows a wide audience to explore the borders of established gender categories and conventions.

Feminist criticism of feminist detective fiction was slow to establish itself as a debate, and for all the arguments over the conservative ideology of the genre, the criteria for the feminist analysis are surprisingly concordant. The more uncritical simply look for strong women, the more complex look for a critique of law, authority and the hierarchy, the scopic gaze, the fragmentation of the individualist self, and a validation of difference and *communitas*. The disagreements arise with whether these complex reinscriptions can be found in specific authors. Paretsky, perhaps because of her success, is a particularly disputed figure.

The feminist appropriation of the detective or crime genre starts in the late 1970s. Munt links it to the ideology of individualism rife during the Reagan/Thatcher decade but I want to suggest a shift in how we see the genre in relation to the political decade. The swingeing success of the early Thatcher government had a profound effect upon the left, and, as discussed in Chapter 1, sent them to embrace and interrogate a number of popular cultures. Detective fiction (traditionally a favourite popular genre for the intellectual) was but one of these appropriations. The continuing success of the right at the hustings also led to a defensive move away from social action to the more supportive 'imagined communitites' of shared values in a variety of feminist literatures. The shared imagined community of the feminist detective audience proved spectacularly favourable to this retrenchment.

When it comes to feminist appropriation of the genre, a couple of earlier proto-feminist writers are often cited. Amanda Cross' Kate Fansler series, beginning with *In the Last Analysis* in 1964, is one but these were straightforward academic murder mysteries. It was not until the 1981 *Death in a Tenured Position* that Cross foregrounded feminist issues. P. D. James' 1972 *An Unsuitable Job for a Woman* with Cordelia Gray, continues to be controversial to feminist critics, but James' consideration of 'female rights' is not informed by feminist involvement[67] and the later Gray novel minimises her sleuthing.

The feminist re-writing of the genre only really starts in the late 1970s. Marcia Muller's *Edwin of the Iron Shoes* (1977), introducing the Sharon McCone series, is usually cited as the first feminist detective book, although Janice Law's Anna Peter series began a year earlier with *The Big Payoff*. M. F. Beal's *Angel Dance* also introduced the bisexual Chicana detective Kate Guerrara in 1977.

The early 1980s saw the publication of three of the bestselling American mainstream feminist private eyes: Liza Cody's Anna Lee series, with *Dupe* (1980), Sue Grafton's Kinsey Milhone with *A is for Alibi* (1982) and Sara Paretsky's V. I. Warshawski, *Indemnity Only* (1982). It also saw a feminist police procedural, with Susan Dunlop's *Karma* (1981), Valerie Miner's class-conscious *Blood Sisters* (1981) and Vicki McConnell's lesbian detective Nyla Wade, in *Mrs Porter's Letters* (1982).

In the mid-1980s, feminist detective fiction began to expand. Marcia Muller developed a Chicana detective, Elena Oliverez (*Tree of Death*, 1983), and Gillian Slovo introduced the racially aware Kate Baier series (*Morbid Symptoms*, 1984). A number of important lesbian detectives also appeared for the first time. Katherine V. Forrest introduced her lesbian cop Kate Delafield (*Amateur City*, 1984), Barbara Wilson her Pam Nilsen series (*Murder in the Collective*, 1984), and Sarah Dreher's *Stoner McTavish* (1985). Sarah Schulman's post-modern lesbian detective novel *The Sophie Horowitz Story* was published in 1984.

The lesbian detective series continues strong in the late 1980s, with Mary Wings' Emma Victor in *She Came Too Late* (1987), Val McDermid's Linsay Gordon series (*Report for Murder*, 1987), and Marion Forster's *The Monarchs are Flying* (1987). Linda Barnes, the fourth of the bestelling American 'she-dicks' began her Carlotta Carlyle series with *A Trouble of Fools* in 1987 (having had a successful male detective series running from 1982). Karen Kijewski's Kate Colorado series began in 1989 with *Katwalk*.

The early 1990s saw Val McDermid switch to the more mainstream Kate Brannigan series, with *Dead Beat* (1992) and the start of Sarah Dunant's Hannah Wolfe series, *Birth Marks* (1991). Deborah Powell introduces her lesbian wise-cracking detective Hollis Carpenter (*Bayou City Secrets*, 1992) and Barbara Wilson brought out the acclaimed *Gaudi Afternoon* (1990) which won the British Crime Writers' Association Award and the lesbian Lambada Literary Award.

British mainstream crime awards seem to have been relatively favourable to feminist fiction. In 1980, Cody's *Dupe* was awarded the John Creasey Memorial, in 1988 Paretsky's *Toxic Shock* won the Silver Dagger (the runner-up to the best crime novel), in 1992 Cody's *Bucket Nut* got the Silver Dagger, in 1993 it was Dunant's *Fatlands*, and in 1995 Val McDermid's *The Mermaid Singing* gained the Gold Dagger award. The American awards did not recognise any overtly feminist crime fiction in the equivalent period.

By the mid to late 1980s, feminist detective fiction was a publishing phenomenon and I have listed only some of the more siginificant feminist authors. *Silk Stalkings: When Women Write of Murder*[68] gave a 'shopping list' for fans of nearly 600 series detectives created by women, in 1988, and in 1998 followed it with *Silk Stalkings: More Women Write of Murder*[69] containing 187 more detectives created since 1976. Though not all of these are feminist by any means, it gives some idea of the publishing phenomenon. As Walton and Jones argue in *Detective Agency*, mainstream mystery fiction was at a boom, with P. D. James, Dick Francis and Elmore Leonard making breakthrough sales.[70] They quote Bantam Books' senior editor, Kate Miciak as saying that whereas women authors had once sold only 20–25 000 copies, by 1989 their sales had doubled or even tripled in some cases.[71] During the 1980s, the feminist presses, Crossing Press, Naiad, Pandora, Seal, Sheba, Spinsters Ink, and the Women's Press, all ran a detective series imprint.

During the 1980s, the more successful novels tended to be more mainstream, and often more hard-boiled, while the more explicitly feminist and experimental, often the amateur, were published by the small feminist presses. Munt argues in *Murder By the Book?* that the genre declined in the 1990s with the decline of the feminist presses, but Walton and Jones dispute this. They argue that the genre continued to be healthy in the 1990s, and to be infused with new energy as it took on more multi-cultural amd multi-lifestyle protagonists.[72] They noted that the more activist writers had shifted to mainstream publishers without compromising the politics of their fiction. Lesbian writers such as Katherine V. Forrest, Mary Wings, J. M. Redman, Phyllis Knight and Sandra Scoppettone had all gone to mainstream publishers by 1990. So had the Afro-American women detectives of Valerie Wilson Wesley (Tamara Hayle) and Eleanor Taylor Bland (Marti MacAlister); the Native American detectives of Jean Hagers (Molly Bearpaw) and Dana Stabenow (Kate Shugak); and the Chinese American detectives of Leslie Glass (April Woo), S. J. Rozan (Lydia Chin) and Irene Lin-Chandler (Holly Jean Ho).[73]

The feminist detective genre continues to flourish within the mainstream, and though some writers may have diluted their narratives for financial success, as with McDermid's switch from Lindsey Duncan to Kate Brannigan, not all of them do and they still continue to sell well, undiluted. Feminist detective fiction has attained the wide audiences desired and often without any diminution of the ideology. If popularity is granted to be a central element of genre appropriation, then feminist detective fiction has proved to be a significant and continuing success.

Case Studies: Sara Paretsky, Gillian Slovo and Barbara Wilson

Sara Paretsky is one of the most successful of feminist detective writers, with her private eye, V. I. Warshawski, introduced in 1982 (*Indemnity Only*). In 1985 at a Baltimore crime writer's convention, Paretsky organised a network of women writers to challenge the invisibility of their work in reviews and American mystery awards. The network snowballed into Sisters in Crime, an advocacy group for women within the genre (writing, reviewing, publishing and selling). Paretsky remained the president or active on the board of this feminist lobby group for most of the 1980s.

Burnmarks (1990), was V. I. Warshawski's sixth appearance. It was published in the UK by the Virago Crime series in 1991, the same year as the disappointing film of V. I. Warshawski, starring Kathleen Turner. By the following novel, *Guardian Angel* (1992), Penguin had noted Paretsky's popularity and acquired the paperback rights to her work.

V. I. Warshawski's first-person narrative accommodates the lone private eye seeking after the truth when all around advise or threaten her to stop. She is professional, active and packs a gun. In this text she scales roofs to break into a building for information, fights her way out of a burning building in which she has been trapped, and finales on a shoot-out, in the shell of a high-rise building project in the dead of night.

But Warshawski critiques the conventions in its recasting of the detective's subjectivity. Warshawski is a loner in that her immediate family are deceased and she is divorced. Yet she has created a new *communitas*, with her downstairs neighbour, Mr Contreras, and the doctor, Lotte, as quasi-paternal and maternal figures; the irascible friend of her father Lieutenant Bobby Mallory; and in this story, the black sheep of the family, Aunt Elena. At times, the demands and pressures from her chosen community are overburdening, at other times they support her and, in the debate around her responsibilities to the elderly alcoholic aunt, she voices the difficulties for the autonomous woman of negotiating a viable space between isolation and self-sacrifice. Warshawski rejects being a constant nursemaid and yet also refuses to cut her off completely, as her Uncle Pete has done, developing a viable compromise that has her coming to her aid when necessary but not 'immolating' herself as a 'Victorian angel'. 'In Chicago people look after their own' (p. 26), but in V. I.'s shifting world, her own community is one of choice as much as family ties. A community that extends to the neighbourhood and the political, in her involvement with the Chicana politician Roz and her feminist supporters Marisa and Velma.

V. I. also critiques the action-figure, focusing on her fears and vulnerability. She is afraid of heights and squeamish about rats as she hunts in derelict buildings. Once she has discovered the bomb in her car, she experiences a 'rising tide of panic' (p. 305) as she takes on influential big business and corrupt policemen. Violence, and its effects on susceptible bodies, are being problematised. Knocked out, Warshawski doesn't just pick herself up and carry on, but spends two days in hospital and worries about the after-effects of Parkinson's or Alzheimer's.

The language of the body is developed further, as she suffers from headaches or hunger. Blood sugar levels create depression and a sense of failure. Gorging also affects her investigations, as the text reflexively calls attention to.

> Gluttony is a terrible enemy of the private detective ... You're disgusting, I admonished myself privately as I paid the bill. Peter Wimsey and Philip Marlowe never had this kind of problem. (p. 222)

Yet cooking and the enjoyment of food is also celebrated as are fits of pique and depression – 'Okay, good. Have fits. They get results' (p. 203). In contrast to over-ratiocination, V. I. Warshawski's character focuses on a healthy emotionalism and the importance of the irrational. Dreams play a significant part in all the novels, usually linked in some way to her mother, in a matrilinear wisdom. They serve as warnings and clues that unsettle her without leading to the easy solutions of the earlier lady detectives. And the maternal presence and 'fierce independence' (p. 96) sustain her on her quests.

> Often when I feel like quitting I hear my mother's voice in my head, exhorting me ... the worst thing I could ever do in her eyes was to give up. (p. 227)

But the feminine is not being reified in preference to the rational. Warshawski's thinking through of the mysteries, and her placing of one piece of evidence alongside another is foregrounded in order to rebuff the overt sexism of Bobby Mallory's 'You don't know how to reason, how to follow a chain of evidence to a conclusion, so you start making up paranoid fantasies' (p. 297). Rejecting his 'repressed-spinster' psychology, mainly because she has an active sex life, Warshawski's resistant subjectivity foregrounds the emotions and the body alongside the rational.

Sex is present but the text refuses to esteem men as essential to her femininity. She is not looking for 'good father material', values her independence and privacy, and while enjoying sex with Robin, has it in perspective. Michael's jealousy about Robin 'was farce, not tragedy – I wasn't about to pretend to be Desdemona' (p. 105).

The politics of the gaze, ever-present in the laconic first-person code of the hard-boiled private eye, is also foregrounded and the traditional apportioning of censure problematised. Paretsky utilises the hard-boiled milieu of the semi-criminal and the dispossessed effectively in her search for her aunt and her meditations on old-age in a manner that focuses on the specular and critiques the objectification involved in looking.

> I stared down at her in disgust.... Her face was flushed. The broken veins on her nose stood out clearly. In the morning light I could see that the violet nightgown was long overdue for the laundry. The sight was appalling. But it was also unbearably pathetic. No one should be exposed to an outsider's view while she is sleeping, let alone someone as vulnerable as my aunt. (p. 7)

The gaze is further implicated in the aunt's boarding-house's indigence.

> What was I going to live on when I was too old to hustle clients any longer? The thought of being sixty-six, alone, living in a little room with three plastic drawers to hold my clothes – a shudder swept through me, almost knocking me off balance. (pp. 32–3)

The objectivity of the controlling gaze is infiltrated with an empathetic subjectivity in relation to old age. The poor and the old, who are usually ignored or marginalised, are one of the central investigations of this text. Warshawski's investigations are informed by an empathetic refusal to reject them from the safe boundary of the young[74] and fit. This open acknowledgement of difference and of oppression through empathy is also demonstrated with the black teenage junkie mother, Cerise: 'She was with a stranger and a white woman at that. She was terrified of the institutions of law and society and I was conversant with them, so to her I was part of them' (p. 60). Issues of oppression of class, age and race are not elided as part of the discourse of the text; indeed Warshawski herself is implicated when Finchley briefly suspects her of racism.

Instead of the autonomous gaze being used to separate, and create boundaries, a more dialectic relationship is constituted between the gazer and the society. In contrast to these empathetic reflections on difference, the men (Michael, Bobby and Vinnie) are condemnatory, laying down the law on the boundaries between the acceptable and the vile. These work across a social range but converge in the views about Aunt Elena, her drinking, blackmail and her soliciting. Whereas the men take an old woman's sexuality as disgusting, V. I. initially finds it comical (given the text's iconoclasm of female sexuality) and later on contextualises the ageist condemnation. 'Just because she's not your type doesn't mean everyone finds her repulsive' (p. 318). A similar rejection of the dominant view informs her fight to be a private eye in a masculine domain.

In this novel the main criminals are a collaboration of powerful big business and community politicians, who corrupt a variety of small business and ethnic politicians. The motive is greed but the opposition are not branded as evil. Both Michael and Roz's corruption are linked to community bonds similar to those experienced by V. I.: Roz to help 'her people', Michael to help 'his pals'. Michael's corruption is also linked to a machismo attitude to women, and his friends' ridiculing his inability to keep her under 'control'. The boundaries between the lawful and the criminal are blurred when V. I. too 'blackmails' a friend to find a home for her aunt, and commits a 'burglary' to find information. Police arrogance and brutality are highlighted throughout the text and two of the most aggressive criminals are police officers.

But although big business, politics and certain policemen are implicated in the corruption, the text does not go so far as to openly question the role of the legal institutions in relation to the social hardship witnessed. Cerise's distrust, discussed earlier, is seen as part of her ignorance (even though a police officer will murder her). That police can be corrupt brings no surprise, but they are presented as the few 'rotten apples'. Despite his gruff arrogance, V. I. has no doubt that once she has produced proof of Michael's crimes, Lieutenant Mallory will arrest him. Through the motif of Warshawski's father, the police are positioned as fundamentally good in upholding order. Her memory of him epitomises police honesty and the number of contemporary policemen who remember his influence stand as a reassuring bulwark against the few who misuse their powers.

The text also valorises the individualism that is part of the generic convention of the hard-boiled, and that has proved such an obstacle for feminist principles of the communal and solidarity. Warshawski's subjectivity has complicated the individual in relation to the community, but doesn't challenge the individualist heroics, rather it champions them, in V. I.'s answer to Lotte's fear of losing her:

> 'So someone else's friend or lover can do the worrying, you mean?' I wasn't angry, only very lonely. 'It will happen inevitably, Lotte. I won't be able to jump through hoops or climb up ropes forever. Someone else will have to take over. But it won't be the police.' (p. 205)

This answer assumes the individual 'lone knight' as the only answer to corruption, with no sense of a group banding together for communal action. Indeed, the issue of feminist solidarity is positioned in opposition to individual integrity, in V. I.'s comment on why she had to damage Roz's political standing: 'Does being a feminist mean you have to support *everything* your sisters do? Even if you think they're abusing you?' (p. 334). Feminism is far from being challenged in this text, with its overt comments on the sexism of business promotion, of institutional sexism in the police, and overt sexism of construction workers and car mechanics, but the issue of political solidarity is, and individualism is being validated, with Mallory's blessing in the final pages. Despite her difference from his own daughters, V. I.'s individualistic stand as a crime fighter brings his acknowledgement that 'you can't do things different than you do, shouldn't do them different' (pp. 339–40). Paretsky's novel ends on a closure not of social wrongs righted and the status quo resumed, since corruption is 'business as usual in this town' (p. 333). Instead, given the centrality of *communitas* and ties of responsibility, it ends with the restitution of harmony between V. I. and Bobby Mallory at his birthday party.

Burnmarks presents an effective feminist critique of the hard-boiled genre, in its complex rewriting of the private detective's feminine, resistant subjectivity and its exploration of the world of the marginalised reliant upon cheap housing. However, it reinforces two of the genre's more conservative conventions: the institution of law and order, and lone, heroic individualism. Nevertheless, *Burnmarks* is overtly and complexly feminist in its ideology and as a feminist text that reaches large audiences, eminently effective as an appropriation of the genre that succeeds in the mainstream.

Gillian Slovo's *Death Comes Staccato*,[75] though reaching a less wide audience, challenged both the heroic individualism of the lone detective and the institutions of law and order. Slovo's text has a much more incisive social awareness, with a socialist feminist political agenda, and it is much more questioning of the liberal humanism underpinning the concept of 'individual autonomy'. Kate Baeier, initially an amateur but, in this third novel, a professional, conforms to less of the hard-boiled features of the detective. She is more domesticated, living with her long-term partner, Sam, for all she keeps her Dalston flat on as a 'bolt-hole' for independence. Through Sam, an eminently relaxed and unjealous partner, Kate experiences both an active sex life and domesticity at one remove, when Sam's young son visits. At work, Kate has one employee, Carmen, and the text is overt about the office politics of their collaboration. But it is a mutual collaboration, with Carmen bringing the insight to the facts Kate has accumulated, or thinking to interview the one crucial witness that Kate has missed. In both instances, Kate deprecates her own role as the 'detective', to highlight how the 'sidekick' is being given an equal status in the ratiocination. Kate's dream about solving the murder invokes earlier detective conventions even more strongly:

> I dreamt I solved the murder. It was very satisfying. Sam and Carmen watched in admiration while I told them how James

Morgan had been asphyxiated by a violin string and that Pete was not dead but merely hiding from the false accusation made by Inspector Crant. (p. 117)

The admiring audience at the fictitious dénouement, and the odd murder weapon invoke the world of Holmes or Christie. But dreams do not come true. On the contrary, it is Carmen who makes the important connection that leads to the solution, and in an inversion of the power structure, it is Kate who becomes the admiring audience: 'I stared at Carmen in admiration. "You're quite a woman," I said' (p. 145). The independent autonomy of the detective is being rewritten here, for a more collaborative, collective investigation. Kate's detective agency takes on two types of work: public cases checking that the GLC's sub-contractors abide by their work practices, and private cases which Carmen spurns as too '*petit bourgeois*', thus establishing her socialist principles. Issues of class and race are invoked as the white, middle-class Kate liaises with the employees and presents the reports, while the black, working-class Carmen collects the background information and delves into the details of the investigation. Carmen, nominally an employee, but needing no supervision, 'saw the pitfalls inherent in a messy division of labour and she would not tolerate any blurring of roles' (p. 12). For all the invoking of the politics of the workplace, when the clash comes between them on grounds of race (Kate thinking a black interviewer will make the black witness talk more easily), the rift is described in liberal humanist terms of friendship and honesty, rather than in terms of social groups ('my people'). What is interesting, though, is how this text invokes unthinking racism and implicates the detective, who has to acknowledge her fault and apologise to heal the rift. Paretsky used a very similar narrative event to invoke institutional racism in *Burnmarks*, but does not allow her detective to be culpable. Kate Baeier's detective, fallible, implicated in the dominant institutions of power, but aware and challenging them, is a much less heroic characterisation. She too is affected adversely by violence, but more emotionally than physically, and allows herself to become emotionally involved with her client even when she is warned off by the mother. Also like Paretsky, she is affected by the appalling lives she witnesses, becoming depressed by the hopeless poverty of the working families.

Socially, the text is set in Thatcher's 1980s when the heady belief that socialism could change the world has crashed, and 'the victories are all work-related' (p. 49). Kate's agency is a watchdog to the work-related anti-sexist and anti-racist good practices, and allows the text to indict capitalist practices of competiton (IBM buying out the small computer firm to prevent it becoming a rival) and of worker exploitation in the main public investigation of Jarvis' manufacturing firm's illegally building an extra floor to expand their factory without planning permission or due consideration of the fire regulations and then buying the silence of the victims when it turns into a fire-trap. Capitalism is exposed as putting money before people's welfare, and the victims, Elmore and Sarah, finally realise that solidarity and activism are the only way to regain their self-respect: '"We've been too passive," Elmore said … "We want to fight," Sarah finished' (p. 161). This sub-plot of the public investigation ends with the knowledge that Jarvis will be prosecuted, but only because, with the union's help, they will make a public outcry.

The main investigation is a personal crime in the milieu of the rich and artistic, allowing the text to represent all sorts of stereotypes about the upper class, from Alicia's mother's frigid control, to the sexual politics of young Toby's monied charm, hiding a bitter mysogyny, and the rival young woman 'brought up to compete with others for male attention and who, inside, hate themselves for doing it' (p. 39).[76] The crimes behind the personal investigation are incest (a favourite with feminist writers) and infidelity, the suppression of the facts of which blight Alicia's life just as the suppression of the incident of the fire has blighted Elmore and Sarah's. The suppression of wrongdoing by the powerful is shown to further damage the victims, and Kate's refusal to stay within her role as hired detective, but insist on exposing the facts, is positioned as a revolt against the capitalism that lies at the heart of such unequal treatment of employees.

> 'I'm not a disposable item,' I said. 'This time if I'm hired I stay hired. The job is over when I say it is over.'
>
> The lawyer in Plastid couldn't take that. 'Surely,' he said, 'there is a conflict of interest here. The right to terminate a contract is at the very basis of our society.' (pp. 118–19)

Kate negotiates a contract of equal power and the elderly European Mrs Morgan sets up an evaluative dichotomy between those who are scared of life and only want to make money, and those who risk themselves and live fully, whether as artists or political activists. Money – at the root of capitalism and the upper classes – and the desire for it above concern for other people, becomes the real villain of the text and the only recourse against institutional and personal exploitation is a positive activism, even though the effort may well fail. This construction of society is a much less safe and cosy place for the readers to find themselves within.

Death Comes Staccato is more suspicious of law and order and of the police as an institution that upholds an unfair society. Like *Burnmarks*, the novel has a corrupt cop who misuses his power in holding Kate and mistreating her for Jarvis. But unlike Paretsky, Slovo does not invoke the good cops to balance the 'rotten apple', neither is Crant represented as the one rogue. The presentation indicts the drugs squad, if not the whole force. Kate's lawyer finally tracks her down because a neighbour 'saw you leave with two men who looked so much like thugs that he guessed they were policeman' (p. 91) and the police who appear at the end to arrest the murderer are deliberately nondescript and muted. The victims in this novel can only get justice by forcing the establishment to acknowledge what is going on in its name. A concept that is far removed from the canonical detective conventions, as Sam's young son is used to comment on.

> It was a hard story to tell since Matthew's emotional inclination was to go with my version while his intellectual upbringing, courtesy of the TV, was to identify with the police. But somehow he made his own compromise with the conflicting ideologies. (p. 116)

In contrast to *Burnmarks*, *Death Comes Staccato* is much more conscious of the political implications of invoking institutions of law and order and of the detective's role as autonomous hero. It has no sophisticated problematising of the 'gaze' of the detective, however, and despite its challenge to liberal humanism in relation to the autonomous self, it reintroduces it in the concept of the 'authentic self'. Alicia is revealed as having three selves, the child, the musician, the rich brat, and Kate wonders 'which one was the real Alicia' (p. 36). Similarly her mother's vindictive expression is encoded as 'her true character' (p. 76). This socialist feminist text still invokes aspects of liberal humanist under-standing of the psyche, while it simultaneously challenges them in relation to the hero, and the schism between the two ideologies comes to the fore with the invocation of how institutional racism exists within everyone, even the politically aware. Indeed the fallibility of the detective is one of the text's strengths. The text is much less effec-tive, though, in its portrayal of Marion, Alicia's mother. Her infidelity, kept secret, and then her blaming of the victim for the incest, makes her the emotional villain of the piece, allied as it is to her unnatural mothering. Richard may have committed incest, Plastid may have murdered two people, but Marion Weatherspoon's female sexuality and her bad mothering make her the originating site of the personal disruption that Kate investigates. In this construction, *Death Comes Staccato* silently reinforces the conventions in relation to female sexuality, even while Kate and Carmen challenge it by their active sexual experiences.

Barbara Wilson, co-founder of the feminist publishing house Seal Press, is the author of the Pam Nilsen series (*Murder in the Collective, Sisters of the Road, The Dog Collar Murders*), where the amateur lesbian sleuth investigates murders that effectively challenge the dominant conservative and liberal conventions. *Gaudi Afternoon* (1990),[77] the first appearance of the amatuer sleuth Cassandra Reilly,[78] is even more subversive in that it ultimately has no crime, no recourse to the legal system, and a 'victim' who is given a voice to demand a specific familial resolution. Christopher Gair, posing the question of how far one can stretch genre conventions, argues that 'it stretches the genre of crime fiction to such an extent that it implodes'.[79] But writers such as Wilson have literally shifted the boundaries of the genre. Much the same questions were raised about the Nilsen trilogy, as are now about the Reilly duo, but Wilson has consistently carried a readership along with her as she contests the shifting boundaries of the genre, and *Gaudi Afternoon* was awarded two mystery prizes: British Crime Writers best mystery set in Europe and the Lambada Literary Award for best lesbian mystery.[80] In public terms, the novel clearly remains firmly within the genre.

Internally, I would argue it does also. In moving from murder as the crime, to the kidnapping of a child, Wilson adopts one of the earlier crimes solved by the many 'lady detectives' before the Golden Age formulated murder as requisite for a 'whodunnit'. Reilly, a literary translator, is hired professionally by one parent to trace the daughter and later, impelled by desire for the 'femme fatale' suspect and a sense of being implicated by her role as sleuth in the further kidnappings, she continues to try to solve the mystery of Delilah's disappearance and apprehend the kidnappers. Reilly therefore occupies the detective role of ratiocination and agency, though it is true she solves the final kidnap by luck rather than reason.

Delilah is abducted four times in all, and the repetition would begin to border on farce, if it were not for two red herrings that give a certain suspense and urgency to her disappearances. The first is the standing of Hamilton and April, linked in some way to Eastern Europe and inexplicably suspicious of each other. The other, more sinister red herring, is the motif of men carrying bags labelled the European Society for Organ Transplantation, within a narrative that stresses the dangers of Barcelona and the parents' final fears that Delilah has been kidnapped by 'white-slavers'.

Gaudi Afternoon's real alteration of the genre lies in its having no recourse to the police, or notions of justice in relation to state institutions, in its dénouement. Given that Delilah's parents, the cause of the 'crimes', are a male-to-female transsexual and a 'bull-dyke' this is explained by their marginal status. The resolution therefore becomes a much more slippery weighing of everyone's rights to custody of Delilah, a communal activity that implicates the reader as well as Cassandra, in the final judgement that Ben and Frankie have to make peace with each other for the sake of the child. The dénouement comes when the silent victim, the six-year-old Delilah, erupts into voice and demands an ending that will satisfy all the parties. In a text where justice or fairness involves the negotiation of competing rights, rather than a simplistic apportioning of blame and punishment, it is the victim, who has constantly been spoken for by all the competing adults, who finally becomes the agent of the resolution and thereby challenges the objectification and silencing involved in the traditional role of victim.

The text also questions the traditional social disruption caused by errant feminine sexuality, reinforced in *Death Comes Staccato*, by the twist it gives to the culpability. Ostensibly, the 'problem' or cause lies with the father's aberrant transsexual transformation into a second 'mother'. But in the careful uncovering of the rights of sexual minorities, the real cause of the disruption becomes located in the gay mother's inability to come to terms with her ex-partner's gender transformation. In this tolerant and inclusive text, it is not the playing 'fast and loose with biology' (p. 130) that is the cause of the social disruption, but the intolerant inability to accept such a transgression. Ben must come to terms with Frankie's change, but the sense of betrayal and confusion she experiences are also understood, rather than condemned. No detective or justice system can impose a solution upon them, the two must negotiate a workable resolution between themselves, under the watchful eye of Delilah. Justice is not absolute, but negotiable and contingent.

Within the detective mystery narrative, the text interrogates two dominant heterosexual conventions: that of the nature of gender identity and subjectivity, and the nature of motherhood and parental rights within the sexual minorities community. Both investigations take place within the context of buildings by the Spanish architect Gaudi, whose monument to the Christian notion of family stresses its 'phenomenally bizarre' and 'tortured form' (p. 81) and significantly favours a 'freer approach to the design of the supporting structure and consequently of the building's ultimate shape' (p. 84). The fact that the family under scrutiny in the text consists of a gay biological mother and a transsexual second mother clearly argues for a more eclectic and open conception of the institution of family that is textually echoed in Gaudi's 'encyclopedic taste' and love of showing 'openly the process of construction' (p. 85). It is significant that Gaudi's cathedral, Sagrada Familia, is unfinished, transitional, and is being further developed.

The nature of gender identity and subjectivity is explored through Cassandra's misrecognition of Frankie and Ben, and her own experience of society's gender confusion around her short haircut. Cassandra's own identity is transitional, having no fixed abode, no sense of country of origin, and a name she has created for herself. Her nomadic life means that no one lover is for ever, only for the brief present. She enjoys travelling the world, 'content to window shop, not to possess' (p. 11).

Cassandra's view of Frankie, of Ben, and of the femme fatale figure of April, are all shown to be at fault, actively negating the canonical gaze of the detective and its ability to delineate distinctions. In this text, male and female, masculine and feminine, blur. Performance and biology meet and co-mingle. The 'husband' is first perceived as a 'muscular adolescent boy' and the gaze is shocked and confounded to discover her mistake: 'Once I realised that, I couldn't understand how I'd been mistaken. The woman had breasts for christsakes, and a rhinestone stud in one ear, and small hands and feet ... recognizably a woman' (p. 41). The assertion comes from a detective insistent that biology defines gender identity, as she pettishly reacts to being called 'masculine' because of her trousers and short haircut: 'I don't look masculine. I look like a middle-aged Irish-American Spanish translator with short hair' (p. 39). But contemplation of Frankie's transsexuality and her own experience of being treated as a 'señor' in her social encounters, modify her view. Frankie's boniness and big hands and feet no longer constitute masculinity. 'In what did her masculinity reside then?' Cassandra muses and decides, 'She was more feminine than I or many of my women friends. It wasn't only surgery that had changed her sex, or hormones, it was a conscious choice to embrace femaleness, whatever femaleness is' (p. 82). Ana enjoys masquerading as masculine, 'I like the idea of playing with my male side' (p. 73) and Hamilton enjoys occasionally cross-dressing as well, to gain 'access to the feminine part of myself, to the softer, gentler aspects of my personality' (p. 152). Masculinity and femininity are constructed upon a continuum, in this text, rather than a binary opposition as Cassandra has a drunken epiphany:

> it was as if I were at a masquerade ball and everyone, at the very same moment, lifted their masks, and I saw gender for what it was, something that stood between us and our true selves. Something that we could take off and put on at will. Something that was, strangely, like a game. (p. 77)

Biology is no safe definition, in this mirroring of Butler's gender as performative, since surgery or body-building can modify gender aspects so that Delilah's father is a woman and her mother has the muscles of Arnold Schwarzenegger. Frankie had always felt herself a woman and she argues that her qualities have not changed, only her sex. By the end, being constantly addressed as señor has Cassandra empathising, 'I wonder if this was how Frankie felt when, as a boy who firmly believed he was a girl, everyone had treated him as a boy' (p. 139). Gender identity becomes an existential choice, and the most complete characters are those, like Ana and Hamilton, who can acknowledge the various sides of their sexuality.

The question of parenthood, within the gay community, begins in the text with Cassandra's architect friend Ana's broodiness, brought on through reading books about childbirth. Cassandra rejects her need to recreate a coupledom to raise a child, thereby demonstrating that maternal feelings are experienced only by some women, not all. Cassandra's and Hamilton's childhood experiences point to the often violent, proprietorial or neglectful heterosexual norm, while Ben and Frankie argue through the rights of custody. The battle for custody becomes a battle for who has the right to be the 'real' mother, with Ben, the birth-mother, arguing from an essentialist, biological conviction, whereas Frankie argues for a post-modern, performative stance. Young Delilah, having friends from AI lesbian couples, accepts variant familial structures so long as they are loving. Ana, who has turned to Gaudi for inspiration, contemplates a different familial structure with the gay Hamilton at the end of the novel. 'It's a little unconvential but I think it might work' (p. 172). Cassandra's dream evokes an hermaphrodite culture, where 'being both sexes as they were they might not understand the intensely proprietorial relationship between mothers and daughters' (p. 141). The issues of propriety and of proprietary within the traditional notion of motherhood are being interrogated in this text in favour of a more open, healthier and experimental familial structure based on love rather than ownership. Linked motifs of the magical-realist novel Cassandra is translating and the birthing house/woman Ana is building, add to motherhood as a site of contestation within the lesbian and transsexual community.

*Gaudi Afternoo*n, informed by queer theory, manages to develop within the detective genre, a complex and transgressive interrogation of the conservative genre formations and of the conservative heterosexual norms of gender identity and the nature of the family, in order to argue for a feminist tolerance and viable improvement on interpersonal relationships. Although less riveting in its suspense than the Paretsky, it still contains enough suspense with the kidnappings of Delilah, to remain firmly within the genre format, but it is infinitely more far-reaching in its subversion of a whole range of genre and gender norms.

5
Science Fiction

No genre has been more comprehensively appropriated and inno-
vated by feminist theory than science fiction, despite its early focus
on technology and intergalactic gun-fights. Few aspects of feminist
thinking have not been echoed, and often predated, by feminist
science fiction writers. The speculative, 'thought experiment' nature
of the genre has fuelled a comprehensive breadth of innovation.
Feminist science fiction has elaborated on all the major feminist
debates from the 1970s to the 1990s: from the explorations of phallocentric language, to strong action-women agency; from ideal feminine communities, to the phallocentric dystopias; from explorations
of the alien 'other', to questions of identity with the cyborg. Feminist
thinkers such as Shulamith Firestone and Donna Haraway have
had a direct influence on certain trends, such as the 1970s utopias and
the 1980s cyborg narratives, but the speculative explorations also
predate the theory. Feminist science fiction does not have a linear
development so much as a simultaneous diversity of exploration.
Joanna Russ' 1975 fragmented selves and cyborg identity (*The Female
Man*) challenges the idea that it is a development of postmodernism
and Haraway, just as Butler's Earthseed utopias of the 1990s rethink
the 1970s utopias of Piercy and Charnas. In this genre, the writers
have also proved amongst the most influential critics, particularly
Russ and LeGuin. Indeed, feminist criticism has at times proved relatively disappointing in the face of such exciting innovation in the
fiction. However, perhaps because of the writers' wholesale appropriation of the genre, or perhaps because of its history of ideological
critique and the nature of its speculative 'thought experimentation',
feminist critics have never argued that it is a genre inappropriate
for feminism. Unfortunately though, while some embraced the

excitement, generated by cultural studies, for popular genres and saw sf as having the potential to deconstruct phallocentric discourse itself, others have been more dismissive of genre. Situating sf in a binary opposition to the literary mainstream of 'serious' fiction, these critics have, at the end of the twentieth century been making a conformist, conservative bid to reject the genre status in favour of literary respectability.

A history of the genre

Early antecedents for the genre can be traced to the seventeenth-century versions of space travel such as Bishop Godwin's *Man in the Moon* (1638) and Cyrano de Bergerac's *Voyages to the Moon and Sun* (1656), or the seventeenth-century ideal future societies eloborated from Thomas More's initial 1516 *Utopia*, where women writers played a significant part: Margaret Cavendish's *The Description of a New World, Called the Blazing World* (1668) ruled by an Empress with a Congregation of Women; the women's societies of Mary Astell's *A Serious Proposal* (1694) and Sarah Scott's *Millennium Hall* (1762); alongside the separatist island utopias of the French aristocrats Madame D'Aulnoy, Mademoiselles de Scudery and de Montpensier. Baron Holberg's *Journey of Neils Klim to the World Underground* (1741) began a long tradition of other worlds found at the centre of the earth.

However, as with detective fiction, most critics agree on the genre, as a genre, beginning with the nineteenth century's expansion in literacy and with the century's complex reactions to increased techno-logical industrialisation. Mary Shelley's two novels are usually acknowledged as the beginning of the genre. Shelley's *Frankenstein* (1818) explores the dangers of unrestrained technology, with the obsessed scientist and the alienated pathos and anger of his Monster, while *The Last Man* (1826) followed the lone survivor of a plague destroying Europe at the end of the twenty-first century.

Poe's short story, 'Hans Pfaall' (1835) about a balloon journey to the moon is another early instance of the genre, before the surge of interest generated by Jules Verne and H. G. Wells at the end of the century.

Jules Verne's first novel in the genre came in France in 1863,[1] *Five Weeks in a Balloon*, closely followed by *Journey to the Centre of the Earth* (1864) and *From the Earth to the Moon* (1865). They proved highly successful and Verne went on to write eighty novels, featuring fixated male eccentrics involved in ingenious modes of travel, such as the submarine Nautilus in *20,000 Leagues Under the Sea* (1869), the flying machine in *Clipper of the Clouds* (1886), or the whole gamut of examples in *Around the World in Eighty Days* (1873). Verne's focus on the invention of travelling machines within an adventure plot, meant that much of his audience was assumed to be juvenile. His British counterpart in the genre, H. G. Wells, was perceived as more serious in his consideration of technology's impact on society, begun initially in response to Mary Shelley.

Wells termed this aspect of his oeuvre, 'scientific romance'. Beginning with *Time Machine* (1895) and *The Island of Dr Moreau* (1896), Wells speculated on the hierarchical divisions within society, or between humans and animals. Power invariably resides with those who hold the technology, but it is a vision inflected by Wells' socialism. The novels that followed, *The Invisible Man* (1897) and *War of the Worlds* (1898) focus more on the scientific, rather than social, speculation. The fascination with how scientific innovation impacts on social structures continues in his twentieth-century works, *The First Men in the Moon* (1901), *When the Sleeper Awakens* (1899), *A Modern Utopia* (1905), *In the Days of the Comet* (1906), and *The World Set Free* (1914). In the later work, however, the scientists and technical innovators have become justified in their social engineering. There is an ideological *volte-face* from Dr Moreau's mad experiments, to the governing technologist 'Samurai' of his Utopia. But Wells, like Shelley before him, uses scientific fiction to raise questions about society, in relation to technology. In Britain, the fiction has been used as a form of social critique from its inception.

In the States, Edward Bellamy used the utopian format to effectively critique society at the turn of the twentieth century. The trend had begun in Britain with Bulwer-Lytton's *The Coming Race* of 1871 and Samuel Butler's *Erewhon* (1872), but Edward Bellamy's *Looking Backward, 2000–1887* (1888) was easily the most influential. Edward James maintains that it was not only a bestseller but inspired 162 political 'Bellamy' clubs and over 50 utopian novels.[2] The direct link between socialist politics and utopian fiction is manifested by these clubs, while the utopian novels written in reaction to, or inspired by, *Looking Backward* continued the political critique. Amongst those challenging Bellamy's particular version of socialist ideals, were William Morris' *News from Nowhere* (1890), and a surge of American women's utopias such as Mary Bradley Lane's *Mizora* (1890), Amelia Garland Mear's *Mercia the Astronomer Royal* (1895), Charlotte Perkins Gilman's *Moving the Mountain* (1911), *Herland* (1915) and its sequel *With Her in Ourland* (1916).

Where Morris' utopian vision challenges Bellamy's enchantment with consumerism and technology, the American women's utopias focus primarily on gender issues. While *Mercia* envisions a world of equality of education and opportunity in which a woman could become the astronomer royal, *Mizora* and *Herland* create separatist societies of women. Situated in the American first wave of feminist agitation for women's suffrage, educational reform and contraception, these texts and their critique of patriarchal marriage and lack of equality are particularly discerning. Mary Griffith, Florence Dixie, Elizabeth Stuart Phelps, Annie Denton Cridge, Eloise O. Randall Richberg, Lena J. Fry and Lois Waisbrook further contributed to the women's utopian tradition at the turn of the century, placing their utopian societies on other planets (for example, Richberg's *Reinstern*, 1900) as well as undiscovered countries (Gilman's *Herland*).

In the States the genre's scientific speculation was not published in the book format of the utopias, but in pulp fiction magazines alongside westerns and detective stories. In 1926, Hugo Gernsback created the first pulp magazine to specialise in science fiction, or 'scientification', *Amazing Stories*, intending to teach the potentials of science through a fiction format. The success of *Amazing Stories* brought numerous imitators, the most successful of which was *Astounding Stories of Super-Science*. In 1929, Gernsback lost the editorship of *Amazing Stories*, and went on to found *Science Wonder Stories* which had an even more rigorous scientification objective. A consultative group of scientific experts vetted all the stories for plausibility. Most of the pulps, though, were untaxed by scientific accuracy. Edgar Rice Burroughs' adventure stories in far-flung planets proved extremely popular, as did the 'space operas' of E. E. 'Doc' Smith, whose 'Skylark' series began with 'The Skylark of Space' in *Amazing Stories* in 1928. Smith's sf stories simply transplanted adventure or western narratives into a setting of spaceships and intergalactic voyages.

Jane Donawerth argues for women writing in the early years of pulp,[3] citing Clare Winger Harris in *Weird Tales* in 1926, and in *Amazing Stories* in 1927. By 1929, she argues, there were a group of women writers using technology and science, though usually only to transform the domestic environment to spotless efficiency: Sophie Wenzel Ellis, Minna Irving, L. Taylor Hansen, Lilith Lorraine, Kathleen Ludwick, Louise Rice and Leslie F. Stone. Despite their using predominantly male narrators and male professionals for their protagonists, a few of the writers, Stone, Rice and Harris, still managed to include women's issues of suffrage and education within their storylines.

In Britain during the mid-1920s, cultural discussion of 'futurology' was being fuelled by the popular sciences of Wells, of the geneticist J. B. S. Haldane's *Daedalus; or Science and the Future* (1924), and of the physicist J. D. Bernal's *The World, the Flesh and the Devil* (1929). These in their turn influenced the speculative social-science fiction of Olaf Stapledon, James Blish and Arthur C. Clarke. In contrast to the American pulps, British writers continued the more earnest and reflective speculation about science's impact on society within the longer, novel format.

The 1930s saw a continuation of women in the US pulps. In 1933, C. L. Moore began writing for the American pulps with 'Shambleau' for *Weird Tales*. Moore created a hugely successful series around her rugged, machismo hero Northwest Smith, but alongside him also created an equally successful series with a strong, female protagonist Jirel of Joiry, one of the earliest sword-wielding Amazons. As well as celebrating Jirel's female agency, some feminist critics have also begun to examine the extraordinary representations of the vampiric opponents to Northwest Smith and to analyse the cultural mysogyny surrounding female desire encoded in them.

In 1938 John W. Campbell Jr. took over the editorship of *Astounding Stories* and introduced many of the writers who were to transform American sf: Robert A. Heinlein, Isaac Asimov, A. E. Van Voght and L. Ron Hubbard. Campbell changed the name to *Astounding Science Fiction*, insisting on the scientific accuracy of the details, but he also argued for a focus on how the technology impacted upon society. This editorial policy to focus on the social impact led to the elaboration of a whole range of imagined future cultures, as with Asimov's 'Foundation' series and closed the divergence between British and American sf. Edward James argues that by the 1940s, *Astounding Science Fiction* set the standards in both the States and Britain.[4] Since Campbell paid the highest fees, he could naturally command the best writers. Ray Bradbury, James Blish, Lester Del Rey, Frederick Pohl, Damon Knight, Robery A. Lowdnes and Theodore Sturgeon were added to his stable. British sf writers such as John Wyndham, Eric Frank Russell and Arthur C. Clarke also wrote for *Astounding Science Fiction*, as did a few women, Katherine McLean, C. L. Moore, Pauline Ashwell and Wilmar Shiras. Shiras' stories about mutant children portrayed them as individuals in need of nurturing, rather than the more usual threats to society of mainstream sf. But not all the women expanded the genre. Leigh Brackett, for example, glorified machismo action heroes so phallocentrically, that she was often praised for writing as well as any man.

The 1950s saw the beginning of an important shift in the production of the genre, with the first science fiction paperback, Ace in 1952. Ballantine, Signet and Pocket followed swiftly in the States while Pan and Corgi started imprints in Britain. Although the paperback was to dominate later sf publishing, the 1950s also saw a blossoming of magazines which introduced a new generation of far more wide-ranging sf writers. Samuel R. Delany, Philip K. Dick, John Brunner, Philip José Farmer, Frank Herbert, Brian Aldis, Marion Zimmer Bradley, Kurt Vonnegut Jr, James White, Robert Silverberg, J. G. Ballard and Harlan Ellison all initially appeared in the magazines of the 1950s. Britain developed its own magazines alongside the popular American imprints, *New Worlds*, *Authentic Science Fiction*, and *Nebula* in Scotland, publishing the work of John Wyndham, Arthur C. CLarke, Brian Aldiss and J. G. Ballard.

The women writers of sf in the 1950s featured 'housewife' protagonists who stumbled ignorantly through their adventures, thereby reinforcing the stereotypes of feminine domesticity being promulgated after the war, to get women out of the factories and back into the home. Ann Warren Griffiths, Mildred Clingerman, Margaret St Clair, Rosel George Brown and Alice Eleanor Jones specialised in these housewife stories. In contrast, Katherine McLean, Margaret St Clair and Zenna Henderson managed to slightly develop women's sf. Henderson in particular created a series around gentle, sensitive aliens very different from the usual bug-eyed monsters. The alien had already appeared as an important metaphor for Shiras and Henderson during the 1940s and 1950s, and no doubt had a symbolic resonance for women alienated by the reinforced patriarchy of postwar culture, however muted and implicit that symbolism remained. Andre Norton began her prolific run of sf stories for children during the 1950s, continuing through to the 1970s. On the whole, however, women's sf in the 1940s and 1950s conformed to the authoritative male narrator and protagonist, upholding patriarchal values, and so accords with romance's gender entrenchment in the same period.

Naomi Mitchison changed all that, creating a very different female protagonist in *Memoirs of a Spacewoman* in 1962. *Memoirs* centres on a professional woman biologist who, in outer space, experiments with reproduction by grafting other life forms onto her own body. The female agency, the exploration of reproduction and mothering, and the sympathetic treatment of alien sex (with a Martian) make this text a quantum leap away from the previous decade's and heralds a shift in experimentalism and assurance among women sf writers.

In 1963 Michael Moorcock guest edited the British *New Worlds* magazine, taking over as editor in 1964. Moorcock and *New Worlds* launched a new phase of science fiction known as the 'New Wave'. Influenced by the 'counter-culture' and hippie drug-culture, the New Wave focused on 'inner-space', rather than 'outer space'. Essentially a British phenomenon, with Moorcock, Aldiss, Ballard, Langdon Jones, Barrington Bayley, M. John Harrison and David Masson, the magazine attracted some of the more speculative American writers, publishing Disch and Sladek and influencing Delany, Ellison, Zelzany and Silverberg. New Wave narratives were more complex and self-consciously literary. They explored distorted mind-states, with a new focus on individual characters. They were also explicitly sexual, as befitted the permissive 'swinging sixties'. A larger number of women started writing science fiction during this period, including Hilary Bailey, Josephine Saxton, Carol Emswhiller, Kit Reed, Sonya Dorman, Pamela Zoline and Phyllis Gotlieb. Pamela Sargent argues that the growth in women writers relates to the concentration upon characters as complex individuals.[5] The late 1960s also saw the emergence of other important women writers, many of whom were to become the vanguard of feminist sf: Kate Wilhelm, Anne McCaffrey, Joanna Russ and Ursula LeGuin. McCaffrey and Wilhelm introduced more complex and more prominent female characters and in 'The Ship who Sang' McCaffrey disrupted patriarchal binaries to create human 'brawn' and cyborgship 'brains' where both brawn and brain could be of either gender. The main protagonist is a female cyborgship. McCaffrey began her phenomenally successful 'Dragonworld' series in 1968, with *Dragonflight*, and moved away from gender issues. Russ and LeGuin, on the other hand, were to develop into two of the most innovative feminist sf writers and critics of the genre.

The 1960s not only saw an expansion in the breadth of science fiction but also a boom in sf paperback fiction. In 1965 both the paperback issue of Tolkien's *The Lord of the Rings* in one volume, and Frank Herbert's *Dune*, became huge blockbusters, alerting publishers to the lucrative potential of science fiction. During the 1970s, science fiction switched from the short story format to the novel and new novels by Asimov, Heinlein, Clarke and Anthony all regularly made the bestseller lists.

The major development in sf during the 1970s was the impact of feminist science fiction, and this will be discussed below. During the 1970s, debates about what signifies 'real' science fiction led to the delineation of 'hard' sf, for the focus on technology and hardware, and 'soft' sf for the focus on psychology, sociology and feminist critiques. Some writers and editors began to argue it was not 'science' fiction at all and adopted the term 'sf' as able to signify 'speculative fiction', or 'speculative fabulation', which they saw as more appropriate terms for the kind of fiction they produced. Just as, during the 1970s 'crime fiction' became a more appropriate name for the expanding detective fiction genre, so 'sf' became the accepted name for the science fiction genre, and it similarly denoted a shift in the predominant ideologies of the genre.

During the 1980s, cyberpunk emerged as the new sub-genre, originating with the computer revolution. The marketing of the microprocessor in the late 1960s and early 1970s, led to the software networking of cyberspace and the internet. Cyberpunk fiction centres on the speculative possibilities of the internet. Bruce Bethke's 1973 short story, 'Cyberpunk' (in *Amazing Stories*) was adopted by Gardner Dozios to descibe the stories in *Isaac Asimov's SF Magazine*. William Gibson's 1984 *Neuromancer*, epitomises the sub-genre with its tale of computer hackers working in cyberspace, told in a sparse, laconic style taken from the hard-boiled detective narrative. Cyberpunk writers include John Shirley, Lewis Shiner, Rudy Rucker, Marc Laidlaw, Richard Kadrey and Pat Cadigan.

Sf, like crime fiction, has become an expansive genre that allows for a whole range of narratives, ideologies and subject matter, from the 'hard' technophiles of outer-space the cyberpunks, through to the alternate worlds and split selves, and the critiques of gender. Sf is, as it has always been, a genre that extends to a whole range of speculative subject matter and the genre has always held within its shifting boundaries, subversive critiques of contemporary cultures alongside imperialistic glorifications of technology.

Feminist criticism and appropriation of science fiction

In 1971, the feminist theoretician, Shulamith Firestone published *The Dialectic of Sex: the Case for Feminist Revolution*[6] arguing for a re-evaluation of society and particularly marriage and child-rearing. Her denunciation of wives as slave-labour, and pregnancy as barbaric, argued for a re-thinking of technology. Technology could enhance personal freedom and destroy the nuclear family, through artificial reproduction; it could destroy the class system through a socialist cybernetics; and lead to a more equitable utopian society. Positing a dialectic between speculative fiction and scientific discovery, she declares 'there is not even a utopian feminist literature in existence'[7] and suggests this has led to a failure to imagine alternative models to the family. Firestone's polemic, while illustrating the obscurity of the utopias of Gilman and Bradley Lane in the 1970s, proved influential to contemporary writers. Lefanu argues, 'many writers took up Shulamith Firestone's challenge and did create a utopian feminist literature in the 1970s'.[8]

Joanna Russ, who had published two science fiction novels by 1970,[9] began her criticism of the genre with 'The Image of Women in Science Fiction' in 1971,[10] arguing that science fiction had failed to place gender roles within the field of its speculations. No exploration of sex differences, family structure or sexuality had taken place. The more intelligent aspects of the genre transplanted contemporary familial norms into their futures, while the pulps took a retrograde view of women as passive prizes for the he-men. While sf written by women attempted to create more active, equal women characters, they still failed to create new ways of imagining family scenes and love scenes. The difficulty of escaping the stereotypes about gender meant that though there are many images of women in sf, there are 'hardly any women'.[11]

The following year, Susan Koppelman Cornilon's *Images of Women in Fiction: Feminist Perspectives* reprinted this essay along with Russ' 'What Can a Heroine Do? Or Why Women Can't Write'.[12] In the latter, Russ continues her argument that patriarchal stereotypes have prevented women being constructed as individuals, within mainstream literature. The alternative was to look to fiction that did not reproduce phallocentric plots, such as the detective story where the focus is on the puzzle rather than the hero, supernatural fiction, and science fiction. Science fiction is now seen more positively, as a narrative of a collective humanity, focused on the spiritual and the cognitive aspects rather than social roles, and as such it holds a potential for women writers.

In December of 1972 Beverly Friend's 'Virgin Territory: the Bonds and Boundaries of Women in Science Fiction' appeared in *Extrapolation*.[13] Like Russ, she argued that women characters in the genre have been seen as domestic robots in 'gadget sf', as passive objects in 'adventure sf'; and it is only in 'social science sf' that there had been any attempt to problematise femininity. Sturgeon's *Venus Plus X* and LeGuin's *Left Hand of Darkness* attempt to fuse the sexes to create androgynous worlds. (A later version of the essay, published in 1977, rethinks LeGuin and Sturgeon's conclusions as 'too pat' in the light of the 'pain' of Russ' *The Female Man*.)

In 1974, Pamela Sargent published her first anthology, *Women of Wonder: Sf Stories by Women about Women*,[14] to be followed by *More Women of Wonder*[15] in 1976. Both anthologies demonstrated the range of women writing within the genre, and Sargent's knowledgeable introductions, particularly for the first volume, argued for a tradition of women writing within the genre throughout the twentieth century. Introducing the work of C. L. Moore, Brackett, Shiras and Merrill through to the 1960s and 1970s, Sargent began the work of uncovering the forgotten history of women sf writers. (A final volume, *The New Women of Wonder* was published in 1979.)

1975 and 1976 saw two notable critical essays by Ursula LeGuin. The first, the important 'American SF and the Other' appeared in a special issue of *Science Fiction Studies* devoted to her work.[16] In it, LeGuin criticises mainstream sf for being authoritarian and power-worshipping, a 'baboon culture' ruled by rich, aggressive males. Arguing that the Women's Movement had alerted readers to the male elitism in sf, LeGuin pushes her analysis further to include class and race as well. Defining alien cultures as 'other', thereby objectifying them, means that only a power relationship can exist. She concludes that sf needs to start re-thinking a paradigm of equality rather than of oppression, especially in relation to women.

In 1976, 'Is Gender Necessary?' appeared in the anthology of feminist sf, *Aurora: Beyond Equality* edited by Vonda McIntyre and Susan Anderson.[17] Written in defence of her novel, *Left Hand of Darkness*, LeGuin argues that although she is herself a feminist and the book was a thought experiment about what would happen if gender were eliminated from society, it still should not be seen as a feminist book. Positing masculinity as hierarchical and femininity as anarchic, meant an androgynous society would have no wars, no class structure, and no servitude. Countering the criticism that the androgynous beings are given the pronoun 'he', she claims she has to work with the given langugage, not reinvent it. LeGuin's later thoughts on this essay, published as 'Redux' (1988)[18] acknowledges earlier feminist criticism that use of the pronoun was a failure of imagination. In the later edition she argued the novel was feminist and that her earlier self had been reacting defensively to a reception that focused purely on gender and did not consider the quality of the work.[19]

Carol Pearson's article 'Women's Fantasies and Feminist Utopias'[20] compared Bradley Lane and Gilman's turn of the century women's utopias with two from the 1970s, arguing for the similarities in their co-operative, non-violent, and non-hierarchical societies. While the early versions sentimentalise motherhood, the later ones eliminate it as part of the rejection of the nuclear family. All adopt intuitive, empathetic knowledge and a closeness to nature to fashion a society that, Pearson claims, transcends the limitations of women's experience.

In 1978, Pamela Annas argued in 'New Worlds, New Word: Androgyny in Feminist Science Fiction'[21] that despite its history, science fiction did have revolutionary potential because of its structural premise to question things-as-they-are. Sf's alternate paradigms could play off dialectically against the given reality to create a non-ethnocentric literature.

The following year, Rachel Blau DuPlessis' essay on women's speculative fiction, 'Feminist Apologues',[22] also championed sf's narrative potential. Science fiction was a form of writing that denied closure by didactically estranging the reader. Further, it focused upon collective groups rather than individual protagonists. From Gilman's *Herland*, to the recent *Female Man* and *Woman on the Edge of Time*, women had visualised worlds where muted groups' values and institutions became dominant. The focus, in this ideological contestation, has been on consciousness, the site of ideology, and the women writers had thereby succeeded in rupturing the norms of writing.

By the end of the 1970s, feminist critcism had moved from its initial criticism of the sexism in mainstream sf, to rediscover women's presence in the history of the genre and to welcome the feminist appropriations of the 1970s with an awareness of sf's subversive potential and its ability to envision a feminine experience, both in its representations and its discourse.

In March 1980, *Science Fiction Studies* devoted a special issue to women. This did not signal a shift in the mainstream criticism, so much as the industry and conviction of Joanna Russ, for the editorial signals a discomfort with the feminism, arguing the criticism is published because it is good, not because it is about women, and reassures its readers that there is no fundamental change in editorial policy.[23] Joanna Russ' 'Amor Vincit Foeminam: The Battle of the Sexes in Science Fiction'[24] argues that whereas neither early twentieth century nor contemporary sf addresses women, the later works allow more violence against women as men become more defensive. Where contemporary feminist utopias see male supremacy as the cause of the problems, these phallocentric 'Flasher' books assume possession of the male genitalia is a guarantee of victory. Susan Gubar's 'C. L. Moore and the Conventions of Women's Science Fiction'[25] considers Moore's creation of the vampire in 'Shambleau' as an evocation of culture's mysogynistic view of female desire as monstrous and alien. Science fiction allows Moore to dramatise the gulf existing between men and women. Other contributors considered the work of Zimmer Bradley, LeGuin, compared the utopias of LeGuin, Jeury and Piercy, and, with Jean Pfaelzer began a consideration of nineteenth-century American dystopias.

In 1981, Marlene Barr's important collection of essays, *Future Females: a Critical Anthology*,[26] celebrated the impact of recent feminist science fiction. Barr's defensive Preface argues that it was time to give critical space to women within science fiction and to begin to speculate about women's future roles. Eric Rabkin, Robert Scheckley, Scott Sanders and Anne Hudson Jones all examine male writers for chauvinism but acknowledge that recent work, such as Panshin's is beginning to change. A revised version of Pearson's 'Women's Fantasies ...' in her 'Coming Home: Four Feminist Utopias and Patriarchal Experience'[27] brought an awareness of the nineteenth-century utopias to a larger audience. Joanna Russ' 'Recent Feminist Utopias'[28] chooses more overtly political utopias to analyse, arguing that Wittig, Charnas, LeGuin, Bradley, Piercy, Gearhart and Sheldon (under two of her pseudonyms), point to a mini boom in feminist utopias in the past ten years. The fictional societies of all these writers are communal and semi-tribal with no overall government structure. They are ecological, classless and sexually permissive (to separate sexuality from ownership and reproduction). The majority are separatist and unproblematically lesbian. All these fictional societies are reacting to contemporary social pressures on women, thus highlighting what the isolated and alienated woman reader lacks in her life. Suzy McKee Charnas' essay 'A Woman Appeared'[29] acknowledged Robin Morgan and Shulamith Firestone's feminist theory as influencing her *Walk to the End of the World* and *Motherlines* and argues that the logical answer to sexism was a separatist Amazonian society. Further essays considered single authors such as LeGuin and Piercy.

Anne K. Mellor's 'On Feminist Utopias', in the more secure feminist confines of *Women's Studies*,[30] gave deeper thought to how revolutionary the recent feminist utopias had been. Mellor illustrated how the separatist, androgynous and bisexual utopias mirrored current trends in feminist political theory. The essay argues that the all-female or androgynous societies were wish-fulfilments that simply critiqued patriarchy, whereas *Women on the Edge of Time* and *The Dispossessed*, about genuinely egalitarian two-sexed societies, could be viable blueprints for a future politics.

Natalie Rosinsky's monograph *Feminist Futures: Contemporary Women's Speculative Fiction* a year later in 1982,[31] considers in detail the range of feminist 'social science fiction' arguing that while the texts focus on similar themes and motifs, their treatment of the themes differed markedly, depending upon the particular feminist stance of the writer. Pointing out that feminism was by now a range of positions, the book analyses the texts along a continuum of American feminisms from gynocentric essentialism to feminist androgyny, or 'cultural' feminism. Speculative fiction is seen as a new space for the merger of feminist theory and praxis, both in the estrangement of the reader and in the interaction of fans with the writers and publishers. Rosinsky was one of the first feminist critics to see audience expectation as productive in the process of shifting the feminist agenda within sf.

The following year, Marleen Barr along with Nicholas Smith edited a disappointing motley of essays, *Women and Utopia: Critical Interpretations*,[32] which had little coherent argument about women and utopias. Many of the pieces remained descriptive, and not all of them were feminist in approach. Of those that were, Lyman Tower Sargent argued for feminist utopias as wish-fulfilment, Daphne Patai argued feminism itself was the most utopian project around,[33] while Barr's own consideration of Charnas is heavily influenced by Charnas' essay in her earlier collection.

In 1984, Carol Farley Kessler's Introduction to the anthology *Daring to Dream: Utopian Stories by Women 1836–1919*,[34] compared the texts at the beginning of the century with 1970s feminist sf, in their similar quest for a spirituality within social equality, and in the focus on domestic labour. For the earlier utopias, co-operative and communitarian solutions to labour were of even more importance than suffrage. The editor's introduction points to the project being a recovery of women's earlier work within the genre.

In contrast, Donna Haraway's influential 'A Manifesto for Cyborgs: Science, Technology and Socialist Feminism in the 1980s' published in *Socialist Review* in 1985,[35] points a way to the future, arguing that the cyborg, having no unified or originary myths involved in its creation, is a new form of being that is particularly relevant to feminism. Cyborgs by their nature question myths about identity, about boundaries, and about language, all of which are central to feminist enquiry. Linking cyborgs to women of colour oppressed by the West, Haraway argues they point the way to a new form of politics devoid of identity, purity and vanguard politics, a politics of the margins rewriting their own bodies and societies. Haraway's essay acknowledges the inspiration of feminist sf writers such as Russ, Tiptree, Butler and McIntyre, but importantly also went on to influence sf writers (Piercy's *Body of Glass*) and sf critics in the 1990s, allowing them a stronger methodology to examine how feminist sf has utilised 'otherness'.

Tom Moylan's *Demand the Impossible: Science Fiction and the Utopian Imagination*[36] singled out four texts for its Marxist analysis, by Russ, LeGuin, Piercy and Delany. Defining these as 'critical utopias' Moylan argues for their ability to subvert dominant ideologies. As an oppositional cultural practice, he contextualised them in the counter-culture of the 1960s and 1970s. These radical writers challenge the utopian genre's tendency to systematise and totalise, bringing a new openness and self-reflexivity to the imagined alternative, emancipatory societies.

In contrast to Moylan's detailed analysis of ideology, Thelma Slinn's *Worlds Within Women: Myth and Mythmaking in Fantastic Literature by Women*[37] has a very different argument. Slinn includes feminist sci-fi in her discussion of utopias, and using Frye, argues that sf can offer new ways of telling the ancient myths buried by patriarchal culture, which celebrate community, communication and ecology. Using, among others, Lessing, LeGuin, Butler and Piercy, the essentialist reading attempts to uncover the ancient myth of the earth mother or the goddess.

Jenny Wolmark's 'Science Fiction and Feminism',[38] also in 1986, thoughtfully argued that feminist literary studies needed to incorporate popular genres, including science fiction, and to consider them as part of the many cultural interventions being made by feminists. Informed by cultural studies, Wolmark considers how feminist sf writers explored anti-patriarchal relationships, within a genre retaining residual sexism in its conventions. Feminist sf, she concludes, use sf at a price. The generic tensions that ensued led to a narrative ambivalence and dislocation, although this was also partly due to the general cultural anxieties of the 1970s.

The end of the 1980s and the beginning of the 1990s saw an increase in production of feminist sf criticism. *Women's Studies* devoted a special issue to 'Feminism Faces the Fantastic' in 1987[39] with special editors Marleen Barr and Patrick D. Murphy. Murphy's Introduction[40] complains that feminist critics have down-played the fantastic in Atwood and Piercy, to focus on the feminism. If they would only focus on the fantastic to note how women have always used it to inscribe the forbidden, suppressed or silenced aspects of their lives, then feminist criticism would catch up with feminist writers. Predominantly gyno-critical in its analysis, the issue included two essays looking at the feminist utopias.[41] Annette Keinhorst argues that the communal, collective societies were a genuine attempt to create emancipatory societies, but that the imagination failed when it came to both dealing with those who rejected the communal values, and trying to imagine non-oppressive male characters. Despite these failings, the estrangement of the reader by feminist utopias made them a medium for emancipatory change. Hoda Zaki's thesis agrees that the spontaneous outpouring of decentralised, anarchic utopias are unable to deal with dissent and develops this to argue the opposite view of utopian politics. They were therefore neither progressive nor subversive but rather still bourgeois in their ideology, extending the known and eliminating all significant opposition. Three of the essays focused on language.[42] Annagret Weimer's French feminist analysis of language in feminist utopias argues for a 'materna lingua', pointing to the prevalence of telepathy as symbolic of the pre-oedipal holistic verbal and psychic mother-tongue. Suzette Elgin Haden, author of *Native Tongue*, discussed how the creation of her 'Laadan Grammar' was influenced by Lacan, Daly and Rich. Since language is a closed system unable to express women's perceptions, she explained that she had been driven to create her own women's language, and the only genre open to such a creation was science fiction. Chris Kramarae argued that most feminist utopias fail in not creating a new language to express the changed social relationships, and singles out Elgin's *Native Tongue* as succeeding in doing so. Overall, the special issue questioned the political implications of the contemporary feminist utopias, while celebrating the shifts in discourse, a manoeuvre that reflected the tensions within the feminist movement away from liberal feminist political activism, towards a focus on language and the symbolic in both post-structuralist feminism and radical feminism. Marleen Barr's essay[43] argues that feminist utopias are not science fiction, but a different genre altogether, that of fabulation, using Robert Scholes' term. At this point in her career, Barr argues that feminist fabulation, rather than an umbrella term for a range of fantastic writing, is an alternative category to science fiction.

Marleen Barr's monograph of the same year, *Alien to Femininity: Speculative Fiction and Feminist Theory*,[44] argued for a dichotomy between feminist theory and speculative fiction. Both discourses share a similar concern and have developed a similar progression, but, she claims, feminist theoreticians have not been interested in speculative fiction and therefore the genre has lacked an appropriate criticism. In using specific feminist theories, Anglo-American, French (though this is minimal), reader-response, and psychoanalytic, to read specific texts by women, Barr argues she is making the 'first step' to providing such an appropriate criticism. The book looks at the separatist communitites created in feminist utopias, the female heroes bringing agency to feminist fantasy, and the ways in which the fantastic allows expression of divergent forms of sexuality, via robots, aliens and cyborgs, and re-problematises issues of mothering. Although perhaps not as innovative as the Preface claims, this is an important intervention in bringing the issue of feminist methodology into an analysis of a range of feminist sf around three highly relevant issues for feminism's appropriation of the genre. But, at the very point when British feminist genre critics in fairy tale and romance are beginning to embrace the valorisation of popular genres by cultural studies, and to try to tie feminist appropriation into the popular, Barr (as LeGuin earlier) tries to divorce feminist sf from the genre in order to ally it to the hide-bound canon of 'serious literature' that cultural studies is challenging.

Sarah Lefanu's equally important *In the Chinks of the World Machine: Feminism and Science Fiction*[45] of the following year, argued to a British audience for the success of feminist appropriation of the masculinist genre. Placing feminist sf as a distinct strand of science fiction, Lefanu points to the genre's history of subversion and iconoclasm, arguing sf had always been a broad church. The book gives a knowledgeable overview of feminist intervention into the genre, from simplistic role-reversal Amazons to the more successfully subversive utopias and dystopias, which challenge heterosexist assumptions while foregrounding women's sexual autonomy. Sci-fi romances further problematised sexual autonomy by making the object of love an alien, robot or cyborg. Lefanu concludes her overview of contemporary women's science fiction by arguing that while some writers seek to transform the position of authority, and others to validate sentiment, the most successful feminist sf seeks to deconstruct notions of essentialism from a more relativistic, ironic stance. Such writers (Zoline, Lerman, Wittig, Carter, Russ and Tiptree) create the successfully appropriated feminist science fiction. The second half of the book was a detailed analysis of four writers, Tiptree, LeGuin, Charnas and Russ.

Lefanu's book was the first British monograph on feminist sf, coincidentally from a feminist press which had a successful sf series. Lefanu, along with Jenny Wolmark and Gwyneth Jones also kept feminism on the agenda of the British sf journal, *Foundation*. In the summer of 1988, *Foundation*'s 'Forum' section was given over to Brian Stableford's reply to a charge of hypocrisy in his review of *A Handmaid's Tale* and four further responses. Under the title 'Feminism and Science Fiction',[46] Stableford argued feminists needed to incorporate the male reader in order to transcend the separatist ghetto and create a truly emancipatory project. Lefanu replied that women have had to put aside their gender for years in reading sf, and questioned why Stableford could not do this in reading women-only utopias. Gwyneth Jones, Jenny Wolmark and Colin Greenland then each discuss Stableford's 'dated' reading position.

In the more academic American sf journal, *Science Fiction Studies*, Jean Pfaelzer was arguing for the convergence of feminist discourse theory and feminist utopias. 'The Changing of the Avant-Garde: the Feminist Utopia',[47] argued that both theory and utopian writers were concerned with female space, the gap, rupture or absence of female inscription in history and discourse. Linking the turn of the century utopias, and the 1970s utopias to the first and second waves of feminism, Pfaelzer cites Cixous' argument that imagining the ideal is empowering. In her post-structuralist consideration of dislocation, history and the avant-garde, Pfaelzer argues that it is not in the worlds that they imagine that the utopias are radical, but in their open-ended narrative strategies which shatter patriarchal determinism and evoke a resistant subjectivity.

In 1989, Roz Kaveney's essay on sf in Carr's *From My Guy to Sci-Fi*,[48] also argues for the radical impact of feminist sf, but concentrated more on feminism's impact and reflexivity upon the genre itself. With its tradition of embodying dissent, sf readers are more accustomed to accepting imaginary worlds with divergent assumptions. Feminist sf challenges genre assumptions of sexism and thereby acts as a 'spoiler', reclaiming and colonising the discourse. Offering a brief but knowledgeable history of women's involvement in the genre, Kaveney focuses on LeGuin and Russ, as 'the soft cop and hard cop of American feminist SF'.[49] Kaveney concludes that the reason so many women writers have turned to sf during the women's movement is that the genre's language enables the expression of radical and feminist ideas.

Where British criticism spanned the range of the sf genre, American critics tended to limit themselves to utopias. Frances Bartkowski's *Feminist Utopias*[50] of the same year, examined the utopias of the past twenty years to question what it was that women desired in their 'not yet' societies. Closely contextualised to the feminist debates and discourses of the time, Bartkowski suggests that feminist utopias are social critiques rather than social plans, less didactic and more ironically critical. Their focus on divisions of labour, power and discourse postulate a redefinition of community, of kinship and family, and of erotic relationship. In generating representations of the hopes and fears of change, Bartkowski concludes that feminist utopias and dystopias are able to articulate social change within a discourse of activism.

The following two years saw further American publications on utopias, the collection *Feminism, Utopia and Narrative* edited by Libby Falk Jones and Sarah Webster Goodwin,[51] and Angelika Bammer's *Partial Visions: Feminism and Utopianism in the 1970s*.[52] The Jones and Webster collection spans the history of utopia from the twelfth-century *forma vitae* to the twentieth-century sf novels and celebrates the narrative ingenuity of the format. Ellen Peel[53] argues for twentieth-century feminist utopias' containment of narrative energy, which is usually dissipated in utopias, because of their narrative scepticism; Libby Falks Jones[54] argues that recent feminist utopias use fictional techniques of reader identification to dissolve the boundaries of utopia, satire, apologues and sf, to produce new models of women's experience. Lee Cullen Khanna[55] compares LeGuin's utopia with More's to argue for a deconstructive creativity in the later one. Kristine Anderson,[56] looking at content rather than narrative strategies, concludes more pessimistically that separatist representations of desire are unconvincing thought experiments. Jean Pfaelzer,[57] asked to comment on the collection as a whole, looks at the celebrations of discursive, fragmented discourse and questions what has happened to history? Do the newly deconstructive utopias allow readers to challenge the empirical reality and thereby shape their view of social change? She concludes that in the profound restructuring of readers' asumptions about contemporary reality, feminist utopias do allow a political engagement with history.

Where *Feminism, Utopia and Narrative* celebrates the subversiveness of fictional utopias, Angelika Bammer's *Partial Visions* uses the fictional accounts to interrogate the subversiveness of contemporary feminist theory. She examines how the literature of the women's movement reflects utopian aspects of 1970s feminism. Bammer divides the utopias into those that posit them as elsewhere; those on the boundaries of the real; and those that deconstruct and transform the cultural scripts. Using Cixous, Bammer argues that feminist utopias are not unreal but voice a desire, a force that moves and shapes history.

In contrast to this American focus, Anne Cranny-Francis' three chapters in *Feminist Fiction* (1990) and Lucy Armitt's edition, *Where No Man Has Gone Before: Women and Science Fiction*[58] (1991) both examine the wider range of Anglo-American sf. Cranny-Francis devotes over half of her book to feminist science fiction, feminist fantasy and feminist utopias and these are the genres she sees as effectively appropriated by feminist ideology. Feminist sf, with its visible challenge to patriarchal norms, is placed along with postmodernism, as a challenge to modernism. Feminist sf 'remakes' the genre, producing stories which denaturalise institutional modes of behaviour and self-representation. The use of estrangement, the questioning of scientific knowledge, and the use of the alien, all create successful *feminist* sf. Feminist fantasy and utopia also create feminist reading positions, which challenge the discourse of individualist subjectivity and estrange the institutions that naturalise sexism.

Lucie Armitt's collection focused on the trope of alien otherness, and on audience interaction in the genre, as well as considering certain key authors, Moore, LeGuin and Lessing. Armitt's Introduction[59] argues that the last decade's interest in women's sf had been instrumental in opening the genre to the general reader, and in bringing it academic recognition. This she accords to mainstream women writers who venture into sf, like Lessing, Atwood, Carter and Piercy. Piercy's *Woman on the Edge of Time*, she claims as 'one of the landmarks of the genre for decades to come'.[60] While Jenny Newman looks at women's use of the monstrous,[61] Lisa Tuttle explores the theme of women turning into animals, in 1980s women's sf, as an investigation into what it means to be human when the human is female.[62] Armitt looks at how feminist sf has tried to challenge patriarchal language structures, using Cixous and Kristeva to analyse how Lessing and Elgin attempt to deconstruct the dominant linguistic and social frameworks.[63] Sarah Lefanu's article, 'Sex, Sub-atomic Particles and Sociology'[64] challenges the expectation that women's sf will be 'soft' sf about utopian creches, and argues that women have also successfully embraced the 'hard' traits of science, machines and bodies. Though not an overview, Armitt's collection points to the breadth of women's sf and to the need for criticism to include film, juvenile markets, and in the case of Lisa Tuttle and Josephine Saxton,[65] the writer as well.

During 1992–3 Marleen Barr continued her attempts to de-genre feminist sf. *Feminist Fabulations: Space/Postmodern Fiction*(1992)[66] was followed by *Lost in Space: Probing Feminist Science Fiction and Beyond*[67] in 1993, although structurally *Lost in Space* comes before *Feminist*

Fabulation. In a Preface called 'Having Nunavit', Barr argues in *Feminist Fabulations* that the term feminist science fiction is obsolete, and that she intends to situate all feminist speculative fiction within the term of feminist fabulation. Arguing that feminist sf has not been valued because it is seen as generic, she attempts to have it revalued by placing it within the canon of postmodern fiction, with which it shares many tropes. The strategy is clearly a way to continue talking about feminist sf while being taken seriously, but is extremely problematic as a strategy. There is an argument to be made for feminist generic fiction being re-valued, but not by denying the value of the genre, in order to be included within the literary. Cultural studies have led the way in re-valuing the popular and feminism's political practice is to be subversive of academic hierarchies and distinctions. Barr's strategy on the other hand is a conformist desire to be included within the hierarchy. The book, nonetheless, is a substantial comparison of postmodern and feminist sf treatments of similar subjects such as flying, the domestic sphere, and egalitarian societies. *Lost in Space*, partially written before Barr's repudiation of the genre, is less notable. Half the book is straight sf criticism, while the other half puts forward feminist fabulation as a criticism. At this point, Barr uses feminist fabulation as an umbrella term to include science fiction, fantasy, utopian and mainstream literature by feminist writers. Sf is not being rejected as a genre but is included as one of the many sub-groups. Claiming to be a reading practice that critiques patriarchal master narratives, what she is actually trying to do is to include feminist fabulations *within* the dominant master-narrative.[68] A Foreword by Marge Piercy applauds Barr's attempt to rescue women's sf from intellectual neglect, arguing that 'The way to get the wildebeest into the tent is to build a bigger and differently shaped tent.'[69] Such a strategy would be applauded by feminist ideology; the problem is that Barr attempts (as *Feminist Fabulation* confirms) to get the wildebeest into the original tent by claiming it is not a wildebeest.

Jenny Wolmark's *Aliens and Others: Science Fiction, Feminism and Postmodernism*[70] looked at the same issues in the same year, and came up with a different strategy, dismissing Barr's 'extraordinary about-face' as a conservative reinvention of the binary positions.[71] Wolmark's own analysis successfully argues for the thematic and linguistic convergence of feminism, sf and postmodernism, without trying to conflate them. Wolmark analyses feminist sf's use of the alien in order to discuss subjectivity, identity and difference. The trope of the alien has allowed feminist writers to create alternative definitions of gender and identity which accommodate, rather than repress, difference. Wolmark examines how feminist sf has used the alien to explore marginalisation by race; to subvert the binary 'nature vs culture'; and to redefine the limits of the self. With the cyborg, cyberpunk's celebration of masculinity is contrasted to feminists' use of it to reconfigure self and other into new kinds of subjectivity. For Wolmark, feminist sf's strength is its emphasis on provisionality, as it destabilises the dominant ideology by confronting the contradictions in gender representation. The subversive potential lies in undermining the boundaries, rather than in trying to re-inscribe the feminine, and this strategy is shared by both feminist sf and the postmodern.

The late 1990s have proved less buoyant in sf criticism. In 1994 the excellent *Utopian and Science Fiction by Women*,[72] edited by Jane Donawerth and Carol Kolmarten, continued the transatlantic focus on the utopian. The editors' Introduction gives a knowledgeable history of the utopian genre from the seventeenth century, although they argue that women writers only begin to use 'scientific' solutions for the utopias in the American women's utopias of 1836–1919. Since the First World War, most feminist utopias have been published as science fiction, and the development of a women's tradition has continued. Rejecting the argument that a break occurs mid-century, they point to Naomi Mitchison as proof for the continuity. By the 1960s, this tradition was in constant conversation with feminist theory, with the flowering of feminist utopias in the 1970s that advanced feminist critiques of much of Western culture. Again, Piercy's *Woman on the Edge of Time* is singled out as becoming 'a kind of scripture for the women's movement in the United States'.[73] The 1980s utopias have proved to be more sceptical of the perfectibility of feminist utopias, particularly by lesbian and black writers, while Atwood explored the failure of feminist heroism. Recent utopian writing by Piercy, Slonczewski and Butler, they conclude, create more inclusive utopias with multiple voices. The collection contains essays on individual writers, Gilman, Mitchison and Butler, among others. It also contains Jane Donawerth's argument for the presence of women in early pulp fiction.[74]

Lucie Armitt's *Contemporary Women's Fiction and the Fantastic*[75] continues the comparison of feminist sf alongside other contemporary uses of the fantastic, such as horror, fairy tale and magical realism, begun by Barr and Wolmark. Armitt's position, in 2000, is that carving fantasy up into different genres 'kills literature dead',[76] and focusing on generic identification has prevented the criticism advancing as far as the literary. While not going so far as to reject the term feminist science fiction as obsolete, she certainly finds it restrictive in her consideration of, among other things, grotesque utopias, cyborgs and mannequins in the marketplace. In itself a fascinating focus on feminist uses of the fantastic, Armitt's rejection of genre terms reflects the turn of the twentieth century's discomfort with feminist science fiction as a genre category. Where detective fiction and romance criticism have embraced the cultural studies validation of popular genres to enrich the debates and the assessment of texts, feminist science fiction has remained wedded to a binary opposition with the literary and, at the turn of the millennium (an sf date if ever there was one), appears to have rejected the genre category for a blurring into the mainstream. Such defensively conformist a strategy belies the excitingly subversive fiction involved and, to a great extent, the rigorous and informative criticism of that fiction.

On the whole, feminist sf criticism has proved less challenging than detective or romance criticism. While there are some very good analyses of specific feminist authors, and some exciting work in relation to discourse and to cyborgs and aliens, the obsession with the literary has meant that critical interventions tend to come from outside the genre, from Firestone or from Haraway. Happily, feminist science fiction more than makes up for this section's critical timidity.

Joanna Russ' *Picnic on Paradise* (1968) is usually cited as the first feminist sf novel, with its strong female protagonist, followed the year after by Ursula LeGuin's *Left Hand of Darkness* (1969), exploring a world where gender is absent except for kemmer (sexually active periods), when any person can become either male or female during different kemmers. In 1969, Angela Carter's *Heroes and Villains* explored a young girl's maturing within a post-apocalyptic world. All three deal with issues of gender and of representations of femininity, but none could be termed overtly feminist in its inflections.

In 1970, Shulamith Firestone issued her challenge for a literary feminist utopia, and a number of writers answered the call, with texts that invoke feminist reading positions. In Monique Wittig's *Les Guerillères* (1971) guerrilla fighters literally wage war on both men and patriarchal discourse. James Tiptree Jr's subversive 'The Women Men Don't See' (1973),[77] argued women are so alienated within a phallocentric culture that they prefer a life with aliens. (Tiptree's other alter egos Alice Sheldon, and the feminist Racoona Sheldon began publishing during the mid-1970s.) Ursula LeGuin's *The Dispossessed* (1974) addressed the question of what a world ruled by feminist principles would be like. While Suzy Charnas' *Walk to the End of the World* (1974) (followed by *Motherlines*, 1978) and Joanna Russ' *The Female Man* (1975) argued for separatist female worlds, Marge Piercy's *Woman on the Edge of Time* (1976), perhaps the closest fictional answer to Firestone, posited a bisexual utopia where no one was valued by gender, class or ethnicity.

At the end of the 1970s and the early 1980s, the fiction was elaborating and exploring any number of feminist issues. Angela Carter's *The Passion of New Eve* (1977) deconstructs the myths surrounding femininity and positions femininity as masquerade, while Vonda McIntyre's *The Exile Awaiting* (1976) and Sally Miller Gearhart's *The Wanderground: Stories of Hill Women* (1979), in contrast, reinforce the myth to conflate masculinity with technology, and the feminine with nature. In 1979, Doris Lessing began her sf series *Canopus in Argos*, with *Shikasta*. The following volume, *The Marriages between Zones Three, Four and Five* (1980), like Suzette Haden Elgin's *Native Tongue* (1984) explored the structures of power within language. The mid-1980s saw the start of Gwyneth Jones in the UK (*Divine Endurance* 1984) and the dabbling of Margaret Atwood (*Handmaid's Tale* 1985), while the African-American Octavia Butler, who began in 1976 with *Patternmaster*, explored issues of race and oppression in *Kindred* (1988). In 1991, Marge Piercy published *He, She and It* in the US (published as *Body of Glass* in the UK), exploring issues of identity and autonomy in relation to the cyborg. Elaboration of a range of feminist issues and debates within the feminist community has always been an exciting aspect of feminist sf.

In the late 1990s, feminist sf has been hit badly by the folding of a number of feminist publishing houses (the Women's Press' sf line begun in 1985 had been a major part of the British feminist sf output). While sf continues to sell and to branch out in a dizzying variety of sub-genres, it was notable that one of London's central feminist bookshops, Silver Moon, expanded their detective shelves by eliminating their sf holdings. While feminist sf continues to be written and to sell, it does not seem to have the wider popularity that it had in the late 1980s and the earlier 1990s.

Case studies: Joanna Russ, Marge Piercy and Octavia Butler

Joanna Russ has been an influential feminist critic of science fiction, particularly at its outset, and also a feminist sf writer. Lefanu calls her unequivocally, 'the single most important woman writer of science fiction, although . . . not necessarily the most widely read'.[78] *Picnic on Paradise* (1968) introduced Alyx, a strong female hero who survives by her wits and her courage. Russ' short story, 'When it Changed' (1972) has spacemen landing on Whileaway, a successfully separatist world of women, and charts their sexist reactions. The short story was Russ' first unaccommodatingly feminist fiction and it won critical acclaim with a Nebula Prize. Yet, *The Female Man*, often cited as one of the first full-blown feminist sf novels of the Women's Liberation Movement, was unable to find a publisher. Initially written in 1968/9 and read amongst sf writers such as Ursula LeGuin and Samuel Delany,[79] the book wasn't published until 1975.

The Female Man's[80] four main characters, Janet, Jeanine, Joanna and Jael, 'a feast of J's' (p. 155), are four variations of the same self, from alternate probable worlds. Joanna, the often disembodied voice of the narrator, and Jeanine inhabit the world of 1969 middle-class America; Jael, the near future, a dystopia that problematises issues of role-reversal between the sexes; and Janet, Whileaway, a utopian far future where women are free to develop their potential. Not till Jael spirits the other three to her world, does the narrative explain that these characters are four versions of the same woman, modified by age, experience, conditioning and education into completely different people. The argument for cultural conditioning is clear. Jeanine, the unreconstructed woman of 1969, abnegating herself to patriarchal constructions of femininity, concerned about her looks, her ability to attract a sufficiently successful man, and to conform by getting married, is obtuse, fearful and permanently depressed. Joanna, the 'female man' of the title, is more perspicacious and rebels against the patriarchal conditioning. Secure in her sexuality and able to voice her anger against the status quo, Joanna has rejected victimhood for self-hood, although it is a self that is often more spirit than body.

Jael, living among the Womanlanders in a rubble-strewn land devastated by forty years of war between the sexes, is a metal-enhanced assassin. With her strength and her love of violence, Jael confounds the other Womanlanders' belief that women are more compassionate than men, loving, gentle and nurturing. Jael is pure aggression, revelling in the violence, although the text reiterates that her vengeance is in reaction to the Manlanders' sexist oppression. In a culture still oppressed by sexism each sex lives a separatist existence, although the women's intelligence allows them to outmanoeuvre the men's complacent power. The men castrate the more feminine of their sex, and sexually abuse the 'changed' and the transvestite 'half-changed'.

Jael's home is a role reversal of the obnoxious 'Boss' in Manlander society. Both privileged to live in houses above ground, rather than the underground norm, their homes are beautiful aesthetic surroundings serviced by a sexually objectified subordinate, in the Boss's case, his wife Natalie, in Jael's, Davy. The narrative, aided by the other selves' horror, problematises the issues of role reversal as an effective feminist strategy, whilst bitterly explaining the attraction of such a course. The rhetorical strategy of the text also makes overt the abnormalness of 'normal' relations through role-reversal as a trope. Jael's having sex with Davy, a chimpanzee cyborg created to be the ideal male body, foregrounds the domination and ownership involved within the sexual encounter, seen anew because woman on man.

> So lovely: Davy with his head thrown to one side, eyes closed, his strong fingers clenching and unclenching. He began to arch his back, as his sleepiness made him a little too quick for me, so I pressed Small Davy between thumb and forefinger just enough to slow him down and then – when I felt like it – playfully started to mount him. (p. 197)

An anti-pornography campaigner,[81] Russ simultaneously allows the woman an active enjoyment of sex and, by imitating the images of traditional erotica, highlights the power and oppression at play within the 'normal' sex act.

Where Jael's world is twisted by the proximity to sexism, Janet's Whileaway has the luxury of developing unhindered by any contact with men. Rethinking how the female psyche would develop without the Oedipal alignment, argued by Freud for feminine subordination, Russ constructs a similar rift and realignment at the age of five. During the child's first five years she is pampered and indulged by her birth mother, who is allowed freedom from work, and fills her leisure with creative pursuits usually only allowed to the elderly. At the age of five, the little girl is sent to school. The mothers, who have been able to indulge their own creative needs, howl at having to go back to work. The text punctures the stereotype about maternal instincts, since they do not mourn being separated from their children, 'the truth is they don't want to give up the leisure' (p. 50). The girls rebel by scheming and plotting to get back to their family, a representation that rejects girlhood as passive or nurturing. They are taught practical mechanics, medicine, to swim and shoot. At puberty, they attain Middle Dignity and roam throughout the land, often in bands, exploring, contemplating, or living rough. At 17 they gain 'Three-Quarters Dignity' and are put to work at all the most mundane tasks. At 22 they attain 'Full Dignity', do the more interesting jobs and are able to marry. Families consist of a group of 20–30 like-minded people, though not bonded by sex, which mostly takes place outside the family. Only in old age, able to induct with machines, are the women free to draw, think, write and collate. The representation highlights, by its divergence, how women are usually isolated within the home, with only low-grade jobs if they do more than look after the family, and little practical expertise. Sex begins at puberty, in Whileaway, with each girl being given her own lingam. Sex is enjoyed for what it is and not invested with the myths of romance, attacked in detail in relation to Jeanine, who wastes her whole life waiting in passive dissatisfaction for romance to 'choose' her. The Whileawayan woman, as exemplified by Janet Evanson, is self-sufficient, confident and agent of her own destiny. The perspicacious Joanna, in 1969, compares her to Jeanine to illustrate exactly how an alternative feminine conditioning could affect women. Janet, like Jael, can be violent and has shot people both in the line of duty and out of anger. This construction of women as dangerous is put to use by the main narrator, Joanna, who grows into rage. For *The Female Man* is a book that employs textual aggression towards patriarchy, to fuel its narrative energy. Highly polemical and engaged, the narrative uses caricature and invective to delineate the normal mid-Western relationships between men and women. The 'Courtship ritual' of the party or the 'Great happiness contest', or the little pink books and blue books that explain the codes of patriarchy, use satire to show how women are expected to be negative, incapable sex-objects, treated without respect in order to aggrandise men's shaky egos. Through the slightly more developed character of Jeanine, we are given the woman who is not listened to, is patronised, and expected to sacrifice herself to any man. Her narcissism and free-floating anxiety are linked directly to such treatment. The feminist meaning of the constructions are made increasingly overt by Joanna, the narrator. At 13 years, Joanna searched in books to find confirmation that women could be ambitious, smart, arrogant, 'OK to be Humphrey Bogart ... James Bond ... Superman' (p. 203), pointing up the silence around female role models in our culture. Joanna posits the thesis that women make up one-tenth of public society, by listing the public roles filled by men, doctor, lawyer, store owner and so on, while women hardly figure at all. Men, as the narrator points out, constitute humanity. 'I'll tell you how I turned into a man' (p. 133) the text states blatantly in Part Seven, arguing that women within the workplace exist as neuters, trying to ignore their sex in order to be treated equally, but that they are turned into a negative construction of femininity by male denigration. The only recourse that enables self-love, Joanna discovers, is to become the 'female man' of the title. This is not an argument for androgyny, but an ironic examination of language. 'Man' stands for humanity within patriarchal culture, so the narrator becomes part of humanity by assuming the nominal title of 'man' that allows her to inhabit all the positive binary constructions within the culture. 'For years I have been saying *Let me in, Love me, Approve me, Define me, Regulate me, Validate me, Support me.* Now I say *Move over'* (p. 140).

The Female Man is a text that utilises the fictionality of it own form, self-reflexively calling attention to the narrator as creation: slipping from inhabiting Janet's consciousness, to Joanna's , to nobody's: 'I was there only as the spirit or soul of an experience is always there' (p. 89). The narrator is as moveable as the separate probable selves of the four main characters. And the playful postmodern mélange of satire, direct engagement of the reader, and story-telling across three worlds, constitutes fiction as rhetoric. The text is not concerned to tell a story for its own sake, but to engage the reader in a consideration of patriarchy and the damage it does to women. It does this with an engaging wit. 'This is the lecture. If you don't like it, you can skip to the next chapter' (p. 29). The non-realism of the rhetoric, locates it as refusing to fit into notions of decorum, and the status quo. The sprawling, bawdy and challenging rhetoric mirrors the aggressive and questioning spirit of the Women's Liberation Movement itself, in the late 1960s, as it stands testimony to Joanna being a 'Female Man'. The 'fictionality' of the selves posits selves as cultural inscriptions, while arguing for the potential to change. Overtly rejecting femininity as intuitive, emotional and nurturing, the text argues for this stereotype as a negative conditioning of patriarchy:

> You will notice that even my diction is becoming feminine, thus revealing my true nature; I am not saying 'Damn' any more, or 'Blast'; I am putting in lots of qualifiers like 'rather', I am writing in these breathless little feminine tags, she threw herself down on the bed, I have no structure (she thought), my thoughts seep out shapelessly like menstrual fluid, it is all very female and deep and full of essences, it is very primitive and full of 'ands', it is called 'run-on sentences'. (p. 137)

While the shift to third person highlights the dissociated alienation of a woman inhabiting the patriarchal construction of femininity, the passage goes on to engage with various beliefs of essentialist feminists, linking their theories to patriarchal constructions. Russ' main rejection of them comes, however, in the use of violence, both in Jael and Janet's actions, and in the narrator's aggression to the reader: 'Listen to the female man. If you don't, by God and all the Saints, *I'll break your neck*' (p. 140).

It is a text which evokes itself, self-reflexively, as a 'little book' sent through America and Europe to have influence, until such time as feminism has been superceded by a more equal culture. It makes overt its influence by such feminist writers as 'Freidan, Millet, Greer, Firestone' (p. 213). It argues, threatens, satirises, and posts various alternatives in a mélange that is itself demanding, lightened by the wit and inventiveness that is exhilarating to the feminist reader. Indeed, in 1969, the text itself takes on much of the work of the 'raising of consciousness' valued by the Women's Movement as a strategy with which to interrogate patriarchy. As such, despite its verve and its humour, it remains an uncomfortable read for many men and could fit into the category of feminist genre speaking to the feminist ghetto. Even some other women sf writers sought to dissociate themselves from what they termed her dislike of men.[82] But it is a breathtakingly avant-garde and inventive text which, while very much a book of its time in the early years of American second-wave feminism,[83] still engages with many of the post-structural questioning of identity and fictionality, in the 1990s.

Marge Piercy's 1978 *Woman on the Edge of Time*,[84] another 'landmark' of feminist sf, makes a useful comparison with *The Female Man* on a number of points. Where Russ focuses on the effects of the state upon the individual psyche, Piercy's aim is a more detailed social critique of institutional oppression, and a more detailed imaginative creation of the social and political workings of a utopia. Where Russ' ideal is for a feminist lesbian separatism, Piercy's is a bisexual utopia that accommodates men by freeing gender from biology. The two texts reflect the best aspects of early American second-wave feminism, initially focused on white middle-class women's oppression (Russ) and then forced to acknowledge that gender was not the only cultural subjugation; ethnicity, class and sexual orientation also needed to be considered in a more complex awareness of social repression (Piercy).

Marge Piercy came to feminism from an active role in radical politics, as she outlines in 'The Grand Coolie Dam'[85] and her realist novels, *Going Down Fast* (1969) or *Vida* (1980), deal with life amongst the radical politics of the counter-culture, trying to change society. *Woman on the Edge of Time* (1976), Piercy's first sf novel, has as its protagonist a poor, middle-aged Chicana, who has already suffered an unwanted hysterectomy, had her child taken away from her, and has been incarcerated in a mental institution. At 15, an intelligent girl full of plans and fire to go to college and travel, by 37 years she is content to subsist in meagre, isolated poverty. '"We wear out so early," she said to the mirror, not really sure who the "we" was. Her life was thin in meaningful "we's"' (p. 35). The social institutions are indicted for abusing her because she is poor, Mexican, and a woman. The text argues that, were she not 'on welfare and on probation' (p. 26), her child would not have been removed after only being hit once. Men, her brother and her niece's pimp, commit her to the mental home, for being a nuisance. 'Some truce had been negotiated betwen the two men over the bodies of their women' (p. 31). A sustained study of the abuses of the mental asylum as places to bury those society finds inconvenient – women, African-Americans and homosexuals – many of the inmates Connie befriends are not mad but simply social misfits. Once incarcerated, the patients are the dispossessed. Treated like 'animals', denied any rights, because nothing they say is believed, they cannot voice their own experience and they eventually become human guinea pigs for scientific experiments. Set as much in the present as in the future utopia, *Woman on the Edge of Time* confronts the charge that utopian fiction is escapist and not relevant to contemporary crisis, by its denotative social realism. The injustice it portrays is recognisable and engages the reader in identification with the protagonist. No hero, Connie is deliberately one of the devalued in contemporary society, in contrast to the future, where everyone is valued.

The other half of the narrative is set in the future world of Mattapoiset, an ecological and egalitarian utopia, to which Connie is transported. Linguistically, the future has eliminated the gender-specific personal pronouns, because neither male nor female is privileged. Instead of 'he'/'she' they have only 'per' (from person). This one word effectively calls attention to the binary opposition implicit within language, although Piercy goes on to create a whole new patois.

Mattapoiset is a mixture of the rural and the technological. Looking surprisingly backward with its small houses and farms, the people raise birds, goats and cows, but converse with them in body language.

Nothing, not even the animals are treated with such abusive disrespect as the contemporary inmates of the American lunatic asylum. In contrast, Mattapoiset respects people who 'go down' into madness, for the different consciousness they convey.

Technology is embraced for mining and manufacturing, where people would be brutalised by the work. Because everyone works, children, women and men, less time is taken and so there is more time for creative pursuits. Once again, they live in communal villages, where everyone has a voice in the decisions of the community. Connie is unable to comprehend a culture without a governing superstructure, but the Mattapoiset have none. People who do not share in the work of the cooperative are simply exiled.

As with the language, desire is bisexual. Mattapoisets fall in love with the person, rather than a specific gender. And, despite having both sexes, child-bearing has become technologised as a basis for equality. The embryos are brought to term within a huge brooder. Echoing Firestone, the text argues,

> It was part of women's long revolution ... as long as we were biologically enchained, we'd never be equal. And males would never be humanized to be loving and tender. So we all became mothers. Every child has three. To break the nuclear bonding. (p. 105)

The rejection of the over-identification of the mother-and-child bond comes both in their mothering (they have no word for fathering, since men nurture and breast-feed as well as the women) and in their lovers, where they have a number of 'pillow friends'. Living surrounded and supported by their families, none could find themselves in the desperate situation of Connie, during the grief and self-distrust which led to her one abuse of her daughter. The Mattapoiset social groupings stand as counter-argument.

They have also eliminated the bond between genes and culture to prevent racism, while holding onto diversity. Now there are black Italians and Chinese alongside the white. Difference is valued for the richness it brings, but cultural identity is chosen by the community as a whole. So black and white, the Mattapoisets share the Wamponaug Indian cultural identity. Racism, class-division and gender differentiation, all the oppressions that damage Connie in the present, have been prevented in this utopian future.

As with *The Female Man*, the children's development has been carefully developed. Following on from Firestone's castigation of the

Oedipal familial structure, the Mattapoiset child has three mothers and learns practically, through attending work along with the adults. They also learn 'inknowing' (p. 140) to prevent internal projection on to others and 'outknowing' to connect with others in the community. No one in the utopia could ever suffer the isolation Connie experiences as the root of most of her troubles. At puberty, they live alone in the wild for a week, as a rite of passage to get to know themselves, decide upon an appropriate name, and return to live with 'aunts' as equal members of society. The mothers are forbidden to speak to them for three months, in order to free the children from the expectancy of dependence. Initially sceptical, Connie realises the value of this upbringing and mentally bequeaths her own daughter to the future world:

> She will be strange, but she will be glad and strong and she will not be afraid. She will have enough. She will have pride. She will love her own brown skin and be loved for her strength and her good work. She will walk in strength like a man and never sell her body and she will love her babies like a woman and live in love like a garden.... (p. 141)

Like *The Female Man*, *Woman on the Edge of Time* argues the need for a culture that grants women an equality of respect, allows them to work at equally valued jobs, to be taught practical skills, and to be comfortable with their sexual desires. The patriarchal, nuclear household is represented as indoctrinating women into being second-class citizens. Lefanu argues that underpinning many of the feminist sf novels of the 1970s is the 'rescue' of a young girl from such conditioning.[86] The utopias are predominantly rural and ecologically sound, respecting nature, but neither eschews technology for the running of machinery. In many ways, these two writers, in common with many other women sf writers, are identifying the same constrictions on the cultural construction of femininity in 1976 (both texts are set in the same year) and putting forward similar solutions to the oppression. In the cultural analysis, both texts function in similar ways. In the rhetorical involvement of the audience, and the linguistic exploration, they differ markedly.

Marge Piercy's text is a realist text, with the concomitant acceptance of how character is portrayed as a knowable, unified set of characteristics. Although refraining from the complexities of fragmentation, the sf element allows for a sense of character as process. In the twentieth century, Connie is exhausted and defeatist until she is given hope and an alternative by Mattapoiset. Then she finds a 'meaningful we' to connect with and finds the courage to stand up to the institutions and to actively fight for a better future. Piercy, too, uses the sf trope of alternate worlds, alternative probabilities, to argue for the necessity of activism. She uses the dystopia of Gildina as yet another possibility of the future, a logical progression from the prostitution of her niece, Dolly, and of the experiments on brain implants in the hospital. In a dystopia where hierarchy is intractably divided into the privileged and the oppressed, the women are divided into those that continuously bear children, and those designed for sexual gratification. These women's bodies are surgically enhanced and any trace of ethnicity removed. They are contracted to the men as sexual companions, from one night to up to a year, depending on the man's whim. By forty they are too old and 'ashed'. The rich have abandoned the polluted planet, and live on space stations, prolonging their life by organ transplants from the poor and dispossessed who live like animals on the polluted surface, 'walking organ banks' (p. 291). The rich, often two hundred years old, are the same 'Rockemellons' and 'Duke-Ponts' (p. 297) of the 1970s, with their multinationals formed into clans, supported by brain-controlled Assassins and the middle-flacks that Gildina services. Money and power rule. Women, having neither, are the despised underclass.

Made aware that this alternative future is what Mattapoiset is fighting, that people in 1976 have to make a stand against the exploitation that, allowed to continue, could mean that the contemporary's future existence could be the dystopia, rather than the utopia, Connie makes her stand. With a brain implant, and heavily drugged, she still manages to poison the doctors involved in experimenting on the inmates, and stops the trials. The story ends on her assertion that she has taken her stand in the war, and has fought on the side of the free.

But the text does not end there. The narration shifts to close on the case notes of Connie, illustrating how the complex, courageous woman we have experienced and identified with, is turned into a lifeless 'problem' by medical jargon. Debates on how femininity was culturally linked to madness, the 'female malady', were current amongst American feminists during the mid-1970s.[87] This final denigration of Connie indicts the medical institutions, and, by invoking the readers' alienation from the doctors, allies them with freedom and with action to prevent such a dismissal of a complex human being.

Realism has been stretched, rhetorically, to include the reader in reactive disgust from the denotative details of known life: to activate the reader to want change the status quo as represented.

Octavia Butler, writing a decade later, has less of the rhetorical didacticism of Russ or early Piercy. (It could be argued that later Piercy is also less didactic in its feminism, in, for example, the excellent *Body of Glass* of 1991.) An African-American woman sf writer, Butler addresses issues of racism in *Kindred* (1988), and of women's political activism against right-wing fundamentalists in the Earthseed series. But right from her earliest sf novel *Patternmaster* (1976), with its use of telepathy, Butler has shown an acute interest in configuring processes of knowing divergent from logocentricism, in the unconscious and in desire. In the Xenogenesis series, Butler uses the trope of the alien to explore how 'otherness' and difference can problematise both gender and ethnicity. In *Imago* (1989),[88] the third book in the series, the alien is the narrator, in order to estrange the reader from humanity. The discourse is of the body, but a body estranged and re-named, because alien. Desire, need and pleasure are re-imagined in a new configuration, that has similarities with Carter's reconfiguration of desire in the fairy tales of *The Bloody Chamber*, but here the configuration is located in scientific language of genes and DNA and pheromones. A biological discourse of the body, that initially appears to invoke determinism, *Imago* succeeds in unsettling the apparent fixities around the genetic definitions of gender and 'race', in a wholesale deconstruction of biological determinism.

The narator, Jodahs, is not only an ooloi construct, but the very first one ever to be born, and hence feared by the Oankali inhabitants of Earth, as a dangerous unknown quantity. Literally constructed by his ooloi parent Nikanj, out of the DNA of his two human parents and his two Oankali parents, Jodahs expects to metamorphise into either an Oankali or a human, of either gender, depending upon which parent he feels most drawn to. Already, through the creation of this metamorphosis, gender and 'race' have become issues of affinity rather than heredity, since the ooloi has hybridised not only race and otherness, but the very genetics that is supposed to underpin those differences, and made adult development a process rather than a fixed given:

> hybridity and the power it releases may well be seen to be the characteristic feature and contribution of the post-colonial, allowing a means of evading the replication of the binary categories of the past

and developing new anti-monolithic models of cultural exchange and growth.[89]

Jodahs confounds expectations by metamorphising into an ooloi, along with his paired sibling, Aor. Ooloi are both male and female in one body, and Jodahs and Aor are the first ever construct ooloi. Difference is doubly defined, since this alien is alien to all of his world. Butler explores the pressures placed upon the different, in Nikanj's assertion that 'You're a new kind of being. There's never been anyone like you before. But there is no flaw in you. You just need time to find out more about yourself' (p. 49) and places responsibility for reacting to difference back upon the bigots with its statement, 'You want to be what you are. That's healthy and right for you. What we do about it is our decision, our responsibility. Not yours' (p. 27).

The Oankali's suspicion towards Jodahs mirrors the intolerance of the humans towards the Oankali and the Ooloi who have come to their planet. Humans are presented, through Jodahs' estranged view, as intolerant, aggressive and needing to dominate, and these charac-teristics are presented in negative terms as a fatal flaw. This human failing is explained as a flawed DNA that makes them hierarchical and hence programmed to destroy themselves, despite their intelligence. The proof of this thesis is the war that earlier eradicated all of the countries traditionally seen as 'first' and 'second' world nations, with only the 'third world' countries surviving in the pockets of still habit-able land. These survivors either mate with the ooloi, as Jodahs' birth-mother Lilith has done, or become resisters, fighting and preying upon each other.

Through Jodahs' superior understanding, humans are viewed as hostile and dangerous. They are shown to want to give physical pain when they are emotionally hurt, sexually betray their mates by sleeping with others, kill animals and each other, and are 'inclined to be intolerant of difference. They could overcome the inclination, but it was a reality of the Human conflict that they often did not' (pp. 185–6).

In locating this hierarchical inclination in the flawed gene Butler, at first, seems to be invoking a biologically determined scenario, with the scientific discourse of genetics. But the text creates a slippage away from this fixity. In the opening chapters, Jodahs characterises human females as open and accepting, while the males are 'suspicious, hostile and dangerous' (p. 31) from his early encounters, and this reads like a definitive gender description. His own mates, however, Jesusa and

Tomas, illustrate the opposite, with Tomas accepting and Jesusa hostile and suspicious. Even more than this, genetics itself is not determinate because ooloi are 'natural genetic engineers' and can change hereditary defects, by altering the genetic make-up. The conflict gene will thus be eradicated in Jodahs' own construct children. In this text, genetic engineering becomes a way of transforming biological determinism into a biological process of becoming, of unsettling the scientific fixities of Western culture.

But it is in the detailed imagining of the ooloi, that Butler most clearly critiques human social and sexual relations, and begins to fashion an idealised language of the body. For ooloi, there is no mind–body split, they are fully integrated:

> Humans said one thing with their bodies and another with their mouths and everyone had to spend time and energy figuring out what they really meant ...
>
> Nikanj, on the other hand, meant what it said. Its body and its mouth said the same things. (p. 27)

The concept of the Ooloi reconceives the mind/body, nature/culture binary oppositions, by eradicating the distinctions. Ooloi are in tune with the landscape around them, the 'Lo', communicating with it, and through it to others, growing it into living dwellings, towns, and fashioning it into food for humans. Inclusively, all life is precious to them and they have an organ, the yashi, in which they hold the genetic material of all the living things they come into contact with. Self and other thereby intermingle in a pleasurable, fascinated appreciation. Vegetarian and pacifist, their acquisition of life forms is an evolutionary need. They travel the galaxies, in their search for new life forms and their desire for compatibility with others. Unlike humans, they are not intolerant of difference, forming partnerships with a huge variety of different life forms and finding potential even in such rejected categories as cancer. Where humans see only the negative, ooloi value the cancerous cell's potential to regenerate. Infinitely accepting, and appreciative of difference, ooloi negate distinctions between us and them, not only by taking seeds of the other into their yashi, but also by neurally connecting with others. 'People who spend as much time as we do living inside one another's skins are very slow to kill' (p. 114).

Their society functions through consensus, not a hierarchy, and even though they are infinitely more advanced than the humans, they still respect the others' needs and wishes. For those who do not wish to remain and mate with them, they have created a separatist human colony on Mars. Ooloi influence by love and desire, rather than by force. 'Ooloi are dangerously easy to love. They absorb us and we don't mind' (p. 147).

The feminine economy of the body is argued by French feminist theorists such as Cixous[90] as one of accepting into one's body otherness, of mutual exploration. The feminine economy is pleasurably excessive, polyvalent and pluralised, disrupting the strict delineation and propriety of the masculine economy. Octavia Butler's invention of ooloi desire configures this feminist discourse of the body, and of pleasure as alien from the phallocentric economy, in the mutual interconnections with otherness:

> Jesusa grew pleasantly weary as I explored her.... Her greatest enjoyment would happen when I brought her together with Tomas and shared the pleasure of each of them with the other, mingling with it my own pleasure in them both. When I could make an ongoing loop of this, we would drown in one another. (p. 155)

Ooloi's body tentacles and sensory arms sink into the nervous systems of their human mates, who then, in a sensory loop feel their own stroking of the ooloi on their skin, feel the same pleasures they make it feel. Looped between its two mates, they feel in touch with each other through the ooloi. Separate being dissolves into a mutual pleasure where each one's skin becomes the experience of the other, and the distinctions and boundaries between participants cease to exist. Acknowledging the proprietorial mastery of masculine desire, Jodahs allows Tomas to experience himself as on top, as he lies beside it, but Jodahs' own pleasure is less appropriating and more about appreciation of the other:

> The smell-taste-feel of Jesusa, the rhythm of her heartbeat, the rush of her blood, the texture of her flesh, the easy, right, life-sustaining working of her organs, her cells, the smallest organelles within her cells – all this was a vast, infinitely absorbing complexity. (pp. 153–4)

Ooloi love life, all life is a treasure to them, and the desire to conjoin with others goes beyond a wish into a bodily need. Without mates, Jodahs' body begins to 'wander' towards dissolution, growing fur, then scales, then webbed feet. Once he finds Jesusa and Tomas, he stabilises and his body becomes like theirs, in order to attract them. Aor, unable to find mates, is shown to deteriorate into a huge slug, its body preparing to beak down even further and lose its individuality. The need for partners becomes a physical necessity of their very being. And, once mated, the partners are physically committed to each other. Neither humans nor the ooloi can bear to be long parted from each other, the ooloi substance Jodahs secretes into his mates when he 'goes into' them, ensures they become chemically addicted to him and unable to bear the touch of rival ooloi.

> ... what she felt now went beyond liking, beyond loving, into the deep biological attachment of adulthood. Literal, physical addiction to another person, Lilith called it. I couldn't think about it that coldly. For me it meant that soon Jesusa would not want to leave me ... (pp. 154–5)

The attachment is mutual, Jodahs is just as vulnerable to being apart from them as they are to him. Need and desire have become bodily necessities, as the mind–body distinction becomes a continuum and the newly embodied desires are described in physical terms as a 'hunger'. Butler envisions a closeness that goes beyond human experience, because more egalitarian and more communal than the usual feminist invocation of the pre-oedipal dyadic union of mother and baby. Mutually vulnerable to each of his four final mates, two human and two Oankali, Jodahs will maintain their health, give them a hundred years of life, and construct hybrid children from the mix of the four. When they die, it will die with them, literally unable to live without them. These mates are co-dependent on each other, in a symbiosis of need and pleasure and love, and in the difference, the alienness that is being celebrated.

> An ooloi is probably the strangest thing any Human will come into contact with. We need time alone with it to realize it's probably also the best thing. (p. 147)

Through the science fiction trope of the alien, Octavia Butler delineates a desire that in its pleasure, its closeness, and its mutual dependence and permanent bonding, far outstrips the male economy. *Imago* imagines a world where both difference and desire are uncircumscribed by the cultural norms of Western phallocentrism.

Notes

Introduction: Unleashing the Genres

1. See for example, Martin Priestman, *Detective Fiction and Literature: the Figure in the Carpet* (London: Macmillan, 1990) and Ian Ousby, *The Crime and Mystery Book: a Reader's Companion* (London: Thames and Hudson, 1997).
2. *Crime on Her Mind* (Harmondsworth: Penguin, 1975).
3. *The Lady Investigates: Women Detectives and Spies in Fiction* (Oxford: Oxford University Press, 1986).
4. Debate rages as to whether it was first published in 1861 or 1864.
5. Kathleen Gregory Klein, *The Woman Detective: Gender and Genre* (Urbana: University of Illinois, 1988), p. 7.
6. 'Tracking Down the Past: Women and Detective Fiction', in Helen Carr (ed.), *From My Guy to Sci Fi: Genre and Women's Writing in the Postmodern World* (London: Pandora, 1989).
7. *Silk Stalkings: When Women Write of Murder* (Berkeley: Black Lizard, 1988).
8. Ibid.
9. Ibid., p. 223.
10. Her later work has shifted position to argue for a more subversive potential, see Klein (ed.), *Woman Times Three: Writers, Detectives, Readers* (Bowling Green, Ohio: Bowling Green State University, 1995).
11. *Sisters in Crime: Feminism and the Crime Novel* (New York: Continuum, 1988).
12. 'Tracking Down the Past'.
13. *Woman Hating* (New York: Plume, 1974).
14. 'Folktale Liberation', *New York Review of Books*, 17 Dec 1970, 42–4.
15. *Loving with a Vengeance: Mass Produced Fantasies for Women* (Hamden, Connecticut: Archon, 1982).
16. 'Mills and Boon: Guilt without Sex', *Red Letters*, 14 (Winter), 5–13.
17. 'Mills and Boon *Temptations*: Sex and the Single Couple in the 1990s', in Lynne Pearce and Gina Wisker (eds), *Fatal Attractions: Rescripting Romance in Contemporary Literature and Film* (London: Pluto, 1998).
18. *The Romance Fiction of Mills and Boon 1909–1990s* (London: UCL, 1999).
19. *Feminist Fictions: Feminist Uses of Generic Fiction* (Cambridge: Polity, 1990).
20. 'The Lesbian Thriller and Detective Novel' in Elaine Hobby and Chris White (eds), *What Lesbians do in Books* (London: Women's Press, 1991).
21. *The Political Unconscious: Narrative as a Socially Symbolic Act* (London: Methuen, 1981).
22. See Daphne Watson, *Their Own Worst Enemies: Women Writers of Women's Fiction* (London: Pluto, 1995).

1. Feminism and Genre Fiction: the Preliminaries

1. Nicci Gerrard, *Into the Mainstream: How Feminism has Changed Women's Writing* (London: Pandora, 1989), p. 14.
2. 'The Problems of Being Popular', *New Socialist*, 41 (September 1986), 14–15 (p. 14).
3. She ridicules the July issue of *Marxism Today* for carrying 'an apparently serious article about how radical Fergie is compared to Princess Di'. Ibid., p. 14.
4. Ibid., p. 15.
5. 'Feminism and the Definition of Cultural Politics', in Rosalind Brunt and Caroline Rowan (eds), *Feminism, Culture, and Politics* (London: Lawrence and Wishart, 1982), pp. 37–58. The paper was based on a talk given in 1980.
6. Ibid., p. 55.
7. Ibid., p. 58.
8. Jean Radford (ed.), *The Progress of Romance: the Politics of Popular Romance* (London: Routledge, 1986), pp. 12–13.
9. (London: Polity Press, 1990).
10. Ibid., p. 2.
11. Peter H. Mann, 'The Romantic Novel and its Readers', *Journal of Popular Culture*, 5 (Summer 1981), 9–18 (p. 10).
12. Nicci Gerrard, *Into the Mainstream*, p. 22.
13. See Merja Makinen, 'Angela Carter's *The Bloody Chamber* and the Decolonization of Feminine Sexuality', *Feminist Review*, 42 (Autumn 1992), 2–15 (p. 7).
14. Peter Mann, 'The Romantic Novel and its Readers', p. 11.
15. *Into the Mainstream: How Feminism has Changed Women's Writing* (London: Pandora, 1989), p. 2.
16. 'The Romantic Novel and its Readers', p. 10.
17. In *Movies and Methods* vol. 2, ed. Bill Nichols (Berkeley: University of California, 1985), pp. 220–32.
18. *Reading the Romance*, p. 61.
19. *Star Gazing: Hollywood Cinema and Female Spectatorship* (London: Routledge, 1994).
20. Ibid., p. 121.
21. Ien Ang, *Watching Dallas: Soap Opera and the Melodramatic Imagination*, translated by Della Couling (London: Methuen, 1985).
22. Ibid., p. 132.
23. Clive Bloom, *Cult Fiction: Popular Reading and Pulp Theory* (London: Macmillan, 1996) p. 129.
24. Ibid., pp. 128–9.
25. As opposed to the reading of it, which elsewhere is seen as 'an anarchic edge on the margin of bourgeois propriety', p. 16.
26. 'The Romantic Novel and its Readers', p. 10.
27. Paper 7, Birmingham Centre for Contemporary Cultural Studies, 1973.
28. 'Pleasurable Negotiations', in Deirdre Pribram (ed.), *Female Spectators: Looking at Films and Television* (London: Verso, 1988).
29. Elizabeth A. Flynn, 'Gender and Reading', in Elizabeth A. Flynn and Patrocinio P. Schweickart (eds), *Gender and Readings: Essays on Readers, Texts*

and Contexts (Baltimore: Johns Hopkins, 1986), pp. 267–88.

30. Ibid., p. 268.
31. Ibid.
32. *Cult Fiction*, p. 130.
33. *Murder by the Book?*, p. 199.
34. *The Alienated Reader: Women and Romantic Literature in the Twentieth Century* (London: Harvester, 1991), p. 143.
35. Sharon Salvator's 1979 *Bitter Eden* was judged to have too complex a plot, to have extraneous political material, and to end unhappily, with the hero's death. *Reading the Romance*, pp. 160–2.
36. *Reading the Romance*, p. 214.
37. At the *Reading and Pleasure: Gender and Popular Literature* conference, 17 April 1999, at the Roehampton Institute, London. I am indebted to McAuley's paper for also pointing me to the Elizabeth Flynn article.
38. *Star Gazing*, p. 47.
39. Ibid., p. 15.
40. 'Angela Carter's *The Bloody Chamber* and the Decolonisation of Feminine Sexuality', pp. 5–6.
41. Philip Schlesinger, Russell Dobash and Kathy Weaver, *Women Viewing Violence* (London: British Film Institute, 1992).
42. *The Alienated Reader*.
43. It would need a sociological study far outside the scope of this book to be able to discuss the varieties of response from both feminist and non-feminist readers to the various genre texts I discuss.
44. (Hamden, Connecticut: Archon, 1982).
45. Ibid., p. 22.
46. Ibid., p. 36.
47. (New York: Plume, 1974).
48. 'Magical Narratives: On the Dialectical Use of Genre Criticism', Chapter 2, *The Political Unconscious* (London: Methuen, 1981).
49. Ibid., p. 106.
50. Ibid., p. 115.
51. Ibid., p. 133.
52. Ibid., pp. 140–1.
53. William Morris' *News from Nowhere* and Samuel Butler's *Erewhon*.
54. *Feminist Fiction*, p. 193.
55. (London: Unwin, 1989).
56. Sara Mills et al. (Hemel Hempstead: Harvester, 1989).
57. Edited by Sara Mills and Lynne Pearce (New York: Prentice Hall, 1996).
58. Chapter 1 of Mary Eagleton's *Feminist Literary Criticism* (London: Methuen, 1991), pp. 24–52, contains the essays by Showalter and Toril Moi which exemplify the polemical divide. Quote, p. 51.
59. Ibid., p. 2.
60. Lynne Pearce and Gina Wisker (eds), *Fatal Attractions: Rescripting Romance in Contemporary Literature and Film* (London: Pluto, 1998), p. 1.
61. (Cambridge, Mass: Harvard University Press, 1998).
62. Ibid., p. 3.
63. Ibid., p. 2.
64. Op. cit., p. 280.

2. The Romance

1. Rachel Anderson, *The Purple Heart Throbs: the Sub-literature of Love* (London: Hodder and Stoughton, 1974), Chapter 2.
2. This is not to deny that the Brontës and Austen also sold well, but to argue a structural difference in the narratives of literary novels and popular romance novels.
3. *Reading the Romance: Women, Patriarchy, and Popular Literature* (Chapel Hill: University of North Carolina, 1991), p. 64.
4. Anderson, p. 103.
5. Anderson, p. 140.
6. Quoted in Anderson, p. 141.
7. Jay Dixon, *The Romance Fiction of Mills and Boon 1909–1990s* (London: UCL, 1999), pp. 13–14.
8. Dixon, p. 58.
9. Ibid., p. 67.
10. Anderson, p. 208.
11. Anderson, p. 223.
12. Mariam Darce Frenier, *Goodbye Heathcliffe: Changing Heroes, Heroines, Roles and Values in Women's Category Romances* (New York: Greenwood, 1988), p. 28. Nancy Friday's *My Secret Garden: Women's Sexual Fantasies* was published by Pocket Books in 1973, and turned on its head the idea that women did not fantasise about sex.
13. Radway, pp. 39–41.
14. 'Heartbreak Comes to Harlequin', *Forbes*, 29 March 1982, 50–1 (p. 50).
15. Nickianne Moody, 'Mills and Boon's *Temptations*: Sex and the Single Couple in the 1990s', in Lynne Pearce and Gina Wisker (eds), *Fatal Attractions: Rescripting Romance in Contemporary Literature and Film* (London: Pluto, 1998), pp. 141–56 (p. 145).
16. Moody, p. 149.
17. 'Mills and Boon Meets Feminism', in Jean Radford (ed.), *The Progress of the Romance: the Politics of Popular Fiction* (London: Routledge, 1986), pp. 195–218.
18. Ibid., p. 204, p. 211.
19. 'For the Love of It: Women Writers and Popular Romance', unpublished PhD, University of Pennsylvania, 1984. Cited in Janice Radway, p. 16.
20. First published in London by MacGibbon & Kee, 1970. Future reference will be to the Paladin edition, London 1971.
21. *Sexual Politics* (New York: Ballantine, 1969).
22. *The Dialectic of Sex* (New York: Morrow, 1970).
23. Ibid., p. 180.
24. Anderson, p. 239.
25. *Red Letters*, 14 (Winter 1982–3), 5–13.
26. In Ann Snitow, Christine Stansell and Sharon Thompson (eds), *Desire: the Politics of Sexuality* (London: Virago, 1983), pp. 258–75. An earlier version had been published in 1979, *Radical History Review*, 20 (Spring–Summer, 1979), 141–68, but as an intervention its effect stems from the later, more widely circulated publication.
27. Ibid., p. 260.

28. (Chapel Hill: University of North Carolina, 1984/91).
29. 1991 edition, p. 73.
30. Ibid., p. 75.
31. Nancy Chodorow, *The Reproduction of Mothering: Psychoanalysis and the Sociology of Gender* (Berkeley: University of California, 1978).
32. Ibid., p. 13.
33. (Westpoint, Conn: Greenwood, 1984).
34. Ibid., p. 4.
35. *Feminist Review*, 16 (April 1984), 7–25.
36. Ibid., p. 23.
37. Ibid., p. 22.
38. Ibid., p. 13.
39. (London: Methuen, 1985).
40. Chapter 7, 'Some Women Reading', pp. 140–54, which argues women use romance in a complex, multilayered fashion.
41. Chapter 5, 'Gender and Genre: Women's Stories', pp. 86–105 (p. 104).
42. 'Marketing Moonshine', *Women's Review*, 2 (December 1985), 16–17.
43. (London: Routledge, 1986).
44. 'An Inverted Romance: *The Well of Loneliness* and Sexual Ideology', pp. 97–111.
45. 'Write, She Said', pp. 221–35.
46. (Chicago: University of Illinois, 1987).
47. Ibid., p. 86.
48. *Women's Review*, 21 (July 1987), 18–19.
49. In Susannah Radstone (ed.), *Sweet Dreams: Sexuality, Gender and Popular Fiction* (London: Lawrence and Wishart, 1988), pp. 73–90.
50. Ibid., p. 75.
51. Mariam Darce Frenier (New York: Greenwood, 1988).
52. Ed. Helen Carr (London: Pandora, 1989), pp. 58–77.
53. (London: Virago, 1991).
54. (Cambridge: Polity, 1990).
55. Chapter 6, pp. 177–92.
56. Ibid., p. 192.
57. (London: Harvester, 1991).
58. Ibid., p. 175.
59. (London: Pluto, 1995).
60. Chapter 4, 'Two for the Price of One: the Novels of Mills and Boon', pp. 75–94.
61. Ibid., p. 9. The collection arises from a conference of the same name, held at Lancaster University two years before.
62. Ibid., p. 34.
63. See especially Stevi Jackson, 'Women and Heterosexual Love: Complicity, Resistance and Change', pp. 49–62; Bridget Fowler, 'Literature Beyond Modernism: Middlebrow and Popular Romance', pp. 89–99.
64. Ed. Lynne Pearce and Gina Wisker (London: Pluto, 1998).
65. (London: UCL Press, 1999).
66. Ibid., p. 195.
67. Cranny-Francis, chapter 6, 'Feminist Romance', pp. 177–92.
68. 'Romantic Readers', p. 62.

69. *Reading the Romance*, p. 64.
70. Publishers such as Fawcett-Crest, Mildwood Towers, Beacon-Signal and Macfadden-Bartell.
71. 'What Has Never Been: an Overview of Lesbian Feminist Literary Criticism', in Gayle Green and Coppelia Khan (eds), *Making a Difference: Feminist Literary Criticism* (London: Methuen, 1985), pp. 177–210.
72. *This Sex Which Is Not One*, trans. Catherine Porter and Carolyn Burke (Ithaca, New York: Cornell University, 1985).
73. 'Rescripting Romance: an Introduction', in *Fatal Attractions*, pp. 1–19 (p. 2).
74. In *Fatal Attractions*, pp. 189–204.
75. Ibid., p. 196.
76. *Deal of a Lifetime*, in the 'Duet' series, 1995.
77. 'There are still no black heroines or heroes in Mills and Boon novels.... There seems to be an in-built resistance to black heroes both at Mills and Boon offices and among their authors', Dixon, *The Romance Fiction of Mills and Boon 1909–1990s*, p. 53.
78. *Tempt Me Not*, 1991, for example, fits the more usual stereotypes in having a sexually naive, domestic and uneducated woman win the virile, intellectual and successful businessman and playboy. Napier is still twisting the genre format, in having the woman secretly married to a dying man, but not in relation to feminism.
79. (London: Pandora, 1986).
80. The two stories by Rebecca Brown, Sara Maitland's, Bobbie Ann Mason's and Fay Weldon's.
81. Ibid., pp. 21–34.
82. Ibid., pp. 106–16.
83. Ibid., pp. 143–68.
84. (Tallahassee, Florida: Naiad, 1995).
85. There are positive characterisations of black and Chinese lesbians, and the trip to the San Diego missionaries includes a discussion of the atrocities done to the Native Americans.

3. The Fairy Tale

1. Charles Dickens' *The Cricket in the Hearth* in the nineteenth century, George MacDonald's books such as *The Princess and the Goblin* and *The Princess and the Curdie* and the works of E. Nesbit in the early twentieth century, and a whole plethora of fantasy writers in the later twentieth century, such as Jane Yolen's *Briar Rose*.
2. *Fairy Tales and the Art of Subversion* (New York: Routledge, 1983), pp. 25–9. The argument is further developed in his *The Trials and Tribulations of Little Red Riding Hood* (London: Heinemann, 1982).
3. *Le Conte Populaire Français*, Vol. 1 (Paris: Erasme, 1957) pp. 373–4. A translation can be found in *Trials and Tribulations of Little Red Riding Hood*, pp. 21–2.
4. 'Grand-mères, sie vous saviez: le Petit Chaperon Rouge dans la tradition orale', *Cahiers de Littérature Orale*, 4 (1978), 17–55.
5. (Frankfurt: Syndikat, 1978).

6. p. 30. The translation is Zipes'.
7. (London: Arnold, 1996).
8. Ibid., p. 8.
9. *From the Beast to the Blonde: On Fairytales and their Tellers* (London: Chatto, 1994), p. 133.
10. Ruth B Bottigheimer, *Grimms' Bad Girls and Bold Boys: the Moral and Social Vision of the Tales* (New Haven: Yale University Press, 1987), pp. 1–2.
11. *From the Beast to the Blonde*, p. 17.
12. Jack Zipes, *Fairy Tales and the Art of Subversion*, p. 21.
13. Ibid., p. 10.
14. The translation is Angela Carter's, from *The Fairy Tales of Charles Perrault*, translated with a foreword by Angela Carter, illustrated by Martin Ware (London: Gollancz, 1977), p. 71.
15. See Karen E. Rowe, 'To Spin a Yarn: the Female Voice in Folklore and Fairy Tale', in Ruth B. Bottinger (ed.), *Fairy Tales and Society: Illusion, Allusion and Paradigm* (Philadelphia: University of Pennsylvania, 1986), pp. 53–74; Marina Warner, *From the Beast to the Blonde*, p. 19.
16. See Maria Tatar's *The Hard Facts of the Grimms' Fairy Tales* (Princeton, New Jersey: Princeton University Press, 1987) which documents how through their revisions the Grimms altered the tales to include more social acceptance and more creative fantasy.
17. Op. cit., 2nd edition, p. 34.
18. It should be acknowledged that there are a number of disrobings in the Grimms' tales, but these tend to be less child-orientated. Ones which were, like 'The Frog King', have had the more erotic elements gradually erased during Wilhelm's re-editing. See *Grimms' Bad Girls and Bold Boys*, pp. 160–1.
19. I am using the two translations in *The Trials and Tribulations of Little Red Riding Hood* for this comparison.
20. *Grimms' Bad Girls and Bold Boys*, p. 21.
21. Warner, *From the Beast to the Blonde*, p. 20.
22. 'Folktale Liberation', *New York Review of Books*, 11 (17 Dec 1970), 42–4.
23. Zipes, in *Fairy Tales and the Art of Subversion*, discusses even more conscious attempts to utilise the form to create socialist normative principles, in Germany during the 1920s and 1930s, a more conscious harnessing of ideology and discourse. See chapter 6, 'The Fight over Fairy-Tale Discourse: Family, Friction, and Socialization in the Weimar Republic and Nazi Germany', pp. 134–69.
24. 'Folktale Liberation', reprinted in Alison Lurie, *Don't Tell the Grown-Ups: Subversive Children's Literature* (London: Bloomsbury, 1990), Chapter 2, pp. 16–28 (p. 16).
25. Feminist social critics such as Simone de Beauvoir's *The Second Sex* (1953), Betty Freidan's *The Feminine Mystique* (1963), and Kate Millet's *Sexual Politics* (1970), use fairy tale protagonists such as Cinderella and Snow White in passing as archetypes for patriarchal role models of passive femininity.
26. Op. cit., p. 19.
27. *College English*, 34 (1972), 383–95. Reprinted in Zipes, *Don't Bet on the Prince* (Aldershot: Gower, 1986), pp. 185–200.
28. (New York: Plume, 1974).

29. *Woman-hating*, pp. 47–8.
30. Ibid., p. 48.
31. (New Jersey: Guttenberg, 1973).
32. 'Things Walt Disney Never Told Us' in Claire R. Farrer (ed.), *Women and Folklore* (Austin: University of Texas Press, 1975), pp. 42–50.
33. In Elizabeth Grugeon and Peter Walden (eds), *Literature and Learning* (Milton Keynes: Open University Press, 1978), pp. 42–58.
34. Ibid., p. 51.
35. Bruno Bettelheim, *The Uses of Enchantment: the Meaning and Importance of Fairy Tales* (Harmondsworth: Penguin, 1978), argues that fairy tales present psychoanalytic fables of conflict and maturation, in a rather fixed Freudian analysis.
36. (New Haven: Yale University Press, 1979).
37. *Women's Studies*, 6 (1979), 237–57. Reprinted in Zipes, *Don't Bet on the Prince*, pp. 209–26.
38. See Kay F. Stone, 'Feminist Approaches to the Interpretation of Fairy Tales', in Ruth Bottinger (ed.), *Fairy Tales and Society*, pp. 229–36.
39. (New York: Dutton, 1981).
40. (Toronto: Inner City Books, 1981).
41. (Albuquerque: University of New Mexico Press, 1982).
42. (San Francisco: Harper, 1983).
43. (London: Bloomsbury, 1990).
44. *Signs*, 15 (3) Spring, 1990. Reprinted in Jean Barr, Deborah Pope and Mary Wyer (eds), *Ties that Bind: Essays on Mothering and Patriarchy* (Chicago: University of Chicago Press, 1990), pp. 253–72. All quotations are taken from the reprint.
45. Op. cit., p. 21.
46. Ibid., pp. xviii–xix.
47. Ibid., p. 238.
48. *Don't Bet on the Prince*, pp. 14, 32–3.
49. For more on Joanna Russ see my Chapter 5.
50. (New York: Tom Doherty Associates, 1992).
51. (New York: Philomel, 1981).
52. *Touch Magic*, pp. 38–9.
53. (London: Dent, 1977). All page references for quotations will be given in the body of the text.
54. Shulamith is an uncommon enough name to link it to Shulamith Firestone, the feminist theoretician arguing for stronger women role models in literature in *The Dialectic of Sex: the Case for a Feminist Revolution* (New York: Morrow, 1970). See Chapter 5 for a more detailed discussion of Firestone's influence on science fiction writers. Dale refers to Dale Spender, and Nancy could be one of a number of feminist theorists.
55. (Dublin: Attic Press, 1989). All page references for quotations wil be given in the body of the text.
56. *The Poetics of Postmodernism: History, Theory, Fiction* (London: Routledge, 1988), p. 126.
57. Ibid., p. 26.
58. Marina Warner, 'Preface', *The Second Virago Book of Fairy Tales* (London: Virago, 1992), p. xiii.

59. Translated with a foreword by Angela Carter and illustrated by Martin Ware (London: Gollancz, 1977). These translations were expanded to include two stories by Madame Le Prince de Beaumont, in *Sleeping Beauty and Other Fairy Tales*, with a new foreword and illustrated by Michael Foreman (London: Gollancz, 1982).
60. Foreword, p. 17 for all quotes.
61. Ibid., p. 18.
62 Ibid., p. 19.
63. (London: Virago, 1991).
64. Ibid., p. xi.
65. Ibid., p. xii.
66. Ibid., p. ix.
67. Ibid., p. xvii.
68. First published by Gollancz in 1979. Future page references will be to the Penguin edition (Harmondsworth: Penguin, 1981).
69. 'Pornography, Fairy Tales and Feminism', in John Foot (ed.), *Forbidden History* (Chicago: Chicago University, 1992), pp. 335–59 (p. 347).
70. See Patricia Duncker, 'Re-imagining the Fairy Tales: Angela Carter's Bloody Chambers', *Literature and History*, 10 (1984), 3–14, reprinted in Peter Widdowson and Peter Humm (eds), *Popular Fictions* (London: Methuen, 1986), pp. 222–36; Robert Clark, 'Angela Carter's Desire Machine', *Women's Studies*, 14 (1987), 147–61; Avis Lewellyn, 'Wayward Girls but Wicked Women? Female Sexuality in Angela Carter's *The Bloody Chamber*', in Clive Bloom and Gary Day (eds), *Perspectives on Pornography* (Basingstoke: Macmillan, 1988), pp. 145–59.
71. See, Merja Makinen, 'Angela Carter and the Decolonisation of Feminine Sexuality', *Feminist Review*, 14 (1992), 2–15; Robin Ann Sheets, 'Pornography, Fairy Tales and Feminism: Angela Carter's *The Bloody Chamber*', in John C Fout (ed.), *Forbidden History* (Chicago: University of Chicago Press, 1990/92), pp. 335–59; Margaret Atwood, 'Running with the Tigers' in Lorna Sage (ed.), *Flesh and the Mirror: Essays on the Art of Angela Carter* (London: Virago, 1994), pp. 117–35.
72. Joseph Bristow and Trev Lynn Broughton (eds), *The Infernal Desires of Angela Carter* (London: Longman, 1997), p. 4.
73. Angela Carter, 'Notes from the Frontline', in Michelene Wandor (ed.), *On Gender and Writing* (London: Pandora, 1983), pp. 69–77 (p. 70).
74. See the 'Polemical Preface' to her *The Sadeian Woman* (London: Virago, 1979).
75. 'The Company of Wolves' and 'The Lady of the House of Love' respectively.
76. 'Is the Gaze Male?', in Ann Snitow, Christine Stansell and Sharon Thompson (eds), *Powers of Desire: the Politics of Sexuality* (New York: Monthly Review Press, 1983), pp. 309–27 (pp. 315–16).
77. Ibid., p. 324.
78. 'fairytale families are, in the main, dysfunctional units in which parents and step-parents are neglectful to the point of murder ...' *Virago Book of Fairytales*, p. xix.
79. 'Embodying the Negated: Contemporary Images of the Female Erotic', in Sarah Sceats and Gail Cunningham (eds), *Image and Power: Women in Fiction in the Twentieth Century* (London: Longman, 1996), pp. 41–50.
80. Lynn Segal, 'Sweet Sorrows, Painful Pleasures: Pornography and the Perils

of Heterosexual Desire' in Lynne Segal and Mary McIntosh (eds), *Sex Exposed: Sexuality and the Pornography Debate* (London: Virago, 1992), p. 79. For a more detailed discussion of this aspect of Carter's work, see Sally Keenan, 'Angela Carter's *The Sadeian Woman*: Feminism as Treason', in Bristow and Broughton, *The Infernal Desires of Angela Carter*, pp. 132–48.

81. See Patricia Duncker, 'Queer Gothic: Angela Carter and the Lost Narratives of Sexual Subversion', *Critical Survey*, 8 (1996), 58–68, and Paulina Palmer, 'From Coded Mannequin to Bird Woman: Angela Carter's Magic Flight', in Sue Roe (ed.), *Women Reading Women's Writing* (London: Harvester, 1987), pp. 179–205.

4. Detective Fiction

1. *Crime on Her Mind: Fifteen Stories of Female Sleuths from the Victorian Era to the Forties* (Harmondsworth: Penguin, 1975).

2. *The Lady Investigates: Women Detectives and Spies in Fiction* (Oxford: Oxford University Press, 1986).

3. See Queenie Leavis, *Fiction and the Reading Public* (London: Chatto, 1932) who makes value judgements between the readerships of romance and detective fiction, based on class and gender.

4. Again, particularly in the 'Golden Age' tradition: literary academics, J. I. M. Stewart (Michael Innes) and Christopher Caudwell; C. J. Masterman the intelligence expert; the Fabian social thinkers, the Coles; the poet C. Day Lewis; and the composer Robert Bruce Montgomery (Edmund Crispin) were some of the more well-known ones. Indeed Ronald Knox, who set up the 'Decalogue' in 1929 and wrote detective fiction was a fellow of Balliol and researcher on the Bible.

5. Stephen Knight, 'Radical Thrillers', in Ian A. Bell and Graham Daldry (eds), *Watching the Detectives: Essays on Crime Fiction* (London: Macmillan, 1990), pp. 172–87.

6. 'Tracking Down the Past: Women and Detective Fiction', in *From My Guy to Sci Fi*, pp. 39–57 (p. 54).

7. They go on to argue a consideration of texts rather than authors, so that the Agatha Christie of *Murder on the Orient Express*, or *The Murder of Roger Ackroyd* can be seen as more fluid and subversive of the form than other Christie texts. Ibid., p. 44.

8. *The Crime and Mystery Book: a Reader's Companion* (London: Thames and Hudson, 1997), p. 15.

9. *The Lady Investigates*, p. 39.

10. No women worked for the Metropolitan police force until 1883, when two women warders were employed for the female prisoners, and in 1905 a 'police matron' took on the role of both wardress and social worker. *Crime on Her Mind*, p. 16. The Metropolitan police were set up by Robert Peel in 1829, and a detective department was set up in the early 1840s. *Crime and Mystery Book*, p. 20.

11. There has been much discussion about whether Mrs Paschal was originally published in 1861 or 1864. Ellery Queen argued that it was really published in 1864, after Forrester's woman detective. Michelle Slung reports the debate but does not take sides, Ian Ousby accepts Queen's argument as

proven, but Craig and Cadogan state that the British Library date stamp on the book confirms that the book was published in 1861, but acknowledge that the BL's catalogue entry is confusing.

12. Cheap editions published for railway bookstalls.
13. 'Radical Thrillers', p. 174.
14. *Murder on Her Mind*, p. 19.
15. *Murder on Her Mind*, p. 19.
16. Martin Priestman, *Detective Fiction and Literature*, p. 78.
17. 'Radical Thrillers', p. 175.
18. *Detective Fiction and Literature*, p. 203.
19. The Decalogue eschewed undiscovered poisons or equivalent appliances, supernatural agencies, Chinamen, or doubles. The detective must declare all his clues and find nothing by accident, nor may he be the criminal. Only one secret room is allowed and the criminal must have been introduced at the start. Cited in Ousby, p. 67. Knox wrote *Viaduct Murder* (1925) and *The Footsteps at the Locke* (1928).
20. *Crime on Her Mind*, p. 23.
21. Kathleen Gregory Klein, *The Woman Detective* (Urbana, Illinois; University of Illinois, 1988), p. 7.
22. Cadogan and Semple, p. 168.
23. Ousby, p. 99.
24. (Penguin: Harmondsworth, 1975).
25. Ibid., p. 14.
26. (Bowling Green, Ohio: Bowling Green, 1981).
27. (Westport, Connecticut: Greenwood, 1994).
28. 5 (Spring–Summer, 1984), 101–14.
29. 6 (Fall/Winter 1985), 85–98.
30. *Clues*, 6 (Spring-Summer, 1985), 2–14. Updated in Glenwood Irons (ed.), *Feminism in Women's Detective Fiction* (1995), pp. 94–111.
31. (Oxford: Oxford University Press, 1986).
32. Ibid., p. 246.
33. *Women's Review*, 8 (June 1986), 18–19.
34. Containing B. J. Rahn arguing for Seeley Register being the first woman detective; Michelle Slung arguing a feminist appreciation of Christie; and Marilyn Stasio discussing her role as a reviewer of detective fiction to bring less known women exponents to notice. See the following footnote.
35. Barbara A. Rader and Howard G. Zettler (eds) (Westport, Connecticut: Greenwood, 1988).
36. (Urbana, Illinois: University of Illinois, 1988).
37. Ibid., p. 225.
38. (New York: Continuum, 1988).
39. Ibid., p. 2.
40. Susannah Radstone (ed.), *Sweet Dreams: Sexuality, Gender and Popular Fiction* (London: Lawrence and Wishart, 1988), pp. 91–120.
41. Ibid., p. 93.
42. Sally Munt, *Murder By the Book*, p. 7.
43. Ed. Helen Carr, *From My Guy to Sci Fi*, pp. 39–57.
44. In Clive Bloom (ed.), *20thC Suspense: the Thriller Comes of Age* (London: Macmillan, 1990), pp. 237–54.

45. In Ronald G. Walker and June M. Frazer (eds), *The Cunning Craft: Original Essays on Detective Fiction and Contemporary Literary Theory* (Macomb, Illinois: Western Illinois University, 1990), pp. 174–87.
46. In Ian Bell and Graham Daldry (eds), *Watching the Detectives: Essays on Crime Fiction* (London: Macmillan, 1990), pp. 48–67.
47. *Feminist Fiction*, pp. 143–76.
48. Ibid., p. 174.
49. (London: Routledge, 1991).
50. Their argument that the sensational, action-packed plot is a further 'ideology' of hard-boiled fiction, and the fair-play puzzle, the 'ideology' of the Golden Age (p. 10) illustrates that at times they mistake ideology for narrative format. This poor grasp allows for the conclusion that Miss Marple and lesbian detectives are similarly marginal to society.
51. In Elaine Hobby and Chris White (eds), *What Lesbians Do in Books* (London: Women's Press, 1991), pp. 9–27.
52. In Lawrence Grossberg, Cary Nelson and Paula Treichler (eds), *Cultural Studies* (London: Routledge, 1992), pp. 213–26. The essay is one of the proceedings of a conference held at the University of Illinois in 1990.
53. (London: Routledge, 1994).
54. Ibid., p. 200.
55. She notes, however, that mainstream detective fiction increasingly carries a feminist message but still sees the sub-genre as in decline, since she does not make the connection that writers from the feminist presses are now published by mainstream publishers. By the 1990s, lesbian writers such as Katherine V. Forrest, Mary Wings, J. M. Redman and Phyllis Knight were all with mainstream publishers. Cited in Walton and Jones, *Detective Agency*, p. 39.
56. (Bowling Green, Ohio: Bowling Green, 1995).
57. Ibid., Margaret Kinsman, 'A Question of Visibility: Paretsky and Chicago', pp. 15–27.
58. Ibid., Mary Jean DeMarr, 'Joan Hess? Joan Hadley', pp. 29–41.
59. Ibid., pp. 143–61.
60. Ibid., pp. 171–90.
61. (London: Pluto, 1997).
62. pp. 62–86.
63. Ibid., pp. 87–110.
64. Ibid., pp. 111–26.
65. Ibid., p. 123.
66. (Berkeley, California: University of California Press, 1999).
67. See 'P. D. James' Stylish Crime', interview with Helen Birch, *Woman's Review*, 10 (August 1986), 6–7.
68. Victoria Nichols and Susan Thompson (eds) (Berkeley: Black Lizard, 1988).
69. (Langham, Md: Scarecrow Press, 1998).
70. *Detective Agency*, p. 24.
71. Ibid., p. 27.
72. Ibid., p. 40.
73. Ibid., p. 40.
74. In this text Warshawski is 37, and so able to voice a mature sexuality beyond the ideal feminine eligibility, but this still places her in the dominant earning-constituency.

75. (London: Women's Press, 1987).
76. Though the upper class is stereotyped, the Weatherspoon's servant is not. Speaking seven languages, independent and sassy, and finally felling the murderer holding everyone else at gun-point, she is the very opposite of the conventional sycophantic, servant ciphers of Christie and Doyle onwards.
77. (Seattle: Seal Press, 1990).
78. Her second appearance, *Troubles in Transylvania* (1993).
79. 'Policing the Margins: Barbara Wilson's *Gaudi Afternoon* and *Troubles in Transylvania*' in Peter Messant (ed.), *Criminal Proceedings* (London: Pluto, 1997), pp. 111–26 (p. 123).
80. Cover of *Gaudi Afternoon*.

5. Science Fiction

1. British and American publication of each of the works following a couple of years later.
2. *Science Fiction in the Twentieth Century* (Oxford: Oxford University Press), p. 20.
3. 'Science Fiction by Women in the Early Pulps, 1926–1930', in Jane L. Donawerth and Carol A. Kolmerten (eds), *Utopian and Science Fiction by Women* (Liverpool and Syracuse: Liverpool University and Syracuse University, 1994), pp. 137–52.
4. *Science Fiction in the Twentieth Century*, p. 57.
5. *Women of Wonder* (Harmondsworth: Penguin, 1978), 'Introduction: Women in Science Fiction', pp. 11–51.
6. (New York: Morrow, 1971). My references are from the Women's Press edition of 1979.
7. Ibid., p. 211.
8. *In the Chinks of the World Machine: Feminism and Science Fiction* (London: Women's Press, 1988), p. 59.
9. *Picnic on Paradise* (1968) and *And Chaos Died* (1970).
10. Initially printed in *Red Clay Reader*, reprinted in *Images of Women in Fiction: Feminist Perspectives* (Bowling Green: Bowling Green University, 1972), pp. 79–94.
11. Ibid., p. 91.
12. Ibid., pp. 3–20.
13. 14 (December 1972), 49–58; reprinted in Thomas Clareson (ed.), *Many Futures, Many Worlds: Theme and Form in Science Fiction* (Kent State University, 1977), pp. 140–63.
14. (New York: Vintage, 1974). Issued in England by Penguin in 1978.
15. (New York: Vintage, 1976). Published in Britain by Penguin in 1979.
16. (Nov 1975). Reprinted in Susan Wood (ed.), *The Language of the Night: Essays on Fantasy and Science Fiction*, 2nd edn revised by Ursula LeGuin (London: Women's Press, 1989), pp. 83–5.
17. (New York: Fawcett, 1976). Reprinted in *The Language of the Night*, revised edn, pp. 135–47.
18. *The Language of the Night*, 'Is Gender Necessary? Redux', pp. 135–47.
19. See the 1975 'SF and Mrs Brown'. Reprinted in *The Language of the Night*, pp. 86–102.

20. *Frontiers* (Fall 1977) pp. 50–61.
21. *Science Fiction Studies*, 5 (July, 1978), p. 144.
22. *Frontiers*, 4 (1979). Revised and reprinted as 'Kin With Each Other: Speculative Consciousness and Collective Protagonists' in *Writing Beyond the Ending: Narrative Strategies of Twentieth-Century Women Writers* (Bloomington: Indiana University, 1985).
23. *Science Fiction Studies*, 7 (March, 1980), 1. The next issue shows a discomfort even by one of the contributors, when Linda Leith distanced herself from Russ and Gubar's 'disdain of men', 7 (July, 1980), p. 234.
24. Ibid., pp. 2–15.
25. Ibid., pp. 16–27.
26. (Bowling Green: Bowling Green State University, 1981).
27. Ibid., pp. 63–70.
28. Ibid., pp. 71–85.
29. Ibid., pp. 103–8.
30. 9 (1982), 241–62.
31. (Ann Arbor, Michigan: University Research Press, 1982/84).
32. (Lanham: University Press of America, 1983).
33. 'Beyond Defensiveness: Feminist Research Strategies', ibid., pp. 148–69.
34. Carol Farley Kessler (ed.), *Daring to Dream* (Boston and London: Pandora, 1984).
35. 80 (1985) 65–107.
36. (London: Methuen, 1986).
37. (Westport, Connecticut: Greenwood, 1986).
38. *Foundation*, 35 (1986), 48–50.
39. Ibid., vol. 14, 81–194.
40. Ibid., 81–90.
41. Annette Keinhorst, 'Emancipatory Projection: an Introduction to Women's Critical Utopias', 91–9; Hoda Zaki's 'Utopia and Ideology in *Daughters of a Coral Dawn* and Contemporary Feminist Utopias', 119–33.
42. Anegeret J. Weimer, 'Foreign l(anguish), mother tongue: Concepts of Language in Contemporary Science Fiction', 163–73; Suzette Haden Elgin, 'Women's Language and Near Future Science Fiction: a Reply', 175–81; Cheris Kramarae, 'Present Problems with the Language of the Future', 183–6.
43. 'Feminist Fabulation; or Playing with Patriarchy vs. the Masculinization of Metafiction', 187–91.
44. (Westport, Connecticut: Greenwood, 1987).
45. (London: Women's Press, 1988).
46. *Foundation*, 43 (Summer, 1988). Brian Stableford, 'A Few More Crocodile Tears?', 63–72. Sarah Lefanu, 'Engaging the Reader', 72–4; Jenny Wolmark, 'There's More to Life than Crocodile Tears', 74–5; Gwyneth Jones, 'The Walrus is Brian', 75–6; Colin Greenland, 'An Interest in Carpentry', 76–7.
47. *Science Fiction Studies* 15 (November 1988), 282–94.
48. (Pandora: 1989) pp. 78–97.
49. Ibid., p. 88.
50. (Lincoln: University of Nebraska, 1989).
51. (Knoxville: University of Tennessee, 1990).
52. (New York: Routledge, 1991).

53. 'Utopian Feminism, Skeptical Feminism, and Narrative Energy', Ibid., pp. 34–49.
54. 'Gilman, Bradley and Piercy, and the Evolving Rhetoric of Feminist Utopias', ibid, pp. 116–29.
55. 'Women's Utopias: New Worlds, New Texts', ibid., pp. 130–40.
56. 'The Great Divorce: Fictions of Feminist Desire', ibid., pp. 85–99.
57. 'Response: What Happened to History?', ibid., pp. 191–200.
58. (London: Routledge, 1991).
59. Ibid., pp. 1–12.
60. Ibid., p. 3.
61. 'Mary and the Monster', ibid., pp. 85–95.
62. 'Pets and Monsters: Metamorphosis in Recent Science Fiction', ibid., pp. 97–108.
63. 'Your Word is My Command: the Structures of Language and Power in Women's Science Fiction', ibid., pp. 123–38.
64. Ibid., pp. 178–85.
65. 'Goodbye to All That ...', ibid., pp. 204–17.
66. (Iowa: University of Iowa, 1992).
67. (Chapel Hill: University of North Carolina, 1993).
68. This is not an ideological strategy for any feminist literature, though it may well be for the critic of feminist literature. Barr's Preface, 'Patriarchal Hocus-Pocus', pp. 1–20, argues for her victimisation as a critic because she focused on sf and on feminism.
69. Ibid., p. x.
70. (London: Harvester, 1993).
71. Ibid., p. 25.
72. (Syracuse and Liverpool: Syracuse University and Liverpool University, 1994).
73. Ibid., p. 11.
74. 'Science Fiction by Women in the Early Pulps, 1926–1930', ibid., pp. 137–52.
75. (London: Routledge, 2000).
76. Ibid., p. 13.
77. *The Magazine of Fantasy and Science Fiction* (December, 1973). Reprinted in Pamela Sargent (ed.), *The New Women of Wonder*.
78. *In the Chinks of the World Machine*, p. 173.
79. James, *Science Fiction in the Twentieth Century*, p. 185.
80. (Boston, Mass: Beacon Press, 1986).
81. *Magic Momms, Trembling Sisters, Puritans and Perverts* (1985).
82. Linda Leith's rejection of Russ' essay I suspect owes more to a rejection of her novel than the essay.
83. It even satirises the impact of ERA's advances, cf. p. 136.
84. (London: Women's Press, 1979).
85. In Robin Morgan (ed.), *Sisterhood is Powerful* (New York: Vintage, 1970), pp. 473–92.
86. *In the Chinks of the World Machine*, p. 55.
87. From Sandra Gilbert and Susan Gubar's *The Madwoman in the Attic* (1979) through to Elaine Showalter's definitive *The Female Malady* (1987) detailing how women were more likely to be described as mad than men.

88. (New York: Warner Aspect, 1997).
89. Introduction to Part VI, 'Hybridity', in Bill Ashcroft, Gareth Griffiths, and Helen Tiffin (eds), *The Postcolonial Studies Reader* (London: Routledge, 1994), pp. 183–4.
90. See, 'The Laugh of the Medusa', in Elaine Marks and Isabelle de Courtivron (eds), *New French Feminisms* (London: Harvester, 1981), pp. 245–64.

Bibliography

General

Ang, Ien, *Watching Dallas: Soap Opera and the Melodramatic Imagination*, trans. Della Couling (London: Methuen, 1985).

Ashcroft, Bill, Gareth Griffiths and Helen Tiffin (eds), *The Postcolonial Studies Reader* (London: Routledge, 1994).

Barrett, Michèle, 'Feminism and the Definition of Cultural Politics' in Rosalind Brunt and Caroline Rowan (eds), *Feminism, Culture and Politics* (London: Lawrence and Wishart, 1982), pp. 37–58.

Bloom, Clive, *Cult Fiction: Popular Reading and Pulp Theory* (London: Macmillan, 1996).

Carr, Helen (ed.), *From My Guy to Sci Fi: Genre and Women's Writing in the Postmodern World* (London: Pandora, 1989).

Chodorow, Nancy, *The Reproduction of Mothering: Psychoanalysis and the Sociology of Gender* (Berkeley: University of California Press, 1978).

Cixous, Hélène, 'The Laugh of the Medusa', in Elaine Marks and Isabelle de Courtivron (eds), *New French Feminisms: an Anthology* (Hemel Hempstead: Harvester, 1981), pp. 245–64.

Cranny-Francis, Ann, *Feminist Fiction: Feminist Uses of Generic Fiction* (Cambridge: Polity, 1990).

Flynn, Elizabeth, 'Gender and Reading' in Elizabeth Flynn and Patrocinio Schweickart (eds), *Gender and Readings: Essays on Readers, Texts and Contexts* (Baltimore: Johns Hopkins University Press, 1986), pp. 267–88.

Friday, Nancy, *My Secret Garden: Women's Sexual Fantasies* (New York: Pocket Books, 1973).

Gerrard, Nicci, *Into the Mainstream: How Feminism has Changed Women's Writing* (London: Pandora, 1989).

Gledhill, Christine, 'Pleasurable Negotiations', in Deirdre Pribram (ed.), *Female Spectator: Looking at Film and Television* (London: Verso, 1988).

Hall, Stuart, 'Encoding and Decoding in the Media Discourse', Paper 7, Birmingham Centre for Contemporary Cultural Studies, 1973.

Hutcheon, Linda, *The Poetics of Postmodernism: History, Theory, Fiction* (London: Routledge, 1988).

Irigaray, Luce, *This Sex Which is Not One*, trans. Catherine Porter and Carolyn Burke (Ithaca, New York: Cornell University Press, 1985).

Jameson, Frederic, *The Political Unconscious* (London: Methuen, 1981).

Johnson, Barbara, *Feminist Difference: Literature, Psychoanalysis, Race and Gender* (Cambridge, Mass: Harvard University Press, 1998).

Kaplan, E. A., 'Is the Gaze Male?' in Ann Snitow, Christine Stansell and Sharon Thompson (eds), *Powers of Desire: the Politics of Sexuality* (New York: Monthly Review Press, 1983), pp. 309–27.

Leavis, Queenie, *Fiction and the Reading Public* (London: Chatto, 1932).

McCauley, Rowan, 'Romance and Women's Pleasure' unpublished paper at the

'Reading and Pleasure: Gender and Popular Literature' conference, Roehampton Institute, 17 April 1999.

Millet, Kate, *Sexual Politics* (New York: Ballantine, 1969).

Mills, Sara and Lynne Pearce (eds), *Feminist Readings/ Feminists Reading*, 2nd edn (New York: Prentice Hall, 1996).

Nichols, Bill (ed.), *Movies and Methods*, vol. 2 (Berkeley: University of California Press, 1985).

Pearce, Lynne, *Feminism and the Politics of Reading* (London: Arnold, 1997).

Schlesinger, Philip, Russell Dobash and Kathy Weaver, *Women Viewing Violence* (London: British Film Institute, 1992).

Segal, Lynne, 'Sweet Sorrows, Painful Pleasures: Pornography and the Perils of Heterosexual Desire', in Lynne Segal and Mary McIntosh (eds), *Sex Exposed: Sexuality and the Pornography Debate* (London: Virago, 1992).

Stacey, Jackie, *Star Gazing: Hollywood Cinema and Female Spectatorship* (London: Routledge, 1994).

Williamson, Judith, 'The Problems of Being Popular', *New Socialist*, 41 (September, 1986), 14–15.

Zimmerman, Bonnie, 'What Has Never Been: an Overview of Lesbian Feminist Literary Criticism' in *Making a Difference: Feminist Literary Criticism* (London: Methuen, 1985), pp. 177–210.

Romance

Anderson, Rachel, *The Purple Heart Throbs: the Sub-literature of Love* (London: Hodder, 1974).

Batsleer, Janet, Tony Davies, Rebecca O'Rourke and Chris Weedon (eds), *Rewriting English: Cultural Politics of Gender and Class* (London: Methuen, 1985), Chapter 5: 'Gender and Genre: Women's Stories', pp. 86–105.

Dixon, Jay, 'Fantasy Unlimited: the World of Mills and Boon', *Women's Review*, 21 (July 1987), 18–19.

Dixon, Jay, *The Romance Fiction of Mills and Boon 1909–1990s* (London: UCL, 1999).

Eagleton, Mary, *Feminist Literary Criticism* (London: Methuen, 1991).

Fowler, Bridget, *The Alienated Reader: Women and Romantic Literature in the Twentieth Century* (London: Harvester, 1991).

Fowler, Bridget, 'Literature Beyond Modernism: Middlebrow and Popular Romance', in Pearce and Stacey (eds), *Romance Revisited*, pp. 89–99.

Frenier, Mariam Darce, *Goodbye Heathcliffe: Changing Heroes, Heroines, Roles and Values in Women's Category Romances* (New York: Greenwood, 1988).

Greer, Germaine, *The Female Eunuch* (London: Paladin, 1971).

Jackson, Stevi, 'Women and Heterosexual Love: Complicity, Resistance and Change' in Pearce and Stacey (eds), *Romance Revisited*, pp. 49–62.

Jones, Ann Rosalind, 'Mills and Boon meets Feminism', in Radford (ed.), *The Progress of the Romance*, pp. 195–218.

Kirkland, Catherine, 'For the Love of it: Women Writers and Popular Romance', unpublished PhD thesis, University of Pennsylvania, 1984.

Light, Alison, 'Returning to Manderley: Romance Fiction, Female Sexuality and Class', *Feminist Review*, 16 (April 1984), 7–25.

Mann, Peter H., 'The Romantic Novel and its Readers', *Journal of Popular Culture*, 5 (Summer 1981), 9–18.

Margolies, David, 'Mills and Boon: Guilt without Sex', *Red Letters*, 14 (Winter 1982–83), 5–13.

Modleski, Tania, *Loving With a Vengeance: Mass-Produced Fantasies for Women* (Hamden, Connecticut: Archon, 1982).

Moody, Nickianne, 'Mills and Boon's *Temptations*: Sex and the Single Couple in the 1990s', in Pearce and Wisker (eds), *Fatal Attractions*, pp. 141–56.

Mussell, Kay, *Fantasy and Reconciliation: Contemporary Formulas of Women's Romance Fiction* (Westpoint, Conn: Greenwood, 1984).

Napier, Susan, *Deal of a Lifetime* and *Tempt Me Not*, Duet series (Richmond, Surrey: Mills and Boon, 1995).

Palmer, Paulina, 'Girl Meets Girl: Changing Approaches to the Lesbian Romance', in Pearce and Wisker (eds), *Fatal Attractions*, pp. 189–204.

Pearce, Lynne and Jackie Stacey (eds), *Romance Revisited* (London: Lawrence and Wishart, 1995).

Pearce, Lynne and Gina Wisker (eds), *Fatal Attractions: Rescripting Romance in Contemporary Literature and Film* (London: Pluto, 1998).

Philips, Deborah, 'Marketing Moonshine', *Women's Review*, 2 (December 1985), 16–17.

Radford, Jean (ed.), *The Progress of the Romance: the Politics of Popular Fiction* (London: Routledge, 1986).

Radstone, Susannah (ed.), *Sweet Dreams: Sexuality, Gender and Popular Fiction* (London: Lawrence and Wishart, 1988).

Radway, Janice, *Reading the Romance: Women, Patriarchy, and Popular Literature* (Chapel Hill: University of North Carolina Press, 1991).

Rudolph, Barbara, 'Heartbreak comes to Harlequin', *Forbes* (29 March 1982), 50–1.

Shapiro, Lisa, *Color of Winter* (Tallahassee, Florida: Naiad, 1995).

Snitow, Anne Barr, 'Mass Market Romance: Pornography for Women is Different', in Snitow, Stansell and Thompson (eds), *Desire*, pp. 258–75.

Snitow, Anne, Christine Stansell and Sharon Thompson (eds), *Desire: the Politics of Sexuality* (London: Virago, 1983).

Taylor, Helen, *Gone With the Wind: Scarlet's Women* (London: Virago, 1991).

Taylor, Helen, 'Romantic Readers', in Carr (ed.), *From My Guy to Sci Fi*, pp. 58–77.

Thurston, Carol, *Romance Revolution: Erotic Novels for Women and the Quest for a New Sexual Identity* (Chicago: University of Illinois, 1987).

Tonge, Rosemary, *Feminist Thought* (London: Unwin, 1989).

Treacher, Amal, 'What is Life Without My Love? Desire and Romantic Fiction', in Radstone (ed.), *Sweet Dreams*, pp. 73–90.

Watson, Daphne, *Their Own Worst Enemies: Women Writers of Women's Fiction* (London: Pluto, 1995).

Winterson, Jeanette (ed.), *Passion Fruit: Romantic Fiction With a Twist* (London: Pandora, 1986).

Fairy tale

Armitt, Lucie, *Theorizing the Fantastic* (London: Arnold, 1996).

Atwood, Margaret, 'Running with the Tigers' in Lorna Sage (ed.), *Flesh and the Mirror: Essays on the Art of Angela Carter* (London: Virago, 1994), pp. 117–35.

Barzilai, Shuli, 'Reading "Snow White": the Mother's Story', *Signs*, 15 (Spring, 1990). Reprinted in Jean Barr, Deborah Pope and Mary Wyer (eds), *Ties That Bind: Essays on Mothering and Patriarchy* (Chicago: University of Chicago Press, 1990), pp. 253–72.

Bettelheim, Bruno, *The Uses of Enchantment: the Meaning and Importance of Fairy Tales* (Harmondsworth: Penguin, 1978).

Bottigheimer, Ruth B., *Grimms' Bad Girls and Bold Boys: the Moral and Social Vision of the Tales* (New Haven: Yale University Press, 1987).

Bottinger, Ruth (ed.), *Fairy Tales and Society: Illusion, Allusion and Paradigm* (Philadelphia: University of Pennsylvania Press, 1986).

Bristow, Joseph and Trev Lynn Broughton (eds), *The Infernal Desires of Angela Carter* (London: Longman, 1997).

Carter, Angela, trans., *The Fairy Tales of Charles Perrault*, illus. Martin Ware (London: Gollancz, 1977).

Carter, Angela, *The Bloody Chamber and Other Stories* (Harmondsworth: Penguin, 1979).

Carter, Angela, *The Sadeian Woman* (London: Virago, 1979).

Carter, Angela, trans., *Sleeping Beauty and Other Fairy Tales*, illus. Michael Foreman (London: Gollancz, 1982).

Carter, Angela, 'Notes from the Frontline', in Michelene Wandor (ed.), *On Gender and Writing* (London: Pandora, 1983).

Carter, Angela (ed.), *The Virago Book of Fairy Tales* (London: Virago, 1991).

Carter, Angela (ed.), *The Second Virago Book of Fairy Tales* (London: Virago, 1992).

Clark, Robert, 'Angela Carter's Desire Machines', *Women's Studies* 14 (1987), 147–61.

Delarue, Paul, 'The Story of the Grandmother', *Le Conte Populaire Français*, Vol. 1 (Paris: Erasme, 1957), pp. 373–4. Translated by Zipes in *Trials and Tribulations of Little Red Riding Hood*, pp. 21–2.

Duerr, Hans Peter, *Traumzeit, Über die Grenze zwischen Wildnis und Zivilisation* (Frankfurt: Syndikat, 1978).

Duncker, Patricia, 'Re-imagining the Fairy Tales: Angela Carter's Bloody Chambers', in Peter Widdowson and Peter Humm (eds), *Popular Fictions* (London: Methuen, 1986), pp. 222–36.

Duncker, Patricia, 'Queer Gothic: Angela Carter and the Lost Narrative of Sexual Subversion', *Critical Survey*, 8 (1996), 58–68.

Dworkin, Andrea, *Woman Hating* (New York: Plume, 1974).

Fairy Tales for Feminists Collective, *Sweeping Beauties* (Dublin: Attic, 1989).

Gilbert, Sandra and Susan Gubar, *The Mad Woman in the Attic* (New Haven: Yale University, 1979).

Kavablum, Lea, *Cinderella: Radical Feminist, Alchemist* (New Jersey: Guttenberg, 1973).

Keenan, Sally, 'Angela Carter's *The Sadeian Woman*: Feminism as Treason', in Bristow and Broughton (eds), *The Infernal Desires of Angela Carter*, pp. 132–48.

Lieberman, Marcia K., 'Some Day My Prince Will Come', *College English*, 34 (1972), 383–95. Reprinted in Zipes (ed.), *Don't Bet on the Prince*, pp. 185–200.

Llwellyn, Avis, 'Wayward Girls but Wicked Women? Female Sexuality in Angela Carter's *Bloody Chamber'*, in Clive Bloom and Gary Day (eds), *Perspectives on Pornography* (Basingstoke: Macmillan, 1988), pp. 145–59.

Lurie, Alison, 'Folktale Liberation', *New York Review of Books*, 11 (17 December 1970), 42–4.

Lurie, Alison, *Don't Tell the Grown-Ups: Subversive Children's Literature* (London: Bloomsbury, 1990).

Lyons, Heather, 'Some Second Thoughts on Sexism in Fairy Tales', in Elizabeth Grugeon and Peter Walden (eds), *Literature and Learning* (Milton Keynes: Open University Press, 1978), pp. 42–58.

Makinen, Merja, 'Angela Carter and the Decolonisation of Feminine Sexuality', *Feminist Review*, 14 (1992), 2–15.

Makinen, Merja, 'Embodying the Negated: Contemporary Images of the Female Erotic', in Sarah Sceats and Gail Cunningham (eds), *Image and Power: Women in Fiction in the Twentieth Century* (London: Longman, 1996).

Monaghan, Patricia, *The Book of Goddesses and Heroines* (New York: Dutton, 1981).

Palmer, Paulina, 'From Coded Mannequin to Bird Woman: Angela Carter's Magic Flight', in Sue Roe (ed.), *Women Reading Women's Writing* (London: Harvester, 1987), pp. 179–205.

Perera, Sylvia Brinton, *The Descent of the Goddess* (Toronto: Inner City, 1981).

Rowe, Karen E., 'Feminism and Fairy Tales', *Women's Studies*, 6 (1979), 237–57. Reprinted in Zipes (ed.), *Don't Bet on the Prince*, pp. 209–26.

Rowe, Karen E., 'To Spin a Yarn: the Female Voice in Folklore and Fairy Tale', in Bottinger (ed.), *Fairy Tales and Society*, pp. 53–74.

Sheets, Robin Ann, 'Pornography, Fairy Tales and Feminism: Angela Carter's *The Bloody Chamber'*, in John Fout (ed.), *Forbidden History: The State, Society and the Regulation of Sexuality in Modern Europe* (Chicago: Chicago University Press, 1992), pp. 335–59.

Stone, Kay, 'Feminist Approaches to the Interpretation of Fairy Tales', in Bottinger (ed.), *Fairy Tales and Society*, pp. 229–36.

Stone, Kay, 'The Things Walt Disney Never Told Us', in Clare R. Farer (ed.), *Women and Folklore* (Austin, Texas: University of Texas Press, 1975), pp. 42–50.

Tatar, Maria, *The Hard Facts of the Grimms' Fairy Tales* (Princeton, New Jersey: Princeton University, 1987).

Verdier, Yvonne, 'Grand-mères, sie vous saviez: le Petit Chaperon Rouge dans le tradition orale', *Cahiers de Littérature Orale*, 4 (1978), 17–55.

Walker, Barbara, *The Woman's Encyclopedia of Myths and Secrets* (San Francisco: Harper, 1983).

Warner, Marina, 'Preface', *The Second Virago Book of Fairy Tales* (London: Virago, 1992).

Warner, Marina, *From the Beast to the Blonde: On Fairytales and their Tellers* (London: Chatto, 1994).

Weigle, Marta, *Spiders and Spinsters: Women and Mythology* (Albuquerque: University of New Mexico, 1982).

Yolen, Jane, *Moon Ribbon and Other Tales* (London: Dent, 1977).
Yolen, Jane, *Touch Magic: Fantasy, Faerie and Folklore in the Literature of Childhood* (New York: Philomel, 1981).
Yolen, Jane, *Briar Rose* (New York: Tom Doherty, 1992).
Zipes, Jack, *The Trials and Tribulations of Little Red Riding Hood* (London: Heinemann, 1982).
Zipes, Jack, *Fairy Tales and the Art of Subversion* (New York: Routledge, 1983).
Zipes, Jack (ed.), *Don't Bet on the Prince* (Aldershot: Gower, 1986).

Detective fiction

Babener, Liahna, 'Uncloseting Ideology in the Novels of Barbara Wilson', in Klein (ed.), *Woman Times Three*, pp. 143–61.
Bakerman, Jane S., 'Cordelia Gray: Apprentice and Archetype', *Clues*, 5 (Spring–Summer 1984), 101–14.
Bargainner, Earl F., *10 Women of Mystery* (Bowling Green, Ohio: Bowling Green, 1981).
Bell, Ian A. and Graham Daldry (eds), *Watching the Detectives: Essays on Crime Fiction* (London: Macmillan, 1990).
Coward, Rosalind and Linda Semple, 'Tracking Down the Past: Women and Detective Fiction', in Carr (ed.), *From My Guy to Sci Fi*, pp. 39–57.
Craig, Patricia and Mary Cadogan, *The Lady Investigates: Women Detectives and Spies in Fiction* (Oxford, Oxford University Press, 1986).
DeMarr, Mary Jean, 'Joan Hess? Joan Hadley', in Klein (ed.), *Woman Times Three*, pp. 29–41.
Gair, Christopher, 'Policing the Margins: Barbara Wilson's *Gaudi Afternoon* and *Troubles in Transylvania*', in Messent (ed.), *Criminal Proceedings*, pp. 111–26.
Glover, David and Cora Kaplan, 'Guns in the House of Culture? Crime Fiction and the Politics of the Popular' in Lawrence Grossberg, Cary Nelson and Paula Treichler (eds), *Cultural Studies* (London: Routledge, 1992), pp. 213–26.
Heilbrun, Carolyn, 'Keynote Address: Gender and Detective Fiction', in Rader and Zettle (eds), *The Sleuth and the Scholar*, pp. 1–8.
Humm, Maggie, 'Feminist Detective Fiction', in Clive Bloom (ed.), *20thC Suspense: the Thriller Comes of Age* (London: Macmillan, 1990), pp. 237–54.
Irons, Glenwood (ed.), *Feminism in Women's Detective Fiction* (Toronto: University of Toronto Press, 1995).
James, P. D., Interview with Helen Birch, 'P. D. James' Stylish Crime', *Woman's Review*, 10 (August 1986), 6–7.
Kaplan, Cora, 'An Unsuitable Genre for a Feminist', *Women's Review*, 8 (June, 1986), 18–19.
Kinsman, Margaret, 'A Question of Visibility: Paretsky and Chicago', in Klein (ed.), *Woman Times Three*, pp. 15–27.
Klein, Kathleen Gregory, *The Woman Detective: Gender and Genre* (Urbana, Ill.: University of Illinois Press, 1988).
Klein, Kathleen Gregory, 'Habeas Corpus: Feminism and Detective Fiction', in Irons (ed.), *Feminism and Women's Detective Fiction*, pp. 171–90.
Klein, Kathleen Gregory (ed.), *Great Women Mystery Writers: Classic to Contemporary* (Westport, Connecticut: Greenwood Press, 1994).

Klein, Kathleen Gregory (ed.), *Woman Times Three: Writers, Detectives, Readers* (Bowling Green, Ohio: Bowling Green, 1995).

Knight, Steven, 'Radical Thrillers' in Bell and Daldry (eds), *Watching the Detectives*, pp. 172–87.

Makinen, Merja, 'Feminism and the "Crisis of Masculinity" in Contemporary British Detective Fiction' in Anne Mullen and Emer O'Beirne (eds), *Crime Scenes: Detective Narratives in European Culture since 1945* (Amsterdam: Rodopi, 2000), pp. 254–68.

Mann, Jessica, *Deadlier than the Male: an Investigation into Feminine Crime Writing* (Newton Abbot: David and Charles, 1981).

Messent, Peter (ed.), *Criminal Proceedings: the Contemporary American Crime Novel* (London: Pluto, 1997).

Munt, Sally, 'The Inverstigators: Lesbian Crime Fiction' in Susannah Radstone (ed.), *Sweet Dreams* (London: Lawrence and Wishart, 1988), pp. 91–120.

Munt, Sally, *Murder By the Book?: Feminism and the Crime Novel* (London: Routledge, 1994).

Nichols, Victoria and Susan Thompson (eds), *Silk Stalkings: When Women Write of Murder* (Berkeley: Black Lizard, 1988).

Nichols, Victoria and Susan Thompson (eds), *Silk Stalkings: More Women Write of Murder* (Langham Md.: Scarecrow, 1998).

Ousby, Ian, *The Crime and Mystery Book: a Reader's Companion* (London: Thames and Hudson, 1997).

Palmer, Paulina, 'The Lesbian Feminist Thriller and Detective Novel', in Elaine Hobby and Chris White (eds), *What Lesbians Do in Books* (London: Women's Press, 1991), pp. 9–27.

Palmer, Paulina, 'The Lesbian Thriller: Transgressive Investigations', in Messent (ed.), *Criminal Proceedings*, pp. 87–110.

Paretsky, Sara, *Burnmarks* (London: Virago, 1990).

Pennell, Jane C., 'The Female Detective: Pre- and Post-Women's Lib', *Clues*, 6 (Fall–Winter 1985), 85–98.

Priestman, Martin, *Detective Fiction and Literature: the Figure in the Carpet* (London: Macmillan, 1990).

Pykett, Lynn, 'Investigating Women: the Female Sleuth after Feminism', in Bell and Daldry (eds), *Watching the Detectives*, pp. 48–67.

Rader, Barbara A. and Howard G. Zettle (eds), *The Sleuth and the Scholar: Origins, Evolution and Current Trends in Detective Fiction* (Westport, Connecticut: Greenwood Press, 1988).

Reddy, Maureen T., *Sisters in Crime: Feminism and the Crime Novel* (New York: Continuum, 1988).

Reddy, Maureen T., 'The Feminist Counter-Tradition in Crime: Cross, Grafton, Paretsky and Wilson', in Walker and Frazer (eds), *The Cunning Craft*, pp. 174–87.

Roberts, Jeanne Addison, 'Feminist Murder: Amanda Cross Reinvents Womanhood', *Clues*, 6 (Spring–Summer 1985), 2–14. Revised in Glenwood Irons (ed.), *Feminism in Women's Detective Fiction*, pp. 94–111.

Shaw, Marion and Sabine Vanaker, *Reflecting on Miss Marple* (London: Routledge, 1991).

Slovo, Gillian, *Death Comes Staccato* (London: Women's Press, 1987).

Slung, Michelle, *Crime on Her Mind: Fifteen Stories of Female Sleuths from the*

Victorian Era to the Forties (Harmondsworth: Penguin, 1975).

Vanaker, Sabine, 'V. I. Warshawski, Kinsey Milhone and Kay Scarpetta: Creating a Feminist Detective Hero', in Messent (ed.), *Criminal Proceedings*, pp. 62–86.

Walker, Ronald G. and June M. Frazer (eds), *The Cunning Craft: Original Essays on Detective Fiction and Contemporary Literary Theory* (Macomb, Illinois: Western Illinois University Press, 1990).

Walton, Priscilla L. and Marina Jones, *Detective Agency: Women Rewriting the Hard-Boiled Tradition* (Berkeley, California: University of California Press, 1999).

Wilson, Barbara, *Gaudi Afternoon* (Seattle: Seal Press, 1990).

Science fiction

Anderson, Kristine, 'The Great Divorce: Fictions of Feminist Desire', in Jones and Goodwin (eds), *Feminism, Utopia, Narrative*, pp. 85–99.

Annas, Pamela, 'New Worlds: New Word: Androgyny in Feminist Science Fiction', *Science Fiction Studies*, 5 (July 1978), 144.

Armitt, Lucie, *Contemporary Women's Fiction and the Fantastic* (London: Routledge, 2000).

Armitt, Lucie, 'Your Word is My Command: the Structures of Language and Power in Women's Science Fiction', in Armitt (ed.), *Where No Man Has Gone Before*, pp. 123–38.

Armitt, Lucie (ed.), *Where No Man Has Gone Before: Women and Science Fiction* (London: Routledge, 1991).

Bammer, Angelika, *Partial Visions: Feminism and Utopianism in the 1970s* (New York: Routledge, 1991).

Barr, Marlene, *Alien to Femininity: Speculative Fiction and Feminist Theory* (Westport, Connecticut: Greenwood Press, 1987).

Barr, Marlene, 'Feminist Fabulation; or Playing with Patriarchy v. the Masculinization of Metafiction', *Women's Studies*, 14 (1987), 187–91.

Barr, Marlene, *Feminist Fabulations: Space/Postmodern Fiction* (Iowa: University of Iowa Press, 1992).

Barr, Marlene, *Lost in Space: Probing Feminist Science Fiction and Beyond* (Chapel Hill: University of North Carolina Press, 1993).

Barr, Marlene (ed.), *Future Females: a Critical Anthology* (Bowling Green, Ohio: Bowling Green State University, 1981).

Barr, Marlene and Patrick D. Murphy (eds), 'Feminism Faces the Fantastic', *Women's Studies*, special issue, 14 (1987), 81–194.

Barr, Marlene and Nicholas Smith (eds), *Women and Utopia: Critical Interpretations* (Lanham: University Press of America, 1983).

Bartkowski, Frances, *Feminist Utopias* (Lincoln, Nebraska: University of Nebraska Press, 1989).

Butler, Octavia, *Imago* (New York: Warner Aspect, 1997).

Charnas, Suzy McKee, 'A Woman Appeared', in Barr (ed.), *Future Females*, pp. 103–8.

Donawerth, Jane, 'Science Fiction by Women in the Early Pulps, 1926–1930', in Donawerth and Kolmarten (eds), *Utopian and Science Fiction by Women*, pp. 137–52.

Donawerth, Jane and Carol A. Kolmarten, *Utopian and Science Fiction by Women* (Liverpool and Syracuse: Liverpool University & Syracuse University, 1994).

Du Plessis, Rachel Blau, *Writing Beyond the Ending: Narrative Strategies of Twentieth Century Women Writers* (Bloomington: Indiana University Press, 1985).

Du Plessis, Rachel Blau, 'Feminist Apologues', *Frontiers* (Winter 1979). Revised and reprinted as 'Kin With Each Other: Speculative Consciousness and Collective Protagonists' in her *Writing Beyond the Ending*, pp. 179–97.

Elgin, Suzette Haden, 'Women's Language and Near Future Science Fiction: a Reply', *Women's Studies*, 14 (1987), 175–81.

'Feminism and Science Fiction', *Foundation*, 43 (Summer 1988), 63–77.

'Feminism Faces the Fantastic', *Women's Studies* special issue, 14 (1987) 81–194.

Firestone, Shulamith, *The Dialectic of Sex: the Case for Feminist Revolution* (New York: Morrow, 1971; reprinted London: Women's Press, 1979).

Friend, Beverly, 'Virgin Territory: the Bonds and Boundaries of Women in Science Fiction', *Extrapolation* 14 (December 1972), 49–58. Reprinted in Thomas Clareson (ed.), *Many Futures, Many Worlds: Theme and Form in Science Fiction* (Kent State University, 1977), pp. 140–63.

Greenland, Colin, 'An Interest in Carpentry', *Foundation*, 43 (Summer 1988), 76–7.

Gubar, 'C. L. Moore and the Conventions of Women's Science Fiction', *Science Fiction Studies*, 7 (March 1980), 16–27.

Haraway, Donna, 'A Manifesto for Cyborgs: Science, Technology and Socialist Feminism in the 1980s', *Socialist Review*, 80 (1985), 65–107.

James, Edward, *Science Fiction in the Twentieth Century* (Oxford: Oxford University Press, 1994).

Jones, Gwyneth, 'The Walrus is Brian', *Foundation*, 43 (Summer 1988), 75–6.

Jones, Libby Falks, 'Gilman, Bradley and Piercy, and the Evolving Rhetoric of Feminist Utopias', in Jones and Goodwin (eds), *Feminism, Utopia and Narrative*, pp. 116–29.

Jones, Libby Falks and Sarah Webster Goodwin (eds), *Feminism, Utopia and Narrative* (Knoxville: University of Tennessee Press, 1990).

Kaveney, Roz, 'The Science Fictiveness of Women's Science Fiction', in Helen Carr (ed.), *From My Guy to Sci Fi* (London: Pandora, 1989), pp. 78–97.

Keinhorst, Annette, 'Emancipatory Projection: an Introduction to Women's Critical Utopias', *Women's Studies*, 14 (1987), 91–9.

Kessler, Carol Farley (ed.), *Daring to Dream: Utopian Stories by Women 1836–1919* (Boston and London: Pandora, 1984).

Khanna, Lee Cullen, 'Women's Utopias: New Worlds, New Texts', in Jones and Goodwin (eds), *Feminism, Utopia, Narrative*, pp. 130–40.

Koppelman Cornillon, Susan (ed.), *Images of Women in Fiction: Feminist Perspectives* (Bowling Green: Bowling Green University, 1972).

Kramarae, Cheris, 'Present Problems with the Language of the Future', *Women's Studies*, 14 (1987), 183–6.

Lefanu, Sarah, 'Engaging the Reader', *Foundation*, 43 (Summer 1988), 72–4.

Lefanu, Sarah, *In the Chinks of the World Machine: Feminism and Science Fiction* (London: Women's Press, 1988).

Lefanu, Sarah, 'Sex, Sub-atomic Particles and Sociology', in Armitt (ed.), *Where No Man Has Gone Before*, pp. 178–85.

LeGuin, Ursula, 'American SF and the Other', *Science Fiction Studies* (November, 1975). Reprinted in *The Language of the Night*, 2nd edn, pp. 83–5.

LeGuin, Ursula, 'Is Gender Necessary?' in Vonda McIntyre and Susan Anderson (eds), *Aurora: Beyond Equality* (New York: Fawcett, 1976). Revised as 'Is Gender Necessary: Redux', in *The Language of the Night*, 2nd edn, pp. 135–47.

LeGuin, Ursula, *The Language of the Night: Essays on Fantasy and Science Fiction*, ed. Susan Wood, 2nd edn revised by Ursula LeGuin (London: Women's Press, 1989).

Mellor, Anne K., 'On Feminist Utopias', *Women's Studies*, 9 (1982), 241–62.

Moylan, Tom, *Demand the Impossible: Science Fiction and the Utopian Imagination* (London: Methuen, 1986).

Newman, Jenny, 'Mary and the Monster' in Armitt (ed.), *Where No Man Has Gone Before*, pp. 85–95.

Patai, Daphne, 'Beyond Defensiveness: Feminist Research Strategies' in Barr and Smith (eds), *Women and Utopia*, pp. 148–69.

Pearson, Caroline, 'Women's Fantasies and Feminist Utopias', *Frontiers* (Fall 1977), 50–61.

Pearson, Caroline, 'Coming Home: Four Feminist Utopias and Patriarchal Experience', a revised version of 'Women's Fantasies and Feminist Utopias', in Barr (ed.), *Future Females*, pp. 63–70.

Peel, Ellen, 'Utopian Feminism, Skeptical Feminism, and Narrative Energy', in Jones and Goodwin (eds), *Feminism, Utopia and Narrative*, pp. 34–49.

Pfaelzer, Jean, 'The Changing of the Avant-Garde: the Feminist Utopia', *Science Fiction Studies*, 15 (November 1988), 282–94.

Pfaelzer, Jean, 'Response: What Happened to History?', in Jones and Goodwin, (eds), *Feminism, Utopia, Narrative*, pp. 191–200.

Piercy, Marge, 'The Grand Coolie Dam', in Robin Morgan (ed.), *Sisterhood is Powerful* (New York: Vintage, 1970), pp. 473–92.

Piercy, Marge, *Woman on the Edge of Time* (London: Women's Press, 1979).

Rosinsky, Natalie, *Feminist Futures: Contemporary Women's Speculative Fiction* (Ann Arbor, Michigan: University Research Press, 1982).

Russ, Joanna, 'Amor Vincit Foeminam: the Battle of the Sexes in Science Fiction', *Science Fiction Studies*, 7 (March 1980), 2–15.

Russ, Joanna, *Magic Momms, Trembling Sisters, Puritans and Perverts* (London: Women's Press, 1985).

Russ, Joanna, *The Female Man* (Boston, Mass; Beacon, 1986).

Russ, Joanna, 'The Image of Women in Science Fiction', in Koppelman (ed.), *Images of Women in Fiction*, pp. 79–94.

Russ, Joanna, 'Recent Feminist Utopias' in Barr (ed.), *Future Females*, pp. 71–85.

Russ, Joanna, 'What Can a Heroine Do? Or Why Women Can't Write', in Koppelman (ed.), *Images of Women in Fiction*, pp. 3–20.

Sargent, Pamela, *Women of Wonder: Sf Stories by Women about Women* (Harmondsworth: Penguin, 1978).

Sargent, Pamela, *More Women of Wonder* (Harmondsworth: Penguin, 1979).

Sargent, Pamela, *New Women of Wonder* (New York: Vintage, 1979).

Saxton, Josephine, 'Goodbye To All That …' in Armitt (ed.), *Where No Man Has Gone Before*, pp. 204–17.

Slinn, Thelma, *Worlds Within Women: Myth and Mythmaking in Fantastic Literature by Women* (Westport, Connecticut: Greenwood Press, 1986).

Stableford, Brian, 'A Few More Crocodile Tears?', *Foundation*, 43 (Summer 1988), 63–72.

Tuttle, Lisa, 'Pets and Monsters: Metamorphoses in Recent Science Fiction', in Armitt (ed.), *Where No Man Has Gone Before*, pp. 97–108.

Weimer, Anegeret J., 'Foreign l(anguish), mother tongue: Concepts of Language in Contemporary Science Fiction', *Women's Studies*, 14 (1987), 163–73.

Wolmark, Jenny, 'Science Fiction and Feminism', *Foundation*, 35 (1986) 48–50.

Wolmark, Jenny, 'There's More to Life than Crocodile Tears', *Foundation*, 43 (Summer 1988), 74–5.

Wolmark, Jenny, *Aliens and Others: Science Fiction, Feminism and Postmodernism* (London: Harvester, 1993).

Zaki, Hoda, 'Utopia and Ideology in *Daughters of the Coral Dawn* and Contemporary Feminist Utopias', *Women's Studies*, 14 (1987), 119–33.

Index